The Storybook Maze

(Volume 1)

By

Bryan S.Godwin

ISBN: 9798474596488

Printed in the United States of America

Published by: Bookmarketeers.com

Dedication

This work is dedicated to my mother,

Kay Chastain,

a singer and songwriter that motivated and gifted me all the tools I need to succeed. As far as I go, thank you for taking me there.

Acknowledgments

I would like to thank my girlfriend Alexis, for believing in me every step of the way without fails, for embracing my vision in a way that made it feel possible every single day. Thank you for propelling me to believe in myself and grind through the time and work to try to take our next step.

I want to thank my family, starting with my mother and father, Tom and Kay, for raising me in a manner that allowed me to explore the things I loved, reading and writing, encouraging me to put the work in every day and instilling within me the discipline to finish what I started. Thanks to my brother, Thomas, who excels in the field and passes on knowledge any time I am unsure. I would like to thank my step-mother and step-sister, Wendy and Tina, for their continual support and interest in my work, for never doubting and living to the standard of any parent and sibling. Thank you.

To all of my friends from home to the places I've been, thank you so much. The positive energy and cheering on I have received continues to humble me each and every day. Thanks for rooting for me. Thanks for being here and thanks for all your contributions.

I want to thank Write My Wrongs LLC, for not only their outstanding work, but for educating me on the path. I express my personal gratitude for Allen, the CEO, and the Chief and Deputy editors just below. Thank you, Chrissy, for enjoying my story and finding relativity to your own life within it. Thank you, Alice, for all your hard work and information passed on.

Lastly, I would like to thank Book Marketeers for getting my work out to the world, opening that first door and showing me the process through each step. From here, I hope to take everything I've learned and apply it to the future. Thank you.

Table of Contents

Wandering Minds

T he sound of her pen scribbling swiftly in her journal faded as the wings of her imagination took flight. Lola was anywhere but where she was, the physical sounds of her fifth-grade classroom passing little more than faint echoes in her mind. Everything else was inconsequential; all that mattered was the world she created around herself, and there she could go to a million places beyond the restraints and rules of reality. Her comfort was the key ingredient, and she was right at home.

Lola Ray didn't like school. Even the harder classes were annoying. Her parents insisted on advanced courses since she had proven to be "gifted." She certainly didn't feel that way. She knew she was smart, of course, but wasn't everyone? When she asked her father that same question, he laughed—a pleasant and infectious sound that, in turn, caused her to do the same. It was a fond memory, but it didn't take away from the fact that the hands on the classroom clock were overly lethargic in their eternal task. She eyed them more than she should have, making it worse, but it was one of those natural habits that humans found themselves compelled to do.

Lola paused her scribbling to soak in the sun draping over her face from the window. Outside, trees soon to fall victim to autumn blew gently in a hot breeze. Elley, Alabama, was a muggy place, thick and uncomfortable for much of the year. It lay south, pressed close to the top of Florida. Her parents had grown up there, though it had little to offer. Lola supposed it had its perks, though. No freezing rains or snows in winter, the beach next door, and, of course, Elley was not lacking in Southern charm, which her mother epitomized.

To Lola's disappointment, the echoes were beginning to demand her attention. Lola hadn't heard her teacher's question. Mrs. Florence was one of the younger, happier teachers, but she had a mean side most of the kids respected.

"I'm sorry, Mrs. Florence. My mind was elsewhere." An unmistakable look of annoyance flashed across the woman's face.

"Just because you're blonde, pretty, and smart, Miss Ray, doesn't mean you don't have to apply yourself," she said. Lola eyed the math equation on the board, feigning interest as best she could. Mrs. Florence pointed a ruler at it impatiently.

"Seven hundred and fifty is what it rounds to, ma'am," she answered, trying to sound interested.

"That's correct, Miss Ray. Thank you." Her teacher's tone was neutral, but her jaw muscles gave her agitation away. "If you could keep your eyes to the front and your mind out of fantasy land?" It was presented as a question but was more of a statement. She didn't wait for Lola to respond before turning back to her whiteboard at the front of the classroom. *Her precious whiteboard.* Mrs. Florence's dry erase marker made a squeaky sound as she wrote another equation.

Lola gave it little thought. *The clouds have so much more to offer.* The itch to write was almost immediate upon setting her pen down. Along with it, and not far behind, came the mental fatigue of sitting at a desk—in prison. It wasn't long before her mind wandered again. Lola studied Mrs. Florence as she spoke to the class. She was young, fresh in the business, and driven to motivate the generations of the future. Her hair and eyes were vibrant, and she didn't smell like cigarette smoke and coffee the way others did. *She wants to spend her*

3

whole life doing this, Lola thought. Despite Mrs. Florence's passion, Lola preferred some of the older teachers, tired and worn as they were. They were representations of life in its later stages, the result of enduring decades of humanity's burdens. It wasn't always cheerful, but Lola appreciated the authenticity of it. And she liked them, anyway. Well, liked them *better*, but it wasn't just the teachers—it was older people in general. She found them more relatable and compelling, often full of wisdom and information. Her parents always told her she was wise beyond her years, and she couldn't argue. Perhaps, too, it was why she didn't have many friends. Kids her age lacked entertainment value; to top it off, they were loud, obnoxious, and, well, big babies.

Lola did spend time with a few peers, though. She tolerated the mild-mannered kids and even had a soft spot for them; they were usually the ones getting bullied or avoiding social interactions altogether. Since Lola was smarter than the older, meaner kids, she waited for opportunities to catch them in their tormenting. The younger victims appreciated her ability to belittle and shame their bullies with her superior wit. Lola supposed she was lucky to avoid physical confrontations thus far, but she also knew the power of her intimidating words. The thought brought a smile to her face. Her eyes moved across the room to a frail boy named Jackson. He was a typical redhead— pale-skinned with a lot of freckles. Unfortunately for him, the insults added to injury were his poor eyesight and propensity for getting sick, which made him an easy target for bullying. He kept his eyes down at his desk as if he feared the air itself would come alive to get him. Even his coughs were nervous. To Lola's delight, she could pull a timid smile out of Jackson occasionally. When he was called upon to speak by the teacher, his responses were broken attempts at the English language. Surprisingly enough, however, he often provided the correct answer after stumbling.

Brandon Melton was another story entirely; Lola hadn't yet figured out the cause of his strange behavior. His folks never paid it much mind, so the boy attached himself to her. Like Jackson, he also wore glasses (come to think of it, each of her four friends did). Outside of school, Lola and Brandon spent many evenings together, parting ways when the streetlights would turn on and alert them of Lola's approaching curfew. She often found him squatting near the gutters lining the street, muttering strange things she couldn't comprehend, like, "Make the voices go away, Annie," and similar references to a lady she didn't know. She never knew what to make of his statements. His mannerisms during these episodes—rocking back and forth with his arms wrapped around his knees—were a clear display of stress in Lola's mind, but he did seem to relax when Lola tried to calm him. Afterward, things would be normal again, and they'd chat and play like the other children did.

It's not like him to be absent, she was thinking, looking at his empty desk when the bell reached its peak, and all the kids scrambled to get out the door. Mrs. Florence managed the flow as best she could, though it was nothing less than organized chaos. It evoked a sense of panic in Lola; had the building been on fire, her inattention could be the death of her. She gave her journal a final fond glance and snapped it closed before collecting her things. When the mad rush settled, she pulled the straps of her backpack lethargically over her shoulders and hopped into the back of the line, which continued to move into the school's one large hallway. Elley Elementary was one of

5

the smaller schools in the county, her mother said. Though Lola didn't suffer from claustrophobia, the crowded area looked much like a disturbed ant bed with kids running, screaming, and laughing. Lola kept her eyes forward, gritting her teeth while passing each giddy child to avoid screaming herself. It was a daily struggle.

Two large silver-handled doors waited at one end of the building, their clear glass windows exposing the freedom beyond. The students spilled out into the afternoon sunlight. Even in October, the air remained thick and muggy. *It never gets cold here,* she thought, crossing the threshold into the outside world and the open air, shirt clinging to her instantly. She hoped for snow on occasion, but that yearning was beginning to fade as her parents drew her attention toward climate patterns in the South. Maybe one day she'd see it, but that would mean her family had to travel somewhere. As frugal as they were, it was a distant hope.

The area for pickup was a half-circle facing opposite of the school. As jammed as it looked, there was usually a steady flow, but Lola's impatience always nagged at her nonetheless. She scanned the cars waiting in line, following them as they stretched out and back onto the street, running parallel to the building. Vehicles of different colors and models made up the order, and she smiled in relief when she spotted her mom's smaller, gray SUV almost hidden down the line. Lola double-checked her bag for her journal, pulled it back over her shoulder, and walked toward her mother. She was quickly falling victim to the humidity, and she looked forward to the cool air conditioning inside the car.

When she approached, Lola could see her mother's smiling face through the windshield. A lot of people said when she grew up, they'd look identical. Tara Ray had a golden mane atop her head—naturally curly, though she was wearing it straight. Lola didn't like how her own hair curled. "Stringy" was her preferred word for it, but somehow her mother made it look majestic. They shared the same eyes. "Green pools with an unknown depth," her dad would always say to her as she grinned. When their eyes met, Tara waved, and Lola's smile brightened. She quickened her steps, bag bouncing gently on her back. It slung to the side with momentum when she stopped to open the car door, the familiar click giving way to the sound of her mother's favorite music: new wave pop. Even at a low volume, Lola thought it was annoying, but she always forgave her mother for it.

"There's my beautiful girl," Tara Ray said as Lola eased into the seat. The air was delightfully cool. "School, okay?" Before she could answer, her mother pulled her into a tight hug and showered her with kisses. Lola resisted at first, trying not to laugh at the ticklish feeling it brought, but eventually, her guard fell, and she pressed her head into her mother's chest. A light floral perfume filled her nostrils; it smelled like home.

"I love you, Mom," Lola said breathlessly before receiving one final kiss on her forehead. Tara Ray settled back into her seat, adjusting the radio before putting the car back in drive.

"I love you too, sweetness. Let me get out of here and get us home."

The car ride was the same slow procedure and headache of getting through school traffic before turning out onto the main highway that led home. Lola didn't ride the bus because they

7

lived so close, and her parents got out of work shortly before school ended. It was a blessing, really. Lola wasn't sure if she could handle another minute of her loud, annoying peers.

"Well?" her mother asked, and Lola knew she was returning to the question about her day. That was their routine, and Lola answered like she always did, only partially committed. Her hands were busy pulling her journal from her pack and flipping through the entries of the day. It worked out, as her mother would stray off subject to vent about her own day. With Tara being a teacher herself at another elementary school, her updates were usually a dull assortment of things ranging from unpleasant teachers to snot-nosed second graders. Lola, uninterested in the repetitive stories, would only tune in when a new event or idea presented itself in the rants. Currently, her mother was talking about how someone used two bags of coffee, instead of one, in the break room that morning, making the day less bearable. Lola understood people, particularly adults, needed caffeine first thing in the morning to get through their days, but she'd sometimes catch her mother drinking it in the afternoon, too. She always liked the smell and taste of her mom's coffee. Her dad's, on the other hand, tasted like dirt.

The scene outside the window shifted to their smaller neighborhood road, flanked with a collection of brick and wood houses. Lola's green eyes peered up at the sky once the words in her journal began hurting her head. Her parents warned her not to read in the car, but she never listened. That act of defiance, though small, made her smile. She searched for different cloud formations to ease the tension behind her brows. Their various shapes and sizes fascinated her; they were unique and different every day.

The Rays resided in the first house on the right of their narrow side road. It was a standard home with lightly faded bricks and a brown shingled roof. It wasn't the prettiest thing in Lola's opinion (her mom had selected it), but it was home. Her father had converted what was previously a garage into a larger living space with a fireplace, so her mother parked in their driveway. To Lola's delight, her father was home.

Thomas Ray ran his own construction business, allowing them to live a comfortable life, but sometimes his work came home with him. It was a small sacrifice, he always said. Once her mother began working part time as a substitute teacher, the extra income afforded them some of the luxuries they had. To Lola, the warmth of a family and home was enough, and she loved her parents dearly for their commitment to her.

The SUV barely stopped before Lola jumped out of the car and pushed through the gate into the backyard. Her mom's laughter followed her, then faded. There was a small door adjacent to the house that led through what her dad called the "utility room," which housed the washer, dryer, and some of his motor equipment. Extension cords hung on nails, and various shelves held cans of paint. Beyond that scene, Lola glided through another door leading into the renovated room, barely feeling the hardwood floor beneath her feet. The house opened into its main living area with the kitchen's small, bordering bar to the right. That was where she found him, reading in the corner spot where the counters met. A few pots were steaming on the stove—always a pleasing sight to Lola. Her father was a bigger man than most, but his size flattered him. He'd transformed the shed in the backyard into a gym with dumbbells, benches, and other necessities. He'd work out and play his music, which Lola far preferred over her mother's.

9

It was heavy and loud, and it rocked. At times, she'd stay with him while he worked out just to bounce to the beats.

Her father had brown hair that was beginning the balding process. His eyes, of the same shade, were kind, and his smile grew when he caught sight of her. Lola crashed into him, throwing her arms around his thick legs.

"Hey there, little thing, I take it you had a good day," he said, looking down at her fondly.

"Better now," Lola replied, still clinging to him as if he might disappear.

"Is your mother right behind you?" he asked, running his rough but gentle fingers through her blonde, curly hair. On the other hand, he marked the spot in his magazine and set it down. Lola could only assume it related to sports or bodybuilding. Though they weren't of any particular interest to her, she enjoyed following and liking whatever he liked.

"Any minute now," she replied. She slid off him, adjusted the strap of her backpack, and bolted toward her room. The living room was attached to the kitchen, and beyond it, a hallway led to the bedrooms. Lola's was the smallest one on the end, but she didn't mind its modest size. Her bed was neatly made, a requirement of hers in the morning, with its pink and black comforter looking terribly inviting. Those were her favorite colors, of course. Lola dropped her bag on the ground, leaving it behind, and clutched her journal to her chest. She gave it a final loving squeeze before tossing it onto the bed. It'd be there for her when she returned.

They ate as a family at the dinner table that night, as they had every night before—a family tradition, her father would tell her. Weekends, when they sometimes went out to eat or to see a movie, were the only exception. It was never unpleasant. The conversations were funny and eventful, and Lola enjoyed the sound of her mother's laughter the most. It was her favorite sound, and her dad knew how to bring it out again and again. The three of them were a perfect trio, and Lola wouldn't want it any other way. The benefits, she supposed, of being an only child.

The chat turned to work, and they talked over drinks, a few beers for her father and a glass of red wine for her mother. Lola was allotted one soda a night but usually preferred juice or milk. Afterward, her dad broke out the tub of ice cream—her favorite part—and they all indulged. The laughter and delight resonated in her, a soft and warm feeling that washed over her body in a smooth, comforting wave. Lola knew one day she'd look back on those moments and recall the sounds and feelings. She took a moment to be thankful for her blessings as her parents had taught her.

Later, long after the kitchen was cleaned and dinner finished, Lola bathed and freshened up before slipping into bed. She left her light on and the door slightly ajar, a gentle reminder that her mom would need to come in and say goodnight. With the small window of time she had before that, Lola grabbed a pen off her nightstand. She propped her knees up, laid her journal across her lap, and opened it—the true treat of her night. She scanned the day's writings as well as a few previous entries. Lola liked to reread them every night before making her final bedtime additions. Her parents, and everyone else in her world, knew that her journal was the most precious thing to her. She needed it to survive. Through her words, she brought the journal to life, too.

She didn't hear her mother arrive. Lola glanced up to see her standing in the doorway with her arms crossed over her chest and a tired but fond smile on her face.

"Are you ready, sweetness?" she asked softly, and Lola nodded, shutting her journal and setting it on her nightstand. Her mom came and sat next to her, reaching her hand to comb the strands of stringy hair out of Lola's face.

"I want you to know that your father and I are extremely proud of you every single day," she started. Lola intertwined her fingers into her mother's hand and smiled up at her. "You are truly an amazing gift, and we thank God for you." Her mom kissed her hand and pressed it against her face before standing back up. "Goodnight, sweetie. We love you."

"I love you both," Lola answered with a smile. "Sleep tight; don't let the bed bugs bite!"

"Your dad wouldn't let them get close to either of us, my love. I'll see you bright and early." After she turned off the light and closed the door, Lola's nightlight came to life with a soft pink glow. Lola pulled the covers up around her and snuggled in. Her mind began to wander almost instantly in the solitude. She thought about what the next day would bring, the events that would transpire, and how she'd record them in her journal. Lola lived an ordinary and perfect little life. What she couldn't predict was that things were about to change drastically—in both her own life and the lives of those around her. She smiled until she drifted off into a dream-filled slumber.

Into the Madness

Wish, whisk, wish you away

The dreams that come are here to stay

Cry and burn and die you may

Or another story and another day

Lola woke in a pool of cold sweat, her breath coming in quick, desperate gasps. Panic was a silent alarm, infesting her mind like an uncontested disease. She didn't scream, though her gut told her to. It told her to cry out for her parents, to scream, and to cry some more. At the same time, her brain was attempting to untangle the confusing webs of fear residing deep within her. It was trying to make sense of it as if the terror had some rational reasoning that could be negotiated with.

Reality settled in slowly, and, as it turned out, her brain was right. A dream. *Only a dream.* Her breathing and heart rate slowed, the frantic confusion ebbed, and her room materialized around her once more. The house was silent and the air still—the same as any night—but the silence felt eerie. Lola knew the nightmare was to blame. She didn't usually have them; her dreams were usually exciting and adventurous. That one, though, embedded itself in her heart, nagging like a starving child, desperate for food. The words rang in her head as if someone said—or rather, whispered—them to her. The visuals were vivid; Lola recalled bodies floating above in a deep red sky, smiling and laughing without sound. Their arms were folded near their chests as if they were to lie in a coffin. She remembered running through the pitch darkness only to slam into a wall and tumble backward. *Trapped forever,* she thought with a shiver. There was a massive floating rock—round yet jagged. Its surface had doors, hundreds of them, wrapped around and somehow engraved into the stone. Every single one Lola tried was locked tight, except for the last one. It swung open into a cold room of wet stone, as small as a prison cell. Brandon Melton stood in the center of the room, facing away from her, rambling with his arms wrapped around himself. When she reached out to touch him, he spun in an alarming way. His eyes were missing, but he stared at her with great black pits. *It's always green,* he said with an angry twist of his mouth. *I told you! They're always green!* He screamed then, mouth opening impossibly wide, and she fled in terror. A million eyeless Brandons lined either side of her, laughing silently, but the whispers remained. *Cry and burn. Cry and burn. Cry and burn.*

The urge to weep became unbearable. It was sudden and overwhelming, and Lola cried out with a helpless, scared wail. Tears streamed down her face, her sinuses congested, and her cheeks began to swell. It was mere moments before she was a mess of broken, choking sobs. She'd never felt so helpless in her eleven years of life. She'd never felt like such a child.

To her comfort, her eyes caught a glimpse of light coming from down the hall, which could only mean her parents had heard her. Her breathing slowed, knowing they were coming, but the pain in her throat persisted. She watched the doorway until her mother appeared, yet everything seemed off. It was as if everything was muted and unraveled in slow motion. Her mother was speaking as she flipped on the light switch and rushed toward her, but Lola couldn't take it in. She just watched in silence with swollen and red eyes, her body flooded with relief. The terror that had gripped and pinned her down faded. Her shoulders slumped, weak and worn. Lola very much wanted to throw her arms around her mother's neck and shove herself into her. She'd do anything to capture that safe and nurturing feeling. It finally came when she felt arms wrap around her. Warm fingers moved the wet, sticky hair out of her eyes and mouth. Her body was settling back into a normal state, the shivers of fear subsiding. *Cry and burn, cry and burn,* the words rang, and Lola squeezed her eyes shut, pleading her brain to shut off.

Her father entered the room soon after. As they comforted her, she became aware of the real-world details falling into place around her. The familiar sights and sounds of her bedroom were returning, and she could hear her parents' consolations. Her mother rocked her, whispering warm reassurances in her ear.

"It was only a dream, my love." Her voice was soothing music. Her dad came to sit on the edge of the bed beside her mother.

"This is unusual," he said, concern lining his voice. "Are you okay, Lola?" She glanced at him and nodded, pressing her face against her mother's nightshirt.

"It is," Tara Ray agreed, still combing her fingers through Lola's hair. "These things happen, though."

"Remember, we aren't going to let anything happen to you. No matter how real a nightmare seems, it's not real, okay?" Her father's voice was strong and sure, and Lola knew she could trust it. Her heart swelled in her chest, and she reached her free hand toward him, her other arm curled and pinned against her mother. He slid over and, together, her parents cradled her between them. Lola took a few more hot, controlled breaths. *They are here for me, and nothing can take*

16

them away. Another tear slid down her cheek, but that one was born from relief.

"Do you want to come to sleep with us, hon?" her mother asked with her face pressed to the top of her head. Lola was tightly jammed between them, and though it was getting stuffy, she dared not move. Not yet.

"You just stay and sleep with me, Momma," she replied. The answer was something a five-year-old would say, but she needed the comfort. The embarrassment and shame were minimal compared to that. She could feel the exhaustion seep into her, both physically and mentally.

"Of course, I will." Her parents smiled tiredly at each other before kissing and parting ways. Her dad rubbed her shoulder one final time and kissed her head, wishing her goodnight. On his way out, he switched off the light and disappeared into the darkness down the hall. Not long after, her mother adjusted the two of them on the bed, so she was lying with Lola's back against her chest.

"Will you be able to sleep again?" her mother asked in a soft whisper. Her voice was the world at that moment, and Lola wanted to say yes, but she knew the truth. The whispers still lingered in her mind.

"I don't think so, Momma." Her voice was helpless. "You can sleep, but just hold me. I need you."

"I'm not going anywhere, my love." Lola smiled in the dark of her room, pressing as tight against her as she could manage.

"Tell me stories about when you had bad dreams, Momma." And so, her mother did. She went on in detail for a while, with Lola hoping the words would lull her to sleep. To her disappointment, it wasn't so easy. While she listened, she had to remind herself to stay focused rather than let her mind wander as it typically did. Never had the fact bothered her, but the disturbing words refused to fade. Brandon Melton's face wouldn't fade. Lola tried to identify a thought, image, or incident from the previous day that could have prompted that nightmare, but no memory presented itself. Locked doors, eyeless people—she couldn't relate it to anything. The dream had come for her so suddenly as if it'd been inserted into her mind. The only detail about it pertaining to her life was her friend, Brandon, but why him? He was already weird enough as it was. Lola wouldn't be able to look at him the same, and he'd never know why. She felt a pang of guilt at the thought, but the image was seared into her.

When her mind began to slow its wild circles, she realized her mother's words were replaced with soft snores. Lola didn't know the time, but the darkness outside her window was shifting to a pale gray. That brought her reassurance on its own, but she also knew she'd be tired for the coming day. She hoped she could sleep at the end of it without any evil surprises waiting in her subconscious. *Everyone has nightmares,* she attempted to convince herself. It *was* unusual; even her father had known it. With luck, in a week or so, the memory would be long forgotten. She was lucky, all things considered. A lot of children and adults were haunted by night terrors on a regular basis. Some were even medicated to prevent such. Lola couldn't help but feel thankful.

As time crept by, Lola watched her room brighten more with the slow, sure rise of the sun. Her dad's alarm sounded, and it wasn't long before she could hear him moving about the house. At some point, he came and peeked his head in her room, though she pretended to be asleep. Her body wasn't near ready to get up. It was Friday, and her mom never worked that day, but she, too, would get up eventually. Lola didn't think either of them had moved, given how comfortable she felt. Her eyelids began to droop, and she wondered if she should fight it or not. Their weight was so overpowering that, half-consciously, she begged for the alarm to go off. If she fell asleep, she'd only feel that much worse when she had to get up for school. Maybe if she could just get up and get in the shower...

Lola woke again, shocked to find her mother was no longer in the room with her. The sun shone through the window, but the rays were deep and lazy like afternoon. *Is it?* She sat up in confusion, her covers sliding softly down her arms. The sleep was still thick in her eyes as she quizzically debated the time. It took a moment to realize her slow thinking, and though she was alone, she looked over at her alarm clock in embarrassment. She felt better seeing that it flashed midnight in repeated blinks; they must have lost power at some point during the night. Maybe her father had reset his clock when he'd gone back to bed, or else his alarm wouldn't have gone off either. When she stretched, her body responded with satisfaction, informing her that she'd gotten a substantial amount of sleep, though she wasn't sure how. Oddly, she could hear both of her parents in another room. *How late is it?*

A thought occurred to her, and the bubbles of panic threatened to rise. Anxiety snaked in, covering her like a blanket while her eyes searched the room. They scanned her nightstand, dresser, and bookshelf. Finally, to her relief, she caught sight of it on the floor, half covered by her thick

19

comforter. Lola expelled a deep sigh before swinging her legs over the edge of the bed and reaching to grab her journal. She wasted no time flipping through the pages to ensure all her memories still waited for her, and she was not disappointed. The thought of losing the diary burdened her, and she made a silent promise to herself to hold on

to it forever. She gave it a final squeeze before setting it silently back on her nightstand.

Lola rose from her bed, her feet hitting the soft carpet and padding out into the hallway. She could see her parents standing in the kitchen, and her dad was leaning against the counter with a lingering smile. Her mother, with a newspaper in her hands, had her back against the corner where the bar and kitchen sink met. She'd been talking and must have said something that amused Lola's father—something she read, apparently. Lola glanced to her left as she entered the living room, crossing the dining area to the sliding glass door that led to the backyard. There were oak trees there with thick limbs, wide and robust, that displayed burly shadows in the sunlight. Even with her brain rattled, she could discern it was later in the afternoon. The only answer was that her parents must have let her stay home from school. On the rare occasion that happened, she was greatly appreciative. And what better day to not have to go than a Friday. Lola smiled to herself and wiped the rest of the sleep from her eyes as she approached them.

"Sleeping beauty has awoken," her father said playfully. A beaming grin appeared on her face.

"Good morning," she replied hazily. Her mom's eyes rose from the paper in her hand, and her smile seemed to carry the warmth of the sun. It was the most beautiful thing Lola had seen, and she rushed to her, throwing her arms around her waist. "You let me stay home today."

"We did," her mother said with delight. "We knew you could use the rest." Her voice was music to Lola's ears. "We are sorry about your dreams, my love. Tonight will be better, I promise." Lola knew people couldn't make guarantees like that, but she hoped her mother was right.

"How are you feeling?" her father asked in a concerned tone. He knew the nightmares had scared her, and they were out of the ordinary. Lola wished she could express how vivid they were—or maybe she didn't. Going into that kind of detail would only bring the fear back to the forefront of her mind, and she wasn't ready for that. Time would have to erase it from her mind.

"I'm fine, thanks for asking. Thanks for everything." She looked through the sliding glass door. "I didn't expect to sleep so long, and now it's going to be bedtime again soon!"

"Yes, it is," Tara agreed. "We'll have to feed you a big dinner and bigger dessert to make sure you're able to rest tonight."

"I'm definitely hungry," she said, surprised at the truth of her words. Her stomach growled in agreement, and she gave it a soft pat. Her father smiled, amused, and glanced toward the refrigerator.

"Well, you're in luck, my little darling. We've had steaks marinating since last night." Lola's excitement was hard to contain.

"Rib eyes?" she blurted as her mouth began to water. Her dad laughed, leaning back to emphasize his cheerfulness.

21

"You already know. With greens and mashed potatoes," he replied. It was hard for Lola not to rush over to him and hug him joyously. He knew that was her favorite dinner, and Lola loved that her parents cooked so much. She'd read somewhere once that home-cooked meals build a solid foundation for a family, much like eating dinner together. She could vouch for it.

And so, the night went much like the evening before. After they'd eaten and cleaned up, Lola took a hot shower and climbed back into bed, the twilight thick and certain outside her window. Lola's stomach was full, and through the satisfaction of the food and her bedtime routine, she hadn't given her nightmares much thought. They worry that they may be waiting for her, however, they rose again and put a sour feeling in her stomach, like an impending sense of doom. She tried to think of anything else—what her family would do that weekend, her schoolwork, or various other things. But lying in bed at night, as darkness surrounded her, brought the memories back to Lola's mind. She leaned over and picked up her pen and journal, hoping the distraction might dispel her fear. Opening it, she began to recall the day in writing. She included sleeping in and the previous night's dreams, wishing for their descriptions on paper to take them out of her mind.

Her parents spent more time with her than usual that time, which Lola was thankful for. Even so, they were gone and in their own bed in the blink of an eye. Her mother left her door open and offered to stay with her again, but Lola declined. She needed to get past it, no matter how she felt or how scared she was. *One stupid, stupid dream.* Yet, the images still plagued her. It was like her brain was fleeing from them, getting caught, escaping, then getting caught again. *Cry and burn, cry and burn.* Pondering the words as if they were a puzzle helped keep the fear at bay for a moment. How was it that such words and images randomly found themselves in the mind of a child? Nightmares happened, she supposed, but where did such evil come from?

Lola's mind started to drift as the groggy state of sleep threatened to overtake. It was a good thing, she tried to convince herself, but she anticipated the other side waiting for her. The once-clear thoughts in her head began to fog, and her subconscious came alive like a slumbering beast, hungering from its time away. She whispered a short prayer in her fading state. A small plea.

Sunlight beamed through her window when she woke. The morning found her safe and sound, to her great relief. Lola stared at the ceiling with tired eyes, expecting to suddenly remember some crazy, wild terror. But there was nothing there. Even if she could've recalled her dreams, she knew they weren't nightmares. She didn't carry the same helpless and lost feeling from the previous night. Her relief was immeasurable. *It gripped and held me, but now it's gone. Only a dream.* She felt so pleased and free that she debated rolling over and falling back asleep. It was Saturday, after all. She heard no sound from her parents. Her bed was an ocean, pulling like a dangerous riptide. While she didn't want to fight the current, she didn't want to waste any of her weekends. Lola's eyes flicked to her nightstand, where her journal rested peacefully. Her lips curled into a satisfied smile, and she rose to start her day.

The weekend was eventful, to say the least. Her parents took her to one of the local flea markets, a larger one, a little north of their hometown. It was one of her mother's delights.

She was a sucker for thrift bargains and stayed glued to auctioning websites on the computer. The sad part was her mother talked about good deals but rarely bought anything. It was regretful at times, but they managed money for the family well and constantly thought about the future, mostly for Lola's sake. That Saturday was different, though. Money was spent on several items, including furniture that would replace what they currently had at home. It made Tara happy, which in turn made Lola's father happy. Lola observed him flashing his special smile at her. Her mother might as well have been a child at a candy store.

They stopped at a small café on the way home, where they all ate happily and quickly. It would take hours to get the furniture moved in, but Lola didn't mind. In the end, the pieces made the renovated family room look very well put together. Lola would playfully jump on the couch under her mom's watchful gaze. She was pleased that the replacements would likely make them all spend more time in the room.

As Sunday rolled around, the morning found the Rays in church, another tradition, and necessity unmistakable in their family's history. Upon returning home, her parents spent most of the day lying around and watching television, rising occasionally to snack. Those were their normal forms of relaxation and rest. Lola sauntered around the house for a time, scribbled in her journal, and then spent the evening outside. She was ever conscious of the streetlights, as she knew her mother would be. She watched them, more out of boredom than anything else, as she strolled down the center of the empty street. She still fought a queasy feeling in the pit of her stomach at the possibility of seeing Brandon, but she wanted to see him. Needed to, she guessed. It'd been a few days since they crossed paths, and the dream had her oddly worried. It'd bring her a sense of clarity—or at least a little comfort—to see that he had eyes and a tongue like a normal person. Lola willed herself to go through with it.

The wind was strangely brisk as she walked toward the cul-de-sac where Brandon lived, but the evening sun was still warm. It seemed to be pushing her along her way. The street was quiet, which was no surprise in a quiet neighborhood. She saw one man outside spraying down a charcoal grill, another unlocking the door to his house and entering, but outside of that, the wind was all she heard. It wasn't a long road, and when it dipped slightly, she could see the small trailer where her friend stayed with his parents. *The Meltons* was displayed across an old, crooked mailbox, hanging pitifully ahead of the last sloped driveway on the street. Rust had masked some of the letters, but Lola could still read them. The wooden post it sat upon was one gust away from collapsing from rot. Often, she found Brandon sitting near that very spot, playing with sticks, dinosaurs, or toy cars. But he was absent from his front yard, and she recalled his empty desk at school, too. *When was the last time I saw him?* Lola couldn't remember. It gave her a peculiar feeling, one that wasn't comfortable in the slightest.

The driveway to the home was small and sloped, curving upward upon a small rise. It was covered in sticks and leaves almost above her shoelaces, but the neglect was nothing out of sorts for the Meltons—they weren't the biggest on yard work. The more Lola thought about it, the more she realized how reclusive they were in general. It was understandable, moreover, that Brandon was so introverted. His father was a writer, and, to her understanding, he stayed cooped up in his office. When she'd first met him, Lola thought he looked like a grown-up version of his son—the same skin and hair, but, more than anything, the same withdrawn and sad look on his face. Brandon's mother worked at a local diner not far from a neighborhood attached to one of the few gas stations they had in Elley. It was only a breakfast and lunch business; Brandon said she made a load of cash serving food. She carried the same somber expression on her face, and Lola could only conclude they were an all-around gloomy family. She felt a stab of pity for her friend.

The driveway curved to the right before transitioning to a small walkway that lay parallel to the house. It veered left at the end to a small set of white stone steps leading to the front door. Lola hesitated at the bottom, questioning herself one last time. Her fingers itched for the comfort of her journal, but it rested on her nightstand at home. While she knew it was there, being without it made her anxious and nervous at the same time. It was a fleeting feeling compared to what she was experiencing facing the door of Brandon's house. Her mouth dried as an inexplicable foreboding came over her. It wasn't just the dream; it was a visceral fear. The air had stilled, which wasn't unnatural, but the timing of it made her uneasy. A chill made its way over her skin, causing her hair to stand on end. *Relax, Lola.* Maybe it was the dream. She was letting it get back into her head.

As she forced her feet to move, rising to take the first step felt like lifting a hundred bricks. The next wasn't easy, either. The door ahead was made of white aluminum, the standard for mobile homes. It sported a few dents near the bottom, only noticeable up close. An image of Brandon being locked out and kicking the door, desperate to get back into his home, flooded her mind. Her stomach turned again. *Just a dream, Lola.* The thought was meant to calm her, but she wasn't sure that it worked. On a positive note, she'd reached the top of the stairs. Without wasting another moment, she squeezed her eyes shut and knocked on the door. The loud, hollow sound it made deepened her irrational fear. Doubt curled around her like a snake, gripping tightly enough that she had to force herself to breathe. The responding silence was thunderous. *Why did I come here?* It took everything she had not to turn around and run for her life. There was a small diamond-shaped window near the top of the door, exposing sheer darkness in the house. The lack of sound and movement tensed her body more. Her heart hammered in her ears as she waited. Her throat began to burn, and her eyes filled with uninvited tears. She stood there for what felt like an eternity, shaking with fear. She didn't know if she was more scared of the door opening or not opening, but she'd taken all she could. Slowly and deliberately, she turned her back to the door and stepped down the stairs, hurrying out of the yard. The urge to run remained, and if there'd been any sound at all, she would have. Lola kept her eyes locked on the end of the small road where her house awaited. She dared to glance back only once. Nothing moved at the Meltons' place. It was almost separate from the world, caught in a still frame. The darkness behind the diamond window remained in her mind like a black hole, ready to swallow her up. She quickened her pace and kept her eyes down until she got home.

That night she lay awake in bed, watching the ceiling in the black of her room. Her parents wished her goodnight normally that time, assuming she'd put the terrors to rest. But if Lola had done anything, she'd reinvigorated her fears. She knew she shouldn't have gone down there. Her gut warned her, but against her better judgement, she ignored it. She glanced at her journal, debating on adding the experience in, but forced the thought away. She just wanted the images out of her mind, out of her life. What was the solution to ridding herself of them? The dread stuck to her like a stain.

Lola was aware of her rising anxiety and knew a great deal of time passed while her thoughts spiraled in the dark. School would be waiting for her in the morning, and her parents wouldn't be inclined to keep her home again. She swallowed a lump of frustration in her throat, desperate to turn her brain off, and squeezed her eyes shut. She couldn't have said when, but sleep inevitably found her.

She was on an empty plain, barren of life. Heat washed over her in dry waves, reflecting off the ground in the distance to form a mirage. As far as she could see, hard-packed dirt and the scattered roots of small brown shrubbery stretched out in all directions. The sky above, however, seemed strange. Artificial, somehow. It was almost solid and so close she could reach out and touch it.

"Touch it then, Lola." The voice whispered from nowhere, soft and elegant. A woman's voice. Lola ran in slow motion, watching the horizon inch closer. The clouds dipped low until she was running among them with arms spread like an airplane. *I will touch it.* It loomed closer, tantalizing and out of reach. Lola ran harder to meet the sky; it enveloped her in a world of white, and she came to a forceful stop, the momentum threatening to topple her. When she attempted to catch her breath, she realized, strangely enough, that she wasn't winded at all. Looking back, she gazed upon nothing. Everything around her—ground and air—was a white so bright it blinded her. *Did I run into a cloud?* It was a stupid thought, but, to her amazement, it repeated itself out loud. Her jaw dropped.

Hello? Her thought echoed around her again as if it'd been spoken.

"Hello, Lola," a voice said from behind her. She spun to find a woman standing several feet away. She was older and modest looking with short red curls, but there was something majestic about her. She was…bright. Her eyes were a deep green, like Lola's. She was dressed in all white, blending into everything so well that she looked more like a floating head.

"Who are you?" Lola asked into the open air. It was meant to sound confident and unafraid, but it came out as more of a squeak. She shifted to mask her embarrassment. The lady smiled kindly.

"I am here to see you off, Lola. You are going to be gone for a very long time." The voice was enchanting, dripping like honey from the comb, but it compounded Lola's confusion.

"Where am I going?" she asked, that time with a more convincing tone. The woman's voice had relaxed her, and Lola could feel her fears and doubts fading into the light around her. Instead of speaking, the stranger simply lifted her hand and pointed a slender pale finger beyond her. Lola turned to look and saw an object in the distance. It seemed to be the size of a vehicle, but she was too far away to know for sure. It was a darker color, but she couldn't discern what it was. She stared long and hard, trying to concentrate her eyes on it.

"You should go, Lola," said another voice—Brandon's voice. "They won't make you feel crazy like everyone does to me. They'll protect you." She turned her head around to take him in, and, to her relief, his face was fully intact. His eyes were the same soft brown she remembered, but they weren't sad. They were relieved. Happy, even. Confusion ripped through her, questions flooding her mind. Her eyes shifted to the woman to find she was gone. Spinning around, she saw the object was gone, too, then Brandon.

"Go where?" she asked nobody. The world of light intensified around her, and her screams made no sound.

Her eyes opened to the sun and her booming alarm clock. It felt like her brain was doing somersaults. Lola didn't recall fixing her clock, though maybe her parents had. She slapped the annoying thing until it turned off, then threw the covers from her body in frustration. She remembered everything vividly enough, but while she was glad it wasn't a nightmare, the real feeling of it had disturbed her. She just wanted her life to go back to normal.

Casting the thoughts aside, she slid across the bed and forced herself to a seated position. Her journal beckoned, so she scooped it up and added a few questioning scribbles. She didn't do that every morning, but when she remembered to, her day always started out better. God knew she needed it to.

Her mom poked her head in her doorway as she was pulling on her shirt for the day: a plain dark-green V-neck tee. Lola received a relieved smile and a *good morning*. As quickly as Lola's mother had come, she was gone, back down the hall and to her bedroom to finish her makeup. She could hear all the different tools her mother used, the brushes and pencils clinking and bouncing. Lola had a smaller makeup set but rarely used it. It was never her thing. People always said how beautiful she was—not that she wanted them to—especially the kids at school. *People are just being nice,* she thought, fingering through her bottom drawer of shorts and skirts. She picked a cotton one with a floral pattern of orange and light green. She slid on a few bracelets and a black necklace with the smallest of gold crosses nestled into the hollow of her throat. Next came her socks and shoes, old-school Converse All-Stars that she had to have. Without tying them, she scooped up her bag, secured her journal inside, and left the room without looking back.

It was a dreary day with a gray-blanketed sky. Lola sat in silence on the short ride to school, her mother juggling some finishing touches for her makeup and making sure they had everything they needed for the day. Most mornings were quiet, a fact Lola never really minded. There were worse ways to spend your mornings than in silence. Besides, she liked to think it primed her brain for the lessons of the day, as boring as most classes were.

Literature started the day, which was one of her better subjects, but things took a downward spiral with world history and physical education following. Science was her favorite but didn't come until after lunch. Then the day ended with math, of course. It was extremely difficult not to be bored with it. Lola thought she needed something more advanced to provide some intrigue as far as that subject was concerned.

The lines to get to the entrance of the school were long and slow: the usual. Her mother cursed under her breath just low enough for Lola to miss the exact words, though one could guess. She watched tiredly as they inched forward, one by one. They were early enough, but sitting idle wasn't her mother's thing. Lola knew that's where her impatience came from.

31

"I can walk it from here, Mom," she offered thoughtfully. It was only a matter of time before steam released from her mother's ears and underneath her collar.

"Okay, hon," Tara Ray said, leaning up and eyeing the rearview mirror to find a quick route of escape. "Just stay on the sidewalk next to the—shit!" A thin tube of eyeliner dropped from her hand and rolled onto the floor. "I'm good. Sorry, baby. I love you, and have a wonderful day!" Her mother's morning struggles were amusing if she was being honest. Lola had to smile as her mother leaned over to peck her cheek. And, with that, Lola was out and on her feet.

The day started normally, like any other. She had a dull throb in her hand from writing in literature class but finished with enough time to browse her journal. Lola flipped through it, checking the dates to see how far back it took her. Her mother bought the book for her at least a year before, but she still hadn't even filled up half of it. It was bound in green with a texture that was rough to the touch. Although it vaguely reminded her of the color of vomit, the journal grew on her over time. A fond smile crossed her face.

Lola tried to keep Brandon and her dreams off her mind and was partly successful, but then odd things—or, rather, odd circumstances—presented themselves between the first and second period. She was crossing through a small paved courtyard between buildings when she caught sight of Jackson. He was several yards away, heading swiftly in her direction through light rain. His face was pale and distressed, which wasn't at all shocking. Behind him, a few older boys were laughing, close on his heels. One of them had the boy's small orange backpack and was shaking it high above his head. With a cruel laugh, he turned it upside down, spilling its contents to the wet ground. It was a collection of papers, some small books, and a plastic-wrapped sandwich. Lola's heart stung.

"Go ahead and run to your girlfriend to save you!" one of them shouted. He was tall and skinny with red hair like Jackson's. His eyes were cruel, though, burning with a hatred that had no business in a child's mind. If she were to guess, the boy was a reflection of his father.

"Aw, sweet Lola Ray protecting Jackson again?" Behind the first, another tall boy stepped into view. *Darrin,* she thought his name was, remembering he got in trouble in history class a few days back. His voice was scornful behind greedy, almost pouty lips. His dark hair was damp in the rain, giving him the look of a diseased rat. Jackson reached her with an intimidating huff and circled behind, his fingers grasping at her wrist.

"Make them go away," he said, pressing his head into the middle of her back. There was no hiding the panic in his voice. Lola was glad to defend him but wished someone had taught him to stand up for himself. *What are your parents doing?*

"Don't you want your books back?" she asked, harsher than she'd intended. *I'm on edge*, she thought with a pang of guilt. To her dismay, he vehemently shook his head. The boy didn't care what he lost as long as it ended. With the boys approaching, her brows drew down and her jaw tightened.

"Pick his stuff up!" she shouted; voice thick with an anger that took her by surprise. She didn't flinch from them as they closed in and towered over her. Her statement, as vicious as it sounded, only sparked an explosion of laughter that washed over her face. Their breath stank, the pungent smell of cafeteria breakfast indicating a lack of dental hygiene.

"Or what, Lola Ray?" It was Darrin again. His smug lips smacked together, and the sound brought the heat to her cheeks. "Does having super-smart, special classes mean you can beat up people twice your size? You know why they call them 'special classes,' don't you?" A variety of insults popped into Lola's head to embarrass the boy; her anger was eager to take control. Instead, she took a controlled breath and tried again.

"Pick up his stuff, or—" Lola's eyes were drawn to something behind them, and she gasped in surprise. The feeling chilled her to the bone and held her in place. A few feet back, in the relentless rain, stood Brandon. He was dressed, as usual, wearing a white-collared shirt, khaki shorts, and high socks stretched almost to his knees. His skin was an unnatural pale white, but that's not what shocked her. A man—an adult— stood quietly behind Brandon, and both were watching her. The man was dressed in a suit of all blue with long dark hair slicked back. His eyes matched the color of his attire with an added depth.

"See? Underneath it all, she's just a scared little brat." Lola wasn't sure which boy had said it.

"Pick up your shit, nerd. Looks like the rain ruined it all," said another voice, and the bullies pushed past them. One shouldered Lola so hard it spun her around, and she wasted no time turning back. To her frustration, or perhaps relief, Brandon and the man were gone.

"Where—" She'd only mouthed the word. Jackson was tugging on her arm insistently until she finally snapped out of her daze. "I'm sorry, Jackson. Let me help you." Her behavior concerned him. But Lola couldn't get the image out of her head. *Am I seeing things?* She tried to busy herself with picking up some of her friend's belongings from the wet ground, but the memory seemed to have solidified itself in her brain, bringing her dreams back to the surface. Her stomach twisted again. Were Brandon and her fear linked? Is that why she saw him? Was there really a man there? A new teacher or a complete stranger? He'd looked far too well dressed for a public elementary school.

"We'll talk to the teachers and tell them what happened," she said swiftly to Jackson as she piled everything into his arms. She wanted to be alone to think, so she ran off without another word.

Lola kept to herself during P.E. The coaches kept the boys and girls separate; girls walked or ran the track in the school yard while the boys played football in the middle. She chose not to participate, which no one paid any mind to, and instead sat on one of four lifted drains around the outside area.

It was elevated about two feet from the ground with a manhole in the center. The gap was big enough to crawl through, even for some of the bigger kids, but everyone was too scared to try. There was only the sewer underneath, which, logically, would scare anyone. But that was the furthest thing from Lola's fears at present. Her mind was wandering so much that she wished she had a mental leash to keep it controlled.

Science was uninteresting that day, likely because of her preoccupied mind. Eventually, math found her calculating some equations Mrs. Florence put together. She watched Lola with a disapproving look that didn't surprise Lola, but she didn't quite understand its cause. Maybe Mrs. Florence wanted to catch her not paying attention or see her fail. Maybe she had a daughter herself, and the looks were born from jealousy. Lola didn't care either way, but she kept her eyes on her work to make the teacher happy.

Near the end of class, Lola forced herself to look toward Brandon's empty desk, and the feeling in her chest grew. Questions plagued her, but her inability to answer them left her defeated. *I'm letting my world fall apart because of a stupid dream.* Was that how all kids were supposed to act in similar circumstances? Was she weak for letting the flashbacks affect her so much? She hoped not. The torment stuck to her like glue.

As if on cue, her questions were answered, but not in the way she wanted. Her doubt vanished in the ensuing moments. Lola raised her eyes to see Mrs. Florence staring at her, but that's not what raised her alarm. The class had turned to gape at her. She looked down at herself, her desk, and anything else in her vicinity that could be amiss and warrant the extra attention.

Lola opened her mouth to speak, unsure if she had or not because no sound came forth. The class was silent. Panic surfaced in her mind like a blooming flower, and Lola wanted nothing more than to scream.

Behind Mrs. Florence, the man from earlier sat on the edge of the teacher's desk in his immaculate suit, watching Lola. His blue eyes penetrated her, but it was the faint smile that she feared the most. It overwhelmed her, and her eyes brimming with hot tears. Everyone was yelling and rushing toward her, though she couldn't hear a thing.

Lola thought of her parents—at work or on their way to get her—having no idea that something terrible was happening. The tears flowed down her cheeks like a river. Her hands were folded in her lap, and when she felt drops on her skin, she looked down in a time-slowed trance. They were a red liquid, traveling through the lines of her fingers and dripping from her eyes. When she raised her head in a panicked, silent plea for help, Brandon Melton stood in front of her. His eyes were missing, but somehow the empty spaces were alive with hate.

Cry and burn

Cry and burn

The
Laughing
Spiral

It was a dreamy feeling, like being submerged in water, the sound of waves crashing with force. Oxygen was sparse, but it was there in small increments, enough to keep Lola from suffocating in the strange place with unknown circumstances. All she knew was that something was terribly wrong. She'd been snatched from her world while she was awake, then thrust back into the evil of her dreams.

The bodies she remembered, with arms peacefully folded in their laps, weren't falling, after all. They were rising. She was simply upside down. It was the first coherent thought she'd processed since the classroom—the first observation that broke through her sickening fright. The bridge between reality and dream, or whatever it was, was a crumbled, broken ruin. The metaphor painted itself in her mind, and on the ruin's edge, Brandon watched her fall. Blood leaked from his ears, nose, and the empty sockets in his head. The foaming at his mouth convinced Lola that she, too, was doomed. She couldn't tell if it was a real, physical scene or if her mind had produced the vision for her eyes to behold. *Am I in my head?* "Yes" was the answer, and she had no control.

Laughter rang all around, a slow and drawn-out sound, resounding like the walls themselves derived amusement from her terror. It was thick and heavy, its cruelty sharp and piercing as if someone were laughing at death. *Am I dying? Am I dead?* Lola couldn't distinguish water from the air, nor could she feel the tears on her face or the panic in her throat. Her terror felt like ice down her spine, and her heartbeat hammered in her ears. There was no covering her eyes or hiding under a blanket. She could only fall.

Her mind darkened. The world shifted until, once more, a stone full of wooden doors floated before her. It was a wide and imposing mass, drifting gently in the illumination of a yellow moon, surreal in its close proximity. She watched it as she fell, coming even with the structure. When near enough, Lola noticed a person, maybe a child, running from door to door and frantically pulling at the knobs. The moonlight shone on the individual, and Lola noticed steam coming from her ratty-looking clothes. They were little more than brown rags, covering the child all the way to her bare feet. It didn't take Lola long to realize that she was watching herself. Door after door denied the other version of her until she began to climb the different levels of the stone. She moved and twisted like an experienced monkey. *I haven't climbed anything as much as that.* But that Lola had, it seemed. Her body writhed and bent in a frightful way, flinging itself upward. The next landing revealed more sealed doors, and she could hear her other self curse violently. Yes, that was a far different version of herself. *But how?* The rock moved higher and higher as she fell, and soon she was looking straight up at it. Lola lost sight of the mysterious version of herself, though she could still hear the explicit language. And then she screamed. Maybe they both did. *Blink.*

The dark, square window at the Meltons' place appeared in a land of blackness, airborne in front of her. It contorted and twisted, shifting back into its normal shape as it approached. Lola's body was still a frozen block of ice, the horror bringing bitterness to the back of her throat. She floated through the window and into the darkness within. Brandon's living room awaited her. There was no light, except for a single swinging bulb in the adjacent kitchen. A small coffee table lay awkwardly on the floor, its glass shattered into countless pieces as if someone had been tossed through it. The silence disturbed her. The smell drifting into her nostrils was riddled with decay, like the stench of a dead animal. *Or human.* The possibility made her body clench, and she knew her senses weren't deceiving her. Her eyes traced the floor heading through the kitchen and down a small hallway, the scent intensifying in that direction. It was the last place she wanted to go, but she was being taken there against her will. The darkness, in its depth, almost looked alive, like a great, towering shadow feeding on the light. Black limbs spread from its core, dominating the walls and doorframes like an overgrown vine. She knew one of the Meltons was down there, or all of them. She cried out, but it didn't pierce the silence. It was swallowing her, and Lola's howls fell on deaf ears.

Time dissipated before Lola came to, but her slow fall continued. Memories of her parents flashed by, recent and older, of the things they did and said their laughter, and their love. The unrelenting torment pushed more tears out of Lola in her present sadness. *What has happened to me?* Lola opened her eyes. The bodies still rose against the red canopy. Their empty sockets watched, seething with blind hatred. She couldn't suppress her ensuing sobs. They emerged from her like an overflowing pot, augmenting the pain in her throat. Her saliva felt thick in her mouth, the desire to swallow eternally denied.

The visions continued, displaying in random order to twist her emotions. Lola saw Mrs. Florence screaming at her to wake up, and when she didn't, the teacher backhanded her across the face, sending her limp head snapping back. The class laughed at the scene. Another showed Jackson back in the small school

41

courtyard, being kicked on the ground time and time again by the bullies from before. The man in the suit was watching from a distance as rain fell, and when he smiled, the vision spiraled off.

Down and down continued the drift, in and out of what she supposed could be consciousness. The sights played out for so long that she felt numb. The endless cycle dragged on while she could only stare up at the thick blood clouds above. *I love you, Mom,* was her clinging thought. *I love you, Dad. Please help me.* Thunder in the distance was the only answer amidst the chaotic silence. It cracked across miles.

Lola wondered numbly of her physical form and whether she was alive or dead. Could she just be suffering a type of trauma? Was her brain plagued by some mysterious disease or cancer? The thought of her own dead body in her classroom desk was enough to deepen the sadness coursing through her. Was that the true afterlife that awaited everyone? Or perhaps she'd been captured by some rare, lurking evil?

The minutes or hours that passed made no difference. Time had lost its consequence in the float. In her daze, Lola allowed her head to roll to the side, and with sudden shock and surprise, she lay on a flat stone surface. Above, darkness awaited. The only illumination was in the area where she lay, lit by an unseen source. Her hands, feet, and the rest of her body were visible to her, and she couldn't help but to look down at herself in wonder. *Is this reality?* Rational thought gradually returned to her, though her fear lingered. Instinctively, her hand shot to her side and around her back, itching to feel the hard binding of her journal. Lola knew it wouldn't be there, but to her surprise, her fingers found it in her bag that lay awkwardly underneath her. Nothing else besides her book of entries resided there, however. Her breathing eased, and she took a few deeper, calming breaths. She noticed her clothes were the same, too—her dark-green V-neck and floral skirt. She then reached to touch the cross at her throat; to her dismay, it was gone. Her mind worked. Was that where she was, physically? It was too real to be a dream. Confusion was a heavy rope binding her limbs.

Lola lifted herself from the ground, dusting her clothes off by habit, though there wasn't any need. She shuffled her bag high on her shoulder and scanned the quiet blackness around her. She wasn't sure what to do from there exactly, so she took a slow, nervous step. She followed it with another, but the light remained only in the spot where she originally lay. *I can't go into the darkness,* she thought fearfully. She spun in a slow circle, pondering her next course of action.

"Hello?" she called, surprised to hear her voice made a sound. It was weak, choked, and frightened, but it was audible and echoed across the great empty space around her. The sound reverberated as if bouncing off walls before making its way back to her. "Hello?" she repeated, to the same effect. Anxiety crept back into her. The light was the only thing she had, and she couldn't help but feel vulnerable confined to its invisible cage. Lola could feel the tears returning to her eyes. "Please," she sobbed softly to the ground. "Somebody!"

"Hello, Lola." She screamed and jumped with such shock that she tumbled back to the ground, her backpack cushioning her fall only slightly. It was a man's voice. For a moment, she thought it was the dark itself that had spoken, but then she could hear the footsteps behind her. They made a light clicking sound—the sound of dress shoes. A smell followed in the air with it, something bitter and sweet. She couldn't say why, but terror pulsed through her, alarms blaring in her head. Lola knew that somehow, she had to turn around.

She found another dim light when she did. Only a few feet away, the lit space revealed a man walking toward her. Lola already knew he would be the one in the all-blue suit. It was smooth and pressed, impressively tailored to his size. His skin was darkened by the sun, and his hair was slicked back and hanging loose at the shoulders. His eyes matched the color of his garb, and in them, a burning intensity blazed. It looked very much like hunger to her.

"What do you want?" she managed her voice a broken mess. Lola stepped backward but remained conscious of her personal pool of light. "Who are you?"

"You don't have to fear, child." He took a casual step forward, the click of his shoe echoing through the dark. "I am called Kalos. It's a pleasure to finally meet you." The man dipped into a formal bow. His movement was smooth, well-practiced. He raised two fingers toward her, and she flinched. He flicked his hand in a dismissive gesture, and as he did, a feeling of tranquility fell over her. She sucked it in like oxygen had been denied her, a chill running through her body. "Think clearly, my child."

"What do you want?" she repeated, her voice steadier that time. Whatever he'd just done, it calmed her somehow. Her fright remained, but it was subdued.

"I don't want anything." His voice carried like an ocean breeze, washing over her relaxing muscles. "I have everything I need, right here in you."

44

"Why?" The question resounded through the dark, emphasized. It burned inside her to know, to have some explanation.

"Because you have a special little soul, Lola. One that has my undivided attention." His lips rose at the corners. It was a kind looking smile, but Lola suspected nothing of the sort lingered beneath.

"Am I dead?" She dreaded the expected answer.

"The mind endures, with or without the body. Were you dead, your mind would not be here," he said. The answer was vague and not what she wanted.

"How?"

He smiled, pleased. "So bright," he said in admiration. "Asking all the right questions." His chuckle was a pleasant sound. "As with any possession, your fear has to be elevated in a way that makes your soul available." Lola didn't understand. Was she…just her soul? Maybe she was simply a stupid child. She could only offer up a look of perplexity.

"I am a demon, my child, in service to my keeper." Even with the calmness he bestowed on her, dread still harbored itself in Lola. It pulsed somewhere deep, and her skin must have lost some color because Kalos's smile persisted. "Walk with me."

Lola could only do as she was bid, trying to swallow a large lump in her throat. The demon was next to her, though she couldn't recall how they became abreast. His smell strengthened with the proximity, filling her nostrils. The light moved with them as they walked, unrestrained and carrying itself.

45

"What does your keeper want with me?" she finally asked.

"Souls carry great power—some more than others," he explained casually as he walked as if describing the weather. "Some are very dull; some are bright and rare. You, my dear, possess a very bright light." As Lola had expected, she still didn't understand. Kalos continued.

"Souls are beacons in the dark to us. This makes it easy for us to locate them. However, I was wrong in my first grab at you. I thought you were someone else." Lola's stomach dropped.

"Brandon," she said, unable to mask her sadness.

"Yes," he agreed. "A necessary sacrifice. After all, it drew you into me." Lola recalled standing on the front porch encased in fear. That must have been the moment the demon realized.

"Is he—"

Kalos looked down at her with his deceitfully tender smile. It didn't leave his face, but she knew it was only a mask. "The boy is dead." Lola had known all along, but it did not save her from the deep grief she felt. It was difficult to keep tears from brimming. *It would be easier if he masked this emotion, too.*

"And you bring these souls to your keeper?" she asked, thinning the saliva in her mouth. The demon laughed again, feigning his amusement. Had she not known what he was, the throaty sound might have convinced her.

"I am a dutiful creature. There are many of us, bound to our tasks."

"Are you taking me to him now?" Another smile followed, lighting his eyes and revealing that hunger again. It was deep and desperate.

"My talents in my employment have allowed me certain privileges. They permit me to indulge in my personal tastes, which we all have. Mine are, well, unique." They made brief eye contact, and she couldn't help but notice an off-putting, unnatural look. Kalos looked like a man, but there was something else there. Lola thought she noticed it in his eyes, but he turned before she could study his strangeness much longer. They walked through the void in the small light for a time until Lola couldn't handle it anymore.

"Why don't you keep the souls for yourself?" she blurted out. He inclined his head to look at her thoughtfully as she proceeded, "If they are so powerful, wouldn't they benefit you more that way?"

"Betrayal bears no rewards for our kind. My keeper has great power, and with that comes great anger if provoked."

"You fear him, then?" He studied her again, eyes weighing. If there was anger there, it was well masked, but she sensed his distaste for her questions. Lola knew to tread carefully, else he may retract his unusual gentleness toward her.

"He holds sway over the bane of all demons," he answered, still indulging her. "Hellfire." The word was a whisper, but for a brief moment, Lola could see a glimpse of fear in his eyes. "It burns eternally, consuming the souls of men, demons, and angels alike. Not something I intend to approach." Lola frowned.

"I thought that's what the devil and his minions lived in," she said. Another laugh erupted, and that time the amusement was genuine.

"The innocence of a church-raised child," he said, cackling. The statement bore a shred of mockery, though she expected nothing less. "Men write books of what things were and what they are with the purpose of serving only themselves. Humanity is a flawed wreck, child. Don't listen to it. Beings suffer in many ways after death. But no, demons don't live in hellfire." A smile lingered on his lips.

"Then where do you live?"

"Wherever I choose."

"Wouldn't people know?"

"Did you?" Kalos spread his hands, twisting in a way that she could look at him fully. No, she supposed not. Lola drifted into thought as they walked, not knowing how to feel or what to expect. She thought of her parents and what could be happening with them at that moment. The idea of their sadness brought more tears, but she bit her tongue and held them in.

"Am I only my soul now? What's happening to my body? My real body, I mean." Each time Kalos looked at her, she attempted to study his eyes. Something different lingered there. She just couldn't put her finger on it.

"Your body remains in a comatose state." The demon didn't elaborate.

"And my parents?"

"They grieve their only child." Her reaction to that thought was visceral—a sharp pang in her heart. The silver lining was that she *wasn't* dead. Not yet. But what would happen here?

"What is it you intend?" she asked in a shaky voice. The only response she received was the clicking of Kalos's shoes. The silence lingered—his mind seemed to be drifting a bit as if he were having a mute conversation with something unseen.

"It's better if I just show you, my dear," he answered finally. His voice was the same low, steady tide that calmed her. She wouldn't allow herself to be deceived, however. Something terrible lay ahead for her. Somehow, some way, she had to prepare herself for it.

"Is there hope for me to ever leave this place?" she asked. A crooked smile returned to his face, yet he seemed reluctant to respond.

"It's a game I have in store for you," he said. "And, of course, all games can be won."

"And then I can have my life back?" Even with the demon's spell around her, it was hard to keep the raw emotion out of her voice. She *was* just a child, and she wanted to go home. Her beaming, cheerful parents flashed through her head.

"All things are possible," Kalos conceded. The possibility brought her a little comfort until her logical mind intruded. *The game must be very difficult.*

They walked through the dark, side by side. His clacking shoes were the extent of their conversation for what seemed like an eternity. She did notice, however, that her shoes made no sound. That realization disturbed her, though she worried it wasn't the strangest thing yet in that place. The light around

49

them followed loyally, constant and unwavering. She was sure the demon could snap his fingers and thrust them into darkness at any moment. With the darkness could come more of Kalos's mental tricks, and what would she do if he altered her other emotions? She needed every moment of alert, conscious thought she could get.

Part of her wondered if he could see inside her head even though he hadn't given any indication he could. She would glance in his direction, trying to get anything from his eyes or movements to no avail. Lola settled for believing the answer was no. Her hand slid down her backpack to find the binding of her journal inside. It was a search for comfort, and it brought some. She wanted to jerk it free and scribble desperately inside, but she was deterred by the thought of the demon taking it from her. *Soon,* she hoped.

A tall door abruptly appeared in front of them. It was made of dark wood and mysteriously illuminated by its own light. The path, hinged to nothing, waited behind the door for them. Lola could see around it, even behind it, but something told her that walking through it would lead to a very different place.

"What is this?" she inquired as she eyed the entrance. Her curiosity grew.

"The beginning," Kalos answered without emotion. They came to a stop in front of the door. Menacing in its size, it towered over her. *If a door could frown, it'd look like this*, she thought. Its design spiraled in complex knots and depicted certain shapes—Lola thought she noticed imprints of claws and webbed feet in the wood. The handle, however, was what stood out the most—a glowing globe of perfect crystal shining a sharp light. Lola marveled at it before averting her eyes. It

burned a circular purple-and-blue afterimage into her vision.
She hesitated in the entryway.

"And if I choose not to go through?" Kalos simply
shrugged, turned back, and pointed a thin finger in the direction
from which they came.

"You could wander in darkness for countless lifetimes."
Lola didn't know what was beyond the door, but she knew
hope didn't lie the other way. "Remember, this is the only path
here. Open it, Lola." She didn't recall when, but somehow,
he'd moved behind her and stood at a distance. His hands were
folded in front of him, and he watched her intently. *The only
path*, she conceded. Whether the truth or a lie, she grasped the
knob, half expecting it to sear her flesh. Instead, it felt cool to
the touch. Lola twisted it until she heard the click, then pushed.
In silence, it opened inward, bending the world around it as it
shifted somewhere else entirely. Lola stepped through with the
demon following behind.

It was a wide red-carpeted hallway that presented itself.
The color was eerily close to that of blood, as deep as a seabed,
serene and undisturbed. To think she would sink once she
stepped onto it was irrational, so she took the step and was
secretly relieved when the carpet acted like carpet. The
surrounding walls were white, with unique designs sculpted
into them. People and creatures were magnificently cut, so they
looked to be moving. Most were naked or half-naked, locked in
different embraces or an eternal frozen battle. It was the best
she could do to keep her eyes forward and advance.

The hall was bright with the light of several ornate
chandeliers, their crystals gleaming. Lola glanced back at
Kalos to see him clearly for the first time, and even with the

additional illumination, he still looked human. He gestured for her to look ahead, and she had no choice but to turn back around. It was a long hallway, seemingly without an end. The farther she walked, the farther it extended. Above, the ceiling was so high, it was lost in darkness. Lola wasn't sure if a roof even existed over that place; the sight overhead was redolent of a starless night sky.

The artistic molds faded farther down, and the walls became a flat, disappointing shade of white. Pictures were hung in place of the art, not nearly as impressive but still intriguing. The ideas were more violent in them, many depicting bloody battles. Some were biblical, some medieval, and some modern, to her surprise. There were individual portraits, too. *Other demons, maybe?* Some were men, others were women, and a few she couldn't discern, to her shock. They were different creatures of a kind she didn't know. One illustrated an older girl with captivating yet childlike beauty. She had multicolored, translucent wings on her back. *A fairy?* Lola always perceived them as friendly creatures of fantasy, but that one's eyes told a darker story than the rest of her appearance suggested. Lola moved onto the image of a sea of violent red waves washing up to a stony shore. Another showed a gray sky with hundreds, maybe thousands of bodies suspended in the air, tangled into a tight, writhing ball. They were living, screaming, and struggling. Lola found it profoundly disturbing. The last she observed portrayed a man with sad, dark eyes dressed—or rather, trapped—in a suit of metal armor. In his hand was a long silver sword, dripping with fresh blood. Guessing how many countless other lives that knight had taken gave Lola a sickening feeling in the pit of her stomach, and she moved on.

Lola was scanning the art for so long she'd almost forgotten why she was there. She spun forward to see Kalos, hands clasped before him, standing in front of her. Behind him, she saw another set of doors—one white, the other black. For an inexplicable reason, the doors signified a finality that brought fear to the forefront of her mind again.

"This is where you shall be tested, child. An intricate game of mine." Kalos's voice was cool, and the smile on his face lacked the faintest hint of warmth that time. His eyes glided over her, and she could sense his hunger for her soul. *He has my soul to deliver, but he wants to entertain himself first.*

"I've built this all solely for you and others like you," he continued, voice livening with excitement. He gestured toward the doors, and they opened on their own accord, revealing a rounded white wall. Two more walls, with a ten-foot gap between, curved in the same direction. *An entrance.* "A maze, Lola."

She gestured to the rounded edges. "A circle maze?" Kalos nodded. "So, if I make it to the center—"

"There awaits your salvation."

"You did something to me. Something to take away my fear."

"Formalities to keep your sanity intact," he said. The demon pointed to her backpack that hung off the side of her shoulder. "Your journal stays for the same reason. I needed you to come this far on your own two feet."

"For your personal pleasure, before my soul passes to your keeper." It wasn't more than a whisper, but Kalos heard all the same.

"The center is your way out, child." His eyes pierced her; two silver globes peered out from their depths. His smile was unnaturally wide, his teeth long. He towered over her, leaning down until she could feel his breath on her cheek. It burned like a flame, and Lola quickly stepped back. Without turning or moving, the world spun around her, and once more, she was facing the entryway. *I have no path, but forward*, she realized with heightening fear. Had he removed his "formality?"

"Go save your soul, Lola Ray." She backed away from him, tears working back to the surface. Laughter poured from Kalos, but that time it was a darker sound. "Run and survive. If you can."

Lola ran.

****

Kalos watched with silent satisfaction as the child ran into the maze. His eyes followed her until she disappeared, and a smile appeared on his cold lips. He knew she'd do well. She was brighter than the ones before, perhaps the most so. *Stronger, too*, he thought. His admiration for his toys was genuine, but then again, so was his evil. He praised his master for his gift with a delightful, muffled laugh. The demon clasped his hands behind his back and turned in the direction he'd come.

He needed no light to guide him. It was his own place, and he knew the path well. He'd constructed every aspect of the reality, and many more were waiting for the child. He glided down the hallway, moving as gracefully as a soaring bird. The blackness around was solid, parting only where he split through it, then closing again. His shoes no longer made any sound, and his feet remained in the air; his movement depicted more of an airborne dance than a walk. A cloak of certainty rested on his shoulders, birthing a pleasure like no other. Another child faced his maze, and while he thirsted for her soul—craved it like the dead craved life—he also longed for the challenge it would present. He would allow the anticipation to build to the maximum level before he took her to his keeper. *Give her hope and let her taste success*, just so he could rip it from her. His booming laughter made a sound in the dark, the noise rising and traveling into the dark heights above. Tears slid down his cheeks, and his human mask slid from his face. His eyes were black houses with two orbs of silver lurking within. With each shifting glance, they moved like disturbed puddles of liquid. His real teeth protruded out of his mock lips. The last of the human slid wetly off his body, revealing a casing of dark blue underneath his disguise. The pile of steaming mush— previously human flesh—at his feet would rot in the darkness once he moved on. In place of his fingers were claws of the color of onyx. Kalos let out a deep sigh of relief, the air coming out in a thick, visible mist in front of him. He delighted in being himself. Even with his mind tricks on the girl, she never could've handled seeing him in his natural form. His laughter rumbled like an avalanche. As it died, his tongue flicked out to either side of his mouth, and he could almost taste the satisfaction of the torment he'd inflicted upon her.

Kalos raised his hands and closed his eyes. Before him, an image appeared. It was Lola in her classroom, body shaking uncontrollably as he possessed her. Around her, panic erupted. Kids pointed and screamed; some ran out of the classroom. The schoolteacher held Lola's head in her hands, trying desperately to help. *You can't*, thought Kalos in amusement. It wasn't long before other adults rushed in, followed by school nurses, then paramedics. As they tended to her, Kalos raised two fingers, extending them with a quiet whisper. In his other hand, an orb rested, black as the night, with a pulsing orange light inside of it. It resonated when he drew on it. Lola's physical form arched, her body rising high above her desk. Her golden hair spilled out behind her, catching the sunlight shining through the classroom windows. *She must sleep now.* With another flick of his fingers, her body collapsed in a motionless heap. Everyone screamed, thinking she was gone until they noticed her chest rising with slow, peaceful breaths.

Kalos knew he would have to monitor the situation closely, even become personally involved to deter her parents from ever pulling the plug. All they would ever see was that Lola rested. There would be no signs of sickness or disease. It would be an inexplicable thing, but he was confident in Thomas and Tara Ray. *They will hold on until the end.* The demon snapped his fingers, and the image vanished.

Around him, the darkness continued its embrace, squeezing him with a gentle caress. He snapped again, and his maze in its entire brilliance came into view, laid out for him like a three-dimensional blueprint. It was a vast creation, and its walls glowed like great pillars of light. On their surface, he knew, were the keys—keys that opened the gates to the other places he'd formed and molded. While he wouldn't be able to see her in the maze's halls, he could monitor her in these realities once she entered them. If she chose not to proceed, well, he had some encouraging creatures roaming about that would see to it. Kalos lifted the dark orb in his hand, staring upon it greedily. *An impressive toy.* The anticipation brought joy to his heart, laughter boiling in his throat. He'd watch and wait. She would suffer and endure; he'd make sure of it. The glowing of the maze's walls reflected on his sharp silver teeth above as he smiled a final time. *Let it begin.*

****

The slow motion of the world continued to haunt Lola. She ran, but everything dragged around her. Her tears were frozen on her face, their movement down slower than that of a snail. The fire in her lungs threatened to burn the remaining moisture from her body, leaving her a dry shell of her former self. The walls stretched around her, twisted and curving. While she never wanted to stop, she was conscious of pathways and intersections as she passed them. *You can't be foolish, Lola.* Finding the path to salvation was a separate thing from her fear, and she had to focus without emotion intervening.

Lola stopped, catching herself from falling by placing her hands on her knees. The world and her insides, however, kept moving. A greenish-yellow spew hit the floor with a wet slap. It was hot enough to numb her throat. Snot dripped from her nostrils and drool from her mouth. Her eyes were wet and blurred. She had to force herself to breathe, and with each exasperated gasp, she remembered it was not a dream. *This is your reality now.* She blinked away the haziness, but her body was not yet finished. She doubled over again, opened her mouth, and choked.

Lola couldn't have said how long the sickness stayed with her or how she ended up seated with her back against a bright wall. It only mattered that it had passed her. She weakly gazed up at the surrounding structures. Their towering presence overwhelmed her, and she could only perceive darkness above.

57

It hurt her head to stare, so she rolled it to the side, taking in the winding path. It curved to the right, down a twisted bend. *One path*, she thought. She had no idea what lay ahead or how she would navigate the structure. She could roam for lifetimes there, the previous offer of being banished to darkness not sounding that bad after all. But she needed to find strength. She had to try. Lola thought of her mother, hair blowing in her face, glistening in the sun. Pressing her back hard against the wall, she put her hands behind her and slid upward with her legs. It took all of her energy to rise, the weakness still thick inside her.

A trace of dizziness lingered when she stumbled forward, but Lola kept her stomach settled. She breathed slow and steady, leaning heavily on the wall for support as she stumbled down the hallway. As the wall's paper-like texture caught her attention, her journal immediately came to mind. The reminder prompted her fingers to search for the binding in her backpack; once they did, feelings of reassurance and comfort washed over her.

It took a lifetime for her to make her way around the first bend. It curved and curved and then curved again, all ending in the same direction. She could take her hand off the wall occasionally, but her weak state wouldn't permit it for long. While only a few steps were granted at a time, her impatience for energy began to burn inside. The idea of sleep crossed her mind, but could she? Was it possible if she was already trapped in her mind? It sure felt that way, given her fatigue. What could differentiate reality from a dream? Either way, something told Lola it was a foolish idea. She fought against her weighted eyelids.

Every ounce of her was pleading desperately for relief, and in her condition, she barely felt herself collapse. The floor was cool and refreshing; Lola's last thought was of how easy it would be to let go, to rest and pretend it was all just a terrible dream.

Lola's eyes shot open. There was a sound pushing through to her mind, but had she imagined it in her slumbering state? How long had she slept? Was the noise coming from another dream? *No*, she thought uncomfortably. Anxiety snaked in, carrying a sense of dread with it. Then she heard it again. *Ssscccrrraapppe.* It was sharp and clear, like stone grinding against stone. She rose swiftly, pushing herself back to her feet with her palms on the ground. The sound came from the same direction she had, and she turned her head toward it. She could only perceive an empty path. Nothing was there. *Please, let it be nothing.* Lola swallowed a hard, fearful lump.

Ssscccrraapppe. There was no mistaking it that time. A large shadow flickered on the walls. Panic struck her, then instinct kicked in; her feet took flight in the opposite direction. Energy surged through her, adrenaline pulsing in her veins. *This is what you wanted.* Lola's legs pumped, urging her forward in the only direction she could go. The maze was a white blur rushing by—so bright she failed to see the wall in front of her. With a hard slap, Lola rebounded off the structure and hit the ground. To Lola's chagrin, unwanted tears emerged. Despite a bruised nose and aching head, she couldn't take any time to dwell on the pain. *Something is coming. Something large.* Where could she find an avenue? She glanced to her left and right, spinning around as she took to running again. *A turn,* she noticed to her right. She made a conscious note not to forget it'd be a sharp *left* turn if she turned from the way she

59

came. Another wall waited shortly beyond the path on the left. *Backward is right, then left. Don't forget.* Another left bend led her to a different blockade, that one with a narrow path to the right. *Left, right, left.* The length was short, but two options stood ahead. Lola pressed hard against the wall and listened for any noise to pierce the eerie silence. *Is it gone?*

Her backpack slid down her arm, and she unzipped it as quickly and calmly as she could manage. Her journal was in her hand and opened in a heartbeat, the other hand finding a dusty pen at the bottom of the bag. Her breaths still came heavy and accelerated, fear sitting on her shoulder and screeching in her ear like a parrot. Lola flipped to a blank page and recorded her turns as best she could with the clock ticking. Her skin was hot, with sweat beading across her soft forehead. As quick as the writing started, it was finished, and she kept her journal and pen in one hand as she dashed to the right. The hall straightened and gave her three options—two left and one right. Without hesitation, she chose the first on her left, logging it in her notes as legibly as she could on the run. The path rounded sharply, reaching a wall and another small opening on the right. Turn and scribble. A short round, two paths left. Second left, scribble. One turn right, scribble, turn, *run.* The pattern went on until Lola collapsed, battling confusion and fear in her lungs. She choked each breath down in her attempted recovery. The maze must be vast. With the silence persisting, she began a shaky sketch to the best of her knowledge of the turns and paths she'd taken. Sadly, the process was interrupted as the sound echoed through the corridor again, seemingly close. Lola was on her feet.

She couldn't let the panic shake her. *Just keep recording your steps, Lola.* She took an option to the left and quickly found a dead end. *Shoot.* She hurried back, daring glances at her journal when she could while keeping her eyes ahead. No shadows on the walls yet, to her relief. A few retraced steps led her back to an earlier option passed by. One turn left a dead end. She spun in a circle, bewildered but referencing her journal to proceed. Another option presented itself, and she moved as quickly as she needed. Her mouth was dry, but alarm surged through her. At the end of the bend, she could see one of two options she hadn't chosen before and pressed hard toward it. Before her second step hit the ground, a moan filled the air, deep and pained. It was capped with a moist swallowing sound, then *ssssscrraapppeeee.*

She could only shriek as she hit the turn so fast that she slid, and her momentum sent her into a wall. Upon impact, she used the barrier to push herself back to her feet. Tears spilled down her cheeks. In her frightened state of mind, there was no time to log the turn. Memory would have to do.

Lola's heart sunk in her chest, and her feet slowed to a deflated walk. In front of her stood a solid white wall with no options to the left or right. The blockade was absolute and unforgiving; all she could do was clutch her journal and turn around slowly. The path stretched back farther than she remembered, and there was no way she could ever make it back to the entry. *Is every path an eventual dead end?*

Ssscccrraapppe.

Whatever it was, it would be rounding the corner in moments, the truth of it undeniable. Her heartbeat felt like it was making its way to her throat, and her tears were unrelenting. The sobs that shook her made her feel more like a child than anything ever had, but in the end, she *was* only a kid.

The sound persisted, and Lola turned her back, unable to face the mystery of what pursued her. The white wall shone in front of her, the glow of it allowing a feeling of comfort amidst her pool of dread. She ran her hands over it, feeling the papery texture that brought her journal to mind. Lola wondered if she could write on it. The thought was silly, but underneath her fingers, she felt something rising from the surface of the wall. Her squinting eyes adjusted to the brightness, and as the light faded at the edges of her vision, she was shocked to see words underneath the sheen. They were impossibly small but laid out on the walls much like the pages of a book. She couldn't read them, as they were scribed in a language she didn't know. But somehow, she felt them. They called to her. Lola followed them up and down in awe, scrubbing her wet eyes to see clearer.

Ssscccrraapppe.

A moan followed the sound, curbed by a rough expulsion of breath. *Some kind of creature.* It was behind her, she knew, and her time ran short. There was something captivating about the words, though. She was almost absorbing them. Her eyes scanned quickly, taking in the inscription, not sure what it meant—if anything. Then, an image appeared in her head, and something else began to happen. The sound behind her dulled, and the world around her shimmered as if she were stuck in a giant crystal. The words rose farther from the walls, chanted in a whisper from an unseen mouth. The surrounding light intensified, but the words stayed apparent. Everything around shook in a thunderous rumble, then the brightness disappeared. Was it death that'd found her? The maze faded from her brain, and again, Lola fell.

The Bright House

One Path

Lola…

The voice belonged to her mother, the sound floating
sweetly through the air. It fell over Lola's ears in gentle waves,
and her eyes fluttered open. The sun beamed down in a world
of black and white, the warmth of a summer day touching her
cheeks. The sky encapsulated her vision, with trees and their
branches dotting the edges of her periphery. The breeze
brought a floral sweetness to her nose, and she felt a peace
she'd almost forgotten. When a shadow broke through like
sudden night, her pulse quickened, but she quickly relaxed.
Above her was a face, shrouded by golden hair and a radiant
smile no sun could match. Tears filled Lola's eyes in the
joyous feeling as she was taken into her mother's arms.

Oddly, Lola knew her mother hadn't spoken. The voice
was separate from where she was. She could only tell because
of the silence that dominated the place. Even her heart
hammering in her chest she couldn't hear or feel, but she knew.
She wanted to embrace her mother forever and never let go. A
memory, however—something very real—told her that place
was a façade. A lurking reality on the edges of her brain
convinced her of it. Her mother's hair, smooth as silk, drifted
in the breeze as if caressing the air. Her laugh was silent when
it burst behind her smile, but Lola didn't doubt its realness.
There wasn't a more genuine sound. The biggest question, she
mused, was why she was seeing it. It had the features of a
vague dream, but Lola was conscious, the maze still lingering
in her mind. The words on the walls, the sound of something

large behind her—all of it remained with her. A part of Kalos's game, perhaps? The thought dug at her. She stared at her mother looming over her and let the tears fall.

The air shimmered once more, and Lola felt a stab of desperation. *No!* she thought as her mother faded. The reality shook violently, the black and white scene around her gaining color and vibrancy around the edges. As the image shifted, the colors swirled in a rushing invasion, all displayed in chaotic array. No sound was made, but the twisting scraped through her head with a type of pain she couldn't describe, making her want to scream. Lola watched the colorful madness resembling a funnel as it encapsulated the trees, grass, and sky. Her body pulled with it as if she were being vacuumed, and she had no choice but to acquiesce. She recalled her mother's smiling face one last time before she was ripped away, falling into the funnel like draining water.

That fall wasn't like the other. It was a rush of colors fading into a blinding white, then running like watercolors. Lola zoomed through the tube, watching the thousands of lines twist and morph. The display was dizzying, and Lola didn't think she was descending anymore. She was flying. The wind was real, blasting her in the face and pushing her hair behind her. As terrifying as it seemed, the motion brought her a deep sense of euphoria. The pleasure and energy caused a friction, and she worried she may burst into flames with the force. Lola closed her eyes against the potency of it.

It began to fluctuate speed, from free falling, to being propelled by unknown means, to drifting gently like a feather. Lola was surprised the experience didn't make her ill, although her stomach was empty. Food was an afterthought, something she wasn't even sure she needed there. If she was only there in spirit while her body remained at home, then Lola had no doubt her parents would see that she was fed. If she wasn't dead. The thought brought a terrible guilt. Her parents deserved better than that.

Lola eased her eyes open, taking in the flowing sea of white and black again. Her speed increased and slowed irregularly until she finally floated again. There was a difference, however, beyond her. A small speck lay ahead. She had to rub her eyes to help them focus in the brightness, but the funnel wound and moved in its direction. At first, the spot looked black, but as it enlarged, it turned out to be a deep brown. Lighter browns speckled the surface, appearing like leaves on a bed of dirt. It grew and shifted directly beneath her. *Leaves,* she thought in surprise. Treetops, too, bloomed in the scene. The silence broke, wind creeping to life in a darkened world. Everything turned to night in a flash, and with a dropping feeling in her stomach, Lola realized she wasn't flying anymore. She was falling.

From that height, the drop would have killed her. It wasn't like freefalling, though. It was more like zipping down a water slide that was raised at the end. Gravity held her in place, then dumped her like a sack of bricks. The impact took the air from her lungs. Lola landed on her stomach, her forehead bouncing off the earth. Dirt and other scum filled her mouth, and pain engulfed her body. *Pain,* she thought through the jolt. A physical feeling in a body she wasn't sure she had. The ground was cold and unforgiving, as was the breeze. It took all of Lola's energy to roll over to her back, and a groan escaped her lips as she did so. She stared at the night sky, her breath fogging above her. The inside of her mouth was dry, which

66

made it difficult to spit out the dirt. Her clothes were moist and covered in the damp filth. The wind shot like an icy stab through a newly torn hole in her shirt, and goosebumps crawled like ants over her body.

Is this the real world now? Had she found a magical path that spat her from the maze back where she belonged? Lola's gut told her not to be foolish. Besides, she had left her real body sitting in a desk at school. To top it off, Elley, Alabama, wasn't close to cold at any time of the year. And it was freezing, considering her attire. As she pushed herself up to her hands and knees, a familiar urgency settled, and her hands shot to her side. It was a relief when she found her bag still with her, the binding of her journal hard against the inside. Mist expelled from her mouth as she sighed. She didn't think she'd be able to bear the hopelessness that would come from losing her journal. Her written words were glue, and they held her together.

Lola looked around, impatient for her eyes to adjust to the dark. The area was heavily wooded, but with sizeable spaces between the trees. They were oaks and pines, mostly, in huddled groups. A combination of large and skinny, they stretched up with branches reaching for their companions. Above, the sky was a deep dusk, speckled with dim stars and no sign of a moon. Silence remained. The nighttime chill was unrelenting, and Lola knew she had to move soon. *But where?*

The thought persisted in her head as she lifted to her feet. There was little choice in what needed to be done. The reality of it was that, in some way, it was part of Kalos's scheme. The only thing she could do was begin walking in one direction. Pine straw, matted and clumped together, littered the ground, giving her steps a stealthy mask. Occasionally, a twig would crack beneath her feet, breaking the silence with a punctuated snap that seemed to echo for miles. It was the only sound; no animals chattered or moved in the night. Only the wind walked with her, a quiet whistle of air carrying a teeth-chattering swirl. The stronger gusts, though infrequent, made her eyes water and her muscles tense. Lola wished she had a coat to pull tightly around her body.

Was she on some lifeless island or barren planet? What purpose would the maze serve by sending her there? Surely Kalos wouldn't bring her to a dead end. The demon wanted to toy with her before he snatched her soul. While the idea heightened her fear of the unknown, Lola could also feel anger somewhere in there. He'd taken her life away, her parents, her school, Brandon…and here she was in an inescapable death trap with a vague and questionable promise of salvation. Was that promise still there? Was it foolish to think she could get out of there with her life intact? *He wouldn't be a demon if he weren't a liar*, a small voice whispered to her. Accepting that would mean accepting defeat, so Lola tuned it out. Her fingers itched for her journal, the only escape she was permitted. She'd find time to write. *Soon.*

Lola wandered for so long that her feet stung and her knees ached. The movement spared her from most of the air's chill, but her mouth was still a dry pit. The thought of water was enticing, and the fact was enough to convince her she *did* need physical nourishment. She dismissed the confusion of it quickly and remained focused. She would stop at points, listening for sounds, praying for a stream or river. To her aching disappointment, only the wind would answer. And then, the swift snap of a branch behind her.

She felt the lost energy burst back into her body, the fatigue fade, and her feet were suddenly moving faster than she could believe. It was the first different sound in the new world, and Lola wouldn't be taking any chances. Trees whipped by her in her near-blind flight, limbs stretching out as if reaching for her and attacking. The thumping of her feet was the only thing she could hear other than the pounding of her heart in her ears, but she didn't dare to look back. The air was comforting in a way as it rushed over her, the iciness of it painting her skin in repeated strokes. Her dry mouth and burning lungs were at the back of her mind, but she knew she couldn't run forever. Desperation drove her, but hopelessness threatened.

The burning sensation shooting through her leg muscles was suddenly absent. For a moment, Lola ran on air, and she only had time to look down for a split second before crashing into a steep hollow. Her body thrashed wildly about, her pack jerking from one direction to the other. It was a thick pile of leaves and straw that found her at the end of it, much lighter than the previous fall, but not entirely painless. Unwelcomed exhaustion overtook her again. She lay embedded in the soft ground beneath, and for a moment, her worries ceased. It was so dark that Lola wasn't sure if she'd opened her eyes at all. If they were closed, maybe it wouldn't be so bad to keep them closed. *Just for a second…*

Mental alarms blared, and Lola's eyes shot open. Had she fallen asleep? If so, how long? A minute? Hour? The urgency was clear. Adrenaline resumed its pumping, and the need to get up and run burned inside of her. Was something chasing her? Only the darkness and wind replied, carrying a gentler breeze as if there was nothing to be afraid of. She squeezed her eyes shut and strained her ears. Still nothing. Shutting out her fear, she rolled over to her stomach—quickly that time to avoid prolonged sound. The same view greeted her as before, an impenetrable black only broken above the treetops. The pines were closer together there; it seemed they were leaning to form a dome over her. *Trapping me in this darkness.* Lola pushed herself to her knees. She felt the worry of standing up and coming face to face with terror without realizing it was present, but she squashed the feeling and expelled a long, exhausted breath. Her eyes followed the air as it drifted, half surprised that so much came out of her little body. Just as it began to fade into the surrounding dark, she noticed something odd. It was a different thing, as unbelonging in that place as she was. A faint glow momentarily reflected against her breath. It was a deep orange color, or at least she thought so in the fleeting moment. As far as she could discern, it was coming from the direction she was going. Lola bit her bottom lip, puzzled at the sight. To dismiss the possibility of her imagination playing tricks, she heaved another heavy breath into the air above. She couldn't tell if it was relief or hope she was feeling, but it bloomed inside her when she saw the same glow again. It was there!

She adjusted her bag, slung it snug around her shoulder, and followed the direction of the light. It was a ditch she'd fallen into, so the way up was steep and painful. She dug her hands in the ground, using fistfuls of dirt and roots to help lift, which in turn made her hands feel gritty and rough. Lola never minded a little dirt, though. *Better grip,* her dad would tell her. Each foothold was secure as she pushed up, but the ground sunk and tumbled at some points. When she reached the crest, the cold had left her once more, and her skin was wet with sweat. Her head fell to the ground from the exertion, the dirt soft and cool against her face. The wind continued, more prominent at the top, several gusts surprising her with their strength. With it, she thought she heard the sound of laughter. Lola's eyes widened, and her ears perked up once more, desperate for the sound. It wasn't an evil sound—like the demon's cackling—but cheerful. The wind whipped again with the same sound in tow. Another laugh, or a combination of two. She couldn't help but feel a sliver of hope. *Please*, she thought with building excitement. *Please be someone who can help me.*

Ahead, the black persisted, but Lola didn't give up in her search, and it yielded her an answer. A light ahead, small and orange, danced in the wind. *Fire?* she wondered as she observed it. The ground sloped downward in a gradual manner so she wouldn't be forced to move too quickly. With the thickening of the trees, it'd be hard not to make a lot of sound, but Lola was upwind, so that could afford her some error. She walked, never taking her eyes off of the flame ahead. The outlines of trees encapsulated it, but she thought she could see several moving parts. Not just two people, but several. That almost gave her pause, given the fact they might not be that nice. The good-natured laughter made her think otherwise, however. She eased on, questions barreling through her mind. What other options did she have? Keep wandering the dark forest? Wait until daylight? Her instincts were screaming at her to approach. *Just go really slowly. Run if you need to. Lose them in the trees.* They didn't sound like kids, so Lola would have the benefit of dodging and hiding more effectively. *Just watch them for a while.*

Lola continued her approach, imagining herself weightless. That didn't steal away from the reality of the wet crunching beneath her feet, though. The wind still worked hard in her favor, so she made a brave pace. When the heavy gusts would roll through, she got braver. They were only periodic but allowed her to gain a lot of ground. The exhilaration and fear inside her were a mad tangle, a feeling she tried to ignore to maintain focus. Sweat dotted her brow. Below, the laughter was all too obvious—that of both men and women. The fact encouraged her. They were carrying on and speaking unnecessarily loudly—the kind of way her parents would late into the night when they'd have friends over for a few drinks. *Are they drinking?* A group of younger adults, camping and drinking alcohol to have a good time? A dangerous possibility, but it still brought her hope. She needed something or someone besides the cold and the dark. There was nothing else for her out there. The prospect of any kind of companionship almost made her forget about Kalos.

She couldn't recall the number of branches and tangles she brushed from her path, or roots and straw she'd stepped over. Her eyes remained locked ahead, her feet picking up steam. Even without the wind, they were so loud up close that they wouldn't have heard her anyway. Besides, they weren't paying any mind. The laughter came in great guffaws, the group slapping words over each other in between. She could hear playful curses from men and women alike. *They're all picking on each other*, she thought curiously, feeling something close to delight. It was a reassuring feeling. When Lola was nearly on top of them, she chose a spot to settle in—a larger pine on the brink of their encampment. She leaned her shoulder heavily into it, standing sideways so she could peek at the scene ahead. The fire was larger than she would've expected, a tall flame roaring high enough to menace nearby trees. It cracked and

72

popped, the coals fresh and glowing a bright orange beneath. The wind was aiding, and the fire was alive in the night. Lola had to stay low to keep from the illumination. The camp itself was a round, open space. It looked natural at first, but a second glance showed it had been cleared and walked upon at great length. *Maybe a common spot for something like this?* It would seem so, and upon closer inspection, there were more than several people. Chairs—plastic outdoor loungers—surrounded the flames. Lola's eyes shot from person to person, counting until she stopped at thirteen. She was right about their age. Younger, probably in college or on the verge of graduating high school. She had a suspicion most were likely too young to drink, at least. They stood around in several small groups, as close to the fire as they dared. Even from her spot behind the tree, she could feel the heat, and Lola craved its warmth. Bottles were in nearly every individual's hand, so that question was answered. There was another smoky smell as well, something potent and foreign drifting to her nose, but she couldn't put her finger on it. There were fewer women than men, she noted. Closest to her, a pair sat on a cooler talking to another large man who stood beside them. Another girl a few feet to the right sat with her back propped against a tree. Her hair was as black as a raven, her lipstick a deep red. Her brows were drawn down to portray an angry look, but there was a softness to her features. A cigarette hung limp and burning from her mouth, and she was scribbling in a small book. It brought a smile to Lola's face—the first in a long time. The feeling was fond, and she gently caressed her journal at her side.

Lola took in the rest of them. Eight of the thirteen were men. She noted some high school football jackets, thick and blue with a gold trim. Two of the boys standing on the far side of the fire were black and identical. *Twins.* Their hair was shaved close to the head to accent the commonality. They spoke to a third who wore the same jacket. He was pale with a full head of hair nearly to his shoulders. His cheeks bore a faint natural blush, complimenting his kind smile. *Kalos had a kind smile*, she reminded herself cautiously. They laughed along in an immature conversation, in turn expelling Lola's doubt. They were giggling so hard they were choking, some even snorting. It made the corners of her mouth twitch upward.

Amidst the noise, Lola took a deep breath and stood. The wind brought a soothing gust of heat to her as she leaned farther from the tree. It was difficult not to stand there and soak it in. They could have spotted her easily, were one to look in her direction, but their attention was elsewhere. She took a careful step forward, convincing herself one last time that she was going to take the risk. Her nerves shot into high gear, but Lola felt it was the right thing. Another step brought her clear from the wooden barricade, the next took her down the short slope onto the edge of the open area. *I'm practically on top of them.* Had she been a bear or a wild animal, they would have been oblivious until they were all being torn to shreds. Maybe she needed a little more of an entrance. With that in mind, Lola jumped the last of the dip into the camp. She landed with a soft thud, sand and leaves moving from the impact. Anyone who wasn't blind would've seen her, and they certainly did. The group seemed to jump at once in surprise, shouts and screams of confusion and fear following shortly thereafter. It was a comical sight, really, but it hardly had that effect in the moment, and for the first time, laughter no longer filled the camp.

"Lord!" exclaimed one of the women sitting close to the fire. She was a bigger girl, and when her seat tilted back, she nearly fell into the sand. The firelight reflected off her short red hair and wild eyes. Luckily for her, she got a hand down in time to save herself from falling.

"Holy shit!" One of the twins was looking at her in disbelief, but still, he came around the fire, approaching slowly. "It's a little fucking kid!" The words caused Lola to frown. She was hardly little. Well, maybe just a bit, but she was no toddler!

"How the hell are you here, kid?" It was the third football jacket with the rosy cheeks. His accent was heavily Southern. The boy looked around, incredulous, as if searching for a kind of portal that could have dumped her out of nowhere. He wouldn't have been far wrong. "How's this possible?" If that question were a cork, it had popped loose. Behind it came mass hysteria—yelling and screaming and questioning. Some were aimed at her; some were shared amongst themselves. A few were asked to no one at all. The one common occurrence was that every one of them was on their feet, eyes on Lola as if she were a ghost. The idea that a fifth-grade girl would pop out of the bushes in the middle of the night was a tough juggle, she admitted, but even with the uproar, she felt an odd calm. It was safer than when she was alone in the dark. There, she felt protected. If these kids were a danger to anyone, it was likely only to themselves.

Everyone chose a position around her, if somewhat absentmindedly. A couple holding hands stared at her from across the fire, mouths still agape. In front of them were three others, two guys and a girl, prodding each other with questions.

If it'd been loud before, the sound pushed to a new level. A few shushed the others, desperate to keep the situation in check and figure out what to do. Lola quietly waited for order to return.

The first girl, the one smoking against the tree, walked straight toward her. Her dark makeup was a scary sight, but her eyes carried an innocent curiosity. When she was within arm's distance, a silence fell over the group. Lola could cut the anticipation with a knife. The girl kneeled in front of her, unafraid. She was very pretty. A silver chain clung tightly to her neck, much like Lola's own cross, but hers was a skull instead. It rested neatly in the hollow of her throat. Eyes of deep blue studied her, and Lola caught the scent of rose petals. The sweetness was curved by the smell of cigarettes, but it was still strong.

"I'm Rosalia," the girl said. Her tone was calm and mature for someone who looked so young, and though her brow was still drawn down to look angry, the sound of her voice was humble and kind. "What's your name, sweetie?"

Lola hesitated before answering, eyes surveying those around her as they closed in a tight circle. They were like mannequins, frozen, hinged on her answer. "I'm Lola."

The girl's deep red lips curved into a smile, revealing glossy white teeth. "Okay, Lola." She reached over and gently pulled the dirty strands of hair from Lola's face. "Are you lost?"

"You don't think!" said another girl who stepped around to Rosalia's side, looking down at them both. "Ros, no one knows how to get up here, much less a child!" Lola bristled. *Up here*, she thought. She suspected they were elevated to some point.

"Let me talk to her, Fiona." Rosalia's voice was sharp but still calm.

"We can't go on here." That came from a shorter fellow with darker skin. He was skinny, looking like little more than a child himself. Luckily, his voice was deep enough to confirm his age.

"We will go on," Rosalia answered with a matter-of-fact tone. The three in the football jackets behind her all voiced their agreement.

"You know where we're going, Ros. Are you going to risk a little girl getting hurt? This is a sign. We have to go back."

"Just hold on, Ricky." Rosalia turned back to her, stroking her shoulder, trying to stay focused. "Are you from town?"

"I'm from Elley," she responded slowly. The gothic girl's eyebrows raised, and Lola clarified. "Alabama." What else could she say?

"How in the world did you get here?" Lola could only shrug at the question.

"I just…woke up here." She couldn't very well say she was forced here by a demon. "Where are we?"

"You're in western Virginia, Lola," Rosalia said, looking at her sympathetically, but there was suspicion in her eyes. *She thinks I'm a kid telling stories*, Lola thought. And she was.

"You must be confused, sweetie. Did your parents bring you here? On vacation, maybe?" The thought of her parents made Lola sad all over again, and she could feel the tears threatening. She shuddered against the chill.

"I'm cold," she deflected. Rosalia turned to look at a black-bearded young man standing a few feet back from her. After hesitating for a moment, he shook his head and stepped forward, pulling off his jacket. It was a heavy thing, army green with many pockets. He watched her uncertainly as he stepped around and draped it over her shoulders.

"Thank you, Jonas," Rosalia said. A look of mutual fondness passed between them before he returned to the spot behind her.

"Hell, just bring her with us," the larger of the twins said. His jacket had more wear than the others had as if it'd belonged to an older relative before him.

"Don't be ridiculous, Corey." That came from Fiona, who was shaking her head. Corey shrugged and smiled with one side of his mouth.

"Shit, I'm just saying. You know how far a hike it is up here? The hard part's over! Let her tag along, and we go through with this."

"And if she tells?"

"Then we'll tell on her." A tall, skinny man with short, spiked blond hair stepped in. His beard was dyed to match, and it was trimmed neatly around the jawline. He stumbled a bit as he moved close to her. "Your parents have to be looking for you, right? Lola?" He leaned in, bending with his hands on his knees, and she could smell the alcohol on his breath. "I bet they aren't too happy."

Lola felt a stab of anger she couldn't describe. It was like the feeling you'd get when you didn't like someone, but you weren't sure why. She fingered her journal nervously and didn't respond. Her eyes turned to the ground.

"Robin, you're scaring her, you dipshit." Rosalia shoved him away without standing up. It was a playful thing, but there was enough force behind it for Robin to raise his hands in defense. Lola could see from the look on the girl's face that she was considering it.

"What would *you* like to do, hon?" asked Rosalia. Well, there was a considerate question, and Lola's comfortability heightened with her.

"I just want to go home." There was some truth for them. She had to fight to keep the helplessness out of her voice. She didn't want to seem afraid in front of these people for reasons she couldn't understand. Her calmness was collected but slipping. Rosalia watched her for a moment, and it took that moment for Lola to realize everyone else was watching Rosalia. *She's, their leader.* Before she could speak, however, Lola stepped forward. "Where are you guys going?"

"We came from King's Burr," Rosalia started, putting both hands on Lola's shoulders. "We are in the Shenandoah Valley on a bit of a…well, haunted trip. This is something all of us have planned for a very long time, okay? When we take you home, you must promise not to tell anyone of this." Lola didn't have a single reason to tell anyone anything, so she simply nodded.

"This is fucking ridiculous, Ros." It was the smaller twin, who slid on a pair of glasses as he approached. "We have to get this girl out of here." Rosalia's jaw set firmly, but it was Robin who answered.

"There's nothing out here, Chris," he said, addressing the twin. "There aren't even any officials anymore in this part, so why does it matter?"

"I get it, bro, but anything happens to this kid, and it's on us. She trips, falls, gets hurt in some unlikely, fucked up way, it's on us! Rosalia?"

"We can't go back," she replied. "Who's to say we'll get another chance to do this—all of us, together? Robin's right. No one's here to stop us anymore."

"Why'd you even ask her what she wanted to do, then?" asked Chris. Rosalia didn't answer, just stubbornly clenched her jaw once more. The big man in the football jacket walked up and kneeled next to Lola. That close to her, he seemed like a giant.

"Lola, I'm RJ." His voice was gentle, but had he wanted, he could snap her in half with the strength of his bare hands. "If you want to go back down, I'll take you." It was a shame she couldn't specify that she didn't want to go back down. She wanted to go home.

"RJ," Corey moaned. "This could be the last shot."

"I'm with RJ," the big red-haired girl put in, easing back into her seat with the fading excitement. "We have to do the right thing."

"Thanks, Brit," the big man said, earning a nod.

"I'm not scared," Lola blurted. She had to admit, her curiosity was pricked. They could ruin their trip by taking her somewhere that would be just as far from home. Or, she could go with them. "I've been worse places." Most of their mouths dropped open again, but laughter spilled out that time. Even Rosalia smiled a bit, still looking at her. Lola noticed how pretty she was when she smiled.

"Well, that might make you the bravest of us all," Rosalia answered, squeezing both her shoulders again.

"I promise I won't tell. But you have to tell me where we're going," said Lola. Rosalia's smile brightened.

"Then you have a lot of catching up to do. Come sit; get acquainted."

Lola couldn't say any single argument was won there, but they were put on standby. They spoke for quite some time once everyone settled back in. As the tone grew serious, everyone found a spot to sit in a tight circle around Rosalia. She talked about their purpose there, and the seriousness of it was not something to be taken lightly. The more they spoke, however, the more comfortable Lola became. She could almost forget she was stuck in a demon's game. These people were real and eased her mood the more they talked and laughed. What they were doing was quite exciting. *Ghost stories and such.* It was right at home with the type of things she liked.

Legend had it there was an old, abandoned asylum deep in the Shenandoah Valley, north of King's Burr. It was called the Arch Ridge Institute. Heavy and illegal experimenting had taken place there, mentally and physically damaging to patients who were already very ill. That went on for years and years. The owner was a rich man named Artur Wendall—no one could touch him since he had many officials, high and low, in his pocket. No one questioned or ventured out near the supposed hospital. Wendall had his own guards, but they became unnecessary over the course of time as explosives were used, instead, to block off any approach. They used large rocks, trees, and debris to bar the path, sneaking in the patients through the smallest planned and well-hidden gaps of the blockage. As time moved into the modern era, these gaps were closed, and people were flown into the secret institute. Anyone who approached without permission was never seen again.

Digging through an old library had yielded Rosalia a report of a King's Burr detective in 1966 who decided to take matters into his own hands, though the library denied its authenticity. The policeman navigated the valley for months in his search of Arch Ridge until one day, he came upon a gap in the forest's blockage, one so small it must have been missed. Once on the treacherous path, he spent days walking and climbing. Weak, weary, and out of food, he crested one final hill, and there it was—Arch Ridge Institute. Its sturdy steel-tipped gates were ajar. Beyond lay the facility, its exterior made of beautiful black stone. To his disturbance and surprise, he found only emptiness within. No employees or patients. No appliances or furniture. Just an empty, abandoned shell. No one knows what happened to Artur Wendall or his staff. The detective reported hearing planes and helicopters but never actually saw one. He also reported seeing flashes of a strange light, vibrant and beautiful. His name was Gordon Plank, the only man to ever come back from Arch Ridge. Not a year later, he was shot in the line of duty; thus, any further details of the mystery were lost or buried.

Lola stared into the fire as she listened, envisioning it as if it were painted before her. She was snuggled close against the older girl's chest, the army jacket pulled tight around her. From head to toe, her body was covered in goosebumps and filled with an intense excitement. She was glad she could stay.

82

"If all that bad stuff was going on, how come no one flew in to help?" she asked. The crackling of the fire was the only sound that joined her voice. Everyone else had taken to a deep silence, enthralled with the story.

"Well, apparently no one who flew in ever returned. The owner had incredible wealth and power. He probably possessed the means to get people to look away."

"Personally, I don't think anybody knew anything was wrong," said Jonas. He'd spoken very little in Lola's short time with them so far. He was a withdrawn type of person, she concluded. "I mean, who'd tell? If word from any of the patients got out, it'd be dismissed as crazy talk at best."

"You're probably right," Rosalia answered, absently stroking Lola's hair.

"You really believe this story, don't you?" Lola asked, twisting around to look up at her new friend. Rosalia's smile warmed her.

"Believe or not, it's the idea that breeds the excitement and the whole reason we're here." Lola could only agree as she wriggled back around to face the fire. Across from her, she saw Robin sitting with his hands clasped. Every time their eyes met, he would smile and wave, but the odd feeling remained with her. There was something off there. It wasn't a fair way to form an opinion; Lola didn't even know him, but the feeling of discomfort was enough for her to keep a distance between them.

The hours ticked away deeper into the night, and conversations passed. It didn't take her long to get to know everyone. It was a silly and happy bunch, and there was indeed a plentiful amount of alcohol being passed around from their stashed coolers. They were all close, and Lola liked the feeling of that. Fiona was one of Rosalia's close friends, whom she'd known through her four years of high school. She was originally from the West Coast and had a type of laid-back California pride. Her hair was a sweeter red with black tips, a similar gothic style to her friend's. Jonas, the man sitting next to them, had already graduated high school and was home for a few more weeks before he had to take over his father's business. It was a photo or print shop of some sort. Lola noticed his obvious attachment to Rosalia, one she wasn't certain was mutual but seemed to be close. It gave her the feeling that maybe one of the two was ready for something more, while the other remained undecided.

Laughter snagged her attention across the fire, where the twins stood near Robin. The identical brothers—Chris and Corey—had apparent differences. Corey was the more athletic and social type, while Chris leaned more to the nerdy side. Both were funny and amiable, however.

The original girl she'd startled, Brit, sat by the fire to Lola's left with Ricky, the one who'd spoken out against her earlier. He was a bit geeky, too, and they shared laughs in a private conversation. He was going to join the Army while Brit worked at a local café with her mother. At one point during the evening, she'd spoken of her close relationship with her mother and even showed Lola a picture that was little more than an older version of the red-haired girl.

There was a second Ricky to her right, who sat next to RJ. He was obviously older than anyone in the group, but he wasn't necessarily more mature. Possibly a friend of an older sibling who got caught up in their little posse. His head was shaved, and a scraggly goatee accented his features. When he wasn't occupied, however, he was the loudest and most rambunctious of the lot. Rosalia referred to him as a "bullshitter," but he was well liked. His mouth was obscenely foul, but it made Lola giggle.

The couple was Josh and Megan. They were glued to each other in a way that annoyed Rosalia. Lola imagined that was normal for young couples. They were the punk rock type with a touch of grunge. Megan wore a black tank that clung tightly to her body and displayed a band Lola couldn't make out due to the wear. Josh wore an overly large white tee with distressed light-blue jeans. She spoke to them the least, but Megan was occasionally drawn into a chat.

Erin was the nicest girl Lola had ever met, although she hadn't noticed her initially. She was a taller girl with short auburn hair; she'd also graduated and was working on getting into medical school. Her smile was incredibly kind and melted Lola like butter, especially mixed with her soft brown eyes.

Lola realized that the large group was having a final adventure before they moved in different life directions. That was something planned out well in advance, and as much as the joking and banter dominated, it was serious to them. She could see the anxiety underneath it all, and maybe even a touch of exhilarating fear. Lola was excited, too, but she had to remind herself the reason she was there. Her mind had drifted from the fact that she was trapped in Kalos's game. *Maybe this is somewhere else. Maybe I'm out of the maze, and these people can help me get back home.* Doubt swelled in her chest, the truth a looming certainty in her heart. So much had happened;

85

was it so impossible to think she'd escaped somehow? She needed to distract herself, so she used the haunted asylum to keep her thoughts at bay. Her anticipation was growing; she wanted to see the legend almost as much as the group around her did.

The fire cracked and hissed as it died down. Cigarette butts bounced off the smoldering logs every few minutes, and she observed them soon rendered to ashy shells. Lola stared at the hot orange glow, feeling the weight of her eyelids. Her physical needs were there, though it would be impossible to ever know how. Hunger gnawed at her, and to her delight, Rosalia was generous enough to split a ham and cheese sandwich from her pack. Each bite was an inexplicable pleasure in itself, so much so that Lola had to remind herself she was raised with manners. Afterward, she snuggled hard against Rosalia's chest, waiting for sleep to take her over. When it came, no dreams awaited her, only the darkness washing up to a shore in calm, repetitive waves.

A gentle shake brought her back to the real world. Rosalia stood over her with a sweet smile, and for a moment, Lola thought it was her mother. Lola was lying on the ground on top of a sleeping bag with a thick wool blanket tucked around her. Bodies moved about the camp, packing things, adjusting straps, and gathering anything needed to move forward. The fire was a gray heap, but heat still simmered from within. Above, the night sky was brightening, the first traces of daylight passing through the treetops.

"Get enough sleep, Lola?" Rosalia asked sweetly. Her necklace hung down from the hollow of her throat as she leaned over her. Lola smiled and nodded, rubbing the sleep from her eyes with cold knuckles. "Good, because it's time." Lola was almost more excited for them than for herself. She could feel the nerves dancing among the camp. They were finally going to do it.

Conversation skipped around in hushed tones during the pack, but a few jokes circled here and there and caused rushes of laughter, mostly from the boys. Given their inattention to her, Lola knelt by her pack and took the opportunity to pull her journal free. It seemed like forever since she'd last held it in her hands. The smell of new paper filled her nose when she opened it, offering her a nostalgic feeling of home. She began scribbling almost immediately with a pen she found at the bottom of her bag. Writing made her happy and sad at the same time—a bittersweet sensation. It was the last thing she had that connected her to a once-normal life. It kept her sanity intact, and without it, she imagined her mind would slip away.

"What are ya writing there?" Lola hadn't heard Robin sneak up on her, and she jumped slightly, turning red and slamming her journal shut. *Sneaky as a snake,* she thought. It wasn't fair, but she felt little guilt as anger pulsed through her. She glanced up at him with an obvious glare, his smiling face fueling the flames.

"I don't think she likes you, bro," Corey said with a bark of laughter. He passed by and patted his friend playfully on the shoulder. Luckily, it drew Robin away.

"There's not a kid I know who likes me," he said, grunting as he walked away. That didn't surprise her in the slightest.

"Don't worry, Lola, I don't like him either," Corey continued as he moved across the camp. She knew he was just picking on his friend, the fact too good to be true, but the thought brought a small grin to her face. Robin began collecting his things and smiled half-heartedly when their eyes met. Maybe she was being mean. He couldn't have possibly known how personal her journal was to her, but it was likely the worst time he could have snuck up. She might forgive him for the mistake—might.

The group, with Lola in tow, stepped up the slope out of the camp and huddled tightly together. Lola stood in front of Rosalia, leaning against the front of her legs. In the gothic girl's hand was a large, expensive-looking compass. Lola didn't doubt how invested they were.

"How are we looking?" Rosalia asked, addressing everyone as a group. Her eyes remained on the compass.

"Packed and picked up, fire's out." RJ was the first to respond, fingering a large chunk of chewing tobacco into his mouth. The smell turned Lola's stomach, but she liked him anyway.

"Check here," said the smaller Ricky. "All gold." Rosalia finally raised her eyes to take in the agreeing nods.

"If we are in the right spot, it's only a few miles to the pass on the map," Rosalia started. Lola could feel the increasing excitement. "Let's all stay together and avoid any extra sounds until we're camped in again."

"Do ghosts have ears?" Big Ricky asked with a smirk, and Rosalia shot him a glare hot enough to incinerate. "Only kidding, dear." He pulled her into a one-arm hug, kissing her on the side of the head. Despite her resistance, she was smiling. Lola didn't miss the flash of annoyance on Jonas's face.

"Seriously now. Are we ready?"

"Aye, aye. Let's do it," Robin said, walking in the direction Lola guessed they'd be going. Packs were lifted and checked one last time as they filed into a single line, leaving the small camp behind. There were fourteen of them altogether, Lola included. Her own anticipation was growing with each step. *A real haunted adventure.* Kalos came to her mind for an instant. Glancing at the sky, she wondered if he could see her; he probably had that kind yet evil smile on his face while satiating his sick appetite. There were times the night before that she felt like blurting everything out to Rosalia. She wanted to tell them all everything and beg for help. *They'll never believe you, though*, a voice whispered in her head. She sighed, deciding again that it'd be best to keep it to herself. Maybe the time would come when she could come clean. Until then, Lola would keep her head up, let the cool wind wash crisply over her face, and walk alongside the rising sun.

The Pass

The journey up the hill began as comfortably as they could've hoped for, but as the ascension progressed, the cold intensified. Even the exertion of the task couldn't save Lola from it, and she blew hot breath into her hands. A short time ago, Erin had given her soft cotton gloves, but they were losing their effectiveness as the cold persisted. An idea was proposed, mostly by the men, that the cold was unnatural—no doubt an attempt at heightening the excitement for the journey. But it failed to take away the chill. What *was* comforting, however, were the occasional wide and sunny openings they'd pass through. They sometimes spanned for several football fields in length, and Lola enjoyed the warmth on her skin. *Breathtaking*, she thought of the view as sharp blades of pale green grass crunched beneath her feet. Lola could see the valley below, the path from which they came. Well, at least where the others had come from. She wasn't sure exactly where she'd started. A thin, winding river ran downward. Beyond, she noticed smoke or something similar. Rosalia told her it was from one of the large plants in her hometown of King's Burr, and Lola was aghast they'd traveled all that way on foot. She shielded her eyes from the sun with a gloved hand, pondering the distance. Her newfound friend called her silly and reassured her the distance hadn't been covered on foot, not entirely. Several cars were used to get them to a point, and once the incline demanded, they climbed the hill the rest of the way. When Lola asked where they'd left the vehicles, Rosalia told her they'd hid them with branches and other sorts of debris from the forest.

To that point, animals remained unseen and unheard. It didn't seem to bother anyone else, maybe because no one was paying attention. It was odd to Lola, though. When she questioned Rosalia again, the girl had fun with the fact, adding that maybe the disappearance of everyone in the asylum took everything in its path. One of the others suggested gas or poison chased everything away—that certainly didn't make any of them comfortable. Lola wasn't convinced either. Something inside whispered that it had to do with Kalos. If it was something of his creation, could it have just been a detail left out? Or maybe it was purposeful. Undoubtedly, something *was* wrong with the animals' eerie absence, and the saddening fact allowed the gnawing feeling in Lola's stomach to persist.

The woods eventually found the group again, and the cold weather intensified with the extra cover. The trees were a cloak, darkening the world close to the threatening shade of night. The pines were pressed tightly together except for a few areas in which they blazed their trail. Lola gazed up, looking to the tops of the pines and spinning in a circle while she walked. The light of the sun pushed through, almost looking desperate in its random-sized punctures. It made her dizzy doing so, but it took her mind off her decreasing body temperature. Others hugged themselves, rubbed their arms, or huddled tight inside their jackets. The sound of teeth chattering filled the air. Lola had no choice but to allow her teeth to do the same.

They were moving up for at least two hours when Rosalia called for a break. The path steepened drastically, and it was decided that there would be a good place for a short rest. Ricky, the smaller one, unshouldered his pack and looked up the incline thoughtfully. Lola followed his gaze.

"Look," he said, pointing. The others walked close, looking in the same direction.

"I don't…" It was RJ who spoke, holding his hand on his forehead, though the sun did little to block his view.

"You don't see how the forest gets darker in a line there?" Ricky looked around for validation, but no one could seem to spot it. She couldn't either.

"I'm not sure what I'm looking for," Erin said as she stepped up the rise. Big Ricky strode up behind her, a bottle from the night before still clasped in one of his hands. He put the other hand on her shoulder.

"The blockade," the big man said, the bottle sloshing noisily as he brought it to his lips. With the same hand, he pointed. "The whole area darkens in a straight line." Erin leaned forward, straining her eyes, and Lola could see the realization hit her. With a smile, Erin snatched the bottle from Big Ricky's hand and took a pull. The others noticed, too, collectively. It took Lola a little while longer, maybe because she was smaller, but it eventually came to her. The growing distance naturally darkened, yet the shade was deeper at a certain point, almost like she was looking at a wall.

"We're close." Rosalia breathed excitedly, not taking her eyes off the blockade. She took the bottle from Erin, and it was passed around to squeals of delight and excitement. Lola noticed in the moment how important it was to the group, and she couldn't help but smile for them. The feeling in her stomach remained, however.

The party decided against acting rashly and instead chose to be patient, sitting on the ground and rustling through packs for food and water. Robin and Corey worked to start a small fire as a conversation circulated about the next approach. Lola seated herself up against a pine and reached into her bag for her journal, but she hesitated momentarily to look toward Robin. To her relief, she saw only his back while he moved farther into the woods to hunt for more kindling. That would give her some time to write comfortably. In his defense, it wasn't *just* him. Lola didn't want anyone to see. She even drew it close to her chest when RJ walked by and rubbed her head. It was a personal thing, but as she prepared to scribble some lines, Rosalia moved close and knelt beside her. She offered a strange smile of understanding when Lola snapped the journal closed.

"Believe me, I know about secrets," said the gothic girl. Her rosy smell filled Lola's nostrils, relaxing her. Rosalia reached into a small leather pouch tied securely to her beltline and pulled free a tiny leather-bound book. "I keep a few myself."

"Really?" Lola asked, interest suddenly piqued. "Do you write everything about your days?" Rosalia laughed, bumping her playfully on the nose with a soft white hand.

"Just secrets, dear. Special ones. Do you know what makes them special?" Lola shook her head, her curiosity bubbling to the surface. "The fact that they're yours and yours alone. They aren't secrets if they belong to anyone else. Keep them that way."

"I plan to," Lola answered happily, excited to be able to relate. "People like to hover a lot, especially when they know you have secrets." Rosalia giggled.

"I'll try not to hover, love. If people didn't want your secrets, though, they'd have no value. We'll just keep them wondering; how does that sound?" Lola could only smile in agreement. "Is any of this scaring you, Lola?" She could hear the concern in the gothic girl's voice. It was genuine. "It's not too late to back out."

"No," Lola replied, but she *was* scared. Not of that place, but of the things she couldn't say. *Secrets.* And not the good kind. She reached out and brushed Rosalia's cheek, receiving a pretty smile in return. Was she real? Her skin certainly felt so warm beneath her fingertips. Was any of it real? It angered her at how unfair it was, but she couldn't allow herself to falter. *One path, Lola.* She had to walk it. She needed to survive. Lola planted her mother's kind face in her mind and used it to give her strength.

Later, after Lola had written nearly a full page in her journal, Rosalia called to break camp and proceed toward the blockade. Lola wondered earlier how the girl knew where she was going, but eavesdropping on a previous conversation between her and Jonas had revealed they'd scouted the area before using the detective's information to isolate the area. That was, however, the farthest she'd gone. You could nearly see the excitement in physical form as it spread throughout the camp. Again, they pulled into a tight group.

"It'd be faster to split into two groups," Rosalia started, breath misting in front of her. "But we have nothing but time out here, so we're going to stay together instead. It's very important that we do."

"We'll freeze if we stand here any longer," said a shivering Josh, looking regretfully back at the fire that was put out moments ago.

"This is it," Rosalia continued, ignoring the statement. "Is everyone ready?" One by one the nods came, including Lola's, her newfound friend looking down at her, and Lola gave her a thumbs up.

The hill steepened before they'd gone thirty feet to the point that it was hard to believe they rested at all. She huffed heavy gasps during the climb, as did those climbing around her. Even Corey was sweating against the cold, his chest rising and falling in quick succession. Around them, the pines stood tall, not bending or leaning with the incline. If anything, the trees got bigger and stronger as they grew straight up, relentless in their task of providing shade from the sun. Feeling moist drops form at her forehead, Lola couldn't determine whether she'd welcome some heat or colder air at that point.

The group was spread wide, but all were in sight of each other. When one would stop to lean heavy on the wood or bend over with hands on knees, so would the others. Their water supply was diminishing fast, and Rosalia was quick to remind everyone that preservation was key up there. It wasn't long before the blockade was looming high in front of them, some of the fatigue masked by the simultaneous exhilaration at what might come. It was nothing but stacked rocks and trees in no specific pattern, but for Lola, it conjured the idea of some old, abandoned fortress. Everything was packed tightly, the size of it intimidating to look upon. Lola craned her neck upward, the height and width evenly displayed. As they approached it and paused no more than a few feet away, its appearance became oddly unnerving. It stood in silence, watching without eyes. But, if anything, the block was a confirmation that maybe the story was true—at least up to that point.

"Good God," Chris said in awe, exhaling heavy. "Really?" Nervous laughter rang through the group as they tried to collect themselves. Lola breathed as evenly as she was allowed.

"It's amazing," Fiona said, her eyes bright as she gazed at the structure.

"You mean big," Corey replied. He gestured to their left and right. "What direction?"

"It has to be somewhere close to this area," Rosalia said with her small book open in her hands. She was reading her notes, her brow drawn down.

"Could it have collapsed?" It was the smaller Ricky who asked, but Rosalia shook her head.

"I sure hope not, but we have to be careful here. Keep your hands off the wall as we move. Anything moves or shifts, then it *might* collapse."

"Or cause a fucking avalanche," Robin pointed out, face still in shock as he looked. "I mean, we really could die for this. *She* could die." He stretched a boney finger toward Lola. His concern was even annoying, but he could be right.

"I'll be fine," Lola said harshly, stepping closer to Rosalia. "If anyone can find a hole and squeeze through, it's me." She looked at the gothic girl. "We continue, right?"

She received another pretty smile. "That's right, Lola. We all knew what this was. We aren't going to come this far and then just say fuck it, right?"

"Hell," RJ said, walking close to the wall. "If I can get my thick ass through, any of us can. I'll go first. Lola, you stay close to me." Lola nodded, perfectly fine with that idea.

"It's decided then," Fiona agreed with a sigh. "Let's do this."

Right was the first direction they chose, if only a temporary path. Lola was first with RJ close behind, and together they scanned the wall for anything out of the ordinary. They'd walk about half a mile before turning back to retrace, making sure nothing was missed. When they reached the starting point, they'd traverse another half mile to the left. Close up, most of the rocks were twice the size of Lola, which still had most of the group gaping. The smallest she noticed was close to the size of her head. An image came to her of one tumbling from the top and squashing her like a bug, leaving everyone around covered in her bloody spray. If anything would turn them back, that'd likely be it. But she found it unlikely. The elaborate game Kalos had set up for her wasn't going to be wasted with a stray rock. Still, she found herself keeping a close eye on everything above.

Hours passed yielding nothing in either direction, so they continued to the left. She heard sighs of exasperation and some minor complaints. Once, she heard Megan say it'd be easier to split up instead of wasting so much time, but Ros quickly squashed the idea. She could tell her friend wanted to, though. She was desperate to find the pass, just like any of them, but insisted they stay together. Lola liked her confidence. She trusted it.

Another hour ticked by, the sun moving down the blue sky. Lola had become desperate to find anything, maybe just the smallest of holes. Exhaustion was setting in. Lola was struggling to walk parallel to the slope; it proved to be just as taxing as climbing the incline. At one point, she even noticed Rosalia getting discouraged, though a stubborn confidence lingered on her face.

"It has to be in…this…fucking…area!" Every word out of Rosalia's mouth was louder than the previous.

"Let's split," Megan insisted again, walking up and pulling some sweaty dark strands of hair from her face. "There are still a few hours of daylight—"

"No," Rosalia interrupted, her resolve not faltering. When she realized she may have said it too harshly, her face softened. "I'm sorry. We just can't lose anyone. We stay together, Meg." If the apology made the grungy girl happy, it didn't show. Rosalia looked toward the sun.

"There's still plenty of time," she continued. "We'll continue this direction, and if we don't find anything by sunset, we'll make camp. Tomorrow, we can use the whole day to backtrack."

Lola caught herself more than once reaching out to run her fingers over the rough surface of the wall as they walked. It was almost subconscious, maybe a kid thing, and hard to overcome when overwhelmed by boredom. And the walk *was* boring. The structure had long lost its luster, so she lowered her hand. It wasn't as if they'd yell at her for breaking any rules. Any shifting of the rocks could bring the whole thing down on top of them. To keep her hands busy, Lola slung her pack around to her front and dug inside for her journal. When she clasped her hands around the binding, she smiled and pulled it free, propping it up on the top of her bag to keep it steady. Lola scanned through some older entries, keeping a close eye out to make sure no one was paying her any mind. She itched to scribble some new ones. Maybe that evening, with a cool air and the light of a fire, she could get some work done. Reluctantly, she stuffed her prized possession back into its spot.

Over time, looking for gaps in an endless wall led her mind adrift. Lola thought and walked for so long that she paid no mind to the sun's drastic descent. Her shadow bounced off the rough surface of the blockade and danced with the trees. The silhouette lengthened while the sun fell, and with the evening, the chill deepened. She kept her hands in her armpits, hugging herself tightly and clutching Jonas's jacket around her. It was the warmth she needed, and she was thankful for the soft-spoken fellow. He still had a sweater, which made her feel less guilty, but Lola still caught him giving his jacket longing looks. Snug as it was, she found herself thinking about being bundled up in one of those sleeping bags.

Once it became too dark to see, Rosalia called for a halt. Their search had uncovered nothing, much to everyone's disappointment. The discouraged mood was felt all through the camp. They moped around silently, settling their packs on the ground. Next to her, Jonas hugged Rosalia tightly, whispering something to her that sounded like an apology. She allowed the embrace to go on for a moment before breaking off, muttering something Lola couldn't quite catch. A pained look passed over Jonas, and Lola felt a stab of pity for him. Did he love her, and she didn't love him back? Lola couldn't imagine the feeling.

It was Robin and Corey again who disappeared to collect firewood. Corey was lighting something as they walked that carried a peculiar smell. Big Ricky squatted with his back to a large pine, drawing his bottle of whiskey out of his back pocket. He took a deep pull, releasing a sigh behind it.

"That's how you warm up," he said, blowing his breath into the air as if expelling cigarette smoke. Lola caught a whiff and wrinkled her nose at the potency of it. Ricky just laughed and held the bottle toward her.

"I suppose one drink wouldn't hurt since you're out here with us." He shivered when he said it, and Lola wasn't sure if it was in response to the cold or the drink's effects—maybe a bit of both. She smiled shyly at the thought. Her parents wouldn't allow it, and though they could never know, that very thought struck her with sadness.

"My parents drink a bit," she said, remembering times with their friends on the occasional weekend. "I'm not old enough." The big man only laughed harder.

"Sounds like your parents liked to have a good time, huh?" Big Ricky pushed the bottle back to his mouth and drew. "Well, no harm in that. My folks are drinkers, too." She noticed a troubled look cross his face, and he held the bottle toward her once more.

"For warmth." God, did she want warmth. First, she had to convince herself that her parents weren't going to pop out of thin air and punish her. Lola stretched her hand out cautiously, but before she could grab the bottle's neck, Brit stepped between them.

"Are we fucking serious here, Ricky?" Her voice was sharp, her eyes sharper. "She's like what, ten?"

"I'm eleven," Lola argued. "I'll be a teenager soon."

"Yeah, like that matters one bit." Brit snatched the bottle from Ricky, taking a deep drink herself. The big man could only throw his hands up. "You got a long way to go, honey."

"It was just for the cold," Big Ricky offered in defense. "One sip's not going to hurt."

"There are other ways to get warm," Brit answered in a cooler tone, handing him back the bottle. "You need to learn some things if you plan to be a father one day." Ricky simply waved her off, and she turned around and unfolded a chair near the center of the camp. *She doesn't like to be far from the fire.*

"It's okay," Lola reassured him. "I know you meant well." With that, she strode off, eager to find her spot and Rosalia. She liked Big Ricky, even if he liked to indulge in alcohol more than the others. He had a tough demeaner that was more mature than the rest, likely due to the fact that he was a bit older. She wondered about that look she'd seen on his face, possibly something to do with his family or lack thereof. But his laugh and smile were more positive to think about. Those warmed her better than the booze would've.

She propped herself against a smaller pine across the camp, waiting patiently for Rosalia to settle in. In the window, she logged her entries for the night. Lola wrote of the blockade and how they'd yet to find a way through. She wrote about the mood of the group that, while temporarily discouraged, remained hopeful. She noted Rosalia's confidence, even though it wasn't something she'd forget. Lola was glad for the

101

therapeutic feelings her journal brought, remembering her friend's words. *Yours and yours alone.* The truth of them rang in her mind. She owned her words. Closing her journal, she looked up as footsteps approached. It was Rosalia with a sleeping bag tucked under her arm. A cigarette hung from her mouth like a flag without wind, its ash almost an inch long.

"Why do you smoke?" Lola asked the gothic girl curiously. Her dark red lips curved up in response.

"There are a lot of reasons," Rosalia answered thoughtfully. "For pleasure. Stress. Relaxation. I wouldn't recommend you start, though."

"I won't," Lola said with confidence and a smile. Her friend's smile widened.

"That's because you're a very smart girl." Rosalia kneeled, flicked her cigarette, and pulled Lola into a warm embrace. She pressed her lips to her forehead, squeezing her tight. "We have a lot of walking to do tomorrow; best we get some rest."

Lola wanted to do just that, but sleep was slow to come. Several still spoke quietly around the fire. She lay on her side, facing the flames. The warm glow lit her face while she thought of what would've happened if she'd never found them. How long would she have wandered the dark woods? The group made it clear on several occasions how large the area was. She could've lost her way and starved, but she didn't think that was what the demon had in mind. She cursed him silently, eyes still on the fire. Could she ever tell those people the truth? What would happen when the trip was over? Was she stuck there? She blinked away tears of anger, confusion, fear, and sadness. It was a surprise she hadn't dried up like a prune given the amount of moisture expelled from her body over a small time. There had to be a way home.

Sleep inevitably found her, caressing her in its peaceful arms. At first, there were no dreams, just a silent, empty blackness. It was a place her brain couldn't follow; she'd typically wake up and remember absolutely nothing. But there, it seemed like she was still aware. On she floated, the quiet easing her during the passage. A small light appeared in the distance, dim and flickering. It was white at first, but it intensified, showing numerous colors. It was like sunlight reflecting glass, a beautiful iridescent glow, but not bright enough to burn her eyes. Lola struggled to look away. It persisted, trying to reach her, but she felt something tugging her away from it. *No*, came the desperate thought. *I don't want to go away.* She reached for the light, unable to see her hand in front of her. Its twisting patterns filled her with an inexplicable joy, a happiness she'd never felt before, even at home. She'd do anything to get closer to it. The tugging persisted, pulling her farther away until she screamed.

And, suddenly, she was awake. The fire had diminished to nothing but ash, and dawn crept around the edges of the night. In her half-conscious state, the light remained, to her incredible delight. Her eyes locked onto it longingly as the sleep faded from her eyes. Lola feared that light would fade, too, but it brightened instead. The rest of the world slowly materialized around her. A grin spread on her face when she realized the source of the light. Her eyes grew large, and an excited squeak escaped her lips. *It's in the wall! It's shining through a gap!* Lola half ran, half stumbled toward Rosalia's sleeping bag, collapsing beside her in the leaves. She urgently shook her with both hands, terrified it'd disappear.

"Rosalia! Rosalia, please wake up! Wake up, wake up, wake up!" At first, she didn't budge, but with Lola's insistence, her body began to shuffle around. The light remained, to Lola's relief, so beautiful that she no longer felt the cold around her.

"What is it?" Rosalia muttered angrily. Lola knew she didn't realize it, so she forgave the mean tone.

"Look! Look! It's the pass!" It was like her words were a strike of lightning because Rosalia shot up, along with others in the group who heard, some out of a dead sleep. Only two remained still. *Big Ricky and RJ.* Her gothic friend wiped her eyes, looking all around until the light found her. She then stared in disbelief.

"What…" No words followed. Rosalia's mouth hung open in disbelief. The light pushed through, illuminating the ground in front of it with a pale, shifting glow. The others stared, too. Fiona was on her feet. Jonas moved closer to Rosalia. The couple, Josh and Megan, were sitting up in their bags. Erin lingered to their left, eyes the size of saucers. The twins approached slowly.

"Where is it coming from?" Chris asked, stumbling over his own words. He pulled his glasses off and wiped them on his shirt. The awestruck feeling remained, but Chris's words seemed to bring everyone closer to earth. They huddled tightly, staring at the light shining through the gap.

"That's it!" Lola exclaimed, pointing. One of the rocks, about the size of her body, was leaning to let the illumination through. It must've fallen. *How lucky is that?* "It fell, so it blocked the path. We have to move it!"

"That's a big rock!" It was Robin's voice, but Lola wouldn't let the sound of it take away her excitement. "It could collapse if we move it!" Even though it was an obvious vote against doing so, she could see the desire in his eyes as he stared. He wanted to go through, too.

Rosalia heaved a sigh in response. "What did we come out here for?" she asked across the camp to no one in particular. "I'm going to move this rock, and God help anyone who tries to stop me." To Lola's delight, no one moved.

"Am I the only one wondering about the light?" Chris said again, but Rosalia covered the space between them in a blink.

"It could be the government. It could be supernatural." Rosalia grabbed his shoulders and shook him. "I have no idea, but don't you want to know?" The adrenaline made her raise her voice. She turned back to the gap, and Lola could sense that Rosalia was drawn to it in the same way—it was almost beckoning. Concern still lingered in the twins' eyes.

"Rosalia, wait!" It was Fiona that time, and she hurried to catch up with her friend. There were a few skeptical head shakes. *Not everyone is feeling the pull,* Lola thought, noting the hesitation. Still, there was no denying the force behind it, and it pushed them all closer to Rosalia. Exhilaration was thick in the air.

Ricky and RJ finally joined them by the barrier. Lola couldn't recall when they got out of their sleeping bags. They eagerly discussed moving the rock and concluded one would push from the left while two others pulled from the top.

"Lola, stand back, baby," Rosalia said, positioned to the left. "Are we doing this?" The others nodded. "Easy, now." RJ stood on the left with her and pushed low when Rosalia pushed high. On the opposite side, Corey and Robin pulled toward them from the top of the boulder. At first, nothing moved, but as they persisted, it started a heavy slide. It shifted with a frightful sound, and Lola couldn't help but watch and hold her breath. Shouts of alarm came from behind, but she couldn't have said from whom. Lola covered her gaping mouth with her hands, watching in anticipation. She hadn't realized she'd backed up several paces. The rock wobbled, small bits of debris shaking loose and dusting those close to it. RJ moved around from the side to the front to support the weight, and suddenly things seemed to stabilize. The light shone through brightly as if cheering them on. It intensified, and her hands went from her mouth to her eyes. *So bright*, she thought. *And beautiful.* Time seemed to stop. They were transfixed by what lay before them; they stood as still as statues with their breath held tightly in their chests. Lola could feel the blood racing through her body. *It didn't collapse!*

"Look!" Robin yelled. He approached, finger pointing toward the stone. Lola moved closer to see what he was referring to.

"The stone's free," Robin continued, running his foot back and forth inside the gap. "Just drop it."

"Are you certain?" asked Rosalia, still wedged against it to the left. Her face was bright red in the light due to exertion. Robin laughed and put his foot through again to demonstrate.

"Yes, drop it!" And they did. The rock toppled forward, landing with a thump. As it did, and even before Lola could raise her eyes from the stone, the light went out. She felt as if something had been ripped from her and replaced with a deep regret. The wonder of the group fizzled and died not far behind.

"Fucking kidding me," Big Ricky said in disappointment.

"We still have the gap!" Chris said, mood improving since they hadn't all been crushed. That was true, and they had a clear path forward, but the light had been so…euphoric. Lola recalled flowing down the tunnel when she'd arrived, the pure rush of energy it brought. It felt something like that. Had someone else come here? Was that what the light signified?

The world was wrapped in a cold darkness with the absent illumination from beyond the gap. But daylight *was* there, just dim in comparison. The sky was a sad gray, pushing through the treetops. Yet the air seemed warmer as a result of the group's excitement. Lola found Rosalia, following her eyes back to the gap. It was just bright enough to see a small passage that appeared to curve to the right, and that's where vision ended. Everyone looked at it. The answer to what was next was obvious, but no one said anything, seemingly at a loss for words. The light still encapsulated most of them, except for Chris, who wore a skeptical look. After a closer look, he scrubbed his glasses and turned toward his brother for a few quiet words. Corey shook his head, eyes on the gap.

Minutes passed, reality gradually sinking in. The rest of the group broke from their statuesque state and were beginning to pack in silence. Lola scooped up her things and helped Corey and Robin cover the fire. It was hard to mask her emotions. She fought the uncontrollable urge to grin. Even though the light was gone, the feeling lingered. Lola kept her eyes on the gap out of fear it might disappear. It wasn't that wide, but hopefully, it was wide enough for an adult to squeeze through. Her eyes went to RJ with the thought. She was never the claustrophobic type, but she felt a little nervous for the others.

When everyone was ready, they shared looks back and forth between each other, Rosalia, and the gap. She was currently crouched over her pack, pulling the drawstrings tight. When she stood, she released a long-winded sigh.

"Well?" Rosalia said, her left arm gesturing toward the path. There was no denying the anticipation, but a worry hung in the air. There it was, right there in front of them, and they were about to walk through. The group had waited a long time to do it. Eventually, the smiles and laughter took over. Even Chris was smiling despite his doubt.

"RJ, are you good with going first? You're the largest of us." Rosalia said it jokingly, but it was the truth. He dismissed the jest with a smile, which in turn made Lola grin. *Contagious.*

"As ready as can be," he answered, shuffling toward the front. Corey followed close behind, then Big Ricky. Brit was next with Jonas in tow. Behind were Robin, Josh, Chris, and Little Ricky. Erin, Rosalia, Lola, Fiona, and Megan brought up the rear, largest to smallest apart from herself. Lola insisted on being close to Rosalia, and her friend didn't argue.

"Shall we?" Rosalia said across the group. She was still cheery as she asked the question. Big Ricky was the first to respond with a hoot, pulling an unopened bottle from his sack and twisting the cap free. *Does he have anything else in there?*

"To us," he said, holding the bottle into the air. He brought it to his lips and tilted it back. Lola's eyes widened when he swallowed more than once. Surely it burned! When he finished, he passed it down the line.

"To us," Brit repeated, taking a swig. The drink progressed, and Lola watched it go over her head twice before it was done. She wouldn't have minded taking a swig then, but she knew better. Besides, the day had warmed with the rising sun. Almost unnaturally so.

She liked her place in line, as it was close to Rosalia and far from Robin. Every time she thought to give him a break, he'd rub her wrong all over again. *It's his eyes*, she thought. They were a pale blue and carried a light she didn't trust. Lola had never been rude or untrusting of anyone without reason, but that case was different—it felt intuitive. It almost made her ashamed of herself. It was a place in Kalos's game, though; could that be why? Could it be an extension of his evil in the form of a test? The questions nagged at her. It was hard to think ill of someone like Rosalia, as sweet as she'd been to her. But was her kindness real? Lola would play along and hope for the best. She opened a little compartment inside of herself and sealed up her emotions. Focus was something she desperately needed.

Final adjustments were made, and they were on their way. RJ led, squeezing into the gap; to her relief, he pushed through. A collective anxiety could be felt in the atmosphere as they began their journey into the unknown. It was hard to imagine what could be on the other side. It was difficult enough to think of anything but the strange light—a guide, just like the light of the group's fire was for her that first night. Into what, she had no way of knowing.

They followed the gap around the curve where it narrowed and then became wide again. There were points where two and three of them could walk side by side, and others where they'd have to shove through sideways. It was never uncomfortable, at least with her size. Lola couldn't speak for anyone else. Beads of sweat decorated all faces, along with it a significant dose of heavy breathing. It *was* hot in the small area with the combined body heat. RJ would curse at the front whenever he had to squeeze, occasionally getting dusted with dirt and small pebbles, but most of the men chatted happily. The conversations had a wide range, not all of which were exactly appropriate, but Lola didn't mind. She smelled the strange cigarette thing, too; and, as always, it was accompanied by lots of laughter. A bottle passed over her head more times than she could count. Sometimes she wasn't even sure if it was the same one. All she could do was play along, adding her laughter and merriment to the noise around her. For a time, she could have forgotten everything. She was distracted from thoughts of Kalos's torment. A warm feeling birthed in her amidst the group's delight, one that felt close to the comfort of home.

An appreciated breeze drifted through the gap as they progressed. Hours passed, and the blockade remained on either side of them. When Lola thought of it, she'd imagined something much smaller, something quick to pass through. Its length and size must have taken weeks, maybe months, to finish. If the story were true, the party responsible really must've wanted to keep people away. They wouldn't have gotten through themselves without a blind stroke of luck. Lola thought about the detective and what his journey would've been like. How'd he find it? What struggles did he endure? And, most importantly, what awaited him on the other side?

The sun dropped, and an unspoken question hung in the air. How far would the path go on? She could see the disbelief in Rosalia's eyes, along with some others. The same feeling was heavy on everyone's shoulders. At that point, the pass had opened a comfortable distance, enough for ten people to walk alongside one another, and that was enough for the leader to call for a halt. The opportunity might not present itself again if they continued. Everyone dropped their belongings and collapsed on the ground. Lola didn't dare lean against either wall; instead, she chose a spot near the middle, let her pack fall to the ground, and sat. Thankfully, water bottles made their rounds, and she drank with appreciation, though she had to remind herself not to chug. She was an extra mouth they hadn't planned for, after all. The enclosed space encouraged the stuffy heat, and sweat still dripped down them as they rested. Had it been anticipated, perhaps they wouldn't have drunk so much. She looked toward the sky through the gaps of rock and trees, and she knew it wouldn't be long before dusk was upon them. As they all caught their breath, Lola knew they'd be stopping for the night.

"We have to call it here," Rosalia verified. "Our resources are dwindling." The water was going fast, and with good reason, but it was important for them to keep in mind they'd eventually have to come back.

"No fucking lie," Corey chimed in, wiping the sweat from his brow. He'd long since shed his jacket and was wearing a black T-shirt underneath. The thought never occurred to Lola, and she cursed herself silently for not taking off Jonas's jacket earlier. She wriggled free and welcomed the air on her skin. It was all she could do to avoid lying down.

"I didn't see that coming either," said Megan, breathing deeply. "How long could this possibly go on?" She was the least enthusiastic of the group, Lola thought, studying the grungy girl. Her face was a bright, flustered red.

"Well, not forever." Big Ricky had a mischievous smile on his face. "Do we have to stop partying?" A few tired laughs were the only responses, but that didn't stop the large man from pulling a fresh bottle from his bag.

They kept the area well lit with flashlights propped against the uneven stones. Sandwiches were passed around, along with booze and water. The silence stretched while they ate, and the sun made its final descent into obscurity, but as the exhaustion faded, things began to brighten. Conversation sparked, eventually evolving into interesting drinking games and laughter. Lola giggled and smiled so much that her cheeks hurt. Even Robin became a little more bearable. She spent most of her time snuggled against RJ, her head vibrating against his soft belly each time he laughed. And it was a lot. Lola would pat it fondly in response, and she concluded he was one of her favorites.

The night stretched on for what seemed like an eternity, and she never wanted it to end. After a few hours, Lola was lying close to Rosalia. They watched the sky together, and the group calmed down as darkness emerged around them. Whispers and small laughs were all that remained, though many sleeping bags were already still and quiet. Big Ricky and RJ both snored peacefully, almost in competition with each other. Lola couldn't determine who was louder. What she did know was she could smell the alcohol seeping from both men.

The only remaining light was the orange tip of Rosalia's cigarette. Its hot ash glowed, intensifying when she drew on it. Lola watched the stream of smoke rise and disappear somewhere among the rocks and sky.

"Ros?" Her voice was soft and tired, and her eyelids were growing heavy.

"Yes, my love?" The moon peaked above them, adding a small scrap of yellow light.

"What is it you really hope to find out here?" There was a pause as her question was considered. Rosalia puffed her lips in an "O" shape, sending rings into the air. Lola watched them distort and drift away as the gothic girl stroked her hair.

"I think we're all just looking for something different, you know? Something outside the realm of our normal lives." The answer was vague but carried a curiosity that applied to both of them.

"That light," Lola said, still watching the sky.

"I know. It was…uplifting, in a way. Driving. Terrifying." Lola felt the same. While they were alone like that, she considered sharing the truth with Rosalia, but the idea didn't linger long. *Yours and yours alone.* The words stuck with her as if they were constantly being said aloud. *What if my secrets are dangerous, though?* She bit her lip and kept it all inside.

Lola was lost in thought for so long she didn't realize Rosalia had started snoring softly beside her. The idea of being awake by herself was unnerving, but the fear had little time to disturb her before sleep came and dictated the rest of the night. She was consumed by a deep swirl of black that dragged her into a peaceful slumber.

It was like the time before. She was aware of the darkness. But, at the moment, she was lying on the ground, not floating. The ground was so hard beneath her that she thought perhaps she'd woken up. But there was a low humming sound, like music that she had to strain her ears to hear. It wasn't a clear sound, but it sang to her heart, cooing and soothing.

Lola…

The voice that spoke was the same one humming. The sweetness it carried reminded her of her mother. Enchanting and mesmerizing like a magic spell easing into her soul and intoxicating her every fiber. As wonderful as it felt, there was uneasiness attached to it. There was hardly a chance to understand the feeling, but it persisted in the back of her mind.

Lola's eyes fluttered open, and she could no longer differentiate between dream and reality. Blackness wrapped her in a blinding embrace, threatening to swoop her away into nothing. The sound had ceased, and she could only plea silently. *Come back. Please.*

Two spots shimmered above her. They were small and close together, and Lola recognized them as two glowing emerald eyes. Her breath got caught in her throat as she was enraptured by their pure splendor. She fought to bring moisture into her mouth.

"Who—" Her attempt to speak was an embarrassing croak.

Shahs. Had she not been asleep already, that sound would've lulled her. She was unconscious, right?

No words are needed here, my child. Lola's heart was pounding against her chest as a warmth spread throughout her limbs. *Is it home you desire?* She sputtered something out of

114

her mouth that was meant to be a *yes*. Luckily, the presence wasn't confused. *Come, and it's yours.* Tears streamed down her face, her mouth and eyes opened wide. She had to say something.

Come. The eyes vanished, replaced by a bright green ring of smoke that floated up and up and up.

Lola shot upright, wide awake, breathing in strained gasps. It was the middle of the night, but she could make out the shapes of those sleeping around her. Rosalia hadn't budged, and snores remained the only sound among the group. Sweat beaded her brow as the exhilaration coursed through her. It was an indescribable line between euphoria and terror, the terror part being that the vision was gone.

It took a while before Lola was able to lie back down, but sleep didn't return. Adrenaline was a coursing, overpowering force that pumped madly through her without tire. She considered getting up, walking, pacing—anything to regulate the feeling. Lola watched the sky, desperate for a distraction. It revealed stars peeking through clouds and a discreet sliver of moonlight. Compared to what she'd seen, it was a subdued sight. The green eyes burned in her memory, the words repeating in her brain. She couldn't shake the intoxicating nature of the sound. *Just breathe.* She inhaled deeply and squeezed her eyes shut. She expelled the air and repeated the process countless times. She thought of the spell that Kalos had put on her to keep her calm and tried to recapture the feeling. The rush was quelled by her determination, and at long last, reality comfortably settled back in.

Sleep eluded her still, but Lola was at peace. Hours passed, and she watched the early hours of the morning unfold. The sun ascended and brightened the passage. Before there was any movement, she took the opportunity to write in her journal, removing it quickly from her bag. Her eyes shot to Robin, who was still a slumbering lump. The pen was nestled tightly in the spot where she'd closed her diary last, and she rolled it gently between her fingers. The words flowed out of her smoothly as she recalled every detail from her dream. Were anyone to ever read it, it would be chalked up to a normal child using her imagination and writing about a fantasy land. But she knew it was no fantasy, and she'd make sure no one read it except for herself. Lola documented the events and emotions with detail, keeping her heart rate under control as the memory transferred from mind to paper. To her surprise, she'd written almost two and a half pages by the time she was done. The light that illuminated the pass for them had been real; everyone had witnessed it. It was something beautiful and alive—and something that wanted to be found. Were they being guided? It was hard to imagine what lay beyond the pass, but she needed to remain vigilant of the possible dangers that could await them. She thought of Kalos to give her strength, reminding herself that she couldn't afford to be foolish if she ever wanted to get home.

It was uncomfortably hot already, and Lola considered waking Rosalia. She ultimately decided against it and was fully packed by the time bodies started to stir. Big Ricky was the first to rise. He walked the way they'd come with a few tired grunts that made Lola think he might be sleepwalking. When she rose to get his attention, however, he stopped, and with his back to the group, relieved himself. Lola turned away with a blush, then realized she needed to pee as well. It hadn't happened since she arrived, but no one seemed to notice. She chose a secluded spot behind a bend to do her business.

Conversation picked up as everyone rose. Breakfast was consumed sparingly, halves of flattened sandwiches from packs for each of them. Rest had done the group well, and the mood was elevated compared to the day before. Rosalia still sat in her sleeping bag, sucking on a morning cigarette. Lola watched the girl gazing at the wall and wondered if perhaps she'd dreamed, too. When Lola asked, she got an absentminded answer saying she couldn't remember. Was she the only one who'd been visited? Maybe it hadn't meant anything.

Her ears perked up when she heard Robin speaking excitedly to Corey about his dream. She busied herself with picking up the camp's trash that was nearest to them, listening closely.

"A what?" Corey asked in a confused tone.

"Crazy and real, dude. It was like I wasn't even asleep. We were right here!" Though Robin was enthusiastic, Corey feigned interest while tightening the straps on his pack.

"So, you saw two shining blue eyes over you, and heard a voice speaking? What did it say?" The twin heaved his pack up and over his shoulders, turning to face his friend. *Blue eyes,* Lola thought, feeling shocked. He couldn't be lying. She'd seen green! Had it been anyone else, she would have blurted out everything right then and there.

"Yes, man. Brilliant, but cold as ice," Robin continued picking up his own stuff. "It was like a kid's voice, maybe a girl." His eyes flicked over to where she was, and Lola was careful to keep her face toward the ground.

"What did you smoke last night, man, because I want some of it!" Corey joked.

"I never have dreams like this, man. It was like real life!" The two stepped away from her and moved down the path, likely to relieve themselves as well. Robin's animated voice faded as they made their way. To her disappointment, she heard nothing more about it. Little Ricky sat with Rosalia, both smoking and speaking quietly together. Jonas was near, as always. Megan was complaining to Josh about something Lola couldn't quite make out. Lola could only stand by herself until they were ready to go.

Once more, they huddled in a tight circle as they prepared for the day's journey. The plan hadn't changed; there wasn't much choice but to move forward. Everyone agreed they should push through to the other side. It was impossible to think that it could go on for much longer.

The pass did continue for a while, though, to their dismay. The gap was very wide at times, but it narrowed uncomfortably at some junctures. RJ even had to turn sideways a few times and duck low. Within the hour, they were sweaty, huffing messes with the strange heat still upon them. Their collective frustration grew. The way was slow going at points, and there were times the smaller openings were tricky. Lola kept her breathing as even as she could but thirsted for water.

The route sloped down, and the overhang persisted. It got so low that most of them had to crouch to get through. Lola was an exception. She heard curses and complaints and reassurances altogether in the span. At one point, they had to squeeze through a gap, stay low, *and* keep from sliding. One of the twins, Chris, lost his footing but didn't go far before bottlenecking in the cramped space. After everything settled, a rumble filled the air, causing an array of exchanged glances. Nothing else moved. Thunder, maybe? *Please let it be so.* They waited cautiously for a few moments before pressing on.

It was around midday, Lola guessed, when Fiona started singing. It was a poppy but classic sound that she didn't recognize. Lola had trouble keeping up with the words, but it brought some cheer. The group was tired and fearful, but the complaints died little by little. Not long after, Erin picked up the tune, then Josh and Big Ricky. Even Megan was smiling while they walked. Rosalia hummed along, and as if by some sort of musical magic, the path widened, the sky was exposed, and the ground leveled out. It was the first time Lola had smiled in hours.

The tune persisted, even becoming comical as Fiona distorted her voice for the effect. Laughter spread like a wildfire, and soon the whole group was chiming in. After the chorus repeated several times, Lola was able to pick up the words and sing along. She turned back, looking at Fiona's goofy, beaming face. As Lola smiled back, another sound joined the air. At first, it was like a growl, but then it hummed low and deep. Song and laughter cut off immediately as the rumble shook the rock around, alarming the group. Fiona stood motionless, mouth and eyes wide, and that's when Lola saw the movement from above. Along with bits of dust and rock, a large boulder was making its way down, bouncing from wall to wall hard enough to jar her teeth.

"Fiona!" The shriek came from Rosalia. Lola instinctively stretched out her hand but was nowhere close. About ten feet away from turning Fiona into a red mess, the rock lodged itself between the two walls. The relief was momentary, however. The walls shifted dangerously on either side, more dust and sand falling to the ground.

"Run!" Lola only knew it was a girl who screamed the word. Everything else was a chaotic mixture of panicked cries. Everyone was running, and Lola could feel a hand on her back urging her forward. Head-sized rocks began to crash all around them, along with branches as thick as Big Ricky's legs. Lola ran as fast as she could. Rosalia was in front of her, sprinting when she could and leaping over fallen debris when necessary. She could see pebbles pelting Rosalia's head, hair, and shoulders, no doubt much of it doing the same to her. Lola's heart was sinking as she ran desperately. Fear for her life was in full bloom. Dust and other particles attempted to blind her, and she wiped her stinging eyes in a futile attempt to remove the clumps of dirt stuck to her tear-streaked face. As she attempted to hop over a branch, something heavy hit her head, and the world went sideways in a slow topple. Something else dropped beside her, pinning her against the crumbling wall. Lola howled as the object scraped down her side; the sound caused Rosalia to stop dead in her tracks and turn around before running back to snatch Lola by the arm. Luckily, she broke free and was on her feet once more, though her vision was significantly impaired. Ahead, she caught glimpses of RJ barreling through the falling pass, both arms over his head with hands clasped behind. Her eyes were on fire, but if she could just keep him in sight, if she could keep pushing like he was…

The rumble had grown loud and powerful. Their screams were muted due to the sound of the collapse. Lola could hear them in her mind, though, and in her heart. Oxygen was absent; her lungs burned, and she could no longer spit the chunks of dirt and wood out of her mouth. The urge to vomit lay heavy on her. Her stomach turned, and dizziness grew out of it. *I am going to die here*, she thought sadly, blinking away blackness at the edges of her vision. She looked ahead one last time as the rumble threatened to tear her apart, and to her shock, RJ was gone. She thought she'd lost him, but then Corey vanished from sight, followed by Big Ricky. One by one, they disappeared in front of her, and she had no choice but to push forward. She closed in on the space where she saw them disappear, realizing soon after that they'd simply dropped. It wasn't a far fall, and she had no time to think. Cool air wrapped her in her flight. Rosalia was below her, on top of someone else, and Lola squeezed her eyes shut, knowing she was going to land on her friend. A gasp of pain escaped Rosalia's lungs. Then, Fiona landed hard on Lola, sandwiching her. The pain and fire in Lola's body didn't cease, but as she struggled for air, the rumbling did.

She couldn't say how much time passed. The whole world had crumbled around her, then seemingly stopped altogether. All around, she could hear the broken sobs, sharp breaths, and painful moans of her friends. The agony of it persisted, despite the fact that they'd made it through. She didn't dare try to move. Lola lay there praying as little by little the pain eased. She could feel Fiona's struggled breathing against her back. All of them were a mess of sweat and grime. Water would be a great blessing, and she imagined gulping it down out of a bottomless bottle. The thought only seemed to make her dehydration worse. Her eyes clamped tight, the thought of dying still not entirely pushed from her mind. The sounds around her subsided except for one—a weeping sound. If anything, it became louder and more desperate.

"Please," a choked voiced called weakly. "Help." It was a girl's voice, and Lola tried to recall whose. Lola recounted the order in which they'd fled the pass. Fiona was behind and then—*Megan*! She didn't think there was a sliver of energy left in her, much less any of the others, but adrenaline drove her to wriggle against the weight of Fiona.

"Fiona," she urged with a few forceful shoves. She maneuvered the top half of her body free and rolled, twisting herself to look uncomfortably back to where they'd fallen. What she saw stung her heart and brought tears to her eyes. "Fiona, Megan's stuck in the rock."

The path had crumbled upon itself in its collapse from both sides. All of them had managed to slip through just in time to avoid being squashed—all but one. Half of Megan's body was out, exposed to them, while the other half was hidden in a jumble of stones. One arm was reached out, the strain on her face turning it a deep, frightening shade of red. One isolated vein bulged on her forehead.

Fiona finally stirred, working herself onto her elbows and spewing out a thick spit of crimson. The disaster had marked her well, scratches evident down the side of her head and face. Her black shirt was ripped at the shoulder and gleamed with the blood soaking into it. Lola followed the wounds all the way down to find the girl was a bruised mess all over. As Lola worked the rest of the way out from under Fiona, she looked back down at Rosalia, who was still, except for her rising and falling chest. Around her was a pile of bodies, all moving and breathing, to her relief. As fast as she could, Lola found her feet and stumbled back toward the wall. Pain shot up her left leg with each step. It was so much that her vision blurred, and she wobbled. A hand on the small of her back prevented her from falling, however. She turned and looked, brushing the hair and dirt out of her eyes, to see Fiona's haggard face.

"Go," the girl said, stepping up behind her. As fast as they could manage, they worked their way to Megan. The trapped girl had her eyes squeezed shut with tears streaming down her disheveled face.

"Meg!" It was Josh, rushing up the slope. A large tear spanned the length of his pants, exposing a pale, bloody leg. His once-white shirt was anything but. RJ followed clumsily behind, still disoriented. One of his ears was a smear of red. *We all look terrible*, Lola thought sadly.

When they reached the wall, Josh grabbed Megan's head with both hands, kissing her face and giving reassurances. It was a wonder the girl could breathe, Lola thought, as she inspected the stone around her. It was compact.

"Easy, man," RJ said, putting a hand on Josh's shoulder and easing him back. "We have to move the little rocks first. And very slowly."

"Please be careful," Josh wheezed, his face stricken. "If it falls again—"

"Never gonna happen." RJ glanced down at Megan, then Fiona. "One little rock at a time."

So, they set about carefully. And there were a lot of rocks, more than Lola had imagined possible. Lola lifted them as tenderly as she could with her sore hands, scared to breathe each time. As they progressed, the sizes of the stones got larger; she eventually had to use both hands. It wasn't long before her little arms were struggling with their weight as she hauled each to the ground. RJ rested a hand on her shoulder, signaling to stop.

"Can you move?" he asked Megan. She lifted her head and shifted ever so slightly. Thankfully, she was the only thing that moved.

"A little bit," she replied thickly. Her eyes had a wild look, shaded with a creeping terror. "I don't know how much longer I can stand this. Please get me out."

"I'm going to get you out," RJ said with confidence. He looked at Lola and Fiona, motioning them to stand on Megan's left while Josh moved to the right. Looking in the opposite direction, Lola saw more of the group struggling up the hill toward them.

"As soon as I pull, I'm going to need you to suck in and make yourself skinny, okay?" Megan didn't look convinced at the big man's words but nodded in response.

"On the count of three." RJ worked his hand into the small gap between her armpit and rib cage. He grabbed her free arm just above the elbow and drew close to her, positioning his feet.

"One. Two—" He never even said three; he just pulled. Megan cried out, but to everyone's relief, she slid free almost effortlessly. RJ heaved her up and out, her legs dropping limp against him. Lola's heart was pounding, but she was able to smile through all the madness. And she wasn't the only one. Josh rushed to his girlfriend, taking her into his arms. She wasn't strong enough to stand, so he scooped her up and carried her down the slope. The rest of them stood motionless for a moment, exchanging looks amongst themselves. Lola felt

Rosalia's arms curl around her shoulders, and she turned to throw her own around her gothic friend.

"Is everybody—" Rosalia started the sentence but didn't need to finish. All of them were a beaten, bloody mess, but everyone was standing. No broken bones. No life-threatening wounds. It was a miracle they'd gotten out alive.

Nightfall found them again when they were a safe distance up the incline and away from the crumbled blockade. They could've pushed forward, but with everyone jarred from the recent event, Lola thought calling it quits for the night was the smart thing to do. A lot of their water had disappeared during the traumatic events of the day, and they agreed to ration the rest out equally and cautiously for the remainder of the journey. It took a while for conversations to begin, the whole ordeal putting a shocked silence on them. Lola imagined that was what followed near-death experiences. But the immediate concern was how they were going to get back.

"We're near," Rosalia said. "With luck it could be over the next hill. It might be out of the way, but we have no choice but to navigate our way back down."

"Where would we even start?" It was Jonas who spoke. His tone was tired and resigned. "We'll have to hike to the bottom if we can even get there without our vehicles."

"Do you think the pass collapsed enough for us to climb and go over?" Chris chimed in. He was looking at Rosalia while clearing an area for a fire.

"It would be an option if we could follow along the collapse," Rosalia answered.

"Too dangerous." Big Ricky was leaning against a tree next to them, and to Lola's surprise, there wasn't a bottle in sight. "Walking over all that shit? For as long as it took to get here? It'd take days."

"Not all of us will be drunk-walking," Chris added in a joking manner. There was no laughter in response.

"And Lola? Is sobriety going to keep her from falling and busting her head open?" A glare lit his face as he turned to Rosalia. "Robin mentioned that wall collapsing a few times, and we all just shrugged it off. Anything to say?" Lola's first thought was that Rosalia would jump to the defense, but her face sunk in shameful admission.

"I don't have to be reminded," she replied. "I'm very sorry this happened. All I know is we're all here now, by choice, and we'll *have* to find a way back." She met Big Ricky's stare for a moment, but he wasn't satisfied. Lola could feel how nervous her friend was. She didn't think Rosalia feared anything, but maybe it was guilt eating at her.

"Well," Ricky said quietly. She could see the anger in his eyes, but there was something else there, too. Compassion? "All I know is we almost died, and for what? Now we're stuck on the other side with no way back." He propelled himself from the tree, dusting his shirt off. "You're right, though. We gotta find our way back. But I have a feeling nobody's gonna like it."

The Bright House

The light was strong against her eyelids. Sometimes she'd take naps outside in her backyard with the intense sun against her face. Lola could remember the feeling of waking up and opening her eyes to find the world a dull grayish color. The brightness had that same effect. Or perhaps she'd already slept into the next day, and it was the sun, indeed. Coherent thought came slowly. She realized she was awake and carefully opened her eyes so as to avoid burning them out of her skull.

It wasn't daylight that found her, though. Instead, the dark of the night persisted. She lay exactly where she had when she'd dozed off, next to a slumbering Rosalia with her sleeping bag flattened beneath her. Her hand shot toward her journal without thought, finding it nestled in her sack. She had paranoid visions of waking to find Robin crouched over her bag, flipping through the pages and laughing. The thought made her squirm.

Before her sigh of relief could even leave her body, the light took her in. It was beaming beyond the crest of the first hill above them, much larger than the light they'd seen through the pass. Her jaw was hanging limp as her eyes traced it upward. A misty haze stood in the air with it, colored across the spectrum vibrantly. It stretched toward the treetops before giving way to the darkness above. Colors—greens and purples, blues and yellows—appeared against the fog. They danced in the direction of a light wind, and Lola knew it was the mist moving while the light remained constant. They rippled and shimmered in a liquid fashion as if painted on the surface of water. The sight was energizing.

127

Lola sat there and watched the light, her mind numb. It wasn't until Rosalia sat up beside her that the trance broke. She first noticed Ros in her periphery and had to peel her eyes away from the illumination to look at her friend. *So wonderful*, was all she could think. She could see the awe in Rosalia's eyes, knowing she felt the same euphoric emotions at that instant. A moment to glance around the camp showed the light pulling everyone from their slumber. It was supernatural—the sight, the feeling, everything. It wasn't something people got to see every day…or ever. It was for them, and only them. Lola felt inexplicably special.

Several were on their feet, gaping with wide eyes. Corey and RJ were the closest to her, both half naked and without shoes, making no attempt to dress themselves. Rosalia and Megan clutched each other, still in their sleeping sacks as if watching fireworks for the Fourth of July. Even Big Ricky looked relaxed, a bottle once more by his side but temporarily forgotten.

"We have to go to it," Fiona said from behind them. She'd snuck out of her sack and was pulling a shirt urgently over her head. By the sudden and desperate movement all around, Lola would say everyone agreed. Lola looked around the group, finding Chris, and once more, he appeared skeptical. *Twice now*, she thought. Why didn't it grab him like it did the rest? Rosalia came to stand next to her and looked over to the smaller twin.

"Chris?" At first, he said nothing, fear evident in his eyes. "Chris!" Rosalia repeated, louder that time. He snapped from his thoughts with a shake, looking startled and confused.

"This…this is crazy!" His eyes were wide with confusion. The gothic girl moved over to him and grabbed him by the shoulders as she'd done before.

"Something amazing is over that hill. Do you understand?" Had she the strength, she would've shaken the smaller twin to pieces. "This very moment is what we're here for! And it's something far greater than we could've ever possibly imagined!" Chris was still visibly hesitant as he watched the light. He licked his lips.

"It's greater than we imagined. But that light could be something terrible and dangerous. Can we…can we just take five fucking minutes to think about this?" Even Lola was taken aback by the escalation of his voice. Rosalia stared at him, perplexed.

"Chris," said a sweet voice from behind him. When he turned toward the sound, Erin entered his line of sight. She stepped close, gently taking his hand into hers. The kind, bigger girl was struggling to keep her eyes from the hill. *It's a battle, I know*, Lola thought, looking toward the crest. The light almost had hands beckoning them.

"I know there are questions," Erin continued. "This is beyond insane, and I get it, I really do, but please. *Please.* It could go away any second…and so could this opportunity. I'm begging you." She squeezed his hand tightly with both of hers, the desire in her voice thick and convincing. Lola closed her eyes, letting the light wash over her. Chris was still having a hard time. He eyed the light nervously as if it would scorch him to ash, but then looked back to Erin.

"Okay," he said in defeat. Lola couldn't understand his resistance, but something about it alarmed her underneath the excitement. Her thoughts were fuzzy with wonder, and she had trouble remembering why it was worrying in the first place. Her eyes were glued to the light.

The group hurriedly packed their gear, looking up at the glow constantly, afraid it would disappear. The feeling of awe remained in Lola's chest as she slung her pack over her shoulders. It felt like she lost something each time she turned away from the brilliance. She'd never longed for something like that before, not even her journal. It was a sad thought, but the feeling left as quickly as it'd come. She patted the binding of the journal through her bag. *It's not like I'm leaving you behind.*

Once everyone was ready, they wasted little time. They ran up the hill like kids out of school when the bell rang. Chris trudged along in the rear, but his brother Corey was there to encourage him. RJ, Rosalia, and Robin led the way, with Big Ricky and Little Ricky trailing. Lola was right there with them, with Josh, Megan, and Jonas at her sides. Erin gave her shoulders an excited squeeze from behind, where she followed with Fiona. Lola looked up at her with a wide, beaming smile. All of them were smiling, and despite all the cuts, scrapes, and bruises, everyone was beautiful in that moment. The collapsing pass was a fading, meaningless memory. It had only served to lead them there.

The hill steepened as they plowed forward. Safety was disregarded, even after the previous event had nearly claimed their lives. Lola couldn't help but feel the same as she pushed herself up the incline. At times, she had to reach and use her hands to help lift her body weight. The odd humidity had sweat dripping from her after a short time, but the breeze against it felt good. She maintained her focus with her torn green shirt completely stuck to her skin—it was so filthy that it wouldn't pass for any color besides brown. It matched the floral patterns, dull and darkened from dirt, on her skirt.

The rise was so close she wanted to reach out and touch it. Lola absently lifted her arm to do so as if she could grab hold of something and haul herself the rest of the way up. The glow of the light washed gently over her fingertips. Her exuberance burned through her fatigue, giving her an extra push. Through the brightness, the only other real things were her pumping knees. The crest was upon them, and her heart thumped in anticipation.

Lola bounced off Big Ricky when he came to a stop; her face rebounded off the side of his leg, and she wrapped her arms around his waist to keep from tumbling to the ground. He was among the rest of them, all halted at the top. She gulped air as if she'd been deprived of it. Most of the group stood with hands on hips or knees, sucking in heavily, but their eyes were all focused on the same thing. With an exhale, she let her eyes gradually slide around Big Ricky to take in the sight below. She squeezed him tighter.

Her brain leapt into somersaults. The communicable lines between sight and thought were a misconstrued blur. Shock and disbelief weighed in. Lola could feel her mind working to decipher how something like that could be possible. Below, a hulking mass of a building waited, a combination of squared and rounded structures. They stretched on, nearly beyond sight, but their vast expansion wasn't the most extraordinary thing. *The colors*. Windows of massive proportion dominated the exterior. Blinding, coruscating light spilled forth from them. It

131

washed the ground below in a spectrum of rainbows. It gleamed and radiated around the perimeter. With a slow, lulling hum, something beckoned them closer. Lola took a moment to look at her friends, their expressions reflecting in the iridescent glow, completely awestruck. Even the trees—not pines but twisting oaks of a size she'd never encountered— seemed luminous. The leaves were the size of her body, hanging heavy as if they might melt and drip to the ground like syrup.

"Wow." Surprisingly, it was Chris, whose glasses were pinned to his head with both hands. The light swirled in his eyes.

"See?" Erin responded, stepping close and wrapping her arms around him. Tears were streaming down her face. "Don't you see now?" No words came out of Chris's mouth. All he managed was a silent nod. Big Ricky's hand came down on Lola's head, and while she thought he meant to stroke her hair, she smiled when she realized he was fumbling around for his bottle of booze. He pulled the warm, half-full bottle and pressed it to his lips. His eyes never left the sight, nor did his body react to the heat she knew was flowing into his stomach.

"This is real." The big man spoke to himself. She heard similar sounds around as she let Big Ricky go and sought out Rosalia. She was crouched in a low squat, hands on her face with her glistening eyes peeking through. Lola hugged her out of pure joy. It took the gothic girl a moment, but she swung an arm around her waist, exposing her trembling mouth. The dark lipstick was pale against the glow.

"What do you think is inside?" Lola asked, trying to speak without her voice breaking. Rosalia didn't take her eyes from the building but shook her head.

"Something more brilliant than any of us could ever hope to see." The response escaped her lips in the form of a breathless whisper. Lola could feel her own anticipation heightening.

"Let's go," Corey urged, bouncing in place. He grabbed his brother by the neck with one arm and hugged Little Ricky with the other. "We're going, right?" A burst of joy spread through them like a raging fire. Lola laughed like she never had before. Her smile stretched across her face until her cheeks ached.

Like ravenous animals, they charged down the hill into the drawing light. Watching where they stepped seemed trivial and unimportant compared to what lay beyond. They tripped on roots, tripped over each other, slid on piles of leaves. The minor setbacks were meaningless as they closed the distance on what looked like heaven. The momentum of the downward movement was increasing step by step, and Lola's teeth rattled hard. The entrance of the place loomed, growing larger in her vision as the ground evened. Lola flew down the hill with impressive speed. Her eyes, however, never wavered.

Double doors, at least twenty feet tall, towered over them. The standard steel unnaturally radiated with shifting colors and an intoxicating hum, incased all around with immaculate black stone. The colors moved from deep reds to rich greens, to blues and oranges. Peace was the only thing Lola felt.

"The eyes!" Robin forced through labored breaths. "The colors are the same as the eyes!" Lola knew he was right, and she couldn't even be upset about it. She'd seen the same thing in her dream. The glimmering eyes were engraved into her mind, hovering over her as they did for him. And they *were* the same. For a reason she couldn't understand, her mind shot briefly to Chris and his hesitations. It was a lone thought in an intoxicating sea, and a queasy feeling came with it. Even so, it paled in comparison to the exhilaration flowing through her. Lola needed to go through those doors.

Enthusiastic whispers passed among them as they debated the next course of action. They'd obviously be going inside, but they needed to have at least *some* plan. The volume of their whispers grew.

"Shhhh," Rosalia urged, pushing a finger to her lips. What followed brought them uneasiness and dubiety. Fourteen mouths clamped shut, yet murmurs filled the space around. The whispers reverberated through the air, echoing back and forth across the group. The colorful doors resonated in response. The sounds didn't cause alarm; they were strangely calming but still something they couldn't quite comprehend. The comfort settled in more as they focused their attention back to the lights, and with a booming groan both doors swung inward. The intensity of the brightness grew until it felt like Lola's soul was igniting. Her eyes were ablaze as the group looked inside and entered without thinking twice.

The grandeur of the interior design nearly brought her to her knees. Lola could faintly hear Erin crying tears of joy. It might have been a few others, too, but she found it difficult to focus on anyone else's emotions. The slightest distraction from appreciating the beauty in front her seemed like a crime. The ceilings were high, much like the hallways she'd walked with

Kalos. Above was a deep onyx with crystal studs spread about the surface. It took her a moment to realize the shapes were those of clocks. Hundreds of them. *Thousands.* It almost looked like someone had taken the stars and organized them in a divine depiction of time. Her eyes slowly shifting downward, Lola saw that the walls were made up of a series of golden doors. The patterns were ornate, and they twisted so much she had to crane her neck in an effort to follow the designs. From top to bottom on both sides, there were three rows of doors. Lola eyed the display in awe, trailing downward until she reached the floor. When she did, the ceiling and walls fled from her mind, and she gasped in surprise. Her first impression was a colorful marble, but the colors were moving! They warped around each other in smooth, graceful rolls. That time, she sunk to her knees to rest her hands on the ground beneath her. Like a magnet, the colors gravitated toward the heat in her palms and fingertips. A squeak escaped her lips, and a single tear dropped from her face. *I will never feel this again. No one will ever feel this.* Lola raised her eyes to see the others were having similar experiences. All of them were inside, and beyond their notice, the doors had eased shut behind. They hadn't made a sound.

"Where do we start?" Corey asked in wonderment. He reminded her of a kid in a candy store, and she giggled.

"Should we just pick a door?" Brit asked. She'd said very little after the pass—so little that Lola nearly forgot she was with them.

"Might as well start with the first one." Little Ricky had donned sunglasses for a reason she couldn't understand, maybe just to look cool. Maybe to dim the pleasure that was beyond his control.

"It's important we all stay together," Rosalia replied, but her voice lacked feeling. The situation had taken that, demanding their undivided attention.

"One door at a time?" Jonas offered, sliding his hand into Rosalia's. She offered no resistance, and Lola smiled. The magic around them was allowing a lot of things to happen.

"Start with me." The voice didn't belong to any of them. It belonged to an angel. It was the essence of pure, flowing waters, cool and refreshing. It was music, but she couldn't locate the sound.

"Where—" Fiona's delight lifted through the air as she looked around them. All of their heads were turning; as the confusion persisted, Lola caught movement from above. Her gaze shot up to find two green eyes near the ceiling. They floated down like a feather, and as so, the body came behind it, revealing itself. It was a *child*!

That was Lola's initial thought, but as she looked closer, she only faced more confusion. It was about three feet tall, clad in a sheer, translucent robe. The cloth was short; the majority of the thing's legs dangled out beneath it, gleaming a silky sheen. Maybe a dwarf, she juggled, but she realized its body was perfectly proportioned and very, well, adultlike. It wasn't a child. It was a woman. Her curves were sculpted with precision, like the shape of an hourglass. As it neared the group, the green eyes shone, and its hair drifted about her shoulders, a vibrant pink that was alive like fire. *This is the one who visited me.* Somehow, the creature was suspended in the air. Lola wondered if it was some type of illusion. Then she peered behind it, and her eyebrows nearly rose from her head. A set of prismatic wings swung gently, easing it down. They fluctuated speed, but the flutters became shorter as to stop the descent. No one could speak a word, only stare in wonder. It smiled a closed-mouth smile.

"I'm called Kyrie," it sang to them. The girls were incredulous while the guys drooled. "Welcome to my home."

"We didn't…we didn't mean—" Rosalia's tone was apologetic, but she couldn't get the words out of her mouth.

"Of course, you meant to come here. You were invited." Eyes of green flame flicked to her. "Weren't you, Lola?" Lola's mouth opened, but she was shocked into silence. It hadn't been a dream. What sort of magic were they witnessing here?

"How—" Her jaw worked, but her mind worked against her. It was like a puzzle with shapes that didn't make sense. "How do you know my name?" She needed water. Anything to moisten her mouth.

"Much is known in this place. In this world."

"There are more of you," Robin whispered up at the thing called Kyrie. "Right? One with blue eyes?" Again, a smile behind closed lips emerged. Another shape detached itself from the wall. Lola never would've seen it had it not moved. That one looked similar as it came into view. Brilliant blue eyes and matching hair that moved like the ocean. Her clothing was the same, and Lola watched Robin lick his lips.

"Essandra, at your pleasure. And yes, there are many, many more of us." The voice rang through the hall like honey, though higher pitched than Kyrie's.

"Are you…" Corey swallowed noisily, trying to find his words. "Are y'all—"

"We're a little large to be fairies, don't you think?" Kyrie quirked an eyebrow in amusement. "But you could say that."

Corey nodded, obviously very pleased with what he was looking at, grinning a toothy grin. The "fairies" inched farther down, and from both sides of the hall more figures appeared, separating from the walls. They were as colorful and mystical as everything else the group had seen thus far; they bore orange and yellow eyes with hair the colors of ruby, emerald, amber, or pink. *Ten*, Lola counted. Ten creatures right there in front of her, of which she'd only read stories.

"Why did you invite us?" Fiona asked curiously. She was still staring but had sobered enough to speak clearly. Some were still struggling. Kyrie continued her gradual descent, the others following behind, swaying gracefully and watching intently.

"We don't get many of your kind up here," Kyrie said sadly. "Not many know the path. Given your persistence, we only thought it fair."

"Thank you," Rosalia said with a beaming smile. "God, thank you. How are you here, though? And why? I have so many questions." The gothic girl's eyes were glistening still. She laughed and ran her hands through her hair. "This is crazy!"

"We can't feel what you're feeling, although we know it's confusing. But you must never speak of this place to anyone." The creature eased forward. "We're orstras. A barrier was breached here, by your people. Torn. We are here because our world isn't as…accommodating."

"Wow," said Josh, hands on his head. "This is like a movie or a really good goddamned dream!" His words caught the attention of a flame-haired orstra, and she floated near him. Their scent was intoxicating. She could see the sweat on Josh's face, the goosebumps rising on his skin.

"I'm Misyrie," she said with a tight-lipped smile. "This can be much greater than a dream." She inched closer, taking his head into her hands, rubbing his cheeks with her thumbs, and sinking her fingers into the curls of his hair. Josh's hands twitched as he fought the urge to reach out and touch her.

If a spell could be broken, it was with the power of jealousy. Megan stepped between them, forcing Misyrie to let go. "This could be much worse than a dream, too," Megan said, voice elevated. The orange-haired creature eased backward but didn't take her eyes from Josh, nor did the smile leave her face.

"Please," Kyrie said, her musical voice breaking the moment of tension. "Let us show you the home we've made. You can enjoy anything here as you like. We, however, have one request."

"Yes, please," Rosalia answered. "Anything!"

"One of you has a weapon. A gun." Kyrie had barely finished speaking before there was a collective intake of breath. Shock spread quickly through the group, and they looked at each other in disbelief. Some eyes even lingered on Lola, to her chagrin. It never occurred to her that any of them might be armed. If so, why not come clean? Having a weapon in a strange area wasn't too unexpected. Whoever had it kept it hidden well, like a secret. *Yours and yours alone.*

"You must relinquish the weapon," Kyrie continued. "It'll be returned upon your departure." Everyone was still exchanging questioning glances before Lola followed Kyrie's eyes down to Corey. When the rest of the group noticed, he threw his hands up in defense.

"You're fucking kidding, right?" Rosalia said hotly. Her brows were drawn tighter than Lola had seen before, looking horrified that those beings might be offended.

"There was no way to know what we'd find out here," he defended. "Or in here. What if these things wanted to, I don't know, eat us or something?"

"Corey." Rosalia's tone was quieter and calmer, but the heat was thick in her voice. He hesitated before shaking his head. Lifting his shirt exposed a black and silver grip, the barrel shoved into the front of his pants.

"Damn, where'd you even get that?" Big Ricky asked, impressed as he eyed the piece.

"My pops. He doesn't know I have it, so don't say shit." It was Big Ricky's turn to raise his hands in response. Corey held his shirt in place, nodding toward the orstras. "Go on, then." Essandra floated down to his level. When she got close, her scent and the power of her beauty were overwhelming. Lola almost couldn't stand to look. She reached with both hands and clasped the weapon, slowly pulling it free. Corey couldn't keep the smile off his face, and Essandra returned it in kind with a wink.

"Now," Kyrie said, grin returning after Essandra handed her the weapon. "We'll guide you on your way." The excitement had again reached a boiling point, and Lola practically bounced where she stood.

"Our magic here is unique," the pink-haired orstra went on. "It's particular about who, what, and where. One misstep can lead to not-so-pleasant consequences, so things must be done a certain way. I can promise you, with our guidance, the reward will be rich for your souls." Kyrie's kind expression filled Lola with warmth, but she noticed the creature didn't have teeth. She found it very curious. Her eyes darted to the others, who didn't bear a single tooth either. Maybe they didn't need teeth? Maybe they looked ugly or creepy if they displayed them? Lola couldn't come to a conclusion.

"The boys must go to the left, the girls to the right." Kyrie gestured toward the doors on either side of the hall with the smallest tilt of her head. No one had a problem with that, save Megan, whose face darkened suspiciously. Lola knew she didn't want to be separated from Josh.

"Misyrie will guide you on your way," Kyrie said to Rosalia. Misyrie shot her leader a glare.

"Shall we?" Essandra asked the men. She began leading them single file through the first door on the left. Kyrie and Misyrie drifted ahead of Rosalia, opening the first on the right with a graceful sweep of her hand. Everyone could feel the anticipation; the air bubbled with it. Lola clutched her gothic friend's leg, feeling her hand come down to rub the top of her head. From the room ahead, a golden amber color spilled forth. Lola moved in a hypnotized daze toward it with the others filing in front of her. She barely noticed she was the last in the line.

Lola slowed her steps to allow the gap between herself and Rosalia to widen. She couldn't really say why, perhaps to take as much in as she could. The light swallowed her friend before gently encapsulating Lola in its warm, soothing arms. It pulled at her in the same way as that place had since the beginning, but it was strengthening. Self-awareness and conscious thoughts were fleeting images in the fog of her mind. Even the effort to remind herself to remain focused and alert fell to the back burner.

The glow's warm caress remained as she took in the next room. It displayed a dining setting, a long table stretching the length of the large room. It seemed plain and out of place compared to the building in which it sat. Two chandeliers of blinding gold hung above them, heavy and encapsulating. Lola stared at them, which almost felt like staring at the sun, but it was difficult to look anywhere else. Around the rest of the girls, Kyrie and Misyrie lingered with a silver-haired orstra— that one unnamed. When Lola slid her fingertips across the wooden surface of the table, she gasped when it reacted as liquid would. She watched in amazement until a sound interrupted. It was the sound of the door closing behind them. The creatures watched them with tight-lipped smiles, and once again, something about it prodded her. It was a subtle feeling in her gut, but present, nonetheless, and persisting.

"This is where we dine," Kyrie started. Her voice was somehow less magical than it had initially been. Something made Lola feel uncertain, but it was heavily outweighed by the warmth in her heart. Lola looked back at the wavering table, noticing that even with its unique nature, it lacked plates, silverware, and any type of decoration. There wasn't any food, either. Lola looked to Kyrie, who was watching her with glowing eyes.

"Where's the…?" Her question hung in the air as she continued to peer into the green-eyed abyss. The more she watched, the more it seemed like they were burning. Alive with something beyond sight. The gut feeling nagged and gnawed. Why wouldn't it go away? Erin's voice broke the gaze.

"How do you dine? What do orstras eat?" Erin said the unfamiliar word slowly. Her voice was filled with curiosity as she continued to survey the room. Misyrie floated down, settling close to eye level. The creature took Erin's head into her hands, and her eyes rolled backward.

"We eat a lot. As a matter of fact," Misyrie said with a giggle, "we're going to eat you." Lola, like the rest of them, didn't initially catch it. When she did, it was almost like an alarm in the distance she wasn't sure she'd actually heard. All of them together looked toward Erin and the orstra, puzzled. When the girl's eyes popped back open, they were filled with confusion. Her mouth quirked into a smile as if unsure if she'd heard a joke or not. That only seemed to amuse Misyrie more.

"Is that funny?" spat the fire-headed creature, and for the first time, it smiled with an open mouth. Lola watched in frozen shock as the orstra's face slid up, skin folding into skin, to expose hundreds of thin, pointed teeth. They were barely the size of toothpicks, but deadly in the sheer number of them. The skin beneath her jaw folded toward her neck to make way for the endless fangs, strings of drool spilling out onto the floor at Erin's feet. All of the feelings—the magical wonderment, the ecstasy, the euphoria—faded into a profound horror. Lola's stomach lurched, and a thick, icy chill passed through her body, paralyzing her where she stood. She wanted to scream, but she couldn't make a sound. It was a struggle to draw breath. She watched the curious expression on Erin's face transform into a mask of terror. The color left her features, and she opened her pale white mouth to scream, but time didn't allow it. The orstra's head shot forward, mouth opening impossibly wide to bite down on the girl's head. Misyrie's grip caught the top of the forehead down to her jawline. With a sickening crunch, the teeth clamped shut. Blood misted in a thick spray, and Erin's body sagged. As gravity took it down, the front half of her skull remained in the creature's mouth, pulling apart from the rest of her. Lola was frozen. *Sweet Erin*, she thought, tears flooding from her. *She was supposed to be a nurse.* It was impossible to look away from the gory mess that used to be Erin's face. Blood flowed like a river from the wound and drifted toward Lola on the floor. It was then that the chill finally broke. The shock let go of her, and the scream escaped her chest, shrill and terror-struck. Chaos followed.

She couldn't say how long the shrieks continued—seconds or a lifetime. The once-beautiful creatures descended upon them, and all of the girls scrambled in a mad panic. Somewhere in the craziness of it all, something hit Lola. Hard. The blow took her from her feet and though the fight to think clearly was elusive, she tried to push herself to her hands and knees, hot tears dripping from her face, landing on the odd floor and causing the colors to respond and gravitate in the direction of the liquid. Each breath was a hyperventilating, wet sob, and her legs were stomping and stumbling as bodies fell from above. She looked up long enough to see Megan hanging in the air,

144

arms and legs flailing about before she suddenly went limp, and the body dropped, but no head dropped with it, just a lifeless corpse ending in a neck. Kyrie had stretched her entire mouth around Megan's head and lifted her from the floor with impossible strength, slicing her skull off completely. Lola screamed again, not hearing herself or feeling more tears pour from her face. She desperately crawled, but something hot and wet dripped onto her back—so heavy that it rolled off the side of her—and when she looked to see a mixture of drool and blood, it fell on her head, spreading through her hair like a burning web, then trickled down her cheek to the floor.

Through the panicked commotion, she could see the door. Fiona was on her knees, frantically pulling at the doorknob with blood-soaked hands. She screamed as she clawed at it, a scream that cut off abruptly. Misyrie latched onto the girl's neck from behind and yanked at the throat violently. Fiona's skin tore open like a rubber band, blood rushing out in heavy dark bursts. Lola squeezed her eyes shut, not wanting to move, and forced herself to keep crawling. The door was the only way out. She felt legs crash against her, then something toppled over her to the other side, causing a splintering crash. It took her only a moment to realize it was Brit. The big girl had fallen through the dining room table as she wrestled with the silver-haired orstra. Splinters of wood, large and small, flew through the air, and Lola did her best to shield her face. When she turned away from the violent spray, she saw Misyrie on top of Rosalia, who was desperately trying to keep the teeth of the creature away from herself. As she did, one hand slipped into the creature's deadly mouth up to the elbow, and all Lola heard was the crunch of snapping bone, followed by a wail of terrible agony. *No*, she thought. *Not Ros.*

145

In front of her stood Kyrie amidst unrecognizable bodies. Her emerald eyes burned into Lola's soul. The creature was on her feet, strolling toward Lola with an arrogant sway of the hips.

"The smaller ones make for the best dessert," she said, a long tongue licking over her bloody lips. "And we always earn dessert." Her lips peeled back, and the face folded in on itself. Her entire head was a mass of teeth—it was a wonder the creatures could even see when they feasted. Teeth glistened white and red as they stretched open. Lola could only submit to the inescapable doom. Yet, in an instant, Brit stepped around her wielding a table leg like a baseball bat. She swung it around madly until it crashed into Kyrie's head. Upon impact, most of Kyrie's teeth shattered like glass, and a screeching howl followed. The sound died after a moment, and the orstra collapsed in a motionless heap. Lola looked toward the table to see the silver-haired one limp as well, a large splinter lodged in her gushing throat. Brit was a red massacre huffing for air. For the first time, Lola felt a glimmer of hope. And then the memory came slamming back. *Ros!*

Brit lifted Lola to her feet with a groan, and together, they rushed toward their distressed friend. Rosalia's arm was still lodged in Misyrie's mouth, while the other had a hold on the creature's throat. The flame-haired monster rained blows down on the gothic girl, clawing flesh away from her face with each swing. Blood oozed from her mouth down onto Rosalia's face, and Lola couldn't imagine how she could breathe. Rosalia coughed and choked. *No, Ros!* Lola rushed behind the creature. Dark eyes buried under folds of skin graced the back of Misyrie's head. Grabbing each side of its skull, Lola dug her thumbs deep into each socket. As the pressure intensified, the

146

eyes popped out and spit steaming blood onto her hands. The creature shrieked. When its mouth opened, Rosalia's arm was free. Lola let go and fell backward just in time for Brit to swing a high-charged blow directly to the top of the orstra's head. A loud crack split through the air. Lola didn't know if it was the table leg or the skull, but silenced followed, and the creature fell off Rosalia like a discarded sack of flesh.

Both girls rushed to their friend. Her face was torn and bloody, and her arm was a broken, shredded mess. Rosalia's breaths were quick and abbreviated at the end, the sound making Lola's stomach turn. Each inhale shook her body. Brit quickly removed her sweater, ripping a long shred from it to tie just above Rosalia's elbow. Lola crouched at her side, tears streaming down her face as she bit her lip. Her best friend's good hand reached up to cup her face.

"Baby girl," she whispered with a violent cough. "I'm so sorry."

"Don't be," Lola replied, wiping the tears and snot from her face. "We're going to get out of here."

"I had no idea," the gothic girl began while crying. "I just wanted—"

"Shhhh," Brit urged. "We all wanted the same thing. No one could've known." The big girl, slick with blood so dark it looked black, looked around the room. Lola followed her gaze, afraid one of the orstras may come back to life. Kyrie still lay motionless. As Lola's gaze drifted, something caught her eye. A black and silver handle, just beyond the creature's head. *The gun!* It might as well have been glowing. Her hope spiked, and she lifted her little arm, pointing a single finger. As Brit followed the direction, a similar expression lit her face, and she

147

shot off the ground without hesitation. Lola couldn't say if she ran or slid to the weapon, but she got there quickly. The girl picked up the gun and slid it into her pants behind her.

"We have to go look for the boys," Brit started shakily, trying but failing to keep the emotion out of her voice. "Ros…"

The gothic girl had turned a ghostly white despite being quite pale to begin with. "I can make it," she struggled to say. "We have to stay together." Brit kneeled, leaning close and wrapping her arms around both Rosalia and Lola.

"Ros, you've lost a lot of blood. We have to do something." Brit's voice was confused and desperate. "I'll find the rest. You and Lola get out of here while you can." Lola wanted to leave that place. She wanted to go *home*. But she knew it wasn't an option, so she vigorously shook her head.

"We're just as good as dead out there," she insisted. "Ros is too hurt to hike with me." Maybe her logical reasoning was coming from the fact that three orstras were dead. Her gaze dropped to Rosalia. The girl's appearance could've been straight out of a horror film. The cuts and tears brewed a deep sadness in Lola's chest—as did the entire situation. If they could only rewind to a few minutes before.

Brit considered her silently, eyes squeezing to push another tear down her cheek. She pulled Corey's gun from behind her and chambered a round. "Okay, but this has to be done very carefully." She gave Kyrie's limp body a glance. The creature hadn't budged from her pool of teeth, blood, and drool. Part of Lola wanted to take the gun from the Brit and blast a shot right into the orstra's skull for assurance. Another part dissuaded her. *She's dead*, she reassured herself.

Together, they lifted Rosalia. She groaned, wincing hard from the pain, but she was able to stand. She nodded with one arm around Brit's shoulder, and all of them moved toward the door. Lola kept her hand on her friend's leg, even if it only offered slight support. One step at a time, they crossed the distance. When Brit was close enough to reach the handle, she leaned a shoulder against the wall, and Rosalia moved behind her to lean against it with her back. Lola brought up the rear and thought about how she hadn't wanted to be in the back when they first arrived. *They might miss me*, she recalled. It devastated her, but it likely spared her life. Megan, Fiona, Erin…they were gone. Lola knew if they got out of there, the pain and shock would both hit her at once. She had to suppress the urge to vomit.

Brit reached for the handle with a blood-spattered hand. Her fingers shook as they slid over the large gold knob and twisted carefully. The object was slick in her hands. She put the gun in her armpit, reached out with a second hand, and gripped again. It turned, though not easily, and Lola held her breath as it creaked. Her teeth were clenched while the process dragged out until the door finally popped open. Her friend proceeded cautiously, and the hinges remained silent, to her relief. It was hard for Lola to see from behind the two girls, but no sound escaped Brit, which was a good sign. No surprises. She took the gun in her right hand, looked back at the two of them, and nodded before opening the door wide. They all stepped through when she let go of the knob with Lola on Rosalia's heels.

The original hallway was eerily quiet. No movement or noise interrupted the thick silence. Lola scanned the walls carefully, looking for one of them to detach itself like they had before, but their stillness didn't budge. Her heart was thumping in her chest, rising with the fear, so she swallowed and reminded herself to stay calm. They could kill these things together, and perhaps the men had an easier time with it. It wasn't too ridiculous to hope for. The girls moved in front of her, each step sure and slow. The doors across the hall could've been a mile away for the time it took to get over to them. She did her best to quell the anxious, terrified feeling that was creeping to the front of her mind.

Brit grabbed the first doorknob leading to the path where the boys had been taken. She turned back to them, placing a finger on her lips. Lola and Rosalia nodded. Beyond there could be anything, and Lola gave Rosalia's hand a squeeze. When the gothic girl looked down at her and smiled, Lola had to fight the turning in her stomach. The bit of skin that wasn't covered in blood had turned impossibly whiter. The sight of it scared her to death, but she knew they had to move forward. She took a deep breath, and Brit eased the door open.

Lola exhaled when nothing happened. She peered forward to get a look as she followed the two into the next room. It was a well-lit hallway of gold that ended just to their right. On that wall was a picture of one of the creatures—a dark-haired one. To the left, the hall stretched before curving to the right. Just as the wall turned, it shifted to glass—large arched windows covering the expanse. As they made their way, the path opened into another large room. A massive door stood directly across; it hummed and glowed in a way that was no longer intoxicating. The trauma of their experience had stripped them of that, and Lola learned that the feeling served one purpose— to lure. On the side closest to them, a staircase spiraled up with a small door nestled at its base. They scanned the room and waited until they were sure they were alone. Confident enough, Brit walked to one of the windows, the other two girls following close behind. Lola put her hands around her eyes and pressed against to the glass, but she couldn't make anything out beyond.

"More fucking fairy magic," Rosalia cursed in an angry whisper. Brit could only shake her head. The big girl gestured at each door as if asking which one they should choose. Without hesitation, Rosalia raised a pale and blood-streaked arm. A single finger rose to point at the larger door. Brit nodded, closed her eyes, and sucked in a deep breath. Lola did the same. She held it for a moment before letting it out. She could see that Brit's hand with the gun was still shaking, and it made her nervous. Were she to fire it, her aim would have to be accurate, or it could doom them? She wondered if Kalos was watching from wherever he was perched. *You threw me into this nightmare.* It was anger that fueled the thought, and she gripped the binding of her journal through her bag for comfort.

They approached the next door cautiously. Brit twisted the knob as gently as she had before until it clicked open. Lola couldn't see inside yet, but she noticed alarm strike the big girl's face. The same look passed to Rosalia, and she looked down to Lola, placing a finger on her lips and then pointing. As Lola came around, she took in a large room with red carpets and walls, dominated by enormous round windows. The room was circular as well. Near the center was a massive canopied bed with a dim light shining through its dark curtains. They watched it for some time, waiting for anything to change or shift, but nothing did. The only sound was a dull hum coming from within. Lola's fear spiked, and when Brit moved forward, she had no choice but to follow. The floor masked their

151

footsteps well, but Brit used it to increase her speed, which caused a giant lump to form in Lola's throat. Brit's hand raised the gun, aiming at the curtains when she was nearly close enough to touch them. They were black and thick, so the light coming from within must've been intense. Brit glanced at them, nodded, and turned back toward the bed with a hard swallow. Lola wrapped her arms around Rosalia's trembling legs and forced herself to watch as Brit reached out and pulled the curtain.

The scene beyond the curtain flooded Lola with misery. She choked and coughed as she took it in. Josh lay on his back in the middle of the wide bed, a yellow-haired orstra straddling him. Their bottom halves were covered with thin silk sheets, and Josh was without a shirt. The creature had his head, seemingly frozen, cradled in her hands, as she lifted it to kiss her. There was a slight gap between their mouths and a light, powerful and pulsating, stretched from his lips to hers. It was responsible for the low humming, and it flowed swiftly out of him into the orstra. Josh's hair had turned a ghostly white and his skin a deep gray, almost unrecognizable to the girls. Lola's eyes were wide, and she didn't even have to blink to free the tears of horror. *She's sucking the life from him. The soul*, she thought. Brit never lowered her arm, instead pressing the tip of the gun against the side of the creature's skull. The orstra's mouth snapped shut, the light vanished, and Josh's head sank back onto the bed. She twisted to study Brit, and when her mouth opened to reveal the ugliness it hid, a powerful blast thundered. The room lit briefly, and Lola's ears rang, but she never blinked. The top of the creature's blonde head exploded in a dark spray that splattered through the curtains and onto the red walls. The orstra's body fell sideways and backward, sliding off the bed against one of the posts on the opposite side. Lola failed to combat the shock she was feeling, and Brit was visibly shaken, too, staring at the gun as if surprised to have it in her hand. Rosalia rushed over to Josh, pulling Lola close behind, but the sight wasn't pleasant. At best, he looked feeble and aged. At worst, he looked like someone who'd been dead for quite some time. Lola choked on a sob, followed by Brit, but Rosalia stared without any expression on her face.

"They're seducing them," the gothic girl said, emotionless. "This is happening to all of them, right now." She looked up urgently.

"They're taking…their souls," Brit said, staring numbly with the gun still aimed. Rosalia moved toward her, putting her hand on top of Brit's and forcing it down slowly.

"And eating us," she answered in a similar tone. Brit carried the same shocked look. It was like everything that'd happened finally struck them. Lola followed Rosalia's eyes farther into the room and past the bed to spot another large door.

"We have to keep moving," she continued, pointing at the weapon in Brit's hand. "Keep that thing handy. Some of them likely heard the gunfire." The girl was willing herself into a clear state of mind with deliberate blinks and deep breaths. After nodding, Rosalia led the way with Lola bringing up the rear. She eyed the dead creature as they passed, then spared a glance for Josh. *They were a happy couple, and now both are gone.*

They wasted no time covering the distance to the door. Rosalia walked with purpose, driven by an anger that was overcoming the terror. The time to be afraid was gone; if they were to survive, they had to remain focused and willing to fight. She gripped the doorknob, turned it gingerly, and swung it wide. She stood to the side to peek through with only her head visible from the other side. She had her injured arm cradled tight to her chest; the blood dried into a dark crust. Another relief, Lola thought. *It wouldn't do for her to bleed out.* As Rosalia surveyed the room ahead, she nodded to them and moved forward. It wasn't far different than the previous room. Once more, it was rounded, stretching to lead to another door directly across. The difference was the stairs, narrow and steep, resting against the back half of the room, leading to an encircling indoor overlook. While they scanned the room, light caught Lola's eye, and she insistently pulled at Rosalia's sleeve.

"There," she said with an outstretched hand. The door on the other side had the same light beaming through the cracks. Her older friend turned to Brit, a grim expression on her face, and held out her hand. There was little understanding at first as to what Rosalia wanted, but then it slowly dawned on her that she wanted the gun. Brit hesitated guiltily but handed the heavy weapon over. Lola felt a stab of pity for her. Her confidence had faded, even after killing three orstras. The gunfire must've rattled her. She gave Brit's arm a reassuring squeeze in hopes of putting her mind at rest.

Rosalia stepped deliberately toward the door on a mission, but before she could reach it, it burst inward with a booming crack. Splinters of wood flew past them sideways, the light darkened by a large figure. It only took Lola a moment to recognize RJ. He was a mass of blood, sweat, and fear. When he saw them, the surprise almost stopped him dead in his tracks. Relief hit them all at once, but it didn't last.

"Run!" he screamed at them, charging by them with nothing but the solitary word. With one huge arm, he scooped Lola up with no effort and plowed back in the direction they'd come. Lola didn't have an opportunity to protest. Rosalia hesitated, watching them flee, but before she had time to make a decision, two flame-haired orstras flew into the room. The two girls backed up as the creatures ascended above them, looking down with boiling eyes.

"We can't leave them!" Lola screamed at the big man, her small hands beating at his chest. "Go back, please! Help us kill them!" He stared at her, cheeks red and puffy. His large chest heaved with desperation as he looked back at the girls. As soon he turned at an angle, she could see, and a gunshot sounded across the area, followed by another. The first was a miss, but Rosalia's second shot blasted through a thin wing, causing the creature to spin from the impact. As it did, to Lola's dismay, it dove and barreled into Rosalia, sending her tumbling backward while the gun slid across the floor. The other descended toward Brit, connecting with the big girl's face. There was the slap of skin, a cracking sound, and a spray of blood from Brit's nose as she fell. Lola wriggled against RJ's grip, but it was useless. She was pinned tightly to his chest.

"I can't let you die. I can't let a child die. I'm sorry." Her stomach sank as he bolted again in the opposite direction. She shrieked in rage and grief, flailing about with what little movement she could manage. She might as well have been mute because her actions didn't sway the man. As he reached for the door they'd entered from, it burst as the last one had. Three more orstras emerged with Essandra at their head. RJ slid to a halt, but their attackers didn't hesitate and rushed him at once. The impact as they dived into him sent him tripping back on confused feet. Lola used the tumble to slip free. A hand gripped her hair just as she popped loose, and she felt a patch tear out. The pain was minute compared to her fear. She hit the ground, and her knees buckled. Lola did her best to roll away from striking distance, looking around to see them swarming RJ like oversized wasps. He caught one in his grip, but the other two were luckier. They chewed at either side of his head above his muscular shoulders. He yelled as he sank to his knees. Lola looked toward Rosalia to see she was running directly toward her, gun hanging weakly in a bloody hand.

"Run, baby! Please run!" She opened fire at the orstras attacking RJ, the first shot drilling one on his shoulder, then another missing wide. That caused Essandra to break free from him and spiral high into the air. RJ's face was a red-painted mask of horror, but his eyes had a thick, empty glaze to them, and he fell face-first onto the ground. As they were watched from above, the original two that'd entered the room sped toward Rosalia. *I can't leave you*, Lola thought, but Rosalia's eyes were pleading. *But you have to survive, or you'll never go home again.* The pain of the decision was unbearable, but she had little time to decide. Lola barely felt her feet on the ground as she ran toward the door, not once looking back.

She felt a rush of wind blast by her face, likely a mad swipe from one of the violent creatures, but she kept running. Lola sped past the bed with Josh and the dead orstra into the room with the spiral stairs. Her first instinct was to go the direction she'd initially come, but shadows on the wall beyond showed movement she couldn't afford to trust. She bolted for the little door under the stairs instead. She crashed into it, swinging it wide, and wasted no time slamming it closed behind her. Her chest heaved, her spit was thick with blood, and sweat covered her entire body.

The scenes of horror that'd occurred replayed in her brain in repetitive flashes. It was a task to keep her breathing under control. Lola squeezed her eyes shut, recalling the images she'd seen while falling into Kalos's reality. *I've seen terrible things before. I must keep it together.* If the demon had possessed her and left her physical body behind, then it was all in her head, right? Convincing herself of that was the hard part. What was the truth? The lines between nightmare and reality and were a blurry mess. Lola knew one thing for sure—she could die there. She had no doubts in regard to that matter.

She opened her eyes to survey a long, narrow hallway. It was dimly lit by candles on either side. Green carpet spanned the floor between vanilla walls, a much less visually appealing area than the rest of the place. It was strange to her how plain everything seemed. *It was all an illusion.* No doors lined the way, though another small one, identical to that which she'd entered through, awaited her on the far end. It was menacing and certain as if daring her to approach. Lola stared at it for a time, considering her next move. Her beating heart had slowed, and her breathing was deep and controlled.

Lola's body slid down the door to take a seat on the carpet. She removed her journal from her bag. Her hands shook, but she needed the words to soothe her. Her last entry was bookmarked by her pen. She found it quickly and began scribbling. Unwanted tears poured from her as she wrote, but she was careful to not let them drip onto the paper. She had to blink to see. Her writing was a jagged mess, but the effort was calming. Over a time, her hands stilled, words flowing from

157

brain to paper in smooth, uninterrupted strokes. It almost took her away from there—to a safer place—but Lola was all too aware of where she was. With a last punctuated mark, she snapped the book shut and slid it back into her small pack. She sucked in another deep breath, whispered a small reassurance to herself, and stood.

She stepped forward but glanced back at the door. At the crack in the bottom, more light shone through, but she noticed shadows darting quickly. *My friends could still be alive out there.* The thought spurred her desire to go back out, to do what she could to save them, but a sudden absence of movement caused her to freeze. In that instant, Lola noticed a lock on the door, and she raised her hand to engage it. As the lock clicked, a sudden and jarring impact immediately followed. Her fright was so intense that she stumbled in the other direction and fell on her back. Her pulse escalated again, and she stared wide-eyed at the small door in front of her. *One more will do it in.* She knew she had little time. Scrambling to her feet, she turned and launched herself down the hallway as quickly as her legs would take her. With each heavy footfall, her goal drifted closer. Lola kept her eyes locked on the door ahead. Behind, the sound of shattering wood split the air, accompanied by the shrieks of orstras. The door grew in her vison, approaching quickly. As her knees worked and tears continued to stream, she could hear the sound of beating wings. As she neared and prepared to drive her shoulder into the wood, her heart sank. A familiar light beamed under that door, too. *They're everywhere.* However, Lola knew there was no other option. Behind her, certain death was speeding her way. In front of her, there was at least the possibility of the unknown. She barely noticed the light vanish as she slammed her body into the barrier, simultaneously gripping the doorknob and twisting. The door flew open so hard that the momentum forced her to her knees, the handle slipping from her grasp. *No*, she thought. *I have to close the door!* As she turned desperately to do so, the orstras were too close; Lola knew she'd never make it. She watched in dismay as Essandra smiled a toothy, blind smile and dove for entry. In the same instant, a large boot flew past Lola's face and kicked the door closed. The blow smashed into the creature, producing a howl of pain. Lola gasped, and she looked up to see Big Ricky standing over her. Blood soaked his bald head and shirt. His hand gripped a broken liquor bottle, the end also dripping with orstra blood. Hope was a beacon of light; she jumped up, throwing her arms around his legs. A slick, calloused hand stroked her hair, and she pressed her face against stained blue jeans.

"We don't have much time," he said in a grim voice. Lola looked around the room—a smaller bedroom bearing similar red and black shades to the others. A headless orstra was slumped over the edge of the bed on her back, and to Lola's swelling grief, a gray and lifeless Chris lay next to her. Her throat was sore from the hard lumps she had to swallow. Her stomach was turning again, and sadness reigned once more. The rest of the room was a massacre of splintered wood and broken glass. Her eyes widened when she saw a broken window and cool air rushing in from outside. Big Ricky shook his head.

"It's too far down, little one." As he said it, an impact shook the door. The middle of it creased and split slightly toward them. Lola knew it wouldn't take but one more thrash.

"The others?" she asked quietly, still clutching his leg. He looked down at her with sad eyes and simply shook his head again.

"The only one I didn't see die was Robin," he said, as quiet as her. Big Ricky stepped forward and eased his shoulder against the door just as the next impact shook it. With the addition of his weight, it managed to stay in place, at least one final time. A few scraps of wood split near the hinges.

"What about the girls?" he asked. When Lola's eyes welled up with more tears, he stroked her hair again, and it was clear he didn't need any more of an answer. "There's only one way out of here, baby." His voice didn't hold a lot of hope, but Lola knew he'd do everything he could. "Are you ready?" She could only nod. "Behind me now."

Big Ricky stepped to the side and flattened them both against the wall next to the door. It was only a few seconds before the door flew, in pieces, across the room. Two orstras, one of which was Essandra, sped in and overshot them. Big Ricky grabbed Lola's arm and darted into the hallway. He ran so fast that her legs could barely keep up, feet skidding more than running. Lola could hear the beating wings and howling behind them, but she couldn't look. As they passed through the ruins of the other door and into the room with the stairs, he quickly bolted left toward the hallway leading to the main hall. It was hard to imagine someone of his stature as quick, but he'd risen to the challenge. They came to a halt, and he shoved her forcefully against the wall. They both knew it'd only be moments before the creatures whipped around the corner after them.

"Close your eyes," he whispered, adjusting his grip on the broken bottle.

"I won't," she replied, looking up at him bravely. She couldn't let them go through it alone—she'd watch it all. He almost had time to smile. Essandra was the first to appear, the heat burning in her eyes, followed by a deep-bellied roar. Big Ricky reached a thick, muscular arm out and caught her by the throat, slamming her against the wall on which they were leaning, then slinging her against the other. The orstra's body distorted upon impact and collapsed to the floor. The next came in lower as if in stealth mode, but Big Ricky wasn't fooled. He clipped her in the head with a heavy black boot, sending the creature sliding into the rounded window across from them. He gave her no time to recover before he leapt onto her. Pinned, the orstra flailed and screeched. With one hand, he pressed her head onto the floor, and using the other, he stabbed her repeatedly with the liquor bottle. Blood boiled out of the creature's body like a geyser. Lola watched, mute, and wondered if he'd ever quit stabbing when a familiar voice snapped her out of it.

"Lola!" *Rosalia's voice.* Lola pushed herself off the wall and saw the gothic girl limping toward them, gun still in hand. Her appearance was shockingly more grotesque than before. Large patches of hair were missing, and one eye socket was nothing but a red hole. Lola's stomach churned, and her heart ached. Rosalia collapsed forward, and Ricky caught her in his big arms.

"Good God," he said, tears brimming his eyes. Lola rushed in to hug them both, crying against Big Ricky's chest. She used his shirt to wipe the moisture from her face.

"Is Brit…" The question hung in the air unanswered until she peered into the bedroom with the large door from which Rosalia had just emerged. Brit lay inside on her back in a thick pool of blood with most of her face missing. Lola choked on the ensuing tears.

"We have to move," Big Ricky pressed, starting to lift them. Rosalia half-heartedly protested for them to leave her, but they ignored her. Together, they moved toward the entry to the main hall. The door, along with every other door, Lola guessed, was a busted ruin. Big Ricky scooped Rosalia up and carried her through with Lola on his heels.

The way out of here, she thought, looking at the giant entrance of the building. Lola hadn't imagined they'd make it that far. It was hard to believe. At one point, she'd been certain of death. They walked toward the front door. Despite its proximity, it seemed far away, and they sped up. Adrenaline was rushing throughout Lola's body. Sweat and blood dripped down into her eyes, impairing her vision, but she kept salvation in sight. Hope, escape, survival—they were right there. Desperation filled her and urged her forward. *Right there. All I have to do is reach—*

Something gripped her foot so tightly that she felt as if she'd been chained to a wall. The suddenness of it evoked a frightened squeal, prompting Ricky and Rosalia to turn around. Lola glanced down to see Robin with streaks of blood decorating his face and body. His skin had lost much of its color, appearing a light gray, but there was still life in him. His eyes were wild and desperate. His mouth worked, but no words surfaced. *He must've fought off the one that got a hold of him*, she thought numbly. As much as she disliked him on their

162

journey, she felt a pang in her chest at the sight of him. Big Ricky was coming around on her right when a small drop of blood spattered directly on Robin's forehead. It took a few moments to process but when they did, they all looked up at once. The only thing she had a chance to see was a swirl of frantic wings, pink hair, and a thick table leg swinging down. *No.* The word passed through her brain, but Lola knew it was over before it'd even happened. As directly as it could hit, the table leg smashed into Big Ricky's skull with a resounding crack. It burst in several directions, and his knees buckled underneath him. He dropped down to her level, eyes crying out to her. They were sad and sorry; her heart broke in her chest. The fright of seeing him in pain made her scream.

"Go," he croaked. Blood emerged from the top of his head and streamed down his face. She wanted to embrace him, but every second mattered. Lola did as she was bid, jerked her leg free from Robin, and ran.

Behind her, a hiss echoed through the room loudly, followed by a gurgle. *It's Kyrie. We should've made sure.* Lola crashed into Rosalia, trying to pull her along, but the gothic girl resisted.

"Go, Lola," she said in a resigned whisper. Lola stopped and pulled at her legs.

"No, I can't survive without you, you have to come!" Rosalia surprised her with a blood-drenched smile. Tears flooded her face.

"There isn't any other way, baby. Keep your secrets, use them, and get out of this place." The older girl pressed Corey's pistol into her shaking hands, mouthing the word, *Go.* As she did, Kyrie hit her from behind, wrapping her arms around

Rosalia's throat and legs around her waist. Her expression never changed; she just watched as Lola backed away. More tears fell from her, and she supposed that they'd never run out. Kyrie's mouth opened wide, revealing a mass of broken, bloody teeth, and she clamped them down over Rosalia's face. Lola watched without feeling. Her body was numb. Behind them, she saw Robin lying motionless, eyes glazed over. *They're all dead*, she thought. *Everyone but me.*

Lola moved her hands behind her back, gripping the gun tightly. When Kyrie pulled free, flesh and blood spilling through her busted mouth, her eyes latched onto Lola. Her lips drew upward in what Lola could've only guessed was a smile.

"A well-earned dessert," Kyrie spat, red gushing from her mouth onto the wet ground. "The best for last." Lola continued to back up with careful steps. The orstra let Rosalia's body loose and crashed toward Lola. Lola's steps had brought her just a few feet from the door.

"You know you'll never make it, child," Kyrie continued to taunt, creeping toward her. Lola knew as soon as she made a run, the creature would bolt, so she just continued to withdraw slowly. It was a surprise when her back hit the door, and she took a deep breath. *One shot to do this.* She watched Kyrie closely, hoping to time everything right. The once-beautiful creature looked dreadful, covered in human blood with her pink hair stained and slick. The worst sight was her teeth, which were a mangled nightmare. As she closed the distance between them, her confidence overtook her, and she couldn't resist. Kyrie darted forward, her wings flapping with a loud swoosh. Skin peeled back, and the full length of her jaw opened wide. The orstra sped at her like a missile. Lola brought the gun around, gripped it in both hands, and whispered a prayer.

The recoil jolted the weapon from her small hands, and the boom made her ears ring again. The bullet flew right through Kyrie's broken teeth and exploded out of the back of her skull. Chunks of bone and blood flew behind. The creature's momentum brought her crashing into Lola, and together, they fell through the front door and out of the house. Lola expected a hard landing, remembering the ground outside, but nothing greeted her besides brightness. The world shook. As she looked back to the orstra's home, it faded—colors melded to become one, then vanished into the blinding light. It intensified with a blazing heat, causing Lola to squeeze her eyes shut and scream. Everything that'd happened, the death and chaos, then her escape, was swallowed up as the world disappeared.

The Gaps

Once more, Lola fell. That was all she'd done since she'd been taken. *I'm falling forever, but I've long since reached the bottom.* The white world swirled around her endlessly. The insanity of it had made her nauseous before, but she felt little anymore. Coherency was a frayed string attached to her mind. She watched it all in a helpless, numb state. Kalos had wrecked her life, and even though she'd managed to escape from his horrors, Lola had lost so much. And only to trade one hell for the next.

The maze suddenly surrounded her again, the impact of her fall knocking the air out of her and bringing reality back home. Her eyes opened weightlessly as the daze of her mind dissipated. The light that spits her back into the prison was nowhere to be seen. White towering walls encompassed her with a darkness looming above. Lola squinted from the shine on either side. Even though she couldn't see, Lola knew there were words etched on those walls, masked by the light. *More horrors.* She sat up and noted that the only path was forward, curving around to the right and out of view. Behind her, a solid wall blocked the path. She struggled to find the motivation to rise. *I haven't lost everything*, she attempted to convince herself. The thought did little to encourage her. *Go on.*

When she leaned forward and set her palms on the ground, it was cold and rough against her skin. Everything seemed so heavy. Her pack might as well have been filled with rocks. All that'd happened, the time that passed and the trials that came with it, she'd brought with her back to that place. The physical injuries and emotional trauma, too. Even the wounds that weren't hers were there. When she opened her mouth, she could feel the dried blood cracking. Her clothes were stained and ruined, her hair heavy and thick with a combination of

167

different filths. Even worse, the fatigue remained. She could feel the tired submission sitting on her eyelids. How she even remained alive was shocking, but she *had* survived. Closing her eyes, Lola tried to take comfort in that. She finally stood.

A small step forward brought a streak of heat up her leg. Her muscles were sore and tired. There was nothing there to nourish her body, which incessantly reminded her that she was both famished and dehydrated. Even if she wasn't in her real body, whatever that place was demanded the same sustenance for her survival. Given all she'd endured, the thought of starving to death in an endless maze was pitiful, and one she wouldn't accept. *I'll find something.* Lola recalled what she ate and drank with Rosalia and the others. It *had* nourished her. That was a hope. But that meant she'd have to go back into another reality to survive. She might have to watch others die again. Lola took one step, no less painful than the first, and clenched her teeth. She took another. *The pain and fatigue will subside eventually, right?* She drifted to the side, feeling the wall catch her shoulder. It was difficult not to use it as a crutch and not to drag herself down its side. Lola kept her eyes off the walls, however, not wanting to absorb the words that would take her to another world. She looked straight ahead while her head slumped against the surface. It was comforting to the touch, and she half-wondered if the dirt from her face would smear on the pristine color.

It took a lifetime to round the bend, and Lola wondered what she hoped for. Nothing encouraging awaited. The path split into three directions; she could proceed to the left, to the right, or continue forward. *Three paths leading nowhere.* Reaching into her pack and withdrawing her journal, she turned her back to the wall and slid down to take a seat. A few glances at her earlier drawings of the maze wouldn't hurt. Expectedly, her mind had trouble piecing any of it together. She could be anywhere in the maze since she'd been carried to another place, so her sketches carried little relevance. She bookmarked them and flipped through the following pages. She drifted past her latest entry and found a crisp, unused page waiting for her. "Which way?" she breathed, then wrote the words as well. Lola only spared a few breaths, knowing she had to move.

Forcing herself off the ground was a task, and she expected the pain of it would be revisited. Lola checked each entrance twice, surveyed what lay beyond, then backtracked. The first was to the left. Her aching legs carried her down to where the path straightened again. Down the straightaway, her feet burned from the effort of walking combined with a lack of rest and energy. Only one opening on the left revealed itself in that direction, but Lola passed three to the right. She took the third, fighting against the feeling of walking in circles. *That's exactly what this is, dummy.* She couldn't argue with herself; the logic was there. But her instincts tracked another path. Her mouth lacked moisture, and her head pounded. The yearning for water throbbed deep within her, begging for even a single drop of hydration.

After her second right, a wall found her, barring her way and leaving no other path, which veered her back the opposite way. Luckily, she'd missed a small offshoot which beckoned to her left. Lola moved quickly through the gap, her thirst and hunger adding desperation to her steps. *Don't be foolish*, she reminded herself. She surveyed the newest stretch of her path and continued.

It was maybe fifteen minutes before she ran out of gas. The paths were twisted and tangled. The exasperation of going backward more than forward added to the exhaustion. Her mind made as much sense of it as her earlier drawings had. *I've turned and walked too much.* She almost collapsed on the floor as she sat down to rest. At one point, she attempted sleep to reenergize herself. It came in small, fearful fits—likely stemming from the fact that she wasn't alone in the maze. The pain of everything made her want to cry. When the tears welled up in her eyes, another option crept into her brain. Could she use the walls to get out of the dead end again? If so, what would she fall into? She felt torn, but what choice did she have?

The question rolled around in her head like dice. As time passed, she considered it more and more. The last journey had landed her in quiet, ominous woods. What else could be in store? Only nightmares would await. *I can't just stay here forever*, she thought, her stomach gnawing at her. Somewhere else might have food…

She backtracked again to her original path, invigorated by a new, hopeful energy. Once she found the first wall that blocked her, Lola knew that would be her place. She couldn't say why, only that perhaps it was the closest link to where she'd come from before. She stepped close, letting her eyes adjust to the brightness. The words came slowly underneath, and she began to scan the odd language as best she could. The writing was smooth and elaborate, almost too perfect. It reminded Lola of printed cursive. They were countless words on the vast wall, continuing endlessly in all directions. It *was* a unique prison, not lacking in a creative stroke. Her captor was very clever and intelligent. But the place was also cruel. Her

170

anger rose, but she let it simmer in the back of her mind. She scanned at a quick pace, eyes darting from side to side. Her mind conjured the image of a house—a large one. Her first alarming thought was that it was the orstra house, but the suspicion faded as the words showed her something different. She leaned in, struggling to focus her eyes. The world around her shifted as it had before, shaking on the edges of her vision as reality dissolved. Color melted away, sucked into a vicious spiral, and Lola could feel it draw her in like an enormous vacuum. As the maze dismantled and folded upon itself, she felt no fear that time. Hope was alive inside her, and she clung to it like a starving child. She wouldn't allow herself to fall. That time, she jumped.

From the Darkness They Rise

Bloody Acquaintance

Chaos waited for her on the other side. It was much different that time. Darker, deeper. There were twisting blacks, reds, and oranges. The combination gave her the feeling that the demon controlling the nightmare was angry, and, of course, that couldn't be a good sign. A pang of regret struck her for deciding to jump, but her will to continue crushed it. Lola was hungry. She was thirsty. She needed to survive. Otherwise, she'd waste away in a stone maze surrounded by nothing but deteriorating bones. The thought disturbed her. It felt like being backed into a corner. *Not just a corner*, she thought, seething. *An entire maze.*

Lola closed her eyes against the rush. She could feel the brightness through her eyelids; it shifted, darkened, then spiraled into something else. The movement was collective, like watching the grace of a school of fish or flock of birds, but there was no euphoria. There was no sense of peace. That'd been ripped away from her and replaced with the pain of very real and recent memories. Lola recalled Rosalia pushing the gun into her hand and the pit in her stomach knowing her friend was about to give up her life. Maybe those events were dreams or hallucinations, the result of some twisted magic. But she had *known* them. They were as real as she—or anything else there—was. Yet they were gone, while she remained.

When she felt herself drifting slower, she opened her eyes. The bending state around her settled into her grandmother's backyard, a half-acre stretching out to meet a thick Magnolia tree. A wooden swing hung beneath, attached by two frayed ropes. The last time she sat in it, she'd been a young child—

173

maybe five or six. It was crooked and worn, forgotten by everything save for age. Beyond, the sun shone, but the world around her lacked color. It was similar to before, during her first fall—some kind of dream stage. Her mother was there again. She stood with her arms crossed, hair dangling around her shoulders, looking toward the ground. Lola could hear her, and the grief broke her heart. A knot rose in her throat as her mother spoke to no one.

"Please," she sobbed. "Bring my baby back. Please." The last word was a strained cry accompanied by an agonized moan. All at once, the emotions in Lola's chest boiled over. Lola screamed, and burning tears slid down the sides of her face. Simultaneously, the image rolled away, and colors laced back together to form her speeding tunnel of travel. The anger had her skin blazing, and her teeth were clenched hard enough to shatter. It'd been a while since she'd felt anything but pain. Lola swore to herself to kill Kalos in that moment. She'd murder him and go home. *I will*, she swore with feelings of empowerment flowing through her veins. *I will*.

Her body dipped downward, and she knew the end would arrive soon. As she sped, the ground revealed itself. Much like before, it was a speck, but it grew larger as she approached. She could discern shades of brown, but an occasional burst of light would flare in different areas. It reminded her of lightning bugs in the summer weather. They intensified so much so that she could hear them. Each spark sounded with a popping noise, louder and more powerful as the distance closed. *Gunfire*, she realized with alarm. Adrenaline rushed through her body as the scene came to life. Two men stood back-to-back inside the living room of a large home. Around them, people were rushing from all directions with angry shrieks. One of the men was dressed as a police officer, while the other wore an orange jumpsuit. Both possessed handguns. The man she assumed to be the prisoner had ebony skin and also bore a large knife. He slashed any time someone got too close. His hair was thick and dark, as was the beard on his face. Lola only had time to open her mouth to yell before she was dropped at their feet. Her impact went unnoticed by the policeman, but the other took a hack at her in surprise, which she narrowly evaded in a half-roll, half-tumble. The landing, of course, did her no favors. The air jolted from her body, and she twisted her wrist in an attempt to break her fall. She ended up on her back, and the man in orange was about to end it for her before they locked eyes. Lola thought she was shocked, but his surprise was far greater than hers. *He can't comprehend it*. From the other side, cold steel pressed against the side of her head; when she looked up, the officer had positioned himself above her.

"Banks, no!" the prisoner cried, kicking his arm at the elbow. As it happened, the firearm roared, and a bullet blew through the ground just to her left. A loud, persistent ring replaced her hearing, muting everything else. The men were yelling at each other. The orange man's finger was pointed at her, and when the cop noticed, his look mirrored his partner's. Disbelief filled his eyes. While her hearing returned slowly, she thought she heard one say, "She's alive, man. She's alive!" While she didn't understand what he meant by that, Lola imagined it was somehow relevant to the current situation. Their attention didn't linger on her long. They continued to repel the assault from the group closing in on them. She hastily forced herself to her knees and plugged her ears as gunshots filled the air. Lola was partially sandwiched between their legs and couldn't get a good look. As she tried to rise, a rough hand

175

shoved her back to the ground, and she took it as a sign it was wise to stay put. With her left cheek to the floor, she looked beyond the feet to see the crowd. It was difficult to see, but they looked like an ugly, angry mob. She'd counted to twelve by the time another body hit the ground. *Eleven now*, she thought. *But they look like...corpses.* One was missing an eye and both lips. He stumbled forward with thick steps; his yellow teeth exposed for all to see. They chomped loudly before a bullet found his forehead, prompting his collapse. Another behind him tripped clumsily over the fallen body—a woman with thin gray hair. She didn't even have one eye. When she fell, her face landed close to Lola's. Her mouth opened and closed rapidly, a hollow hole in her skull that was hungry for something. Lola expected to be afraid, but adrenaline overtook her. A heavy, booted foot came down on the lady's head, and it exploded into bloodless chunks of skin and bone. *The policeman.* Lola looked up to see him blasting more shots into the few that remained, rotating positions with his partner. Blood oozed from a large cut on his forehead, mixing fluidly with the sweat around his face. His intense expression conveyed anger and exhaustion. A soaked thin brown beard lined his haggard features, but his green eyes burned with life.

A thud caused her to whip her head around. The large knife had been pulled free as the man in orange wrestled a few corpses on his side. Digging his thumb into one dark socket, he pressed, and the head snapped backward, opening at the throat to reveal dried insides. It fell to its knees, but the others persisted. The broken head flapped open and closed as it dropped the rest of the way to the ground. The remaining eye, dead and glazed over, locked onto her. A skeletal hand reached out, hungry and frantic. Lola tried to squeeze the opposite way,

176

but the officer's legs blocked her. Her only other option was the blade on the ground, so she snatched it and lifted it in the air. It was a dull thing, beaten and chipped from heavy use, though there wasn't a drop of blood on it. Lola didn't doubt that it'd carved a good deal of the dead creatures around them. *They're rotten*, she thought, the words passing through her mind as she brought the weight of the weapon down on her attacker's head. The knife sunk an inch and stopped, not seeming to discourage its grasping fingers at all. The cold limbs curled around her ankle, and Lola shrieked, yanking the blade free and stabbing it downward again. A different spot on the skull yielded more depth, but the grip on her foot tightened. She rained blows down, again and again, until her arm was burning from the effort. Her fingers had gone numb. The last blow jerked the blade from her hands, but the corpse luckily didn't move again. She noticed the skull was nothing more than battered bits of bone and dry, crusted brain. Lola expected relief, but the sight was disturbing enough to keep her distressed. Gunshots still rang above her and abruptly ended in a metallic clicking noise. It was hard to tell from her position, but as she surveyed the area, it appeared as though there were only a few threatening corpses remaining. Two of them were crawling. One heavy leg stepped over her to move toward the remnants.

"They busted right through that rotten heap of shit," the cop said in a not-so-kind tone.

"Fuck you, Banks," the prisoner replied dismissively. He reached out and grasped the only standing one under the chin. Lola watched him slam it into the wall across the room over and over again until its body was in pieces. The policeman—

Banks—smashed the other two heads with the heel of his heavy boot.

"Besides, it's the best of what we've found here." The prisoner walked in a circle back to Banks, stepping over the dead. "You're welcome to find something better."

"I'm telling you, Burris. There's something back there, beyond all that shit rubble. We need to dedicate some time to digging through it."

"Well, if the last week hasn't been enough, then I don't know what will be." Burris continued to walk around, browsing through the dead. Lola couldn't say what in the world he could be looking for on a corpse. They were pointedly ignoring her, however. She didn't know what to say about it— or if she should say anything at all. She stayed where she was, making no sound. The surrounding windows and doors were all beaten in or broken down. The only door that remained was the front one, which was actually two heavy doors. A wide hole was visible near the bottom of the right. The room itself was extremely large with high ceilings—the place obviously belonged to someone of wealth. The floor was lined with a light red carpet bearing golden designs that Lola couldn't make out due to the debris of wood shards and rotten pieces of corpses. The place was a wreck. A set of narrow stairs lined the right wall, but every other step was busted. Similar to the orstras' dwelling, a small door was tucked beneath the staircase. The upstairs space was lost in darkness. Beneath the second story and heading across the opposite wall, an empty hollow sat that'd been a double-door entry at one point. It was currently blocked by numerous collapsed rocks, wooden planks, and pillars from the other side. The far wall had no doors; as it stretched around to the front, two empty sockets—former windows—decorated it like empty black eyes. How ironic.

Lola looked across at the two men to find them staring at each other in some kind of silent debate. The cop raised his hands in submission and turned away.

"Go ahead, Burris. Just say it." His tone was angry once more, and Lola concluded he was just an angry person.

"Okay, so just ignore the elephant in the room?" the prisoner asked, gesturing in Lola's direction. His voice was deep and loud, but there was a gentleness to it.

The angry policeman spared her a glance, one that wasn't nice. "A little girl's unlucky enough to survive that fucking nightmare outside and ends up in here with us. What do you want from me?"

"We have to do something," Burris returned, kicking a skull from beneath his feet.

"She'll die. Or get us killed. Not an option."

"Banks—"

"No, Burris. I'm not looking over my shoulder to take care of some ratty child. We'll never make it like that." Lola felt a stab of anger, and her jaw dropped. *Ratty?* Subconsciously, she reached up to pinch her hair between her fingers. It was thick with filth, and she could only imagine the scum on her face.

"How're you just gonna make that choice, man?" Burris grilled, gesturing in her direction again. "It's a fucking kid. Come on. It's the right thing to do."

"Tell me all about the 'right thing to do,' Burris."

179

The prisoner heaved a heavy, resigned sigh, avoiding eye contact with Lola. "So, this is your idea of 'right?' Leaving a child to die? Maybe *you* should be wearing this." Burris gripped his collar and flipped it toward Banks to emphasize the statement.

Once more, the cop's eyes found her. "I took his handcuffs off not even two days ago. See what I get?" Burris scoffed in response.

"I'm sitting right here, you know," Lola said, looking at the pair of them with an angry frown. They had the audacity to look surprised that she spoke.

"How the fuck you get here, kid? What, you just fell out of the fucking sky?" Banks asked, ignoring her comment. His eyes still carried a disbelieving look as if his brain were trying to catch up with the sight in front of him. They both kept their distance, understandably skeptical after the horrors they'd dealt with up to that point.

Lola pointed to Banks. "You were right. I just got lucky enough to survive it out there."

"Ain't nothing lucky about it, and I promise you won't survive long. We can't look after you, kid." Banks turned toward the small door under the stairs. Burris was shaking his head.

"I killed one of them not five minutes ago!" she said proudly, pushing herself to her feet. Lola pulled Burris's knife into view and pointed to the motionless corpse at her feet. "I smashed its head!" Banks turned and considered her coldly, then shrugged, unimpressed.

"When they're crawling out like roaches and coming at you from all sides, and you survive *that*, then come find me."

"Banks!" Burris yelled from across the room.

"Maybe I have!" Lola fought on stubbornly, feeling the heat emanating from her face. "I've seen worse, much worse. And I've killed worse!" A bark of laughter from the cop was all she received in response, and her anger deepened. *What an insufferable person!*

"Well, one thing you can do for sure is lie," he spat. "Your mother teaches you that with all your survival skills?"

"I have!" she argued, but her voice and rage seemed to have no effect on him. "You see this?" She yanked her fingers through her thick, matted hair. It was dry, cracked, and painful to pull through it, but she didn't care. Her eyes stung as she stared at Banks. "This is the blood of flesh-eating fairies! They killed my friends, but not me!" It sounded ridiculous, and Lola instantly regretted saying it. But, given that the undead were walking around there, maybe it'd sound more real.

Banks threw his head back and roared as Burris continued to shake his head. "And your mother taught you to entertain! Perfect. Maybe we should keep you around." The man continued to laugh hysterically as he opened the small door and disappeared beyond, slamming it shut behind him. Lola was fuming. Her fists were clenched tight. Why did a stranger insist on being so intolerable?

"Don't worry about it," Burris said, continuing to rummage through the dead as if the whole conversation hadn't taken place. "We've been here for a long while. Gone through a lot of shit."

"Then why aren't you like him?" Lola asked, still hot behind her ears. The prisoner gave her a sad glance she didn't understand.

"He's lost a bit more than I have." His booming voice had gone quiet, so she decided not to pry. She felt a stab of sympathy—only a small one, though. Lola knew about loss. Everything had been taken from her. What had Banks lost in whatever nightmare they were in? A son? A daughter? A wife?

"Where is this?" she asked, changing the subject. It was a better route to take and might lead to some enlightening answers.

"Texas," the man responded, facing the other direction. He knelt, digging through some pockets, but only found dust.

"What are you looking for?" Lola took a step toward him, mindful of the fallen dead underfoot.

"Anything, really. Anything that could help." He paused, holding up a coin in the light that was gleaming down from a large set of bulbs connected to the ceiling. Cords ran from it in several directions, stretching down to line the walls, with one thread disappearing under the small door Banks had retreated through. "Some of these bastards are armed and don't even know it." Lola took another few steps, gazing over the bodies out of curiosity.

"What are they?" He looked up at her from where he knelt, amused.

"The dead, come again," he answered, and he spread his hands wide. "I know a smart girl like yourself has eyes to see that."

"Yeah, but how?" she asked, letting her growing interest get the best of her.

"I don't think anyone knows, but if they did, we might not be stuck in this damn house with a little girl who asks a lot of questions."

Lola flushed. "I'm sorry. I just want to understand."

"We all do." Burris was quiet for a while after that. Together, they dug and rooted through the bodies on the ground but found nothing of any real help. The closest thing Lola found to a weapon was a pair of small sewing scissors and a fingernail clipper with a filing knife, rusted shut. The majority of the corpses looked elderly, maybe dead for quite some time before they came back, but she did notice a few that appeared younger. It was hard to tell, but she could gauge it somewhat by the clothes. No children, thankfully. The image wouldn't do well with her, she knew. *I've seen enough dead already*, she thought, looking out of the dark, broken windows into the silent night beyond. She walked in the same direction, glass and wood and bone cracking beneath her feet. She thought her eyes would adjust and be able to discern something as she closed the distance, but they found nothing. She strained to hear, too, but it seemed like nothing existed out there at all. There was just a blank, soundless world.

A hand on her shoulder caused her to jump, and Lola smothered a squeal that tried to escape. Burris stood behind her and gently pulled her away.

"Not too close now." She nodded, allowing him to guide her back toward the center of the room. Questions still nagged her, though.

"Why can't you leave?" she asked, looking back at the bleak view. Her companion only sighed and shook his head.

"The darkness out there is deep, kid. And it doesn't end." Her brow rose, and he answered her unspoken question.

"You should know. It all started about a month ago, by our count. Everything went dark. Middle of the day. Couldn't even penetrate it with a flashlight. And the black ain't lifted since." Lola found it odd. What exactly had Kalos built here? The realness of it was no less convincing than the nightmare she'd escaped previously.

"Banks was transporting me to the next county, back home, but we never made it. Couldn't see." His voice was low and calm as he sat on the edge of the broken stairs. She could sense the faintest touches of fear in his recollection, however.

"He pulled me out of the car, and we ran. God, we ran. Ran forever. Tangled with these things. Talk about being scared, fighting something you don't know in the dark. They were everywhere. Banks kept track of me, but he didn't need to. I never thought once of escaping. Separating from him was the last thing I wanted, especially being cuffed. Banks was all I had." Lola listened intently, half wondering how the black beyond didn't swallow the light inside the house as well.

"Man saved me more than a few times. Held on to me." Burris was impossibly quieter than before as if he were telling a ghost story, but one that was real. "We fought and stumbled until we finally saw something holding light. This place." He spread his hands wide again.

"Whose home is this?" Lola inquired, looking around the large place. "Did anyone else make it here?"

Burris shrugged. "You're the first we've seen. Alive, that is. Whoever stayed here, well, they're long gone." The prisoner reached out and patted her on the head with a curious smile. "Tell me more about these fairies."

Lola didn't want to at first, but she went ahead with it anyway. Telling him didn't change her situation. At worst, he'd surmise it was a child's fantasy. Whether he believed her or not, she needed to hear herself say it and have someone listen. So, she started from the beginning. She told him about being taken from her home through her dreams. How she'd been in class when Kalos had seized control of her mind. She described the maze in great detail and even showed him some of her sketches in her journal, though careful not to let him see any of her entries. *My secrets.* He asked questions throughout her story about the demon and the maze. His eyes even widened several times when she elaborated on certain things that'd happened, mostly from the orstra stories. Burris played along politely, but Lola could tell he didn't believe her. He was nice enough not to say it. Not directly, at least.

"So," he started slowly, recollecting the pieces of her story in his brain. "We're in one of these…nightmares you've been forced into?" When she nodded, he leaned back, looking perplexed but curious.

"Then I guess we're in for one hell of a show, huh?" He crossed his arms over his chest, mentally debating something. *Probably better that he doesn't believe me*, she thought, feeling a stab of worry. If they didn't take her in, maybe they wouldn't be caught up in the horror that was likely to follow. But what chance did she truly have out there in the dark, alone? No choice was going to be easy, but the hardest ones to make were going to be those needed to survive.

"Listen, kid," the prisoner started. "I'm gonna convince Banks to let you hang around, but you can't repeat any of that stuff to him, okay? He's not as receptive as me."

"Not a word," Lola promised quietly. Banks was already bad enough. Hopefully, she could avoid him all around.

"In the meantime, stay close. We have a lot of work to do, and it ain't gonna be easy." Burris walked toward the small door under the stairs and opened it softly, waving her forward.

"How do you know when the—" Lola wasn't sure what to call the dead, other than the obvious.

"Fucking zombies, kid. You can say it," Burris returned as she stepped through under his arm. "They come randomly. Most of the time with a few hours between. Sometimes, we can hide deeper in the home and ride it out, but that allows them to disperse inside, spread out, and surprise you if you aren't so lucky. But it's been over a day since we've seen any. Longest stretch yet." Lola envisioned one sneaking up on her, clamping those rotten teeth onto her soft, exposed throat. The hallway through the door was small and ended in rubble. It was dimly lit by another room to the left.

"Close now," Burris reiterated to her, and she slid her hand in his, trailing behind. He stepped into the lit room, which turned out to be a tiny bathroom with a busted yellow toilet. They passed through it into a connecting bedroom, almost too dark to see, but Lola could make out piles of old clothes and assorted cloths stacked on a small bed in the corner. It smelled like rotting, unwashed fabric mixed with wet wood. They went

186

straight across another dark hallway into a large kitchen that had an additional entry on the other side. In the center of the room was a large island with pots, pans, ladles, and spatulas hanging above. They looked rusted and forgotten, though some had been used recently on a dirty stove behind. Lola guessed the two men had to eat. To her left was a wash area and a large rectangular window that spanned the entire wall. Just next to the door they entered, Burris pushed open a smaller door, almost child-sized. A set of stairs about a foot wide and jet black dipped steeply below, and Burris allowed her to go first. It wasn't uncomfortable for her to make her way, but the prisoner had to turn sideways and take slow steps. His breathing turned frustrated; she could tell it wasn't the most pleasant thing for him. Lola knew that he must've made that trip a few times before.

Once they reached the bottom, the area opened into a wide space with dusty green tiles. Several tracks of footprints could be seen walking both ways. The ceiling was a gray stone with flickering, fluorescent lights in a line down the center. To the right, the wall was made of dirty glass, with steel-handled doors finely cut into them. It was difficult to see the details of the rooms on the other side, but she noticed stainless steel trays and carts with wheels at the bottom. *Maybe medical spaces of some sort?* Odd to think, being as it was under a house, which led to the question of who those people were. Secret experiments were a more likely conclusion. Lola recalled Rosalia telling the story of the asylum and its history, feeling an eerie chill down her spine.

The left side held standard rooms. White plastered walls stretched, interrupted by narrow doorways that led into each space. Furniture lined most of the areas, leathered and cushioned. Some had small beds that were shoved into the corner. None of the rooms had a window, and she felt a wave of claustrophobia. Did the patients of that place stay here? She envisioned the imaginary traffic of people, doctors asking questions and writing things on clipboards. Her thoughts carried her back to the other side, where the examiners cut them open while still awake, their screams carrying through the hall. The new ones would have to walk the halls to hear and see. She had to fight to suppress her imagination and the disturbing visions that came with it.

The end of the hall hooked to the right in the shape of an upside-down L. The corners were filled with piles of shattered rock and wood, much like the first room she'd seen under the second story. Slivers of white light shone through the rubble beyond.

"What is this place?" Lola asked softly. Burris led her into the patient room at the corner. That one had no bed, but a pallet lay on the hard ground, topped with a discolored pillow. There was a table to the left, round and leaning with several canned goods scattered atop. Some were open and empty, others untouched. Was that where Burris stayed?

"Your guess is as good as mine," the big man responded tiredly. "A house converted for medical use, or vice versa."

"Everything is so modern down here compared to the house." Lola eyed the food again. "Is this your room?"

"For now. You hungry, kid? Thirsty?" Since she'd arrived, her hunger and thirst slept, but the idea she could eat at that moment seemed to wake the giant, slumbering hollow in her stomach. Lola managed a nod, a desperate anxiety building inside of her. Burris reached beside the table, lugged a large dust-covered water jug out from under it, and held it out to her. Lola wanted to display a sense of patience, but her thirst got the best of her, and she greedily snatched it from his hand. If it offended him, Burris didn't show it; he turned back to the table and began to dig around. She ripped the cap off the bottle and pressed it roughly to her dried lips. The water was warm but blissfully wet, and it was like sucking down a piece of heaven. It flowed through her insides, and her throat worked methodically as she gulped it down. Lola drank until her stomach hurt and would've continued, but a big hand closed around the bottle and pulled it away.

"Easy now," he said. "Water's on short supply."

"I'm sorry," Lola said, feeling a bit ashamed. That didn't keep her eyes away from the remaining liquid in the bottle, though.

"It's okay. I know it's probably been a long time." His words made her feel a little better about it, and she found her eyes wandering to the cans behind him. Burris smiled, and it was a pleasant thing to see.

"Here," he said, handing her a can. It was already open, half full of what appeared to be baked beans. "You can have the rest of those, just don't eat too fast." The words were barely out of his mouth before she grabbed the can. The beans were cold and thick as she spooned them out with her hand, but she gobbled them down, chewing and swallowing as fast she could. The prisoner had warned her, but her impatience rewarded her quickly with an empty can.

"We don't have a lot," Burris continued, taking a seat on the ground near the end of his pallet. "But we can last another week or two."

189

"Then what?" she asked, wiping the sauce from the inside of the can with her finger and cramming it into her mouth. He regarded her silently, and Lola could see the worry deep in his expression. *Then we'll starve.*

"Then we're just going to have to make a run for it, I suppose." The thought made her wish for a third option.

"You've made it this far," she said, eyeing the empty can with regret. Burris chuckled lightly at her positivity.

"I suppose we did, kid." He pointed to a few separated cans on the table. "Those are for you. We've only got one can opener, though, so don't lose it." Lola looked at the cans curiously. There were green beans, corn, and chickpeas. She wasn't sure what a chickpea was, but she was fairly certain she wouldn't mind. Her desire to open and devour them right then and there was tempting her, but patience prevailed for the moment. Her stomach growled loudly.

"The next room down is Banks's. His door is closed, so just go on by. The last room before the rubble is vacant and has a door. Might be some stuff stored in there, but plenty of room, given your size." Lola stood facing him as he turned his back and lay on his side. She still felt like there was much to say, so much information to take in, but her mouth couldn't get the words out. *Am I supposed to just go now? Hide in a room? For how long?* It seemed to be the only option she had. If she was lucky enough, she might even get some sleep.

"Goodnight, I guess?" she offered quietly. Burris's only movement was to shift his pillow farther beneath his head.

"You guessed right, kid. Goodnight."

The Grind and the Find

The next day started in a worse way than others. Lola guessed it was the next day, given there was no sunlight. She'd slept, God knew she needed it, but couldn't say for how long. The situation allowed it to be enough, however, as she felt revitalized. She woke that first day with Banks beating her door down, thankful for the fact it had a lock in the first place. He was pissed, she knew, and despite everything she'd seen, Lola was afraid. She pressed herself into the corner of her tiny room and wrapped her arms around her knees. The things coming out of her mouth were obscene, and it deepened both her fear and sadness. Relief joined her torrent of emotions when Burris's voice joined Banks's angry sounds. They engaged in a noisy argument, one that Burris was struggling to gain any ground with. *Why is Banks so stubborn and cruel?* She felt a stab of resentment, quickly calming it with deep breaths. With the argument persisting, Lola took the time to pull her journal free from her pack and write some more on the first blank page she found. There was much to log since her last opportunity. She needed to escape. Escape Banks. Escape Kalos. Escape into herself.

The voices had moved farther down the hall after a time, closer to Burris's room. One of the two men would occasionally louden, but overall, rational words had taken place of the enraged slurring. Lola wrote and wrote, detailing her fall, the dead, and the strange place she found herself in currently. She scribbled the way she felt, including her longing for her home and family. At one point, she must've dozed off, and she came back to life startled, frantically searching for her prized journal. To her great relief, it'd only slid from her lap to the floor, pinned upright against her thigh. She knocked the dust from it, ensuring the pages escaped the damage of the fall.

Rereading her entries had become a necessity—mostly involving her scanning for errors. By the time she slid it back into her pack, the hallway had grown silent. Lola prayed that the arguing ended in her favor.

As if sensing her curiosity, she heard a soft knock at the door, followed by Burris's voice coming from the other side. Lola pushed herself off the ground and ran to the door in anticipation, twisting the lock and pulling it free. She only allowed the slightest crack in case Banks was lurking nearby. An orange jumpsuit stood in the dim light.

"Come with me, kid. Time to go to work." His words were a good sign, and she felt a spark of hope as she scooped up her pack and darted out into the hallway. Burris didn't say more; he just turned, and they made their way back up through the halls, kitchen, bedroom, and bathroom to the living space above. Upon entering the large room, she noticed—to her surprise—that all of the dead had been neatly stacked against the far wall, starting near the rubble under the second story and stretching all the way back to the shacky front door. Banks stood where the line ended, stripping the clothes off one of the corpses. Lola felt a sickened feeling, not understanding the scene in front of her, but Burris gave her a reassuring pat on the head.

When Banks saw them, he stopped what he was doing and walked their way. A cigarette hung loosely from his mouth, the way Rosalia liked to let hers hang, smoke filling the dusty air. It looked like one of those self-rolled ones. Lola's stomach clenched at his approach, and she held her breath. Burris's hand dropped protectively to her shoulder.

"Burris went to bat for ya, girl," the rough policeman said, taking a deep draw from the stick. "I didn't want you. Didn't want the responsibility. To be honest, I was pinning the blame on you for this most recent shit show. But my friend here may have convinced me otherwise." Lola looked at him blankly, not sure what he was blaming her for, and he continued to stare her down. It wasn't making her any less nervous.

"The dead," he continued, blowing out a smoky cloud. "They didn't come back until you came here. Longest it's been since the start."

"How long…?" With the isolation of her room and the bit of sleep she got, she wasn't sure how much time had passed.

"Would've been twenty-eight hours." Banks stepped closer, and while his presence was intimidating, he carried a pleased look in his eyes. "Before that, three hours was the max. Is that fucking crazy, or am I?"

"I don't—"

"Don't say anything, girl. My partner did all the talking for ya." He was close enough that he was looking directly down at her, looming like a great giant. Her fear wasn't at ease yet, though his tone was favorable.

Banks knelt and pulled the cigarette from his mouth. His eyes were brown and hard. The lines on his face were drawn in as if he'd frowned his entire life. He reminded her more of military than police. Her grandfather on her dad's side had the same look.

"You're going to contribute," he said in a stern but not cruel voice. "You're going to carry your weight and look after your own goddamn self. We work together, we might get out of this shithole. Do you understand?" Lola's mouth was too dry to speak, so she nodded instead.

"Good. My partner here is Eli Burris. I'm John Banks. Your turn."

"Lola," she managed with a croak. She swallowed hard. "Lola Ray."

"Good." Banks reached out a rough hand, covered in dirt and dried blood. When she took it in hers, Lola could feel the heavy callouses. *Strong*, she thought. He could crush her had he wanted to, but the grip was gentle, respectful. "Now…"

Lola made little sense of what she saw when she first walked into the room, thinking back on Banks taking the clothes off the corpses' bodies. Apparently, however, the two had concocted quite a strategy. The first day of work, Burris gave her a pair of scissors and tasked her with cutting the hair from the deceased. It was disturbing and unpleasant, but she was surprised at how quickly she got used to it. What bothered her more was *why* she was doing it, and the fact that the question had yet to be answered. All they told her was the hair was brittle and easy to break, so she ought to knot it up tight and thick. The work was time consuming, but tranquil in a way. Even so, a sense of urgency remained in her gut. Everything was peaceful with Rosalia, too, for a time. The memories plagued her—all the death and pain. They lingered in her mind, stubborn and unyielding.

Burris and Banks stripped the dead down to nothing, exposing the skeletal bodies underneath. There were patches of old, dry skin clinging to shins and elbows, a greenish-gray in color. Lola wondered how long they'd been dead until they were, well, undead and cannibalistic. The two men laid them out in lines across the living space, making a few rows with what they had. It reminded her of some shows her dad used to watch, when she had to sneak out of her room and hide behind the couch after bedtime. She recalled one in particular, in which the military quarantined a certain area and lined a parking lot with the deceased in body bags. Lola followed them down the rows, scissors working swiftly in her duty. Most of the bodies with hair remaining were women, at least from what she could discern. She cut the longer strands and bunched them together, leaving the shorter clumps alone. Lola wasn't sure what purpose her role was supposed to serve, but she didn't stop to ask any questions. Banks likely wasn't as receptive to them as Burris was. She did as she was bid, eager to show the policeman how willing she was to work and contribute.

The two men stood off toward the stairs in a conference of whispers she couldn't hear. As she finished the last of the corpses, she added the rest to the pile she'd bundled on a scummy off-white sheet she found in the small bedroom. Lola smoothed it as flat as possible, given the condition of the floor and all the scattered debris. A lot of the hair was straight, but some strands remained curled. When she stood, Lola surveyed her work and felt proud at the amount displayed. With a smile, she turned to the two by the stairs.

"What's next?" she asked, twirling the scissors on her index finger. Burris smiled but gave her a pitied look. Banks just laughed. It was a cruel sounding thing, but Lola resolved that to be his natural demeanor. She had a feeling she wasn't going to like the answer.

"Let's take a trip up these busted-ass stairs, Lola Ray," the policeman said, exhaling a huff of smoke. A piece of ash caught in his short brown beard but went unnoticed. Lola looked at the stairs and felt she could make it up, but against Banks's weight, surely the rotten wood had no chance. To her surprise, he hopped right up, skipping lightly over the smashed steps on his way. He looked down at her as he crossed the upper lever, taking another vacuum pull from his cigarette. She glanced at Burris for reassurance, receiving a nod and a gesture in the direction of the stairs. Lola approached slowly, wishing there were a handrail, but she convinced herself it was foolish to be afraid of some stupid old steps. She hopped delicately, avoiding the broken ones entirely. When the top was before her, her breathless excitement quickly vanished when she saw what decorated the second floor. *More bodies*. Her heart sunk, and she realized she wasn't even close to being done with cutting hair. On the bright side, it wasn't a large area. The roof, even at its peak, was close to Banks's head. It might've originally been a storage area. Stretching back about thirty feet, it stopped at a short wooden wall with a small round window revealing nothing but blackness outside.

"Back at it, kid."

The task was annoying after the time she spent doing it, but it wasn't laborious. Lola completed it with relative ease. The following day made things more painful, however. The dead remained quiet with no new intrusions. The black that lurked beyond the house was still. For the first few hours, the three of them pulled and broke the bodies apart. In separate stacks, they piled skulls, limbs, spines, and ribcages. If anyone ever asked how she spent her day, Lola couldn't imagine explaining it to anyone. And that was the truth. She didn't know why they were doing it, but there she was. They carefully moved the bodies down the stairs to the main living space.

When she asked Burris why they'd moved them up there in the first place, he answered that he wished he'd initially realized their use.

"Barriers," he responded to her questioning look, and it all seemed to dawn on her at once. *Of course.* Cutting and knotting the hair suddenly made more sense, as she supposed it'd be an attempt at rope. It was a surprise they didn't have more real rope, given the size of the place.

Another day's time passed, or at least she thought so between her sleeps. It was hard to tell. Banks and Burris drew out plans for how the bone barriers would be constructed while Lola spent more time braiding the hair. The brittle strands weren't very strong. She gave them one tug and watched them split apart. However, Banks showed her that, in the right places, knotting them could make just enough of a difference to bind the pieces. With his dark receding hairline, she pondered how he knew so much about it. Regardless, the two men wanted to be prepared. And she did, too.

Keeping busy was the best possible option for them, and she finally understood why. They didn't just build and plan, they cleaned as well. Lola didn't exactly understand the purpose, but Banks said it kept their minds off eating, and she couldn't argue the fact. Her stomach *did* growl most of the day. She'd eaten two of the cans Burris had given her and drank more water than she should've. It was difficult not to. Lola knew she was malnourished, knew the inconsistency of sustenance in her life at that point. Was it her soul that craved nourishment? How was it that she needed it without her real body? Thinking about it made her head spin.

The kitchen got little use, which was a shame, given that the power somehow worked despite an apocalypse going on. Banks would let her heat soups up, though, and their warmth made everything a bit more bearable. During her time in the kitchen, Lola would prowl for other foods, digging in cabinets and drawers, but to no avail. There wasn't much beyond the canned goods, and the men had already accepted the fact.

Another day. Lola woke to a breakfast of warm water and a shared cup of beans that Banks had warmed up. The three of them ate in silence, as usual—it hadn't taken her long to discover neither of them cared for conversation in the mornings. Burris ate his share with grim determination, the sauce from the beans dripping into his curly black beard. It was a messy thing, thick and tangled. Banks smoked while he ate, which was appalling, but he seemed to enjoy both at once as if they normally went hand in hand. *Is it enjoyment, though, that I see?* Usually, a smile came with the feeling, but those were seldom seen on the man's face. She wondered how many cigarettes he had and how long they'd last. Perhaps he believed he'd die before he ran out. He looked across the table and caught her watching him, and she quickly averted her eyes. They were getting along fairly well since the rough start, and Lola didn't want to mess that up.

Later, the cop and prisoner were latching ribcages together, and she continued her work of securing them. To Burris's dismay, Banks began prattling on about the rubble near their rooms again. The man in the orange jumpsuit would half-heartedly argue there wasn't anything back there, but the policeman would press on. Lola was actually curious herself after seeing the rays of white light penetrating from underneath. Burris said there were more hallways, with the same lighting they had above, but Banks insisted otherwise. He believed it was purposely blocked off or sealed—maybe protecting a stash of emergency food and supplies for the house's owners. Lola wasn't shy about expressing her excitement about that idea, and she received a smug smile from the cop. Burris remained resigned.

"See, you got the kid thinking we're going to dig for lost treasure or some shit."

"Hey!" Lola spurted, hurling a rib bone at Burris. "I'm not six!" *And I wouldn't do stupid kiddy stuff like that, anyway!* "There isn't exactly a lot of promise up here, except maybe starvation!" The stubborn set on the prisoner's brows persisted.

"And when we're shoveling through that shit down there while these things are filing in up here, then what do you wanna do?" Burris raised his hands, and Banks scoffed.

"They can file in while we sleep, while we eat, while we're in a different room," he responded roughly, lighting another smoke. "They haven't shown up for days, a new record by the way. Something is different. Smells like opportunity."

"Smells like fucking cigarettes," Burris said with a shrug of his shoulders.

"It's settled then," Banks announced with arms spread. "Let's finish this shit up here, and tonight we can dig around a bit." Lola beamed.

The largest construction of bones was put against the windows across from the staircase, but the size of the barricade was creating difficulties, given how closely they were tied together. They worked the ribcages as best they could to avoid substantial gaps, but it took a large part of the rest of their workday. When they called it quits, Lola couldn't say she was upset. Her hands were rough from working with the bones. Red lines laced across her palms from pulling and stretching. Her knuckles bled in spots where she'd rapped them when something snapped or slipped. Banks had cussed at her more than once, so she hid the pain she was in for both of their sakes.

For much of the night, they pulled the smaller debris from the rubble downstairs, but looking at it up close made Lola realize how sizeable the task was. Large chunks of concrete and rebar were stacked without much give. The wood was thick and splintery, and her motivation quickly faded. They worked for an hour before Burris elected to rotate sleeping and was the first to go. She and Banks continued, mostly in awkward silence aside from occasional grunts in the effort. Some sections of the pile wouldn't budge. Even with Banks's strength working—she'd noticed his arms were corded with lean muscle—nothing gave way. He spat and cursed enough to teach her a second language, occasionally kicking the pile in frustration.

The cop was next in the sleeping rotation, but Burris told her she could sleep as well if she needed. Lola declined. They went about the business a little less aggressively, however. The prisoner didn't share Banks's enthusiasm, so there was more conversing.

"My wife, Darma, and my son," Burris continued during their talk. "They're out there in this shit." His eyes carried a distant look, and Lola could relate to losing family. *That's why he's so sad all the time.*

"How long has it been since you've seen them?" she whispered, pulling a sliver of wood from the pile and tossing it to the side. The despondent look remained, but something changed in his face as if he were shaded with regret.

"Man," he sighed and shook his head slowly. Lola gathered enough from that to know it must've been a long time.

"Are you innocent?" The question just popped out of her mouth, and Lola felt a stab of fear, even having grown comfortable around these men. He was still a stranger, and getting too personal probably wasn't the best idea. Burris looked at her with a smile that didn't touch his eyes. His reaction was as good as she could've hoped for, thankfully.

"No, child," he said. She could tell he didn't want to frighten her, but he also didn't want to be dishonest. A redeeming quality, she thought. "None of us are, and not me, especially." Lola knew not to ask what crime he'd committed, so she simply nodded.

"I wonder sometimes if this is my punishment." His voice was deep but soft. Burris leaned back and wiped his face with the front of his orange jumpsuit, drying the sweat. "Anywhere without them is a prison, and in this darkness, they could be an eternity away." When he looked at her again, it seemed as if he was debating something. "Maybe you're right, kid. Maybe this is some kind of horror story." *He doesn't truly believe that*, she thought. Even with the dead crawling through windows and doors, it was all still so unbelievable to him. She could see it in his eyes. Lola feared she'd remain alone in that regard. *All you have to do is survive. Survive and go back home.*

Lola didn't feel tired, but she knew she needed rest. She rotated with Banks and could tell sleep didn't do him any favors, if he'd even slept at all. His eyes carried the same hunger as before.

"Did you two actually do anything or just bullshit the whole time?" His voice was angry as she made her way to her room. Lola didn't care to wait around and hear more. Inside her small cove, her dusty blankets awaited her, and she curled up tight in the corner. It was dark, the only light coming through the cracks under the door, but she knew she had nothing to fear. The walls were her protection there, as was the darkness. *Much more disturbing things beyond*, she thought. Her mind didn't linger on the thought. She drifted off to the muffled sounds of Banks and Burris outside. Sleep was dreamless and peaceful, but very brief. It seemed that as soon as she'd closed her eyes, Burris was there, shaking her by the shoulder. He pressed the can opener into her hand and told her to eat before meeting them in the hallway. With that, he was gone, leaving the door open behind him. She wasted little time, her stomach gnawing at her almost instantly at the reminder. She noticed she was down to her last can as she stumbled across the dimly lit room. *Chickpeas*, she read on the can. Upon opening it, she dumped a small wet pile of them into her mouth. Lola didn't taste them, though she was too starved to care either way. A few gulps of water followed, and it was difficult to make herself put the cap back on the bottle; she thirsted for more. Wiping her mouth after one more spoonful from her can, she shouldered her pack and stepped out into the hallway.

The lights flickered as they normally did. Lola noticed the two men had removed a large wooden beam from the rubble, but the gap leading to the light within was still only the width of an infant's arm. Banks had his face pressed against it, desperate to see through to the other side.

"Anything?" Burris asked, sounding disinterested. Banks cursed once, looked up, pressed his face back against the debris, and cursed again.

"Fuck no," he spat. "It's just…light. Like a large and empty white room."

"Salvation isn't waiting in an empty white room," Burris responded. Lola could sense the prisoner's exasperation. "Let's finish these barriers, man. We'll come back to it." Banks could only glare and curse, but he eventually agreed.

"Did a lot of thinking," Burris continued as Banks dug for a cigarette. "If we split the barrier and put one in front of each of those windows—"

"It won't be heavy enough or have enough leverage to hold unless we stretch it the length of the wall," Banks returned, shaking his head.

"We don't have the bones for that, Banks. And we don't want—" A shriek from above cut him off, and they all looked at one another in surprise. It was loud and full-bellied. *Angry*, Lola thought. She stepped closer to the two men, looking toward the narrow staircase.

"You heard them sound like that before?" Banks asked, incredulous. Burris shook his head.

"Fuck no, man, and I don't like it." He pulled Lola close to his hip with a protective arm.

"Come on, Burris. We need the bones." The policeman darted toward his room, and the prisoner rushed after him with Lola on his heels. As they entered the small space, Banks flipped on a single hanging lightbulb. In front of him was a stainless-steel cart, much like the ones in the glass rooms across the hall. On top of it sat a dark bag with a metal zipper spanning its length. He yanked it open and fished around inside.

"What's left?" Burris asked urgently, receiving a head shake and a curse.

"A dozen shots for the Remington," came the answer. Banks pulled out a jet-black police-issue shotgun and tossed it across the room to his partner, who caught it with one hand. "I guess it was too much to ask for those fuckers to stay away for good."

"Still a round chambered in here?" Burris asked, eyeing the pump-action weapon.

"Just the one, ready to go." Banks stretched his arm across the room, handing Burris a green box. "It'll hold eight." Another cry came from above, sending chills down her spine. It sounded sick, haunted. *Hungry.* Lola could feel her heartrate increase. The cop pulled a pistol from the bag and shoved a long rectangular clip into the bottom. *A 9mm*, she thought, remembering her father's gun. The officer eyed her, debating, before digging back into the pack. Next came a silver revolver, one almost small enough to fit in the palm of his hand.

"Ever fired a weapon before?" he asked. Instantly and unbidden, her mind went to Rosalia pushing the gun into her hands. Lola swallowed and nodded, not looking particularly confident. *There isn't any other way. Keep your secrets.*

"Don't miss," he returned. She could tell his blood was working up, too. The anticipation on his face was clear, and he looked more alive than any other time she'd seen him. *He enjoys it. Maybe even lives for it.*

"I didn't," she blurted without meaning to speak. Banks gave her an odd look, but it carried approval at the end of it. That's what she needed. She needed him to trust she wouldn't let them down. When he handed her the gun, she looked down at it, tinkered with it until she got the round clip to pop out to the left of the weapon, then snapped it back into place.

Banks moved to the other side of the room and pulled a red ax off the wall. Burris, still standing near Lola, pulled his knife from its leather sheath on his hip, flipped it, and held it out to her, hilt first.

"For close binds. Aim for the head or joints." His voice shook at the edges. She knew well enough he hadn't been scared before, but something was different that time. The unknown. All of them had adrenaline pumping through their veins. Lola inhaled and exhaled slowly, then reached out and took the blade. Another hand gifted her a box of rounds for her small weapon.

"Shoot only if you can't get it done with the blade. If they group, you'll have to fire a lot. Make each shot count."

"I will," Lola promised. He smiled and rubbed a hand through her tangled hair before stepping around her toward the door. She nestled the ammo close to her journal inside her pack and whispered a quick prayer. Banks, gun in his belt and ax on his shoulder, put a finger over his lips and stepped out of the door. Burris positioned her behind his body again, and she stayed as tight against him as she could. He turned and looked down at her, pointing to his eyes, then behind her. She nodded, knowing that meant to watch for surprise attacks from the back.

Lola and the two men slowly and deliberately made their way up. More shrieks sounded from above—some loud and furious, others quieter and desperate. It sent a chill down her spine, one that was clinging to home with no intentions of letting go. Banks led the way, the two men in front of her voicing their frustration while easing up the narrow stairs. The policeman reiterated the need for silence in each passing room—first the kitchen, then the dark bedroom beyond. It was when they reached the small in-between bathroom that connected to the last hallway that Banks held up a fist, signaling for them to stop. From where they were, she could see into the hallway and noticed the light pouring in from the massive living space. *Funny*, she thought, unable to remember Burris leaving the door open. Shadows moved against the shine, but it was too bright to discern how many. Lola knew there was more than one. She breathed slowly to ease her fear and made sure there was little distance between herself and the prisoner. In preparation, she eased the big knife around and into her pack, then gripped the small pistol with both hands after. She wouldn't miss. She promised herself she wouldn't.

Banks stepped into the hallway, impossibly silent for his size. He moved fluidly but torturously slow. Her eyes were locked on his tense back. The shadows danced across his face, and both he and the policeman watched coldly. No sign of panic touched him, so Lola could only hope that meant the situation wasn't overwhelming. It made her relax, if only a little. He turned to Burris and held up his hand, showing five fingers. He squeezed it shut and repeated twice, then held up two fingers. The man in orange nodded, but Lola remained unsure. *Seventeen?* That was more than she'd anticipated, given the expression on Banks's face. Burris stepped out into the hall as his companion moved forward, then turned to look down at her. After a brief hesitation, he swiftly knelt.

"Don't cross through into the light," he whispered urgently. "We'll handle it. If we get flanked, don't be afraid to fire, but do it from where you are!" It was a difficult angle, just inside the frame of the door, but she had a small window of view. That could prove better—smaller window to aim, smaller window to miss. Still, she was scared. As scared as she was in the house with the orstras, but her desire to contribute was equally powerful. Banks told her she had to; else she'd be on her own. Lola could only nod to Burris. He rubbed a hand through her hair one more time and stood, looking back toward Banks, who was creeping forward, step by painful step. He reminded her of a crocodile, slowly drifting for its prey on still waters. His fury would be just as deadly; Lola was sure. The light shone on his arms and shoulders when he stepped into the main area, Burris moving behind him—out and to his right. Another prayer fell from her mouth, and she pulled back the hammer on her gun.

It was hard to say if the delay occurred because the dead didn't see them or because they thought Banks and Burris were dead, also, but the two were in plain view for more than a few seconds before the shrieks intensified and became angrier. The sounds were terrible, agonizing rips of pain. They were in need, but Lola couldn't say what the dead truly desired. To make them the same? The noise became rhythmic, reverberating off the walls once they spotted Banks and Burris in the room. Lola watched the shadows on the floor, only able to see the men's backs through the small window. The corpses moved frantically and grew in numbers. She could guess they were grouping up to make a rush at the two men, and her body seemed to move on its own accord. She stepped out of the bathroom and into the dark hallway. Lola was still obscured from view, and she crouched down low. *Maybe Burris won't notice.* The view was better from there, but not by much. Numerous boney legs bearing rotten clothes clamored toward them from what she could see behind Banks and Burris. The first gunshot sounded, and her ears rang. It was Burris's pump-action, the blast spitting flame and buckshot into the center of the group. Several pieces of human bone and dried flesh were sent the other direction, and all of them fell backward. Taking advantage of the momentum, Banks bolted forward, swinging the ax in a whirlwind way. The first blow demolished a head entirely, while the next swipe aimed low to sweep some legs. The cop came back around with the weapon in full arc, knees flying apart in a spray of dust. Roars of anger followed. Banks stepped back, Burris forward, and another powerful blast boomed in the room. Everything from the torso up on several of the frontrunners blew backward and fell—or, rather, crumbled—to the ground. Banks rotated in again, raining death with his oversized wood cleaver. He lifted his arm and landed a crushing blow downward, splitting a skull like wood on the chopping block. Surprisingly, a thick and red liquid burst from that one, looking very much like a watermelon. Lola's heart stopped. *Hadn't all these things dried up?* The confusion spread through the two men as well, and they exchanged worried glances. It was brief, but enough time for the dead to momentarily recover. Lola heard the sound of splintering wood from Banks's left. The additional shadows breaking into the light confirmed her suspicion.

"Nine o'clock!" Burris screamed, driving the hilt of the shotgun into the eye socket of an approaching corpse. Banks had just enough time to look before one of them attacked him. Lola inhaled, raising her weapon to her eye. The window was small, but the memory of her bullet passing through Kyrie's skull gave her confidence. The exhale came, and she pulled the trigger. A bang and a zip blew up another head. Once more, it ripped apart into pink chunks and red spray.

"Jesus, that's fucking cold!" Banks shouted with the viscera splattering onto him. He gave her a look of surprise, and she smiled. *Told you.* Burris blasted another round into the crowd, but more still came from the left, closing the gap too quick for Lola to get a clean shot. Banks grappled with two in front of him, taking a step back before driving forward. They fell, but the denser part of the crowd behind caught the corpses' bodies and pushed forward as one.

"Drop back, baby!" Burris yelled as he and Banks stepped back into the hallway. Lola swallowed and eased the same direction, almost tripping on the wrecked debris covering the floor. The dead were howling in anticipation, so close to the living they could already taste their blood. Another blast. All she saw was dust, bone, and wood flying past the bathroom door.

"Fuckin shit's in my eye," Banks cursed, and Lola heard two more shots—that time from a pistol. Burris entered the room first, followed by the policeman who was clutching his face.

"Keep goin', baby. Keep goin'!" Lola didn't hesitate; she stepped through the bedroom and into the next hallway, waiting for them to catch up. They were driven back slowly.

Her panic was threatening to rise, her throat opening and closing. Banks fired more rounds to little effect. When the ringing in her ears faded, she heard the smallest shuffle coming from behind her, near the kitchen door. It was almost inaudible, something to be ignored, but her gut told her something different. Above her, one of the dead loomed, looking down. Its empty sockets seemed surprised to find her there, but when the shock passed, it howled, the sound piercing and powerful. The kitchen door was open, and more were piling in through the large kitchen window. Lola screamed, raised her pistol, and fired. The round blew through the corpse's teeth and spit bone against the ceiling, but it didn't seem fazed. Skinless fingers, save for the pinky, grasped her hair. It squeezed with more strength than she would've thought possible, so hard its index finger snapped backward. The other hand flailed near her face, and the slaps were painful when they connected. She screamed again and reached around to her pack to grab the hilt of Burris's knife and yank it free. *I can't scream for help*, she thought, feeling vulnerable. Lola grabbed the hand that held her head and pushed the wrist up. She took a swing, trying to dodge the blows of the dead. The first attempt resulted in bits of dust and bone, but its arm remained connected. Her second was thwarted altogether, the other arm coming around in time to knock the knife from her hand. As it did, she jerked free from its grasp and darted down the hallway. She tripped on debris and fell, immediately crawling with desperation while turning to glance behind her. The thing had the odd, surprised look on its face again. In that small moment, a pair of giant hands flanked its skull and squeezed. The head burst, and blood—a thick, deep red—ran like syrup over Burris's knuckles.

"Banks, they're behind us, too!" More flowed in from the kitchen door. The prisoner raised a boot and kicked, gaining enough from it to unload another shotgun shell. Bones exploded in a dark haze of blood.

"How the fuck?" Banks said as he was being shoved through the bedroom door into the hallway. He kicked low, collapsing the knees of one body, grabbed the side of the head of the next, and crushed it against the doorframe. He pulled it down and let go, then with both hands, pulled the first corpse and yanked up hard. Bones snapped on both of the dead, sounding like a chiropractic's office. The two were jammed together, forming a skeletal blockade, though only about waist-high. Burris worked the other direction, shoving one corpse back enough to reach in and grab the kitchen door. With both hands, he pulled it, desperate to get it shut. It was close, only a crack showing, but several fingers were clawing their way through, pinned between door and frame. As he struggled, Lola pushed herself up and ran to him. When she tapped him on the shoulder, he turned to her in surprise, ready for anything. Sweat poured from his head around bloodshot eyes. He nearly dismissed her until he caught sight of her holding his blade up to him, hilt first. He snatched it, and in the same motion, hacked savagely at the knuckles pinned in the door. It took a few blows, but the blade wouldn't be denied. Severed fingers piled by his boots, and the door shut with a click.

"Maybe a little help, if ya don't mind." Banks was wrestling with a few more, attempting to climb over his barrier. Burris swung the blade over his partner's head, connecting with a sickening crunch, and repeated the motion several times. A few more piled up on top of the blockade, closing them in for the moment with the dead desperate to get through.

212

"God help us," Banks breathed, leaning against the thrashing pile of bodies behind him. With one arm, he ripped open his police top, exposing a white tank beneath, drenched in sweat. "That's definitely more than last time."

"Just by a few," Burris answered, spitting a large green glob on the floor. "We need to think of something fast, or we're going to die in this hallway." Banks answered by firing a few more rounds through the gap at the top of the bedroom door. A head burst and a body collapsed, another stepping in to take its place. He fired again to drop another, then repeated the act two more times.

"That should add to the blockage a bit." The pounding on the kitchen door from the other side was becoming more forceful. The two men pulled a few more corpses through the bedroom door, stacking them high enough to reach their chests.

"How many rounds left in the Remington?" the policeman asked, lighting a cigarette. Burris shook his head.

"Four, maybe. Five in the box." Banks pondered the answer with a long draw, turning to blow the smoke into one of the skulls jammed in the doorway. He looked back at the kitchen door, which was close to being beaten down. *How is he not scared at all?* Lola knelt and pulled the box of ammo from her pack. She only needed to reload a couple rounds, but she liked snapping the magazine back into place.

"We have to get downstairs," Banks said quietly, almost as if to himself.

"Dead end down there, partner." Burris was still trying to regain his breath, speaking with large gaps between every few words.

"Dead end up here, too. At least down there, they can only come at us from one direction." Burris considered it, but Lola could tell he didn't like the idea. She found it hard to imagine there'd be any agreeable options. She glanced down the hall, which ended with more debris than they could hope to pass. The bedroom was blocked, and the kitchen door was about to give. They'd be stuck in a small hallway, outnumbered by bloodthirsty corpses.

"Give me the shotgun, Burris." The man in orange hesitated, not sure what his partner had in mind, but begrudgingly held it out to him.

"The ammo, too. Come on." Burris pulled out the green box and handed it over.

"Why do I feel you have a stupid idea forming in that thick skull?" the prisoner asked, reluctant to hear the answer. Banks only spared him a glance and, surprisingly, a quiet laugh. *He's crazy. That's why he isn't afraid.* Strangely, she found herself wanting to trust him.

"Stupid or dead—your call," Banks said as he reloaded the shotgun. When he finished, he handed the red ax to his friend and walked to Lola as the kitchen door started to splinter.

"When I say go, I want you to run for that corner in the kitchen and get down them fucking stairs, you hear me?" Lola could only nod, looking up at him through a haze of smoke. He looked down at the gun in her hand and smiled. "Felt good blowing that fucker to hell, didn't it?" When she nodded again, his laughter was a wild sound. "You sure didn't miss." He turned to Burris.

"Lord, man," Burris said as if he knew it was going to be outrageous. "We gonna make it through this one?" The cop smiled again. Come to think of it, he'd smiled a lot since the dead arrived. *He thrives on it, lives for it.*

"I never anticipated shit getting this bad," Banks said, taking another pull from his cigarette. "Spray and pray, right?"

"That ain't really what you're gonna do." Burris grabbed his partner by the shoulder, and Banks returned the gesture.

"This is the end," he said in a puff. "Just not for us." With that, he shouldered the shotgun and spun toward the kitchen door. Taking aim, he sent a blast that demolished the door and caused the dead to shriek. When they made their way to claw through the wooden wreckage, Banks cocked and blasted again. Then again. And again.

Lola couldn't hear him through the fiery rampage, but he turned and screamed a word to her, and she knew the word was "go." She darted for the door and ducked in, putting her fear to the side and functioning on pure adrenaline. The shots pushed the dead back halfway across the room into the large island. Spoons and ladles were rattling and toppling from where they hung, but she couldn't hear them. Pieces of bone and a river of cold blood dominated the tiled floor beneath her feet. As she turned the corner, she slipped and slid past the door, looking back to see the corpses raging behind. Banks and Burris filed into the room, unloading more shots. Lola crawled toward the stairway door, knees and feet struggling for traction against the slippery surface. Out of the corner of her eye, she could see the two of them moving past her to push the dead back, and her hope of survival deepened. She reached the knob, jerked it open, and turned back.

"Go!" Banks roared. As much as it terrified her to leave them and continue down alone, she did. Lola prayed they'd follow right behind her. She went down quickly, careful not to tumble downward. Her eyes stayed on the room below. To her relief, none of the dead were awaiting her.

"Neck 'em at the door like before," Banks yelled as he backed through the doorway. There wasn't a lot of room for the men, so Lola knew it'd be a tough trip for them. "Use them for blockage. It's our only chance." Lola waited at the bottom, and the cop turned to look at her.

"Put your gun in your pack and catch this!" he said, indicating the shotgun in his hand with a nod. She did as she was bid, and a blink later, the Remington hit her hands. The heavy steel shocked her bones, but she managed to hold on to it. Banks took a few more steps down, and Burris backed in at the top.

"We ain't gonna be able to do this, man," Burris said, breathless again. "I ain't got no fucking room."

"Make it work, Burris. I'm right behind you!"

"Just get the fuck down there, man. I'll hold them off here as long as I can."

"You don't get to die here. I'm still taking you to state when this shit is over," Banks replied. Burris laughed, and Banks followed. *They are both crazy!* "Make it work!"

The first group of the dead pushed through the doorway, shoved in by the second, then a third. They were bottlenecking, but there wasn't an end to them. Lola swallowed and forced herself to watch. *Please*, she prayed. *Please find a way.* But the prisoner was struggling. The walls were close against his shoulders, and the two of them together lost a step down the stairway. Burris swayed, and Lola's heart leapt in her chest. *I can't just watch this happen!* Dropping the shotgun, she bolted up the stairs. Banks didn't have room to squeeze up there with Burris, but she did. The cop watched in awe as she flashed past him and moved right up against the back of Burris's legs. She wrapped her arms around his right thigh from behind and gripped her six-shooter in both hands. Lola whispered another prayer.

Six shots sounded from her pistol in quick succession. They impacted knees, legs, and feet, causing the dead to collapse in the middle of the doorway. Burris looked down at her in surprise, barely aware of her presence, before returning his focus above to start jamming the corpses in. He pulled and yanked and twisted, shredding bone against bone, tearing clothes as he forced them together. The door was jammed about waist-high, but the dead wouldn't be stopped. One was reaching across the tangled mass, so Burris smashed its head with a couple of shorthanded swings of the ax. He pulled it farther in, draped it across the pile, and waited for the next. Another reached in, and the prisoner yanked it halfway through. He handed the ax down to Lola and pulled his knife free, hacking at its neck. With the limited range of motion, it took several small swings, but the head finally snapped free, cold blood spilling down in a wet gush. *Not all of them bleed.* The next one he pulled through made the hole smaller and tighter. Within a few moments, only a hand could reach through near the top. The furious shrieks from the other side persisted.

"Good God!" Burris breathed, putting a bloody hand on her shoulder. "I could use a nap." He half laughed, half wheezed, and Lola, unable to muster a laugh, forced a smile for him.

It wasn't easy getting Burris down the stairs, but together with Banks, they took it one step at a time. The narrow way was slick and dangerous. Lola was finally able to breathe when they reached the bottom. It was then that they all took a moment to pause in exhaustion. Banks leaned on the shotgun, blood oozing from under an eye. The sight of it made her cringe—his eye looked like a pool of blood nestled in his face. Burris lay against the glass wall on the right side, heaving in and out.

"That ain't gonna last forever," he said, leaning his head back and closing his eyes. "We're sandwiched in here."

"The pile of shit back there," Banks said, a twisted smile playing on his lips. "It's the only way." Burris's shoulders slumped as he shook his head and began to laugh hysterically.

"Goddamn, Banks. You had this shit planned out all along, didn't you?" Lola couldn't tell if the prisoner was actually angry or just tired.

"Just a coincidence, partner." Banks was still smiling. She knew the man wouldn't purposely play at having them trapped down there, but she knew he wasn't upset at the prospect of having no choice but to get through the blockage. Part of her wanted to know what was beyond, too. There was light down there. And light meant hope.

The dead were howling at the top of the stairs. Lola watched the jammed pile budge here and there against the pressure. Burris was right; time wasn't on their side.

"The dead," said the prisoner, still gulping air like a prized possession. "They're bleeding now. They're—"

"Stronger," Banks finished. "Must be a fresh batch."

"They've never been able to push us like that before," Burris said. Banks could only nod.

"And never in those numbers," Burris finished. They breathed collectively, and Lola looked back up the stairs.

"The numbers are growing," she said, watching the pile shift even more. "Nothing discourages them." The two followed her eyes, then exchanged a glance.

"Well," Burris said, pushing himself off the glass wall with his back and shoulders. "Time to dig."

The three of them together pulled, hacked, and yanked at the rubble blocking their path. Burris sent blow after blow with the ax. With his hands, Banks pulled any of the larger pieces that broke free. The pile was deep, though. Lola cleared out the small pieces and anything in their way, and she was also responsible for keeping an eye on the door, which the dead could break through at any moment. She'd walk back around the corner, and each time she saw the barricade in place, she'd exhale in relief.

Lola kept her eye on a hole in the pile the size of her arm—the one she'd noticed earlier. It enticed her, and she couldn't help thinking if they focused on that part alone, it'd be their best bet. The two men seemed to be of like mind, but they weren't gaining much ground. Once, Banks let her reach through the hole, and her entire arm up to her shoulder fit. Beneath it, however, everything was solid and wouldn't budge. It was frustrating with their time dwindling down. She could hear the dead raging, still, and knew the clock was ticking. Shutting her eyes against the sting of her sweat, she whispered another prayer. She needed hope. Lola tuned everything out as her companions worked. She didn't hear Burris's agitation as he slammed the red ax against the stubborn pile. She didn't hear Banks's cursing fits of rage. Only the words in her mind continued. Or rather, one word: *please.*

Reality struck her when the wails from above shifted. They became more urgent, hungrier, and alert. Lola pushed herself to her feet and rushed back around the corner to take a quick look, her heart thumping in her chest. Something inside told her she didn't need to look, that she already knew, and that her gut instinct was right. To her dismay, the opposite of what she prayed for tumbled down the narrow stairs. The dead pushed and rushed over each other, bones twisting and snapping as they struggled through the bottleneck. Dark hollow eyes all looked toward her, and their hunger heightened, their goal within reach. Most of the ones she could see had the majority of their skin intact, though it was gray and dry. A "fresher batch," Banks had said. They seemed louder and deadlier than before, strong enough to resist, to corner them, then attack. Her stomach turned, and her heart sunk. Tears came without resistance as the dead filed into the open space of the hall, quick and closing in.

"They're through!" she screamed, darting back around the corner. Her words snapped the men away from their task and turned them away from the pile. Once more, Banks tossed the shotgun to her, and she awkwardly caught it for the second time. The steel didn't hurt that time, though. She didn't feel it at all.

"Take it and get behind us," Banks said with a grim tone. It didn't raise her expectations. Eyes on the floor, she hurried to the far side of them, but as she did, Banks caught her arm. She swung around from the momentum as he leaned close.

"Last shot," he said, handing her an open green ammo box. The remaining shell rolled to the front of it. His eyes found hers, and with one hand on the side of her face, he pressed their heads together. "If hope is lost, eat it."

"I won't miss," she said, though the prospect was devastating. *Could I do it if I didn't have the choice?* Lola shakily pulled the shell from the box, dropping the cardboard to the ground, and pressed herself against the pile as deep as she could go. The weapon was more difficult to load than the six-shooter. She strained to push the round into the slot. When it popped in, she exhaled and propped the gun against the rubble. Pulling the smaller weapon free, she attempted to reload and sadly noted only five rounds remained in her box. *Well, at least we'll go down shooting.* Dying wasn't something she wanted to do, but maybe it'd finally take her out of that hell. Lola just didn't want it to hurt.

The dead surged around the corner, but their clumsy momentum drove them into the opposite wall. To say the impact was rough would be an understatement. The snapping bones could be heard over their howls. Some fell, but the horde pushed on. Banks and Burris both had pistols in their hands; after exchanging brief looks, they opened fire. The shots rang out and echoed in the hall, making it sound as if they were firing double with each squeeze. The disorientation it caused dared Lola to cling onto hope. The explosions caused some of the dead to lunge sideways into one another; more corpses fell, while some screamed. Others lost their heads or parts of them. Lola watched a skull burst and another jaw dismantle, bits of it flying into another's eye. Bullets ripped through chests, throats, and heads. Knees blew out, their bones splintering and sending them tumbling. It thinned the herd a great deal, but in the brief moment when she felt like they had a fighting chance, more emerged from around the corner. Their hunger was yet again more desperate, their cries deeper. She pressed the five rounds into her small revolver, but the men reloaded faster than she would've thought possible. They barely missed a beat, but the dead still gained on them. Round after round burst forth, devastating body parts with each, yet still more came. When Lola couldn't watch anymore, she stepped up between them, rose her weapon, and drained her remaining rounds as fast as she could. There was no way to miss; it was like shooting into a wall, and the damage was felt. Her first two shots struck one in the chest, the third ripping into its face, and it collapsed immediately. One of her last two took one in the hip, sending it sprawling. The other was a gut shot that punctured through its bones and sent its spine out of its back.

"Last one," Burris said, indicating the fresh clip as he dropped the empty one to the floor.

"Make them count," Banks yelled over the gunfire. "I got four rounds left." Lola knew their time was limited and stepped back against the rubble. Discarding the pistol, she hefted the shotgun and snugged it against her right shoulder. Burris was steadily dropping the dead with each shot he took. The cop, however, was empty. Dropping his gun, he swept the ax off the ground between them and didn't hesitate once the melee of dead was in range. He used the back of it on the first swing, sending a skeleton sprawling. Coming back around, he sent another to the opposite side, where it exploded against the wall. At first, it seemed like they were willfully running into a buzz saw, but as she began to hope again, Banks's swings became sluggish. Pressing the ax head into the chest of another corpse, he shoved it backward and took out the next one with a haggard but sturdy swing. Burris was empty, too, and he sliced and hacked with his knife. Two yards quickly became only arm's length, then vanished altogether as the wall of the dead pressed hard against them. The men would swing, then hold their arms wide, blocking the corpses' path to Lola. The cop and prisoner pushed and leaned with force against the bodies, but the dead were more forceful, even with little more than bone. Arms flailed and clawed, jaws chomped, and the two men struggled to resist. A few corpses were trying to slide through the gaps of their legs, empty eye sockets locked onto Lola. *It's like they just want me.* Burris thrust a leg out, blocking the path and buying her another moment. He brought the hilt down on one skull, then another, and another, with each caving at the blows. The motionless bodies were suspended between the living and the dead. Beyond her control, Lola's vision began to blur, and her bottom lip started to quiver. The horrific sight in front of her turned into fogginess. Her hands trembled on the shotgun. Lola debated which way to go would take more courage. It was the only thing left to think about. Should she blast one last zombie to pieces and go down fighting or…? She turned the weapon up and peered down the black hole into its unforgiving certainty. The act would be quick. But did it really matter? She squeezed her eyes shut, knowing her time was coming to an end. Tears trickled down, and when she opened her eyes, the light from the gap in the rubble flashed in her periphery. Lola looked at it, the shine beaming through the narrow, arm-sized hole. *Light at the end of the tunnel,* she thought vaguely, and it suddenly gave her an idea. It was a small child's hope, but she was going to die anyway, right? She turned to look at her two guardians, struggling to hold on, taking blows to the head and shoulders— bites that drew hot blood from their flesh. Their yells had joined the screams of the dead. Boney hands reached through the gaps between the men's legs, around their sides, and over their shoulders. Why did it seem like the monsters were solely focused on her? That alone bought the men more time. Knowing she had to act, Lola turned to the pile and jammed the nose of the shotgun into the hole. The barrel sunk smoothly in before stopping against the cocking handle. *Well, what do you know, it's like it was meant to fit?* She repeated her one-word plea in her head, hoping that time it'd be heard. *Please.*

The shot was heavily muffled, but it pushed through and produced a metallic ring below. Nothing followed, and her hopes sank to the ground, but before she had time to turn and meet her doom, a groan filled in the air that caused a universal pause. The men turned, and the dead looked around in confusion. Lola's breath caught in her throat as time froze at that moment. And then, like someone snapping their fingers, the world fell. The pile dropped as if it were being sucked into some endless abyss. The foundations of the building shook so hard, many of the dead fell apart, collapsing and toppling over one another. Banks's eyes lit up as he took in what ensued, and he roared a chaotic sound that chilled her to the bone. The laugh of a madman. Grabbing Burris by the shoulder, he aggressively spun the man around, and before she knew it, both men were rushing directly toward her. Banks mouthed a word, and while it wasn't her favorite prospect, it was better than death. *"Jump!"* Lola didn't have time to debate, lest she be run over. She turned and jumped. Into what, she didn't know.

She fell long enough for her stomach to drop, then she crashed into something flat and solid. Lola had jumped facing forward, but somehow landed on her back. The breath escaped her body, not for the first time, and she gasped in shock and pain. Banks landed to her left on his feet, his legs failing him. The impact sent him tumbling out of her sight. Burris fell near her right, bouncing roughly on his front side before rolling away. The dust from the crash muddled her vision and burned her eyes. The light she'd previously seen creeping through the pile dominated the area around them, intense enough to blind. When the world settled back into place, her ears tuned back in to the howls of the dead. Other sounds were there, too. The sound of bones falling on stone and bursting, then bouncing roughly around. The sound of wet slaps as those with blood and a bit of life still in them splattered on the ground. The sounds continued, so Lola painfully forced herself to a seated position to survey the scene.

The three of them had jumped, but the dead simply fell, the lack of brainpower propelling them mindlessly forward. One by one, two by two, and more, they continued with gaping mouths and eyeless confusion. With the clearing dust, Lola looked up. A few more fell, though some teetered on the edge, screaming as they spotted the three of them below. She strained for breath as she watched, but the relief flooding her was almost sweeter than oxygen. *Somehow*, she thought, shaking her head in disbelief. Somehow, she'd survived, at least for another moment. *Thank you, God.*

Lola couldn't say how long the dead stood there howling, or how long she lay there recovering. She breathed in conscious efforts until it evened out. Her panic fled, and her chest rose and fell evenly, her heart rate slowing. Glancing up from where they'd fallen, Lola noticed the gap was a rotted staircase that'd caved in. Looking to the left and right trying to get a view of her companions, she realized she was lying on something elevated above the actual floor. Piles of stone and wood lay scattered beside her, and it was a wonder nothing had smashed her head or caved on her chest—there were some heavy pieces. Angling herself to look beneath, she realized she was on the hood of some type of vehicle. Even with the brightness in the new area, the haze of dust was thick and clouding. It was heavy steel she sat upon, a tan color with horizontal ridges lining the center of it. Lola, not painlessly, forced herself to turn over and found that she was looking at her reflection in two square windows. Above that, on the roof, was something else substantial. Bearing the same tan color, it looked like a rounded, protective wall of some sort.

The sound of coughing took her attention away from it. Banks stumbled up from her left and collapsed on the hood. He was a bloody, dusty wreck, but a smile danced on his lips. A red one. He really was crazy. What she'd taken as coughing, she learned quickly was actually him struggling to laugh. Lola looked at him wide-eyed as he wheezed and his body shook.

"It's a fuckin' Hummer," he said between choking fits of laughter. He forced himself up, the sound from his chest intensifying. "Burris, you asshole, it's a fuckin' military Hummer." Lola didn't know if he realized she was lying right there in front of him or not. He slid back off the hood, collapsing to the ground once more, and he seemed happy to do so. She heard a groan from the other side and quickly rolled in that direction. All types of broken wood littered the floor, and right in the middle lay Burris, forearms crossed over his face. His head rolled to the side, and an eye peeked in her direction. When he saw her, he started to laugh, too. *Both of them,* she thought. Both were nuts.

"You all right, kid?" the prisoner asked tiredly. She sat back down and twisted to dangle her legs over the edge of the Hummer.

"Better than them." She pointed at the dead that'd flattened themselves during the fall. Burris laughed quietly.

"Two lives to live, and they still fucking blew it." Burris forced himself up to the seated position, chunks of wood and dust rolling off him. "About time for that nap now, wouldn't ya say?" He smiled, and for the first time, it spread across his whole face. It was the smile of someone who couldn't believe he was still living, and Lola's heart swelled in her chest. A laugh burst from her, and she jumped down, navigating her way to him. When she arrived, she threw her arms around his neck.

"Easy, easy," he said, patting her on the back.

"I'm sorry," she answered, fighting the swelling tears. "I'm just glad we all made it."

"Glad is an understatement," he replied, pulling her away from him and looking behind her. Her eyes followed his back to the hulking vehicle. *"Hummer," Banks called it?* The prisoner scanned the thing, but when his eyes looked up, they brightened.

"Motherfucker's got a turret," he yelled across the room. Laughter was the first response he got. Lola heard Banks rustling around on the other side.

"And what's in the middle of that tootsie pop?" the cop returned, and Burris stood, smiling in disbelief. He started to laugh as if someone just told the world's greatest joke.

"You won't believe me if I say it starts with an 'M' and ends with a 'two'."

"Fucking Browning?"

"Yep," Burris answered. Lola looked at him, puzzled.

"Brownie?" she asked, and the black man smiled, running his hands through her hair.

"Browning," he repeated, emphasizing the "g." "Or you can just say about sixty-five inches of death." Still, she understood little, but those were a lot of inches of death, so it had to be good. Lola stood and dusted her dirty, ruined clothes. *Despite it all, my clothes have taken the worst of it.* When she looked around, she realized they weren't just in a bright room with a vehicle, but in an expansive room with so much more. Aisles lined the far wall about fifty feet behind the vehicle, loaded with things she couldn't make out due to the distance. Her eyes continued scanning and widened at a wall with numerous weapons mounted, ranging from primitive to modern. Assault rifles, shotguns, smaller submachineguns. Big boxes sat in front of the displays with glass tops, ones she could only guess were filled with ammo. *What the hell is this place?* Had the owners gotten blocked off from their own safe haven, their own place of defense, and perished? Past the guns, more aisles lined the wall. It was difficult to say, but she

228

thought she could make out bags and cans and bottles. The first idea that came to mind caused her stomach to rumble loudly. *Food.*

Lola realized she was smiling like a kid at a candy store and hadn't noticed her two companions came around to stand on either side of her. All three of them were covered in sweat, woodchips, and blood.

"Don't even say it, man," Burris said, shaking his head and turning around to pace. Banks could only laugh.

"I fucking told you so!" The cop laughed so hard that he bent over and placed his hands on his knees. Lola thought they were going to argue, but the prisoner only laughed. The sound was full and hearty.

"Of all the things that could've been under this goddamn pile of shit," Burris said, struggling to contain his laughter. "This is the only thing that could've saved your ass because I was goin' to get ya anyway."

"Saved us,"

Lola said, smiling up at Banks and sliding her hand into his. The act caught him by surprise, but Lola wasn't fooled. She saw for the first time a flash of kindness in his eyes. A flash of heart.

"You saved us, kid."

Looking down to the edge from where they jumped, they noticed the dead had gone quiet. They watched in seething silence from above. It was a disturbing sight, but it was a death sentence for them to make the jump, given the state of their decaying bodies. Banks pulled a cigarette from his pocket and sparked it up, blowing out smoke in a haze of certainty.

"Nothing, though," he said, nodding toward the corpses, "is going to save them."

Seven Quiet Days

Lola dreamt of the dead. They surrounded her in a suffocating crowd, stretching boney fingers with skin dangling between like loose rubber bands. Mouths gaped, and dried tongues hung limp before a throat shrouded in darkness. Darkness deeper than the moonless night—darkness eternal. The dead's empty sockets matched, while the ones with eyes remaining looked cut from stone—cold and cruel. Rotten yellow-green teeth clamped shut in repeated hungry chomps, each one driving them to the taste of her flesh, closer and closer, inch by inch. She could only watch helplessly, sitting in the middle of the crowd. She screamed, but in the dream, it made no sound and felt like yawning. As always, two would break free to close the gap first. Burris and Banks grabbed her, their rotting corpses deteriorating with each moment she looked upon them. Skin melted from their faces and hit the ground with a sizzle. Their eyes boiled and burst, sticking to their cheeks like glue. Her scream of silence to a higher power went unheard as her former protectors tore her apart, the rest of the crowd following in to feast on the scraps.

Lola always woke with a scream, and Burris would be there to calm her. By their count, seven days had passed since they'd battled the dead. And the dream had come to her seven times. It plagued her like a disease. She often wondered if Kalos was doing that to her brain after witnessing her survival, once again, in the face of certain death. Could he control things like that? What was he capable of seeing and doing? It was all his creation, and as far as she was concerned, the demon walked beside her in each waking—and sleeping—moment.

It wasn't as if the dead were fresh in her mind, but perhaps the trauma of everything that'd happened. She had to remind herself she was just a child, though she didn't like to admit it, and these things had a way of infesting the development of young minds. That was likely the point of it all anyway. Each passing day, the dead failed to show themselves again. From what she could tell, there was no way for them to get down there. Given what they'd discovered, the three of them could easily survive for quite some time.

The first day had been the brightest and most exciting; they found countless supplies, food, endless gallons of water, and weapons. *Lots* of weapons. Lola happily scribbled about their findings in her journal while describing her surroundings. It was impossible to say what that place was or how it came to be, but it was a stroke of great luck for Banks and Burris to end up there after their flight from the dead and the dark. The policeman said it was the old Forester house—she didn't know who or what that meant—that was set on high ground overlooking their small city. It was built in the late 1800s on the former site of a medical building. According to him, the family must've discovered the lower levels of the place, near the foundations, and initiated some upgrades. For what purpose, Banks was unsure, but it could be said the proper situation had arisen, granted the family wasn't there to utilize it as intended.

The area they fell into was a large well-lit room. The high ceiling and the stretching rows of fluorescent lights reminded her of a grocery store. The "Hummer," the two men called it, with the turret and mounted .50 caliber, was at the far end, closest to the collapsed stairs where they made their jump. It being a military vehicle, they surmised the family must've been affiliated in some way. That wasn't the only indicator, as almost the entire back wall housed a variety of weapons, most military grade, much to Banks's delight. Fully stocked, operational, and with enough ammo to start a war. It hadn't taken him long to test things out, either—much to Burris's dismay. The prisoner argued the sound would bring the dead upon them, to which Banks only responded, "Come and get it," and did what he wanted to anyway. That first day, while she and Burris ate, the cop bolted straight for the guns. His weapon of choice was an assault rifle with some sort of grenade launcher attached to it. It could only load one round at a time, but that didn't slow him down. He set spare rounds in a line on the hood of the Hummer, then surprised the dead above with a lot of explosive destruction. As they were blown apart, they screamed and jumped. Lola couldn't discern how many were up there, but Banks cleared the lot of them, all the while laughing. Had he had it his way, he would've gone back up and devastated every single one he could find, but Burris urged him against it.

There was a reason she was smiling so much that first day. They browsed the aisles of food, including one with nothing but chocolate, and laid claims to their favorites. Everything was there, from bread, to cereal, to sodas, to canned goods. Rows of five-gallon containers, all filled with water, sat adjacent to the various foods. There was even a large walk-in cooler that still worked, housing a great deal of meat, milk, and eggs. They'd essentially found heaven in the middle of hell. Lola didn't know who those folks were, but they'd been prepared. Even though it hadn't saved them, it saved her and her companions; for that, she was thankful.

On the same side as the food, water, and cooler, a large downward ramp sloped away about fifty yards toward a massive steel-enforced garage door. While the men investigated, Lola kept her distance. She knew what was out there in the dark, even if she couldn't see it. It was the only other way out of there, other from where they'd jumped. She envisioned making an escape with the Hummer, down the ramp, through the garage, and out. Burris mentioned the idea several times, but Banks didn't seem to want to go anywhere. There was nothing but the blackness out there, and Lola knew he was right. They were well-equipped, moreover, and Banks was thirsty for blood. Hot, cold, or dried, he didn't care—he wanted to obliterate the dead. Lola witnessed the obsession in his eyes, but she didn't blame him. Someone had taken everything from her, too. And she also wanted to destroy him.

Across the wall of weapons were aisles of different supplies. To their relief, there was a row of soap and shampoo. Lola dreamed of a shower to wash the filth from her body, even if it was a cold shower from one of the jugs. Most of it was hardware, though: nails, bolts, wood, and cans of paint. There was a fair share of electrical stuff, including extension cords and surge protectors. To her exasperation, there was rope. Lots of it. All of that hair cutting from those decaying corpses was time left behind. They also found ladders, one of which Banks took over to a personalized pile of gear he was gathering. It was a large extension ladder, coincidentally tall enough to reach the top of the fallen staircase. They knew he was planning something. Banks wasn't trying to escape, and neither was she—not in that way. Her escape would have to be much different because she had no idea where to start. Exiting the house with the orstras had brought her back to the maze,

235

but strolling out into the darkness here offered no assurance of the same. Lola remembered Burris pulling her back from one of the windows. Not even light could push through it, but somehow, there was light inside. A purposeful design. Kalos's design.

There was bedding near the back of the supply aisles, including sheets and heavy blue blankets. There weren't any pillows, so they grabbed extra blankets to substitute. There were no separate rooms either, save for the walk-in, so they lay their makeshift beds in front of the Hummer. They slept two at a time, with one person always keeping watch. Near the back wall next to the guns, a large lever controlled the lights and could shut them all down at that one point. When they pulled it, a string of red lights glowed dimly, circling all the way around the structure. Banks fixed a spotlight onto the hood of the military vehicle and adjusted it upward toward the spot they'd jumped from. Occasionally, they would flip it on to see if they had any visitors. Thus far, only wreckage, scattered bones, and scorch marks from exploding grenades shone in the light. Lola wrote about their anticipations while lying, propped up on her elbows, the smell of her journal and ink filling her nostrils. Sleep came easily that night, but the nightmare waited for her.

The second day was more eventful. Banks wanted to go back up, and Burris initially argued, but was finally convinced after a while they couldn't just lie down and eat for the rest of their lives. The thought didn't sound that bad, though. They had to take all measures to properly protect themselves, including executing their original strategy of the bone barriers. Besides, they had plenty to work with. After hearing Banks out, Burris grudgingly got on board. Lola did, too. However, she wasn't happy she had to stay behind while the two of them went up. She resisted and argued, though all in vain. Banks's word was final. She was to lock herself within the safety of the Hummer and wait. She stupidly asked how she ought to repel an assault. Banks sarcastically answered she should man the turret. Lola couldn't imagine being physically able to operate a gun that size. It was longer than her! Burris paid no attention to the comment, and they let her take her pick from the wall. Stubbornly, Banks showed her how to fire the .50 anyway. He showed her the design, how it was set up so she wouldn't have to support the weight of the weapon, and how she even had free range.

"All you have to do is pull the trigger," he said, pulling up a green steel box with yellow writing and placing it into a holder to the side of the weapon. He pulled the top of the Browning open, lay a string of alarming-sized bullets into the slot, then clamped it shut.

"There's a lever here." Banks pointed to the right side of the gun. He yanked it back one time toward them. "It's ready to fire. You squeeze the trigger by pressing down with your thumbs. Hold it only in burst to avoid extra heat. A weapon like these jams, too, because of the rate of fire, so reach over and pull that lever again when it does, and fire again." She attempted with one arm but was only able to get it back with both. It didn't make her any less doubtful. She desperately wanted to go with them, but Banks was having none of it.

"We're going to hear the gunshots if you need to fire," he reassured, pulling her into a surprising hug against his leg. "Those rotten sacks of shit won't have a clue how to get to you."

237

It turned out he was right, but she hated it. On that day, the two of them went up, and that was the last sign of movement she'd witnessed. Lola jotted angry notes, pressing the pen near hard enough to tear, but while documenting her lesson with weaponry, she felt herself relax. After, she watched the gap upstairs until her eyes hurt. Hours passed, and she didn't see or hear anything. Down there, that was. From above, occasional shots went off. It worried her, but they were capable and well-armed. They were likely clearing out lingering dead, those hiding in corners or dark hallways. Banks had taken a small automatic strapped around his shoulder, along with an AR-15, a larger assault gun he carried in his hands. Burris went with a shotgun, which was decidedly his style, that had a round ammo clip which slid into place underneath. Aside from that, a few pistols decorated each man's hip.

As those hours passed, Lola shifted and turned in the uncomfortable seats of the military machine. More worry nagged at her, and she couldn't seem to suppress it. Her dream came to mind, and the vision made her sad. She pictured them getting trapped up there again and how lucky they'd been the first time just to get out. Would they be able to do it again? The possibility had a higher chance, she supposed, since they didn't have to look after her, but that consideration only angered her more. *They didn't have to babysit me*, she thought, frustrated. *I carried my weight. Even saved them. What do I get? Left down here.* While she was fuming, she thought about how unfair it was, but as time went by, she calmed, knowing they were just trying to keep her safe. They were helping her survive, and that was the one thing she needed to do.

Lola stifled a yawn and wondered how long they'd been gone when she spotted movement from up top. Her breath

238

caught in her throat, and she tensed before relaxing with a sigh when she recognized Burris dropping the ladder down. Part of her still wanted to be mad, but she was excited they were back. The prisoner didn't look tired, sweaty, or bloody, so that was a positive sign. Banks followed shortly behind, looking much the same. When Lola asked them about the gunshots, it was as she suspected. There were a few left up there, wandering aimlessly or trapped under fallen dead. They succeeded in what they wanted to do and planned to move forward the following day. When Lola experienced the dream again that night, it was less vague. It was much more vivid to witness and remember. Burris held her as she cried against his chest. She was afraid to tell him about the nightmare as if speaking it would make it come true, but he pushed her to tell him. In the end, it did make her feel better talking about it, and even stopped her tears.

The third day, she put the dream behind her, more pleased than anything that they were taking her along. Not before they engaged in some target practice and weapons education, however, which was equally exciting. Burris set up a target down the ramp made of large containers of corn, flour, or meal. Her first weapon was something Banks called an *Uzi*. As a high-powered automatic, it was deceptively small. He warned her she'd have to use two hands to manage the high rate of fire. She gripped it firmly and planted her feet like he showed her. The cop balanced his strong arm over hers and told her to squeeze the trigger. As much as she was prepared, the spray still shocked the weapon from her hands. The effect was not positive for Banks, who screamed and cursed in surprise. Lola glared at him while Burris laughed.

On the second try, he brought her some thin black gloves he'd found to help with her grip. They were a little large, but the idea worked. She yanked them tightly over her skin, gripped the weapon again, and set her sights.

"Remember, you don't have to hold the trigger down. Small bursts. Until you get used to it." The advice turned out to be sound, and she got the hang of the weapon quickly. Lola blasted the array of random cans and sacks all over the place, even though it took a few tries to keep it steady. Banks showed her to aim high, to squat or crouch and shoot low, and to turn the weapon sideways and spray in a line. When they were done, she smiled up and him, and the two men laughed together.

"I think you got it down, kid." Burris seemed impressed.

Target practice only took up the first few hours of the day, but they shot a lot of weapons. Handguns, shotguns, semis— anything they could test. Banks showed her how to disassemble and reassemble and introduced her to the tools she'd need to clean them. He showed her the safety settings on each one, taught her when to shoot and when not to and, above all, to always be aware of what she was pointing at. The rest of the day entailed blasting bones to pieces near the top of the staircase. She and Burris did most of it together while Banks stayed below, cutting different lengths of rope.

"He likes to be by himself, huh?" Lola asked the prisoner as they worked. He looked up and gave her an agreeing nod.

"Some people need their own time," he suggested.

"But why, do you think?" She watched Banks sitting on the end of the Hummer, going about his business in silence.

"Life just shapes people in different ways. It'll show you how you work most efficiently." He sighed, yanking a skull free from a corpse. "For Banks, solitude is probably the ticket." Lola pondered the words.

"Do you think that means we're holding him back?" It was a serious question, but Burris quietly laughed.

"I wouldn't think of it like that, kid." He leaned against the wall, popping an arm free at the shoulder. Lola busied herself with a ribcage. "Deep down, I don't think he wants to be alone. Sometimes, I think people just need to be. Do you understand what I'm saying?"

"Kind of," she answered, though not really following. Burris only smiled at her again.

"You will, kid. One day." His eyes were sad as if he knew there were some hard lessons for her ahead. She'd had some hard ones already. Lola wondered if he still didn't believe her about the story, she'd told him. In that setting, it was hard to imagine it couldn't be grasped. Hell, if the dead were walking, anything was possible, right? Chances were, he hadn't given it much thought. She knew he just wanted to go home, like she did. He wanted his family back. Her mother's wail entered her mind, and she clenched her teeth. Every time she got scared, she reminded herself to think of that sound. The anger it birthed would give her strength.

Later that day, they grabbed all the sheets and blankets they didn't need and used them as sacks to carry the bones. It took all three of them to force the sacks up and through the narrow staircase leading to their former rooms. She didn't feel like she was doing much pushing from the back. The men, however, were vocally frustrated as they pulled one at a time. They were huffing and puffing by the time the eight sacks were cleared. Lola's arms and fingers hurt from pulling apart corpses, and it wasn't long before she was thinking about sitting idle inside the Hummer again. Funny how that worked. Still, she pushed herself, knowing how much needed to be done.

They ate lunch at the island in the kitchen. Lola made a few peanut butter and jelly sandwiches, but when Banks threw a few steaks on the grill, her stomach soon forgot them, and her mouth watered.

"If you want one, you better take that shit back to the cooler and grab yourself one," Banks said without taking his eyes from the grill. Lola snatched the sandwiches from her plate without hesitation, running like she never had, even with fairies and zombies giving chase.

"From the pack that's already open!" Banks's gruff voice faded as she ran. Her feet glided down the ladder. In those moments, Lola forgot everything in the world, excitement surging through her. She jerked the cooler door open, darted down the length of it, and snatched the meat. She set the sandwiches on a box where they'd likely be forgotten.

Not long after, she was savoring a bite of beef, resting both elbows on the table. Her eyes were glazed over as she looked thoughtlessly up at the ceiling. Nothing had been that fulfilling for a while, and she took her time with each glorious bite. Lola recalled her parents' steak night—her favorite of the week. Even though Banks's steak wasn't nearly as good as her dad's, it was wonderful after being deprived for so long. She hoped they could eat steak every day.

They worked their way from the bottom to the top of the barriers, which made the kitchen the starting point. Wrapping up their meal, they got to work. Banks pulled out different lengths of rope and instructed them on how it'd be done. They could barely fit two on one, and sometimes the second one had to be tied. They had to remove a middle rib from each side to ensure the skulls fit or stacked properly. Upon completion, they'd shove a few heads into the hollow middle to fill it out, then they'd stack the resulting products side by side in the window. The kitchen window was long and wide, previously a pushout window. They were able to place five sets across, almost perfectly spanning its length. The last one took a little jamming, but Banks told her the tighter the blockade, the better. They got another row to fit on top, jammed tightly together, then secured with rope as a single piece. A hands-length gap remained near the top, so they lined it with skulls—facing out, of course, to Banks's morbid delight.

The process repeated by the small window in the bedroom. In the bathroom with the ugly, busted toilet, they lodged a cage in the tiled frame around a window over the sink. It was so tiny it'd even be a tight squeeze for Lola to try to push through, but the men weren't taking any chances. Moving out into the living area, the group's task wasn't so simple. The front door was obliterated, explaining how the dead had flanked the two men before. They used the first structure they built to cover the door, moving it from its original spot for the windows. Given its size, it had to be heaved across the room into place. Banks tied the bone structure tightly against the frame. With the additional rope, they'd be able to use the ribcages for the two remaining windows. They stuffed the dark, hollow spaces full of them. It was difficult as the ribcages—somewhat standard in size—didn't fit perfectly in the windows, so they filled the remaining gaps in the frames with limbs. Banks ran rope through, binding it all together. Lola couldn't help but smile at their progress. The idea was genius. The dead would have to *really* fight to get in.

"The dead," Burris said, taking in their accomplished work. "They were much stronger this time. Do you think they'll be even stronger when they return?"

"Could've been a coincidence," Banks replied, lighting a smoke. Lola knew cigarettes were one thing they hadn't found down in the big room. He'd cussed the owners of the place upon that realization, calling them all sorts of names she'd never even heard before. She wondered how many he had left. Moreover, what would happen when he ran out?

"Even so," he continued, blowing out a monstrous cloud and giving the door's barrier a tug. "We're better equipped now. Real men could assault this place. Strong men. And they'd fail." Lola liked his confidence, but Burris wasn't convinced.

"The barriers, though. Who's to stop them from beating all this shit down while we're down there sitting pretty in our newfound area?" Banks's expression was never pleasant when the prisoner questioned him. But the questions needed to be answered.

"They're there to buy us time, Burris. We'll check daily as best we can with just three of us. Regardless, whether they can break through or not, it's gonna be what it's gonna be."

"I get it, Banks. I really do. I wish we had an indication down there that'd let us know when they're up here." Just as Burris finished speaking, Banks threw back his head and laughed. It was a rough noise propelled by billowing smoke. Burris could only raise his eyebrows.

"Indication, huh?" His laugh continued, morphing into a haggard cough. "If you hadn't been so occupied with all that food, I suppose you'd know, as a matter of fact, we have plenty of indicators." Burris threw his hands up, and Banks's smile widened.

"Y'all come on," he said, waving them to follow as he started back toward the door under the stairs. "Let me show you fools something."

Back below, in the large area, Banks took them to the wall with the weapons. He dug around in the glass cases for a few moments until he found a large green box that resembled a metal suitcase—like one that'd be seen, full of money, in a mobster movie. After struggling a few moments to slide it to the front, Banks lifted it free and set it on the glass. With a smile, he spun it around to face them.

"Are you ready?" Burris looked skeptical, but Lola was antsy with anticipation. She bounced on her feet as she waited, hands on the glass counter, struggling against her own height. When the cop popped the case, she had to push herself up with her hands. Burris's eyes widened, but Lola didn't recognize what it was, to her disappointment. There were six round metal casings the size of a coffee mug. The top of each was wrapped with a thin, golden metal full of holes. Sticking out of it was a cylindrical object about the size of a pencil. Above was a kit of some sort with some wiring. Lola looked at Banks, who was staring at Burris and nodding excitedly.

"Those are—" Burris started, breathless.

"You got it, partner. M-sixteen mines." Lola didn't know what that meant, but mines were familiar to her. *You step on them, and they blow up, right?* Her excitement deepened.

"Damn, they come with the whole kit and everything," Burris said, eyes lit. "You know how to wire these up?"

"You bet your ass," Banks replied, looking half offended. He reached in the case, pulled out a small stack of folded papers, and pressed them against Burris's chest. "The two of you will learn too as well." Lola's brows were still drawn as she looked at the equipment. Burris gave her a gentle pat on the head.

"Trip wires, kid," he said with a smile.

"Like booby traps?" she asked, and his smile widened, a chuckle escaping his lips.

"Yeah, kid. Like booby traps."

Banks leaned on the countertop with his elbows, studying the bombs closely. "The doorway under the stairs, the kitchen door, and the narrow stairway coming down to our old rooms." He was speaking quietly to himself, then his voice rose. "After that, we'll line the hallway leading to us with the remaining three, spaced evenly apart." Lola could tell Burris's comfort level had improved, as had hers.

The time to sleep came and passed, as did the dream. She still couldn't shake it; every time it felt as if she were seeing it for the first time again. Her subconscious was unable to adapt, and Burris, once again, comforted her after she woke with a scream, covered in cold sweat.

"Just dreams, kid. Just dreams. We'll get by. Together." His words brought little comfort, but he meant well. Until they got moving and busy during the day, she could only see him and Banks as they were in the nightmare. After, though, the images would fade. That fourth day, she spent the time it took the men to get ready to write about her weapons training, defense preparations, and, of course, the steak she'd eaten. After, they spent the first few hours shooting weapons and cleaning them. Banks timed her on her assembly time, which was still sluggish, but got better by the end of the run. Her aim had improved, as well. The cop took her through mobile firing, clearing areas, and proper concealment, using the aisles as obstacles. It was by far her favorite part of the day. After, they wired up the mines, or booby traps, as she liked to call them. The men had taken to calling them that, too, once she'd said it enough times. Lola busied herself cleaning debris—chunks of wood, big and small—with a shop broom she found in the hardware area. It was heavy, and the bristles shaped the bottom in a rectangle as she pushed the trash from the hallway and the fallen staircase. She swept and bagged the debris from the kitchen, too, and cleaned the small bathroom. Near the end of their workday, Banks let her help him with the last of the traps, showing her in detail how they worked, then guided her through it with his words. She did the last one all by herself and earned a rare smile.

That night, they were lying in their makeshift beds behind the Hummer with Burris fast asleep. He'd taken the toughest of the tasks—removing a great deal of the larger fallen debris and piling it near the back corner of the room, by the ramp. The prisoner worked hard, and his exhaustion proved it. Lola lay awake, journal open in front of her, attempting to sketch her mother in the low red light, trying to avoid any unwanted images of her recurring nightmares. She lay on one arm with her back to Banks, who was oiling one of the assault rifles he fancied, and it gleamed in the dim red lights. It seemed to be a therapeutic thing for him, something he repeated every night after lights out. Lola couldn't imagine what he thought while he did it, but it seemed to bring him peace.

"I know about dreams," he muttered quietly, but the suddenness of it caused her to jump. She didn't know what to say or if she should say anything at all. Was he talking to her? Did he know she was awake? An uncomfortable feeling caused her to shift in the darkness.

"Your eyes close when you sleep," he continued, voice grim. The cloth in his hand glided down the barrel of his weapon, smooth and silent. "But your mind sees. Your mind sees the things that you can't unsee." He cocked the weapon, startling her again and evoking a gasp.

"Sad thing is"—he held the weapon up in the red light, eyeing its length— "here, you don't need to be asleep for the nightmares." Lola could feel his eyes on her back. "Here, the nightmares are real, kid. The quicker you accept that, the quicker the dreams become harmless." He knew she was awake. She should've known. Banks knew a lot of things.

"But you and Burris are dead in my dreams," she whispered back to him. Banks didn't stop in his task, nor did he look back in her direction.

"A possible reality," came the reply. "You've seen it several times. What better way to be prepared?" The thought made her sad, and the policeman wasn't helping, but Lola knew he meant well in his own sort of hardened way. He regarded her thoughtfully again, then reached toward his bed to dig through his things.

"You know, kid, music is a really good thing to keep your mind in the right place." Turning back toward her, he reached over and tossed something heavy onto her blanket. "I found this a few days back. Tinkered with it but couldn't get it to pick up. Maybe you'll have better luck." Turning and looking behind, it was hard to tell what it was. Lola rolled and picked it up, feeling some wires and a plastic box. It was an electronic device she didn't recognize.

"What is it?" she asked curiously, eyeing it closely.

"An escape," he replied, his attention reverted to his weapon.

"Thanks," she said hesitantly, inspecting each side of it. She touched several edges that felt like switches or knobs. "Does it work?"

"Yeah," he replied, reaching to show her. "It turns on, I just can't get it to—"

"That's not what I meant." She looked up at him, sad but hopeful in the red coating her face. She'd do anything to make the nightmares go away, even if their reality wasn't much better. To her surprise, Banks gave her a sympathetic look.

"If you can find the right jams, kid, you can make a lot of shit go away." She was sure he spoke from personal experience. Lola did have an appreciation for music; she just never found time to listen to it with obligations like her schoolwork and family time. Church music, of course, was present on Sundays as well as her dad jamming while he worked out in his shed. Those tunes were some of her favorites—maybe she could find something like that. The anticipation made her smile, and, surprising Banks, she leapt up to throw her arms around his neck. Several moments passed, but finally a muscled arm crept around her to pat her gently on the back.

"Save the sappy shit for Burris." Burris was the preferable one for that, like a big teddy bear, but that didn't stop her from hugging Banks just as tightly. Days ago, she'd been scared to come within ten feet of the man, afraid he might scream at her or bury a knife in her skull. They'd come a long way, and her heart swelled for him.

"There's a pair of headphones on the back end of the supply aisles, too," he continued. He set his rifle aside, propping it against the vehicle that loomed over them like a giant protector. He adjusted his blankets and lay down. "Look for the boxes at the bottom loaded with random shit."

Those were the last words he spoke to her before he was out. His snores filled the air softly in tune with Burris's, and she lay on her back, running her hands over the little radio. Part of her was tempted to get up and look for the headphones, but it was too dark, so she'd wait until the lights came on. It was good to feel something a little different. The nightmare, however, wasn't lost; when she slept, it came with vivid intensity. The screams were so loud they hurt her ears, drowning out her own screams. The worst part for her was the eyes of her two friends. Hate fueled and enraged as they clawed at her. She could never forget the eyes.

On the fifth day, the three of them began to relax a little more. Most of the work was done, so they trained for the majority of the day, with a bit of journaling for her in between. Banks extended the sessions a few more hours, and Lola got some good work in with a smaller, three-round burst rifle—an M4. It fit her well, and her aim was dead-on. Her assembly time improved drastically as her interest in weapons continued to peak. It was enough to make Banks proud. They practiced clearing and infiltrating as best they could without going through more ammo, then called it a day. Afterward, the two men spent their time building some lengthy elevated ramps that spanned the mines and trip wires, lest they forget. One misstep, and they'd join the dead. While they did so, Lola dug through the boxes in the supply aisle to find headphones. To her surprise, she found two pairs, but the first fit her ears better. They were a soft clear rubber, and she couldn't imagine getting much sound out of them, but the tiny things surprised her. She lay in Burris's original room, up the ladder in the long hall, while the men worked outside. Lola fidgeted with the device, twisting the knobs left and right, and got nothing but blaring static. She had to turn the volume down. It was a small hope to believe she could pick anything up, given the world had gone dark, but then again, for inexplicable reasons, they had electricity and enduring light there, while everything else outside was black. It was enough to keep her trying. Sometimes she could discern the faintest sounds of music, but she wondered if she was just imagining them. *Surely there's something here.* The old thing wasn't offering her much promise, but it'd occupied some of her time. Her brain needed a distraction.

As she was about to leave it and try again another time, a short blast of radio clarity came through. It disappeared back to the static as quickly as it came, but Lola held her breath excitedly. As slowly and carefully as she could manage, she twisted the knob back in the opposite direction, only so slightly, hoping to bring it back to life. It boomed through, clear again and surprising her a second time. Her smile climbed

251

to her ears as an old classic rock melody blared through the earphones:

> *Blues on the river*
>
> *Or on the green of grass.*
>
> *How them days felt like forever,*
>
> *But them days, did they pass?*

Her smile remained glued to her face, and she rocked her head back and forth to the sound. It reminded her of her dad's music, the classic feel of his time and generation.

> *Her smile deep as an ocean,*
>
> *A smile meant to last.*
>
> *How them days, how them days*
>
> *Did they pass?*

She was careful to set the radio softly to the side as she lay on Burris's former blankets. Lola didn't want to lose the signal. She closed her eyes and soaked it up for as long as she could. Burris and Banks would occasionally drop in to check on her, the prisoner giving her a nod and smile, the cop nodding in understanding. She'd found his escape; he knew, and she returned his smile and a thumbs up in appreciation. The music continued, following the same standard with each passing song. It must've been a classic rock station of some sort—no doubt old recordings just cycling through and playing over and over. It took her back home, if only in thought, and while the image saddened her, it brought her comfort as well. Lola's eyes found the ceiling, her lids fluttering lazily as consciousness became a struggle. Her mother and father were laughing at the dinner table, arms stretched toward each other and hands gripped firmly. Lola sat with them, laughing in tune, and cutting into her meal. She knew in her mind the sounds they were making—how happy they were. Tears tracked a path down her cheeks as the memory faded. She imagined them at church, in the car, or picking her up from school. Her mother's words floated through her brain, talking about work and the kids she taught, the mean ones and nice ones alike. Lola remembered that, most days, her mind would drift in the car, and her eyes would find the sky. The words were heard, but she never paid much attention. She would stay lost in her head, deep into her imagination, wondering what was beyond their universe, what was beyond the sky. And she knew. Maybe that's what got her there in the first place and piqued the demon's interest. Lola thought about how many smart and advanced children there were in the world, and as she had a million times before, asked herself, *why me?* Kalos popped into her mind with his strangely shaped smile. "Next in line, one at a time," the monster said without moving his mouth. The grin widened too far for a human face. His teeth were long, silver spears. Lola ground her teeth, and her body tensed with the boiling anger she felt. *You took my world.*

The thoughts and feelings drifted once she found sleep. No dream awaited her that time. Lola woke sometime later with static booming in her ears. She must've bumped into the radio during her slumber. Banks stood just inside the doorway, leaning against the frame, and Burris was across the hall, facing him. The two were laughing about something. Lola sat up, pulling the headphones free with a soft, earwax-coated pop, and the voices of the men became clearer. She was groggy and knew from their smiles that she wore it all over her face.

"Got all the time in the world to sleep, kid," Burris said from across the hall. Some life had come back to him over the last few days. She could see it, finally, as his smile touched his eyes. It made her happy.

"How about some cards?" Banks asked. He flipped a small, rectangular box into the air and caught it as it fell. Lola knew it was a deck of standard playing cards, and a grin spread across her face. It brought more memories of family, and although she rarely won at home, the competitive part of her was always up for the challenge.

Down below, they set up a small wooden box in the center of their sleeping area where they'd play. Banks took Burris down one of the food aisles to show him something while Lola searched for music on her radio once more, unplugging the phones so it played out loud. If she could find the station, they'd be able to listen while they played.

Upon their return, Lola found the tiny spot where the music played clearly and looked up at the men, excited and proud. They responded with shocked expressions that turned into matching smiles. Banks had a small box in his arms, and he sat to her left. She could hear the clinking of glass bottles and guessed he'd found the booze. Judging by the looks on their faces, it was probably the expensive kind. Banks fired up a cigarette, taking a deep draw as Burris sat on the other side of her.

"Where'd you find that?" she asked, looking at Banks's haggard face. Another cloud of smoke whooshed by her face, and the smell nearly made her cough. It was Burris who spoke, however.

"Back corner on the bottom. Hiding from us." She was surprised to see him light up a smoke, too. It was the first time she'd witnessed him doing so. When he noticed her look, the prisoner shrugged.

"You only live once, right?" He looked over to Banks who laughed, all the while pulling the glass bottles from the box and inspecting them.

"Quite the selection here," the cop said, casually tossing a green bottle over to Burris. "Irish." He lifted another. "Ugh. Fuckin' rye." He tossed it to the side onto one of the blankets and pulled another. "Ah, American." It was a clear bottle with a brown liquid inside. When the cop noticed her peering over into the box, he chuckled.

"I don't think so, kid," he said, giving her a playful shove backward. She didn't want to drink any of it anyway. Not really—she was just looking. "God knows when we get out of this shit, we'll have to find your folks. We can't be returning you as some boozy, smoky, dirty rat." He laughed at his own comment, and she glared at him, snatching the playing cards off the wooden box. Lola wished it were that easy for them to take her home. It wasn't possible, though, so she shied away from the subject.

"You really think we can get out of here?" she asked quietly, and if the cop hadn't looked amused before, it was all over him then.

"Of course, we will." He twisted the cap off the American bottle, tilted it back, and took a deep swig. Lola watched his face, expected it to scrunch up like it did when she'd seen other people drink. Instead, it stayed the same as he took a pull from his cigarette. He set the bottle down to his right, well out of Lola's reach.

"You ever play Rummy, kid?" Burris asked across from her, drinking from his own bottle. The liquid in his was much darker and stronger, smelling something like liquorish. Her nose wrinkled and her insides twisted as if she'd drank it herself. *Gross*. The question he posed, however, pulled her mind far away from the smell. That was her parents' favorite game.

The next two days were much the same. Training in the morning, though they didn't fire anymore. They mostly pieced the weapons together and worked on mobile aiming, strategic movement, and taking cover. Banks was dedicated to teaching her, and she'd learned a lot from him. Outside of that, they played cards, listened to music, and told funny stories. They took turns bathing themselves in private with the water jugs and soap. Lola was thankful for cleanliness, but filth clung to her when she had to put on her same tattered clothes.

They'd picked out meals each day and headed up the ladder, crossing the wood ramps to eat dinner together in the kitchen. While Burris was slow on the alcohol, Banks had no problem draining several containers. It perplexed her how he still seemed the same after drinking so much, though he occasionally got quieter. His eyes never lost their hard set, no matter how much he smiled or laughed. If Lola could peer inside his mind, if only for a second, she knew she'd see him waiting for battle—for war. She accepted that was how he'd always be. He believed the dead were coming back, whereas she just prayed that the horror was over. Deep down, she knew better there in Kalos's game. Banks would get his wish; she just hoped beyond hope it wouldn't cost any of their lives.

Burris was quiet, too. She knew he was constantly thinking about his family. She couldn't help notice how much they were alike. *All of us are stuck in the darkness, alone.* She blinked back the tears in her eyes the harsh truth often evoked. The prisoner did seem cheerier, though. Lola knew he had a soft spot for her, and perhaps she was the reason he'd become more optimistic. She'd sure like to be. She could tell because his eyes softened when he smiled, whereas before they hadn't. He was learning to live with the pain, though there were demons that haunted him. The laughter, food, and music were helping. Lately, Burris had been telling them family stories—such as comical and predictable holiday mishaps from previous years—that had her and Banks in fits of laughter. Banks had good stories, too, though they weren't all amusing. Some were deep and intriguing with darker themes, and she liked those, too. Some were about his job and investigations, though the two men avoided the subject of how Burris became a prisoner in the first place. She was curious, but she dared not bring it up. They kept it secret for a reason.

Time rolled on. There were instances when Lola could forget it all, and she even looked forward to their activities. Their time together made her happy, a feeling she never thought to have in that place. She'd put these things in the front of her mind, and she wished they could somehow be locked into that spot. That seventh night, after another day shaking her nightmare away, had them settled and playing a game of poker. She wasn't that good at it, so she watched them a few rounds before getting dealt in. She miserably lost most of the time but managed to win the last round before they put the cards away

257

for the night. The three of them lay on their beds in the shape of a T with heads together. Banks turned out the main lights, and the red light reflected on their faces.

"We have to get Lola out of here," Burris said quietly, sometime later. She figured he thought she was asleep.

"I can't think of a better plan right now other than to wait this out, Burris," the cop replied, equally quiet. "We're equipped to do so."

"You think they'll come again, don't you?" The prisoner's tone was somber.

It seems to me there is a pattern of a sort." When Burris didn't respond, the policeman worked himself up onto his elbows and looked at his friend. "Haven't you noticed?"

"Yeah, a pattern of dead fuckers trying to make us the same."

"Seriously," Banks pressed. "The gaps between attacks become larger each time, but they come back stronger, fresher." He shook his head. "And higher in numbers."

"I thought you said it was a coincidence?"

"It was a suggestion, asshole."

"You really think these things can…plan?" It was Burris's turn to roll over. He propped himself on one elbow and faced his partner. "Gotta be coincidence. These things are just roaming out there. A group of them see the light of this place, and it draws them in."

"I don't know anymore, man." Banks reached toward the box in the middle of them and grabbed a bottle, taking a small sip. "I think a fight's coming." He turned toward Lola. She could feel his eyes weighing on her as she peeked through her eyelids.

"No child should have to go through this shit," Burris said, barely whispering.

"Do you believe how she got here?" Banks's face was shadowed, but Lola knew he shifted his gaze back to Burris. She held her breath, waiting for the reply.

"I didn't—" Lola had to strain her ears.

"Maybe there's a lot more going on out there than we know," Banks interjected before the prisoner could say more. "But you're right. We have to ensure she makes it. One way or another."

"Girl's got you soft, Banks." Burris laughed as he grabbed the bottle from the cop's hand and took a swig. "And you're a cold son of a bitch." Banks scoffed and shook his head but remained silent. Lola smiled, and Burris continued to laugh. "No shame in it. Girl's a good kid. Reminds me of mine."

"Good," Banks answered. He pulled the blankets up over his arms and rolled over, his back facing them. "Keep her close. And don't let her go."

She knew the comment was meant well, but Burris was right. The cop was a cold man. If there was anything adults taught her, it was that the truth hurt. She was learning that for herself early on. And it was more real than anything else out there.

As silently as she could, she pressed her headphones into her ears, trying not to let them know she was still awake. Neither of them moved or gave indication they noticed. She was thankful, as Lola was sure they wouldn't be happy with her eavesdropping. She closed her eyes and felt sleep wrapping itself around her. She drifted slowly and waited for the dreams, the harsh reality of it all—the *truth*—to come.

The Eighth Day

Thump. The sound was quiet and inconsequential, but Lola's eyes shot open. Suddenly, she was very awake and afraid, though she couldn't say why. It wasn't the nature of the sound that alarmed her. Rather, it was out of place in the routine they'd created. Abnormal. After a moment, her stomach sank as she realized her headphones were in, and the music was chiming on as it had when it lulled her to sleep. Lola hadn't heard the noise. She *felt* it. Her body jerked into a seated position; the movement almost involuntary, instinctual. She tore the headphones from her ears and noticed her two protectors were already on their feet. Burris was sliding on his boots while Banks ran for the lights.

"One of the mines," Banks yelled across, the lights blinking to life and turning their world white. "Hopefully it's not some stray fucking rodent." Banks had his trousers and white tank on, the latter decorated with large spots of dried blood.

"Hopefully it is," Burris replied, lacing a boot tight. He pulled his new shotgun against his body with the strap, flipping it around to his back. The older shotgun he took into his hands. "That'd explain why they didn't…" The two men exchanged urgent looks, and Lola looked back and forth between them, puzzled.

"The fucking ramps," Banks said, and her mouth dropped. *Not good.* They'd forgotten to pull the ramps yesterday, so the dead would be able to walk over the mines if they were indeed coming. The cop slung his own weapon over his shoulder, the AR, followed by his other rifle with the grenade attachment. *M203*, he'd taught her. The large rounds were layered into a band that he strapped across his chest. Banks buckled on his gun belt with two side arms holstered tight.

"We have to move," he said, pulling on his shoes while standing. "With luck, the first explosion may have barred their way." Lola stood and pulled her own shoes on, her dirty Converse All-Stars. If one had tripped a mine, that meant something had pushed through at least one of the bone barriers. Her hands were shaking as she tied the laces together, but she tried to reassure herself they were prepared. They had more weapons and more ammo that time around. *Lots more. Plus, a way out. Well, sort of.* If it came down to it, they could plunge out of the garage into the darkness in the Hummer. That was the last resort, though. Her adrenaline, anxiety, and fear were all spiking in that moment. *You've seen it all, already. Be strong.* The sobering truth brought little comfort.

"What about the kid?" Burris asked when they started to move toward the ladder.

"I have a name, you know," she answered, delaying Banks's reply. She tried to sound unafraid but wasn't sure if she'd succeeded. They looked at her, at each other, then at the Hummer. Anger propelled her confidence, scorching away the feelings twisting her insides.

"I don't fucking think so!" It was the first time she'd cursed in front of them that she could remember, but her voice was calm. Leaving her there wasn't wise, she knew that, and not just because she wanted to tag along. Lola dipped down, swiped up her M4, and slung it across her back. She grabbed the Uzi as well, along with her original pistol. "We didn't train so I could sit down here in a goddamn car. You can't protect me down here, and I can't protect you. The horde will be bigger. Right, Banks?" She knew they couldn't argue, but still, they hesitated. She decided for them and made her way to the ladder.

"Alright, alright, take it easy." Burris grabbed her gently by the shoulder.

"Girl," Banks said roughly, coming around to face her. "Just like last time, then." She looked up to him, putting on the meanest face she could muster.

"Yes, sir." That seemed to please him enough as one side of his mouth slid upward into a half-smile.

"Burris, close to me. Lola, stay at the rear with a small gap." Banks put his hand on the first rung of the ladder and took a few steps before looking down. "We go over the first few ramps until we get to the point of impact. Scope the area, engage if necessary, and fall back, taking the ramps with us. Watch the flanks, or we might be in for a shitstorm." Nothing sounded appealing about a shitstorm, but she and Burris nodded, and the cop hurried the rest of the way up. The two of them were not far behind. She looked up to see their weapons casually bouncing against their backs and adjusted her grip on her own. She double checked the safety on her primary. *Can't afford any accidents now*. She had to prove herself again, and she would.

Once atop the landing, they hustled across the ramps and down the long hall, making the left at the L. The ramp remained butted up against the frame of the narrow stairway opening, as did the mine underneath. There was no sign of the dead, but Banks slowed the pace anyway.

"Easy here. Remember, second step." Lola nodded, but the policeman didn't look back. He stepped onto the ramp, then hopped to the second step of the stairs. Burris followed suit with Lola right behind. She held her firearm low by the waist, right arm hanging limp as they crept up. At the top, everything was still in place, and the kitchen was untouched. The M16 mine rested in the kitchen doorway against the frame, tripwire undisturbed. Banks slowed again, and all of them strained their ears, listening for anything. Nothing filled the air save silence. It should've been a good sign, but Lola was still nervous. She couldn't say why. *They aren't clever creatures*, she thought— at least not the ones they'd encountered. Banks crossed the ramp into the hallway, then through to the bedroom, where it was much darker. Lola glanced at her feet, careful with her own steps, keeping the smallest of gaps between herself and Burris. Collectively, they continued forward until she noticed dust and dirt filling the air in a cloudy haze. It reminded her of Banks's cigarette smoke. *It could've only been one mine.* Through the process of elimination, they discovered the mine that'd gone off was the first one, the one on the door under the stairs. Banks eased forward at a slow, steady creep. His rifle was planted firmly against his shoulder, his cheek on the stock, ready to fire. Closing on the bathroom, Lola noticed orange light flickering against the clouded air. Something was burning in the aftermath of the explosion, and she could hear the flames crackling. It was the only thing she heard, however. Lola had cleaned the bathroom up a couple days before, but chunks of burning wood and stone lined the entryway as Banks stepped into it.

Banks held a single fist in the air, and she knew from her training it meant stop. She couldn't say why he did it, but he could see more than she could, given his position. They'd been there before. *We should just go back now, pull the ramps, and hold out below.* As if it heard her thoughts and had a different idea, a large, silent corpse suddenly stepped directly into their line of sight. His shoulders were wide, and he towered over the cop. Skin completely intact, it was an ugly shade of greenish-yellow. It even had all of its hair—a matted brown bowl, disheveled and dry. Stooping down to Banks's level, it opened its mouth and released a booming scream. Rotten teeth fell from its face with the wail. Its eyes bulged from its skull, bloodshot but alive, locked onto the cop with a pointed anger. Lola recalled his words. *They come back stronger, fresher.* Her heart thumped in her chest, and she planted the stock of her own weapon against her shoulder. Lola didn't remember doing it, but she'd backed up a few steps.

"Hell, not hot enough for you, ya stupid fuck?" Banks laughed in its face and pulled the trigger. The assault rifle ignited the air, flames shooting out of its end and drowning the zombie's screams. Round after round punched into the creature's face before blasting it into chunks of skull, blood, and skin. Lola almost expected Banks to keep firing madly, but the shots died with his laughter. It collapsed to the ground, and the cop turned back to them with fresh red blood splattered on his face.

"Lola, you pull the ramps. We'll jump over," he commanded in a roar, almost as loud as the corpse. "Go, now!" She didn't hesitate, but as she turned, more screams—as loud and powerful as the first—echoed through the air. She bolted through the bedroom and hallway, then across the ramp and into the kitchen, turning back to lift the wooden platform. Luckily, it wasn't that heavy. Looking back, she saw Banks crouched low with Burris standing above him, both of their weapons locked and loaded. Even as they began their powerful assault, the howls endured. Fresh bodies poured into the bathroom doorway, piling against each other in unrestrained rage, and the two men shifted back. While most of the dead weren't as large as the first, all of them looked much sturdier than the skeletons before; they were fully skinned, even bearing muscles. They exploded in fairly the same way, though their blood was thicker and hotter that time. Something was giving these creatures life. Steaming red streaks whipped and arched and splattered. Fear gripped Lola's gut as she shuffled backward toward the small stairway door and clutched her weapon close against her. Burris breached the doorway into the hallway, looking back to step over the newly exposed tripwire and move into the kitchen. Banks slapped the button on the side of his weapon, and an empty clip dropped. In a blink, it was replaced, and the spraying continued into the bottlenecking crowd. Lola's breath came in arduous gasps, and she backed up more. She reached up and looped her fingers through Burris's belt. They were going together, she promised herself. She couldn't handle being separated from them, not like that.

"Come on, Banks, keep coming, goddamn it!" Burris screamed it loud enough for her to hear, but she knew the cop couldn't over the gunfire. He was still standing in the doorway that led into the bedroom. His feet were planted, and he drove the dead back with careful, calculated blasts. Another magazine hit the floor, then another was driven home.

"Banks!"

"I got these fuckers," he screamed back at them, slinging his AR behind him and pulling the M203 around. He didn't have to aim too much with it; the weapon hung low by his hip, and, with at least thirty feet between him and the swarm, he unloaded a single blast directly into the heart of it. Black smoke, blood, bone, and chunks of flesh erupted in every direction. Shrapnel lodged in the surrounding walls, while one piece jutted through the cop's shoulder. *You're fucking crazy, Banks!*

"Woo-fuckin'-hoo, assholes!" Banks screeched.

"Banks, damn it!" Burris's attempt was futile once again. As the prisoner made to step back over the tripwire toward him, a sudden impact shook the entire wall to her right. A chill passed down her spine as she turned her head with wide eyes to the large kitchen window with bone barricades. She swallowed hard but didn't have the opportunity to do much else. The bones burst inward, and a million shattered pieces spread through the room in a series of violent cracks. Dozens upon dozens of the dead spilled in behind it as if dumped out of a truck, jumbled and tangled, all at once. Their screams were loud enough to cause ringing in her ears, while her own was drowned out. They clamored and clawed against the tide of one another, frantic and eager to get to the three. The horde split around the island like a river, intent on converging on the living. While most barreled toward them, others made for the kitchen doorway. With an unheard shout, Burris turned toward her, swept her under his arm, and crashed through the small, stairway door. They tumbled down a few steps before landing with a heavy thud, inches away from the tripwire and ramp at the bottom. Burris landed on his butt with Lola crashing on top of him.

"Banks," the prisoner whispered as the kitchen mine detonated. The explosion shook the walls and stairs, blowing the top few, along with the doorframe, into busted bits. Her teeth clenched together painfully as shrapnel ate through the walls around them. One caught Burris in the dead center of his arm, a large steel shred, but luckily it only sank about an inch into his flesh. Like Banks, he didn't even react. Both were covered in the following rain of dust and dirt, and before she could suck in a breath, the wails above peaked again. She could hear broken bones snapping and sliding across the floor, and footsteps rumbling on the ground. Lola looked up to see several dead staring down at them with gaping mouths. Burris struggled to his feet, pulling Lola up with him. He flipped his old weapon behind his back and shouldered the new one with the rounded clip. *The AA-12*, she thought. Automatic. With one arm, he fired a blast upward, the strap allowing him to maintain control. He pumped more rounds, clearing the doorway with a sea of red spray. Again, it filled with more bodies. Many more—so many they were jamming themselves, despite the widened space. Burris turned and stumbled down. Lola was afraid he'd forget about the wire, but he consciously stepped over it. Her ears were bleeding, and stars danced in her vision. The prisoner cradled her in his free arm against his chest, almost too tight for her to breathe. He kicked the ramp against the doorframe aside and turned, picking up his pace. They locked eyes, and she knew they were thinking the same thing. Banks was gone.

"Prepare for a ride, baby girl," was all he said when he started to run, kicking more ramps to the side. She squeezed her eyes shut, chin bouncing against his shoulder while she tried to avoid biting her tongue in half. The screams echoed

269

behind them, continuing to grow. Lola was compelled to open her eyes; when she did, she saw them. They moved swiftly down the stairs, the wall of them so wide they crushed each other to bloody wrecks on the edges. They clawed their way down over each other, moving faster than they had before, more determined. Drool fell from their mouths as they snarled and hungered for human flesh. Burris couldn't get away from the mine fast enough, seemingly moving in slow motion. The corpses reached the bottom, and the M16 bomb leapt dutifully into the air. Lola witnessed a brief moment of the horde observing the object, stunned, before it introduced them to hell. Red blood was buried in flame and smoke, and the blast knocked Burris off his feet. They sailed against the far wall, right toward the L. Lola was jolted from his arms and landed on her knees and elbows, her Uzi sliding on the ground with them. She coughed and choked for air, finding nothing but fumes. Her head was pounding, and she'd lost track of where she was through the thick curtain. *My gun.* Lola frantically ran her hands over the ground through splinters of wood and glass, searching for the weapon. To her left, Burris slid to pin his back against the wall, his face buried under a crimson mask. With her ears ringing in pain, it was hard to discern, but in a moment's time, the distinct screams came to her clearly. Lola choked back a sob.

"Go, baby, let's go! Finish the job!" The prisoner's voice was urgent. He forced himself to his feet, using the wall for support. He lifted her by the elbow and guided her forward.

"Get across the ramps, kid! Come on! I'll pick them up!" Lola did as she was bid, the rage intensifying behind the two of them. She could hear hundreds of footfalls, and the dead rushed down the hallway. She hopped across the first platform, and

Burris yanked the wooden plank up with one arm behind her as she closed and crossed the second. He turned and heaved the first back the way they'd come just as the angry mob poured around the corner like an unforgiving flood. They jammed each other's bodies against the wall and pushed on with angry, bloodthirsty shrieks. Burris picked up the second ramp and tossed it between the two traps. *Anything to help*, she thought as she crossed the third and reached the ladder. The man in orange repeated the same on the third and final plank, but as he did, the first mine ignited. It lifted and spun, blasting their faces with a furious discharge. Burris lost his feet again, sliding on his back and almost taking them off the edge. *Wouldn't be the first time.* Lola clung to him as terror clung to her. The dead charged through flame and death. Burris swept her up once more, twisting her to his back, and made the descent down the ladder. The second mine burst, and she thought her eardrums were going to explode. Blood ran freely down the sides of her head, and tears rolled down her dirtied face. Burris ducked, and the ladder lifted off the edge briefly before crashing back down. The shrieks heightened as if the bombs were making them stronger. *How many are there?* When the two reached the bottom, the third mine exploded, and Lola could feel the heat of it on top of her head. Chunks of wood, glass, and limbs rained down as her companion pulled the ladder away, cutting off their path down. Blood fell in hot waves, drenching them below.

"The Hummer, kid!" the prisoner boomed as he tore her off him. She did her best to stay on her feet, and hearing him behind her gave her strength. She wildly grasped the handle of the heavily armored passenger door and swung it open. Burris did the same on the driver side, and together, they charged into

271

the vehicle so hard they almost collided. They slammed the doors shut, but she didn't hear them. For the first time, silence met her ears. No ringing stuck with her. With dirty red cheeks and swollen, tear-stained eyes, she watched the dead approach the edge. That time, it wasn't enough to discourage them. They stampeded forward. Some of them fell in front of the car with a wet splat, while others crashed onto the hood. But they kept coming. Each impact evoked a fearful gasp from Lola, and Burris watched beside her in awe, his chest heaving. Some of the dead survived and regained their footing; if anything, they seemed even angrier. As the bodies piled up, the fall was becoming less detrimental to the horde. The dead were starting to roll without harm, proceeding to stand and rush the vehicle. They beat against the thick windows and hood, climbing onto the front to slam their enraged faces against the windshield. Lola was beginning to panic; she knew her fear would consume her. Her heart raced so fast it felt like it might burst out of her chest, and the urge to vomit was overwhelming. She wanted nothing more than to look away but she…couldn't. Some were beating themselves to pieces against the glass, and when the first crack appeared, she finally screamed. All she could see were teeth and hair and skin and red. The dead howled in agony as they neared closer to their goal.

"Burris," she sobbed, her voice breaking apart around her constricting throat. "Burris, please." *Please.* The man turned and looked at her as if he was surprised, she was sitting next to him. It was like he'd been taken to a different place, and his mind had to recollect everything. *Shock*, she thought.

"Burris, we have to go," she pleaded, her nose running down to her mouth. "We have to go, Burris! Please!" Lola broke down, and her body shook as she cried. Thoughts of her mother and father did nothing for her—they just tore her apart more. Death was coming; she was going to die. The vehicle rocked as the corpses shook it from both sides, and Lola wailed. *"Please!"*

It was Burris who screamed then. Anger, hatred, and rage bellowed out of him, and he twisted the ignition switch, engine roaring to life. It was loud and powerful. Lola looked over to him as he was hitting all the switches, looking for the wipers. When he found it, it helped little, only smearing the chaos that was present. Yanking the shifter into reverse, he slammed his foot on the gas. The Hummer shot backward so hard that Lola flew against the dash and smacked her head on the glass. The resulting dizziness induced vomit right into her own lap as she sunk down to the floorboard. Blackness surrounded the edges of her vision and continued its invasion of her sight and mind with each passing moment. She felt something hot and wet sliding down the middle of her face, thicker than any tears. As it ran into her mouth, the last thing she could recall was the taste of iron, warm and soothing, as she fell deeper into darkness. *You don't have to fight anymore,* her mother's voice cooed. She looked up to see Tara Ray in front of her. Lola tried to smile but choked on blood instead. A soft hand reached for her, and she stretched out her own shaking hand.

"Momma," she gurgled thickly. It was all she wanted.

I'm here, darling. It's over. It's all over. Her mother pulled her into a warm embrace, smiling a sharp silver-toothed smile.

Wake up, Lola. Her eyes fluttered open to the sound of the voice, not sure if it was real or in her head. Emptiness stretched around her, black and impenetrable. She floated in the barren void, drifting as weightless as a feather. There was no up or down—there was nothing. The voice was familiar, the voice of another…*child.* Not that of her mother, even though Lola remembered falling into her embrace. That was the voice she longed for. It was distant, but strong enough to wake her to the abyss. Lola looked down at her body, realizing that she was visible by some unseen light. Her clothes weren't torn and tattered. They weren't covered with scum or stained by sweat and blood. Confusion settled quickly, but as it did, the memories penetrated her, and she realized why she was there. The numb thought came: *I died.* Everything had been going so well, too, until the final wave arrived. In the blink of an eye, it'd all changed. Without feeling, Lola recalled tumbling down the stairs with Burris, while Banks was caught in the kitchen explosion. She remembered the shock on the prisoner's face when he watched the dead slam themselves against all sides of the Hummer, desperately trying to get inside. Last, she remembered her mother, who welcomed her home before the world went dark. But if she'd gone home, then how was she there?

"Is anyone there?" she called out, her voice echoing across the blanket of darkness. She felt cold and achingly alone. The place made her helpless.

"I'm here, Lola." She stopped breathing, straining her ears toward the sound. It rang in her memory but seemed so far away. *Who—?* Her eyes opened wide, and she gasped.

"Brandon?" Her voice carried again, making her feel like she was talking to herself.

"Yes?" came the response, and she exhaled a sob.

"How? How are you here? You're dead?"

274

"I am," his voice responded, sad. "But Annie let me stay here. For you." Lola felt puzzled. Annie? Why did that ring a bell? And if Brandon could help her, why hadn't he before? Then she remembered.

"I'm dead, too." Admitting it made it more real, more certain. "I failed."

"You aren't dead," Brandon said with a childish giggle. "You're unconscious." A vivid flash of smacking her head on a windshield came to her mind.

"Unconscious…" Lola spoke the word slowly, pondering the possibilities. Kalos had taken her mind from her body, so in true reality, her physical body was a vegetable. She was in the maze in her mind. Did that mean if she were knocked unconscious again, she'd enter a third plane of being? There was no making sense of it.

"You're very real, Lola, and very much here," Brandon voiced in the dark. "Your body is just a vessel. Your mind is you, and you have many layers." Her head hurt.

"I still don't—" Brandon appeared out of the black in front of her, and she gasped in surprise. It wasn't the eyeless, angry Brandon from her dreams, but the boy she knew in school. His brown eyes searched hers.

"Annie will explain it to you. She's good at making all of us understand." The named tugged at her still, but something about the obscured memory troubled her and made her nervous.

"You have to wake up," he continued, reaching out his hand and laying it against the side of her face. "I can't come back with you because he'll see, but here I can help!"

275

"Brandon," she said, choking as the tears boiled back to the surface. "I'm so alone—"

"You aren't," he responded before drifting away from her. Lola reached out for him. "Use the allies you find. Use the resources available. Just stay alive." He floated farther, and Lola felt a rising sense of panic, wanting to rush toward him. "Look between the lines." More words she couldn't understand. She needed more time, more answers.

"Wait," she urged desperately. "Help me. Please!" The boy had faded from her vision, and the tears spilled down her cheeks.

"I did," he said, his tone suggesting she was being silly again. Then he was gone. Only his voice remained, and Lola screamed his name across the empty, black void. Two words echoed back to her.

"Wake up."

Urgency was the first thing she felt. It surged through her. Sight and awareness followed, and she found herself crammed into a floorboard. An engine roared, tires screeched, and Lola saw Burris behind the wheel of…*the Hummer*! The heavy-armored vehicle hit something solid, the crash almost rocking the prisoner from his seat and pressing her tighter against the passenger door. Blood boiled out of Burris's arm around the lodged shrapnel and also oozed out of smaller cuts on his face. His eyes were wide as he shifted into drive and slammed on the gas pedal. The momentum pressed her against the seat, and she used the opportunity to painfully force herself back up. If Burris noticed her, he didn't show it. Looking out the blood-doused window, she could see they were still in the large room. The crash was from hitting several of the supply aisles, sending everything toppling and breaking across the ground. Shelves had burst apart and were still sliding. In the rearview mirror, the unfaltering dead were there, still giving chase. Rows upon rows of them ran madly after the Hummer. *An army*, she thought. Lola grabbed the seat as they slid again. The blood on her face was still warm. While she was unconscious, it'd felt like forever; in reality, however, only a few seconds had passed. She watched the ground dip in front of them, knowing they'd hit the ramp. She dared to hope as Burris sped down its length. The garage door grew in her vision, and she clawed for her seat buckle. When her hands found nothing, she could only scream.

The Hummer plowed through the structure, steel groaning and twisting as it exploded outward. They rocked up and down, shouting together while sparks rained on top of them. What was left of the door collapsed to the ground behind the vehicle. The light only illuminated it for moments before the living darkness swallowed everything up. She turned back to face the front and gasped. The black was a suffocating curtain laid before them, headlights illuminating a few feet in front, but no farther. Burris, with no other choice, let off the gas. Sliding to a coast, they held their breath, expecting anything.

The Hummer stopped after a few seconds. No other sound beside their heavy breathing penetrated the darkness. If the dead pursued, they were silent, or perhaps they'd been swallowed up, too. *No,* she thought. *The dark is where they came from.* It was a terrifying notion, worse than all of them beating the doors in and crawling through the windows. At least inside they'd been able to see. Lola struggled to get her breathing under control, the fear weighing heavily on her. Burris flipped off the headlights, reached up, and clicked on the interior light. In that moment, she and the prisoner were the only things that existed in the whole world.

"You alive, kid?" Burris's low voice surprised her, and she jumped, looking at him with wide eyes. He sat slumped over in his seat, one arm across his stomach, the other bleeding and hanging limp by his side. Her heart dropped. She reached out, fingers lightly brushing across the metal in his arm, and he winced. She recalled Brandon's words, but stifled them. *I won't use him. I will save him.*

"Kind of makes me ill, pulling it out, ya know?" He looked down at the wound and gave a half-hearted chuckle. "You gotta do it." The thought didn't sit well with her stomach, either.

"Can we leave it?" she asked, hopeful. What if it was keeping the blood from flowing out? Burris shook his head.

"Nah, kid. It'll fester." He reached over and grabbed her hand weakly, pulling it up to the steel. "Come on, now." Lola didn't want to, but she didn't want it to get infected at the same time. She reached her other hand up, breathing nervously, and grasped it. The piece was sharp, so she had to be careful, but maybe the pain would help the feeling twisting her insides. Burris squeezed his eyes shut and nodded. She took another breath and hesitated, trying to will her hands to stop shaking. When she tightened her grip, a breath escaped from his mouth, and she yanked. It remained stubborn, and Burris groaned loudly, beating the steering wheel with his other hand. She kept on, determined. His pain hurt her, but it had to be done. Lola leaned back, gripped it hard, and pulled again. He leaned his head back and screamed. She pressed her foot against the shifter and gave it her all, a sigh of relief escaping her lips as it slipped free. Blood pooled over her hands, and Burris slumped forward, sweating profusely. In momentary panic, she slapped her hands over the wound, but the cracks between her fingers filled with red. The prisoner reached down inside his orange suit and ripped at the white fabric underneath. Still in pain, he held a strip of the tee out to her, breathing hard.

"Tie it over top, kid," he whispered, and she did as instructed. Lola pulled it around and through, then repeated the loop above the first. When she yanked it tight, another groan escaped his lips.

"You didn't answer my question," he said weakly, reaching out and grabbing her by the side of the head to inspect her cut. It was high and wide, but not deep. Her dad always told her cuts on the head bled a lot.

"I'm fine," she answered in the quiet around them. Burris surprised her with a smile, then another wheezing chuckle.

"We're some nasty motherfuckers," he said, ending the sentence with a gurgling cough. She didn't want to see him that way, so she couldn't force herself to smile at his humor.

"Not as nasty as they are," she replied, which earned her another small laugh. She wasn't sure if it was true or not. They might as well be dead, given the state they were in. Maybe they could get out there and walk among them, unnoticed, but she wouldn't bet on it. The reality was unavoidable—at least the reality in *that* place. As her emotions rose and fell, something else came to her mind: grief.

"Banks…" she whispered, mostly to herself. Burris sighed and shook his head.

"He's gone, kid." It hurt him to say it, Lola knew. They had created a close bond in their time together. Circumstance had driven their relationship to not only friends but partners. If there was a silver lining to their story, that was it—something that would've never been otherwise. They watched each other's backs and had survived.

"There's no chance, huh?" It was a hopeless question, but her heart wanted to make it so. Burris stared straight ahead, his mind in places she couldn't imagine.

"Explosion that big," he started, cut off by a thick cough. When his body shook, blood pressed through the cloth on his arm. "He was right there. And so was the horde." Unlikely wasn't the answer to her question. Impossible was. Accepting it was the best they could do. They needed to be thinking about their next course of action, but the drive to stay alive, and their morale, was low. They might as well be sitting on the peak of a mountain, a bottomless drop on all sides, waiting for one stray wind. She stared out the blood-streaked window, her mind as empty as it was beyond the glass.

"I believe you, kid," Burris said, eyes never wavering. "The hell we've gone through, after that…I believe ya." Lola was at a loss. She knew it should make her happy, but it did the opposite. They sounded like words from one's deathbed. Her mouth worked as tears reappeared in her eyes, but no words came.

"You're just jumping through hells," he continued, attempting to smile through the pain. "You get out of here, you just land in another?" The truth was a miserable reality. She nodded, and he turned to look at her. She watched his face, drenched in blood and sweat. His eyes were hard to see.

Bloodshot and weightless. The burden of it made the night seem darker. *The fight is gone in him*, she thought. Lola wondered, if she weren't there, would he keep pushing on? Would she, if she were alone? *You are alone, child.* Her own thought, lest she forget the truth.

Lola couldn't say how long they sat there in the silence. She lost herself in her mind for an unknown period of time, and her head ached. She pressed her thumbs and forefingers to her temples, then peeled them off, sticky with Burris's blood. The blood from her own wounds stopped flowing, half-dried on her cheeks and nose. Her mouth was dry and tasted of iron and vomit. None of it mattered compared to the empty hole growing in her chest. Lola dozed off a few times with the numbness, as did Burris. Once, she woke to see him slumped with his head pressed against the wheel, blood dripping in a slow string to his lap. Her fear that he might be gone lit in her heart, but a light wheeze from his nose with each exhale relieved her. The other times she drifted were interrupted by her subconscious playing tricks, convincing her that the dead were there, tearing her apart. It was her nightmare coming to life. Her eyes would open to find nothing but Burris and silence, but the real world did nothing to subdue her fears.

A light shuffling sound caused her to lift her eyelids. In her exhaustion, she wanted to dismiss it as an imaginary sound. Lola almost concluded it was just Burris shifting to get comfortable in his seat, but the insistence of it pulled at her. When she lifted her head from the window, a dizzy feeling swept over her—one that was all too familiar. Sleeping it away would have been too easy, and reality wouldn't allow it. Her companion snored lightly, and Lola tried to listen beyond his breathing. At first, there was nothing. As she eased her head back to the cool, comforting glass, the noise came again. It was as if someone were dragging his or her feet. *If it's not coming from inside, then…* she thought. She pressed her ear to the glass, and the shuffling was suddenly closer, though still muffled. It wasn't just one sound, but several. It was close— maybe just outside the door. She strained to hear, squeezing her eyes closed and shutting everything else out.

A hand smashed against the bulletproof window so suddenly she leapt back with a scream. It was tough to make out, but the skin she could see was gray and discolored. The fingertips curled and dragged downward. Another hand slapped the glass beside it. The fist angrily beat against the window, and her chest started to heave. Her body was frozen as she watched, but her hands worked. She clutched the seat with bloody white knuckles until a face came into sight. The corpse roared, cheekbone popped loose as it crushed and smeared its blood-soaked face on the glass. It was toothless with little pink left in its gums. The dead's skin pulled free, sticking on the window like glue and peeling off its skull. Lola pushed herself farther toward Burris.

"Wake up!" she screeched, but she received no response. Lola looked back at the sleeping prisoner and pried her fingers from the sticky seat. With luck, she connected with the fresh wound on Burris's arm, and his bloodshot eyes snapped open, followed by a long-winded gasp of pain. As it happened, he jerked his body off the steering wheel, and his legs moved upward. When he did, he accidentally hit the switch for the headlights, and the true horror revealed itself.

A wall of the dead stood in front of them, clamoring madly against one another. They looked shocked in the sudden light,

282

heads and bodies whipping around in surprise. Lola and Burris watched as the screams returned, rage driving them forward in a jumbled mass. They came in a frantic wave, pouring onto the vehicle. The Hummer shifted back against the weight, steel groaning while the dead crawled onto the hood, pulling and fighting for a chance to get inside. Rotten hands beat at the windows from all sides, but it was the steps on the roof that sent the chill down her spine.

"Burris, they can get in through the turret!" The black man looked at her, then back to the opening where the heavy machine gun rested.

"No choice now," he said, and she couldn't tell if he was relieved or resigned. Burris flipped the switch, and again, the engine roared to life, its rumble throwing a few of the weaker ones to the ground. The prisoner slammed it into reverse, pressed the pedal to the floor, and they lurched backward. Lola was ready for it that time, a foot planted against the dash to hold herself into place. The scream of the motor blazed in her ears. It rocked and heaved, crushing into something behind them. The Hummer lifted over it but didn't settle back on the ground. Bodies, she guessed. Burris gunned it again until they lifted more than dropped. He twisted the wheel around, spinning them in a donut, and the lights revealed rows of the horde—an unimpaired line of gaping skeletal mouths and eyeless skulls. The vehicle skidded to a halt, and Burris shifted into drive, glancing over at her.

"We're gonna go till we can't, okay?" Lola took a deep breath, controlling her fear. *I've survived before*, she tried to convince herself. She could only nod, and Burris gave her a nod in return.

"When we stop, I'm gonna get on that gun. I'll hold them off as long as I can, but I'm going to need you to hand me the ammo boxes." It sounded straightforward enough. Lola looked over her shoulder and gasped. Three rows of green metal cans that were previously stacked had fallen over and scattered around the back of the vehicle. Two wooden boxes sat on the far side opposite of them. Was it too much to think that could be a way out? With a .50 caliber machine gun, they could do some serious damage, but the dead were attacking from every direction. The fight wasn't the worst part; accepting the inevitable end was what frightened her the most. Lola recalled a movie her dad once watched in which a character stated that being dead didn't hurt at all—dying was the hard part. *I understand now.* Lola counted the seconds and recalled each intake of breath in that moment.

Burris hit the gas, plowing into a wall of corpses. They raged, crushed beneath the weight of steel, bones snapping to compliment the sound of grinding wheels. They made progress for a while; the Hummer would slow against the load, and Burris would kick it into reverse, slamming into the bodies from the other side, then he'd shift back into drive. When he saw a gap in the beam of their headlights, he'd yank the wheel and shred through more of them. *It's like a tank,* she thought as the vehicle took down countless at a time. Some of the dead broke apart easily, shattering into boney bits. Others bore more flesh, and therefore added weight, but they still went down. And yet, they were replaced by more bodies. What was worse, those that'd already perished were taking up space, and soon the options would be very limited. To prepare in advance, Lola leapt into the back amongst the piles of ammo. She whispered a prayer in thanks when she noticed several M16 rifles stacked on racks on either side of her. She pulled forward a few ammo cans and snapped open the lids. Rows of gold destruction—bullets the size of her hand—were stacked on top of each other. When Burris smashed the vehicle into the dead again, the equipment stayed steady, but Lola fell over. Looking at the .50 caliber as she pushed herself up, she noticed a can already attached to it. Banks's instructions came to mind. *It's locked in. I don't have to support the weight of it.* The Hummer whipped around, and she tumbled again, that time into the backseat passenger door. *Gold destruction,* she thought as she pushed herself up. With a moment of stability, she climbed into the turret and ascended to where the handles of the gun waited. Lola grabbed them to help lift her weight and pressed her back against the rounded steel in an effort to lock herself into place. She had to stand on the tips of her toes to peer out. The barrel of the weapon was facing the direction they were moving, the headlights lighting their way, which was partially coated with a deep red. The black beyond was tightening its grip on her fear, and she was careful not to watch it for long. It felt as if it'd seep into her. Burris rammed through the blockade of groping bodies, slowing against the flood. Lola rotated the turret to face behind them, aiming as low as she could. Her trembling palms were sweating against the surface of the handles, while more beads formed on her forehead. Her nervousness swelled as the sounds drifted up to her from the blackness. She couldn't see them, but she knew. *Thousands,* she thought, aghast. Their feet rumbled like a stampede. Lola's fingers found the trigger, and she squared her shoulders as best she could.

"Woo-fucking-hoo," she whispered, a call to Banks. She squeezed hard on the trigger, and the weapon erupted, quick as lightning and booming like thunder. It rattled hard in her hands, and she felt like one of the dead skeletons, about to shake apart. Somehow, she held on. Flames emerged at the end of the barrel, much like a fire-breathing dragon. The orange blaze clutched at the night around it, spanning at least a foot and a half with giant bullets exploding out. The light reflected on the dead long enough for them to witness their end. The top half of the first corpse disappeared completely. The next lost its head and most of its shoulders. After, they became so massed she was blasting into a wall, which was exactly what she needed. It reminded her of a woodchipper's effects, but crushing flesh and bones instead. Arms and legs and heads burst in every direction. Their insides whipped by her face. Some landed and stuck with splatters on the back of the Hummer. Even fingers managed to fly by—a few pelted her head, while some reached her collar to slide wetly down her back. She barely noticed. When Burris realized she was making a hole, he shifted into reverse and began to ease back. As he did, the weapon jammed, and she panicked as the dead surged forward without hesitation. They waded and climbed through the pieces of their counterparts. Lola watched, frozen, until Banks's training rang in her ears, and she yanked the lever on the side of the gun. Squeezing the trigger again, the onslaught continued and forced the dead back. They weren't discouraged, though. They closed on their flanks, so Burris gunned it back into drive, turning the wheel and smashing through another thick wave. He used the sides of the Hummer to do more damage. The impact shook Lola free, and she fell back to the floor of the vehicle with a thud.

"You okay, kid?" he screamed back at her, not able to turn and look while they rocked and lifted off the ground.

"Yes," she yelled back, trying to climb back into the turret. The front wheels rose off the ground, the dead massing from the front and sides. Lola fell farther, as far back as she could go, the slap of the steel shaking the breath from her. Above, she saw hands gripping the rounded metal top of the roof's opening, struggling to climb up and in. Ammo boxes tumbled back to her, smashing loudly against the back, but luckily leaving her unharmed. The wooden boxes burst open as they fell, and dozens of red sticks spilled out of them. *Flares,* she thought in surprise.

"Hold on, Lola!" She only had a split second to grab hold of something, and she managed to slip her fingers into one of the gun racks. She heard the engine revolutions heighten as Burris slammed the gas, and gravity pushed her to the trunk of the vehicle. A slow climb ensued, the Hummer tilting more as she screamed. Lola was looking straight up to Burris, and he was practically lying in the front seat, screaming and cursing as he urged them forward with determination. If they were working on sheer will alone, the vehicle would have crested the hill of bodies. With headlights facing the sky, it was pitch black, but they could hear enough not to need sight. The howls filled the air, an infection to existence itself. They rocked back and forth against the tide, and when Lola thought they would finally topple, a savage horde rushing from the right sent the Hummer tumbling to the left. She screamed again, crashing into the weapon racks. Ammo boxes fell like rain, spilling or already empty. She ended up sprawled against one of the passenger windows. Pain laced up her arms and knees. The cut on her head reopened and throbbed as blood pumped out. Burris was still in place, but she noticed fresh blood on the inside of his window, as he'd crashed against it. The glass was

287

intact, but a large crack stretched the distance across the windshield. Lola knew the dead would soon be crawling inside in a swarm, but, to her vast relief, the Hummer rocked back onto its wheels before coming to a stop.

"Go!" she screamed at Burris. He didn't need her encouragement. Even better, the headlights shone onto nothing but the dark, meaning their path was momentarily clear. The engine roared, and they sped blindly ahead. As terrifying as the prospect was, she didn't want him to ever stop. *Just go forever,* she wished like some foolish child. As they gained speed, Lola couldn't take her eyes from the front. Burris had the same idea, his foot pressing the pedal all the way to the floor. *Just go,* she thought again as tears streamed down her face. If they crashed into a tree or drove off a cliff, at least the dead couldn't have them. She recalled blasting them to pieces with the mounted .50 caliber and smiled a bloody smile. No wonder Banks had enjoyed it. The adrenaline and power she'd felt, and the burning desire to feel more, was almost enough to forget everything else. That was why she wanted it, she concluded. *To forget.* In that moment, she wanted nothing more than to squeeze the trigger again.

Eventually, something solid appeared in front of them, but it wasn't a tree, wall, or barricade. To her surprise, double doors grew in her vision, illuminated by the headlights. The right door had a gaping hole at the bottom. She inhaled, and Burris screamed. Lola didn't know if it was shock or frustration that she heard, but she'd never find out for sure. The Hummer struck the doors, and wood and bone from their barrier burst into hundreds of pieces. The well-lit main room of the house was littered with dozens of corpses. Burris hit the brakes, and the tires screeched, tearing through the floor and bodies alike. Lola flew forward, colliding with the back of Burris's seat, and they shifted sideways. A dim awareness of the staircase flashed into her vision. The Hummer slid into the wreckage under the second story, pressing her tighter against the driver's seat before coming to an abrupt halt. The two of them were surrounded by large clouds of brownish dust that worked their way into the opening at the turret. She coughed when it filled her lungs, and she looked toward Burris when he made no sound. He was lying on the steering wheel, as he had while he was sleeping.

"Burris?" she said with another hack. Lola crawled around and pressed herself between the front seats to get a better look at him. "Burris…"

A small, tired moan passed through his lips, but he didn't move. His head was supported by the wheel, and blood dribbled from his lips, dripping onto the glass above the odometer in a gooey string. Lola sighed in relief. He was alive, but she wasn't sure how much he had left in him. The shred of shirt she'd tied around his cut was hanging limp with the wound freshly opened. His hair, face, and beard were thick with blood as well, resulting from several lacerations. She eased herself back into the front seat, and another wave of nausea hit her. It was a terrible feeling, and she reached up to touch her head. The cut was wide enough to stick her finger in, and it made her retch. Here she was, worried about Burris, but severely injured herself. Her arms, elbows, knees, and legs were torn up as if she'd played twister in some thorny brambles. Another cut lay under her collarbone, working its way across her chest and down her right side. Lola had no idea when that'd occurred, but when she traced her fingers down the length of it, she found something foreign beneath her shirt.

Grabbing hold of it revealed the object to her: a rotting finger of one of the corpses she'd blasted apart. Lola held it in her red-stained hands and stared at it, squeezing the skin from the knuckle and pushing the bone out. She was shocked to hear herself laugh at the display. *What a mess.* She looked at her tattered clothes. Her shoes were one of her most prized possessions, and they seemed to have endured the best, even if stained. Her skirt was a nightmare, almost black from filth and gore. The shirt was in a similar condition, hanging limp around her shoulders, laden with everything else she'd faced. Looking at it brought her exhaustion back home. It was all so…tiring. She considered it a blessing she'd made it that far, but Lola was tired of fighting and running. As the fatigue returned to weigh her down, she rested her head against her window. The dead were coming, she knew, but Burris didn't seem to care either. They'd fought their battle and ended up back where they started. No mines remained. The way to the big room was likely blocked from all the explosions, not that it would've mattered. There was no longer a garage door at the end of the ramp, so the dead would be able to flow in freely. Nor was there a way out from the darkness encapsulating them. No escaping the everlasting night that'd been thrust upon the world. What a hell Lola had found herself in. The thought passed through her mind as her eyes closed. Sleep beckoned. Maybe she wouldn't feel anything that way. Maybe—

A sound delayed her passage into the nightmares waiting beyond her conscious mind. *A song*, she thought dimly. A familiar one. One she'd heard not long ago. Her mind struggled with coherency, and she debated whether she was actually hearing the sound or imagining it. *My little radio?* No, that was impossible, as it'd been left behind. Lola attempted to lift her head, but she lacked the energy. Her thoughts twisted. *How...*

"Her smile deep as an ocean, a smile meant to last. How them days, how them days, did they pass." Somebody was singing it, she concluded, convincing herself she was still awake. Whoever it was, they were singing with a delirious merriment. Lola listened, a fraction of energy worming its way into her body spurred on by curiosity, but maybe it was she who was delirious.

"Banks, you son of a bitch." It was Burris who spoke and answered her questions. When the realization finally hit her, Lola burst into a laugh. It was an insane sound, but to her delight, Burris's body began shaking with laughter as well. *Banks's voice! But how?*

How them days, how them days, did they pass...

Sunshine
and Silence

When Lola woke, Banks wasn't singing any more. She stared at what appeared as a wooden, peaked ceiling, trying to recall where she was, but her mind was blurry. The distance between dream and reality was a small gap, and she tried to fit the puzzle pieces into place. *Banks is dead.* Her mind spoke the thought, and she heard it as if it were spoken out loud. Lola remembered his voice, however, singing one of the songs she'd heard on her tiny portable radio. Her mind couldn't comprehend how that'd be possible. She remembered the explosion in the kitchen, the swarming horde on all sides, the way it separated her and Burris from the policeman. She remembered their escape out of the big room and into the darkness. And then—

"Burris!" Lola intended to sit up, but her body lacked the strength. She worked her way onto her elbows with difficulty. She was scraped and bruised from head to toe. Before her lay the second story of the main living area, where she'd stripped so much hair from the dead. The area served mainly as an open attic area. There were piles all around her, which she thought were old clothes, but as her vision cleared, she saw they were stacks of bodies. Understanding eluded her, and pain rushed into her head. A groan escaped her lips, and she dizzily settled back onto a makeshift pillow. It wasn't soft or comforting in the slightest. Lola swallowed and squeezed her eyes shut against the nauseating feeling.

"Easy now, kid," a voice said from across the room. It was thick to her ears as if spoken under water.

"Burris?" she asked the ceiling. Her question was met with a rough, deep-pitched laugh.

"You should be more worried about yourself." The voice became louder, punctuated by heavy, echoing footsteps. It sounded like Banks, but her mind knew that was impossible. *Then who?*

"Jesus, kid, you're worse off than Burris," the voice continued, defying all logic. The steps were booming, mind-piercing thuds, and Lola moaned again. A shape appeared on her side and knelt beside her. He was fuzzy in her eyes, but familiar. Her visual disorientation was interrupted as he pressed something against her lips, and water flowed. It was refreshingly cool, and she reached up to grasp the bottle greedily. As soon as it hit her throat, pain ignited, and she coughed and sputtered, her body rising in protest. A firm, strong hand pressed against her chest and eased her back down.

"Easy, I said." The voice was harsh around the edges but laced with concern. A cloud of smoke drifted above and away from her, and through her blurred sight, she couldn't grasp the plausibility.

"You're—" she started, her throat raw and scratchy.

"Dead?" the voice asked, amused. "Dead is right, kid. For a long time now." He turned his head to look beyond her, down into the room she and Burris crashed into. "Therein lies their predicament, huh?" Another puff of smoke. "I could walk among those rotting shit sacks, and they might never know the difference." Lola blinked; certain the image of Banks would disappear. How odd would it appear to Burris, talking to herself?

"Killing them is more fun, though," Banks continued, laughing like a crazy man. "It's like they were given another chance to come back and die better. Luckily, that round they got front row tickets to me." Lola couldn't fathom laughing right then. Nothing gave her the urge to smile. She felt terrible. But she did remember giggling just before she passed out. She remembered Burris laughing, too, with the ghost of Banks singing that sweet song. *The dead are the sanest of us all, here.*

Lola's vision cleared more, but keeping her eyes open was a task in itself. The ghost of Banks lingered over her, pressing the bottle to her lips again. She drank carefully that time, but it still hurt. Her throat was sore beyond any sickness she'd ever carried back home. Lola cringed as it went down, bittersweet.

"I can see it in your eyes," Banks said with a smirk. "You think I'm in your head." His features sharpened as she watched him. His smile was a red nightmare, his face a mask of long-dried blood. He was bare-chested, save for the strapped grenade round belt dangling over his shoulder. "The dead have been here all this time, and yet you're still frightened of a ghost." He chuckled, and Lola felt heat rise to her cheeks. She was *not* frightened.

"I'm dreaming," she said, lying her head on the boney pillow beneath her. "How long will I dream before I die?" The amusement faded from the cop's face, and his eyes hardened.

"There are no dreams here, Lola." He screwed the cap back onto the bottle while he watched her with a pitiful look. Surely not—not from Banks. Another indication he was gone, and it was merely an illusion. "The gap between dreams and reality has disappeared. You didn't wake up screaming this time, did you?" She knew he was right, although its kind of just happened on its own. There was no sense of accomplishment for her, no victory over the plague in her subconscious mind.

"Then how do we know what's real and what's not?" she asked weakly, looking up at the ghost. Banks's smile was sad, still.

"You don't, kid." He reached his calloused hand down to stroke her knotty hair. "We live, and it is what it is."

"Do you want to live?" Amidst everything, the question caught him by surprise. The policeman hesitated.

"No one should have to live through this," he dodged. "Least of all a child." His fingers pushed gently through her hair, and Lola closed her eyes to cherish the comforting feeling.

"But here we are," she replied and drifted again into darkness.

When she woke again, the ghost was gone, but the same peaked ceiling remained. A dragging sound below was the first thing that came to her ears. An image of the dead shuffling their feet appeared in her mind, but the urgency was absent. Something told her it wasn't the same sound. How had she gotten up there, anyway? Lola closed her eyes, searching her memories, but everything was vague. She configured the image of Burris grabbing her out of the Hummer and bringing her up there, but that was only a conclusion, not a recollection. Her last coherent thought of him was his body slumped against the steering wheel, blood draining out of him from multiple wounds. *No way he could've mustered the strength to get us both up here.* Come to think of it, Lola wasn't sure Burris was there at all. Had she gotten out of the vehicle and climbed the stairs to pass out? The mystery compounded her headache, but she supposed the pain was the only reminder that she was, in fact, alive.

Lola attempted to sit up, that time with more success. She dimly wondered how long she'd slept. It had to have been long enough to restore some energy in her because she *did* feel better. Looking behind, she discovered her pillow was a rotten corpse—mostly bones—then sighed. *That's not disturbing at all.* To her left, a full bottle of water rested with the cap on. *Banks...*No, she told herself. It was only a dream. Still, no explanation presented itself to her, and she was more surprised when she noticed a fresh bandage around her elbow. Lola eyed it, then reached to her chest. A large patch was placed just under her collarbone, and she inhaled sharply. *The cut on my head.* Her fingers drifted up, and the tips felt another fresh cloth pulled tightly across her forehead, up to her hairline. Someone had cleaned her wounds and cared for her, but how could—*Burris.* Her jaw dropped as she noticed that, across from her, he lay propped against a stack of bones. He was shirtless and heavily bandaged as well, with several empty bottles next to him. Not all of them were water.

Lola pushed herself to her feet, wobbling on weak knees. She felt better, but the dizziness still lingered as if a reminder it'd be happy to return if she pushed it. She stared across the room toward the prisoner, deeper into the second-story space. When she made to cross the distance over to him, the dragging sound persisted below, prompting her to look down. A shirtless man covered in sweat worked below. A black strap stretched across his chest. Corpses stacked in two long lines flanked the main door on either side, leading to the wreckage just beneath her. Blackness awaited through the hole where the doors used to sit, but no sound came from its depths. Not yet, at least. The Hummer was parked against the wall between stacks beneath her, too, while also facing the door. But it was the man who

297

held her attention. She stared down at him, incredulous, squeezing her eyes closed then opening them again. He was still there, working in silence, enforcing the manmade walls with each dead body. *Impossible.*

Lola turned back to Burris, inspecting him as she approached. His stomach rose and fell as he slumbered, and it relieved her. How they survived, she'd never know. Twice, the odds were stacked against them, and yet…

"Here we are," she said to no one as she turned toward the stairs. Looking down, she didn't notice any steps, assuming all had been completely destroyed. In their place were more bodies of the dead, mostly the weaker, skeletal kind bearing loose, tattered clothes. They were tangled in a most convenient way to form a bridge between the top and bottom floors. *Creative,* she thought, glancing at Banks as she stepped down. His body glistened with sweat from the light of the heavy chandelier above. The bulbs of one side had been broken and destroyed in a previous blast, but still, it remained in place. Beneath, Banks heaved another body onto his pile, chest rising and falling from the exertion. All indicators suggested he was very much alive, but she struggled to convince herself. In all honesty, if she and Burris survived what they had, was it unrealistic to think that Banks could've, too? They should all be dead.

"Banks," Lola said as she hopped off the stairs onto the debris-littered ground. He looked up only for a moment before turning back to his work.

"How's the skull, kid?" Lola absently reached for her wound as she watched him, feeling the bandage above her eyes, wrapped tight.

"Better," she answered appreciatively. If he noticed the gratitude in her tone, he didn't show it. The cop only shrugged and laughed quietly.

"That thing's pretty thick," he said, slinging another body over his shoulder. He carried it toward the wall under the second story and dropped it on the right side. "I think any other little girl may have been toast." It was an acknowledgment of her toughness, she knew. Lola beamed at the compliment.

Banks reached into his pocket and pulled out a soft, semi-smashed pack and pulled a thin white smoke from it. Lola walked to one of the walls and gave it a gentle shove. It was packed tight and tied, but still, it shifted.

"These were disappointing last time," she said of the barrier. Banks struck a match and sucked in the first hit from his cigarette with visible relief.

"It was too much to hope for," he answered, walking toward her and eyeing the walls. "These have a slightly different purpose, though." He traversed the length of the room, from the Hummer to the open front door, then turned back toward her and pointed to the vehicle.

"A straight line?" she guessed.

"Straight as an arrow," Banks replied, sounding pleased with himself. They'd failed before, so his voice wasn't without doubt. "They're strong in numbers, but they aren't smart. Susceptible to a good bit of goading, I'd say."

"If that's the only direction they come from," she offered, and he nodded with a half-smile.

"If an open door doesn't encourage them, I don't know what will." He furrowed his brows and spoke grimly. "Buy us some time and space."

"You don't think we'll make it?" It was more of a statement than a question. Banks only sighed.

"The horde gets bigger and stronger each time they come." The smoke filled the air in a giant cloud as he expelled it from his chest. "It's only by miracle any of us are still here."

"How did you survive?" she asked, dying to know. "The explosion—"

"I saw it coming." He flicked the useless butt of his cigarette out the front door into the darkness. "I stepped inside that bedroom door just as it went off, and the wall took the best of it. "Then…" He gestured as if he had one of his rifles in his hand and made weapon sound effects as a kid would. She smiled in response. "I blasted my way up to the second story here." Lola's eyes traced the wall to the stairs and then up.

"You blasted away the stairs with your grenade thing and picked them off," she finished for him, still grinning. He laughed with a deranged look in his eyes.

"Some of them made it up anyway and gave me a good fight, but the idea was sound." Banks lifted another corpse, bringing it toward the end of the left wall next to the Hummer.

"So, what's next?" she asked, though it was easy to figure out. *A final stand. No running.* The finality of it didn't sit well with her, but then again, there was nowhere to run. She knew Banks would have a job for the three of them, assuming Burris had time to restore his health and strength enough to fight. That time, they wouldn't have the advantage of limitless supplies or a tangle of rooms to work with. The small door under the stairs was in shambles, bogged down with splintered chunks of wood and stone. It wasn't hard to imagine the rest of the destruction along the way, especially since the policeman had battled his way back with a heavy dose of firepower.

"You aren't going to like it, kid." Banks displayed a fond smile, but it did little to warm her. Lola frowned, crossed her arms across her chest, and waited. His chuckle was pure amusement.

"Burris is gonna be up top," he started, pointing to the second story. "All the weapons we have are gonna keep him company. All but one." Banks pointed to the .50 caliber mounted on top of the Hummer. She remembered her fingers on the trigger, the life filling her body as the weapon tore through the dead. "I'm going to man that big daddy right there and—"

"And I'm going to hand you ammo boxes?" she angrily finished for him. "Did you hear it firing while you were in here?" He nodded, and she drove on. "That was me. I blew them to pieces. Lots of them." His expression turned serious and sad, and he knelt, placing bloody hands on her shoulders. The gesture didn't ease her stubbornness, and neither had his words.

"I know what you can do, kid. You—"

"Then let me do it!" she pleaded, shoving his hands and stepping back. Sitting within the confines of their military vehicle was not her idea of contributing.

"You will, Lola." His voice rose as he stood and looked down at her. "You'll do plenty of shooting, I promise. After."

"After what?" she said, louder than she intended. She eyed the dark hole that used to be the door. What was worse, she knew the answer already. *After they take him.* Lola pushed the thought away.

"Burris and I have to do everything we can to make sure you get out of this shit hole. I'm sorry, that means you have to go last." Tears brimmed her eyes as the painful idea of it pushed her anger away.

"Are you really that ready to give up?" She turned her back, not wanting him to see her tears. "None of us are going to die. We're going to walk out of here." Banks didn't need to respond. But he might as well have. *Out of here and into what?*

Lola helped Banks complete the barricades against two walls, and afterward, they made their way back upstairs. Burris slumbered on. More color had returned to his body, for which she was thankful. How close to death he'd been. How close they'd all been. Lola reflected on how lucky they were, but the possibility of escape didn't leave her mind; as hopeless as the policeman was, they *could* still get out of here. She looked at the piles of corpses from above. He'd constructed the blockades to buy them time and space. He wouldn't have, however, if he didn't have a scrap of hope. Lola knew he did— so did she.

Banks tasked her with gathering the ammo and weapons together to clean them as best she could, then fill up empty mags for all the M16s from the Hummer, Burris's shotguns, and a few more assault rifles. She was happy to say that she still had her weapons, too, including the Uzi she'd become so fond of. It wasn't long into her work when Banks approached her and held out his dirty hand. He revealed something wrapped in a stained white cloth. Lola looked up at him, expecting an explanation, and reached for it. When her fingers closed around the soft rag and felt the shape within, she couldn't help but beam. She uncovered the cloth to find her little radio with the headphones still attached.

"How did you—" she blurted, unable to contain her excitement. *If you can find the right jams, kid, you can make a lot of shit go away.* It wasn't a lie. She was thrilled to have it back, though she wasn't sure she'd have the opportunity to use it.

"I scooped it up before we came back up a while ago," he said with a grin. "I envisioned this exact moment. Imagine that." Lola bolted to her feet and threw her arms around his legs.

"You didn't even want to take me in at first," she said. It was a joke, of course, but there was a hint of scolding in her words. He laughed and smoothed the hair on her head.

"Nah, I didn't, you little shit." Lola had never imagined their relationship blossoming into what it was. Burris was much sweeter than the cop, that was certain, but she loved them both the same. *My protectors,* she thought fondly. After everything, they were still together. Together, they'd successfully fight off the dead.

Several hours passed, and the two of them covered most of the prep work. They huddled against the piles of the dead, close to where Burris slept, still unconscious. Once he woke, it wouldn't take much to understand his job, assuming he was physically capable. He'd fire down into the "slaughter area"— the name Banks had given it. Lola liked it. The policeman sat on the other side of his partner, reconstructing one of his handguns while she tinkered with her radio. Glancing at Burris to check if he was still asleep, she dared to pose a burning question.

"What did Burris do?" Lola asked quietly without looking up. Banks pushed the top of his pistol onto the handle, and the piece came together with a series of clicks.

"What?" came the absent reply. Lola knew he'd heard her, but perhaps didn't grasp her meaning.

"Burris," she said again slowly. "To have to go to jail, I mean. What did he do?" The cop paused in his work to look up at her. He was debating whether to tell her.

"I'm not sure you'd want to know, kid." He picked up another pistol and began smoothing it down with an oiled cloth.

"I do," she persisted. Lola waved her hands, gesturing all around, and shook her head. "What does it matter, right?" Banks sighed, setting the weapon on the wooden floor.

"Burris was accused of killing his family," he conceded, showing little emotion. "You could've gone the rest of your little life without knowing that, huh?" Her mouth hung open. The urge to defend Burris came, but Banks waved her off.

"I told you," he continued. "He was only accused. Never convicted. We were on the way to the neighboring county when, well, you know." It was difficult to hear. Lola recalled the prisoner telling her he wasn't innocent, but that could have meant anything. She didn't want to believe it.

"Do you think—"

"No, kid," Banks answered quickly. She knew that he didn't want her to have any doubts. "Not anymore, at least. Not after all this."

"Good," she said, feeling better about it. "Me neither." It was no wonder Burris was so sad when he spoke of his family. Lola fought every day to survive and see her family again. She could only look over to him in pity. *What are you fighting for, Burris?* What would she have to fight for if her family were gone?

"Vengeance," Banks said suddenly, disrupting her thoughts. He stared at her as if he could read her mind. "There's no mistaking that burning look. If anything, that proves his innocence." He lit a cigarette, the tip glowing orange and hot in the darkness of the upper floor.

Lola slept first in the following hours. When Banks gently shook her awake, she felt better, but nowhere near completely rested. The cop didn't sleep easy, she knew, so she sat as quietly as she could against a boney pile. She thought about putting some entries into her journal, but her pack was still in the vehicle, and there wasn't a lot of light. It'd been a while; her fingers itched to write, but if she survived, it'd be there waiting for her.

Her thoughts drifted again to Burris and his family. Lola couldn't imagine him being capable of something so cold, so evil. But if that was a place constructed by Kalos—with people created by Kalos—could she really rule it out? She had to stay prepared, but even with her caution, she wouldn't believe it. Rosalia hadn't turned on her or tried to kill her. If anything, Kalos had put these people here to die, if they were real at all. Lola pushed the thought from her mind as the silence endured.

305

The dead were out there. When they'd finally come was the question. But she knew they would.

Banks woke on his own, maybe after a single passing hour. He threw on his boots and busied himself with checking on the two walls below. Lola leaned on the rail and watched him, lost in her mind, when she caught movement in her periphery. Her face brightened as she turned to see Burris sitting up. Her first thought was to throw herself at him, but she resisted because of his injuries. The bearded prisoner winced as he leaned forward and rubbed the sleep out of his eyes. She had no doubt that he was trying to piece together where he was. She'd done the same. Lola watched him fondly until she heard Banks climbing the corpse stairs. When Burris noticed them, he attempted a grin, but winced instead. Then he laughed, and her jaw dropped.

"They knew your ass wasn't worth killin'," he said to Banks with choking laughter. His voice was low and raspy, but the cop grinned.

"Something like that," he returned. He walked over to Burris and knelt. "I think that thick hair on your head cushioned some of them blows. And there are more than a few." The prisoner pointed toward Banks's receding hairline.

"You're just lucky that skull is so thick," he said, and the two of them laughed together. Burris's eyes drifted to Lola as she approached, and that time, his smile remained. It was hard to say in the dark second story, but she thought there was moisture in his eyes. From pain or emotion, she couldn't say.

"This one's tougher than us both," he said with a hint of pride, and she felt her heart swell in her chest.

"Much more and beyond," the cop answered with an approving nod. Burris held his arms out toward her, and she had to fight from running.

"If you're coming, then come on." He barely had time to finish before Lola closed the distance between them. She was careful, though, not wanting to cause him any more pain. She eased her arms around his neck, nestling her face against his chest.

"Banks saved us," she said, unsuccessful in holding back the tears. He gingerly gripped her around her own shoulders, stroking her hair out of her face.

"I think we need to quit taking turns saving each other's asses and get the hell out of here." Lola couldn't have asked for better words, but deep down, the dark truth wouldn't be so simple. She cried against him, nothing able to take the present moment away from them.

"Out of here is much farther than through the front door," Banks answered grimly. "Got a nice setup, though. Safe to say the attempt will be a blast." Burris looked up at his partner, then softly pushed Lola back to arm's length.

"Run me through it. Our time is sorely limited, I'm sure." And that's what they did. Banks ran the idea by his friend, from his post to their own. It wasn't a mood-lightening subject, but the three agreed it was their best chance. Banks went on to explain how everything had come to be, along with outlining his own survival after being separated from them. Burris would occasionally shake his head, not only shocked at the cop's luck, but also at his and Lola's.

"Everything we've been through, just to put our back to the wall once more and fight to the end." It wasn't a question, but Banks answered anyway.

"We can't make the run out there in the darkness, even if you did survive the first time. No chance it goes the same way."

"They came pretty hard the last time." Burris's voice was increasingly somber. "They looked…alive."

"They grow with every new horde." Banks walked down the line, inspecting their weapons against the railing. "Doesn't mean we ain't gonna stack them pretty high." Burris smiled in appreciation for the motivating words, but it faded fast.

"I'm sorry you're in this, kid," he said to her. "I wish there was some way I could change that." Lola crossed her arms over her chest in response.

"We're walking out of here. All of us," she said firmly. She hoped the confidence she felt lined her voice. Both men glanced at each other and forced a pair of smiles. They only did it for her sake. She wished she could convince them of the truth of her words.

Lola slept again. Banks, too, while Burris kept watch. The prisoner healed more with each passing minute, and she was thankful for his quick recovery. Lola didn't have the chance to dream; a hand was shaking her awake, but that time it wasn't so gentle. It was urgent, and the pit of her stomach knotted up as she came to her senses.

"They're coming, kid," Banks said, and she bolted upright. Burris stood at the rail, setting up the weapons.

"We're walking out of here, okay?" Lola attempted to keep her voice from shaking against her escalating pulse. The policeman's face was a dusky mask.

"We're walking out of here," he replied. Lola closed her eyes, driving her fear back with anger—with her will.

It wasn't until she stood that she heard the low rumble. Her breath caught in her throat. *Breathe, Lola.* An intimidating sound, one that meant there were many and more. Much more. Banks sped away from her in the darkness, and she pushed herself up and followed him. When she got to the rail, Lola threw her arms around Burris's thick legs. He hugged her back, muscles tense.

"This isn't goodbye," he swore. She looked up at his face, dimly illuminated by the chandelier. His eyes were sad, but there was no fright in them. *He's ready,* she thought, and she owed it to him to be ready, too.

"Rummy, after?" she asked. Burris smiled and ran his fingers through her filthy hair.

"You bet. No crying, though." He surprised her by pressing her radio into her hand. "Hold on to it."

"Lola, come on!" Banks yelled from below. She gave Burris one final squeeze before breaking free and half jumping, half sliding down the boney staircase. Banks started to muscle the bodies free as soon as she was clear, and she did her best to assist him. The rumbling was louder, accompanied by a few distant screams. Lola swallowed, helping the cop pull the last body free from the makeshift stairs. Left behind was only an empty gap. She looked up to Burris, holding up her thumb. *No way they can make it to him.* The prisoner nodded, shouldering

Bank's assault rifle with the grenade launcher attachment. The world slowed as she fixed that image in her mind.

Snapping out of it, she followed Banks to the Hummer. He didn't enter from the interior, but rather leapt onto the hood and pushed himself up to the turret. Even with the damage to the vehicle, the havoc-wreaking weapon had fared well, though the attached ammo box was missing. Lola opened the armored door and slid into the back. She tossed her radio aside, and using both hands, yanked the door shut with a slam. Spinning, she noticed five ammo cans remained in a straight line, orderly and convenient for her to push up. Popping the first open to reveal a row of gold, she made to lift it up as Banks's legs slid down the turret slot into place. She strained against the weight of the box but managed to get it up effectively. A hand reached down, and he said something. She couldn't exactly hear, but it sounded like, "Hurry the fuck up." Lola grunted as she held the box with one hand until he grabbed it by the handle and hauled it away. She could hear it sliding into place, the top of the gun opening and closing onto the sheet of rounds.

"Burris," Banks called, voice hard against the rumble of the oncoming dead. "You locked and loaded?" Banks knew the answer was yes, but she could tell he liked the verbal reassurance. His hand scrambled into his pocket, searching for his smokes.

"Would you like me to hand you those as well?" she said sarcastically, and the man only laughed. She tried to keep the heat from her cheeks.

"You know it, you ugly motherfucker," Burris answered from above. "Try not to have too much fun with that monster of yours." Lola had to strain to hear him through the reinforced steel. Banks looked down at her and winked, working to get the crushed soft pack open.

"She's well under wraps, partner." He looked into his pack and frowned. She could hear Burris laughing from above.

"I meant the gun, you sorry asshole," Burris replied. Lola didn't share the amusement passing between the two, and she smacked the cop's leg hard enough to sting her hand. That'd show him.

"Jesus, kid," he said while laughing. He held the pack of cigarettes upside down, peering into it. After a moment, a wrinkled single slid free into his cupped hand. "What do ya know? Last one."

"I was curious when that was going to happen," she said from below. "Hope it's a good one."

"You know it will be." He flicked a match, and the flame burst to life, igniting the round tobacco tip. As Banks took the first drag, he leaned in and looked straight at her, face devoid of smiles and laughter.

"Keep them eyes open and get them boxes to me fast, you understand?" Lola could only nod and watch as the cop stood up straight. The rumble felt closer and louder with each second. She turned to face the windshield, watching the empty black space beyond the door. On each side, a line of bodies stretched toward them, stacked about four feet high. She glanced at the windows on the wall to the right, noticing the bone barriers there had long since been torn through. Those were the entryways Burris would cover from the top. Banks had the main door. The stampede was coming, and through the steel doors, Lola could clearly hear the shrieks. She barely noticed the sweat rolling down the side of her face. *Tears, sweat, or blood—it's always one.*

"Get ready!" Banks screamed up to his partner and yanked back the lever to the right of the weapon. Lola's eyes locked onto the front entrance, burning as she tried not to blink. It was so loud the Hummer shook. She wasn't certain, but she thought she could hear Banks laughing above her. His feet were stomping and bouncing in anticipation. She only had time to shake her head when, at long last, a shape ahead broke the darkness. Another appeared beside it, then another. Her breath caught short, and she swallowed dryly as the space filled with the dead, clawing and screaming at each other while they rushed forward. A quick glance at the window showed it was still dark, but the door was packed full, some corpses squashed against the tattered frame. They spilled into the large room, flowing down the lane as they'd hoped. Each one that she could see had its skin fully intact, looking little less than alive and well. A far cry from the rotted skeletons she'd first witnessed. Their screeches boomed across the open space. The first thing they saw was Burris up top, aiming down, and the hesitation couldn't have been timed more perfectly. Doubt blossomed in their lifeless, cruel eyes.

A thump sounded from above. A trail of smoke sped down to the crowd, impacting near the door, a good fifty feet from the Hummer. The explosion was deep and powerful, rocking the vehicle backward, raining bits of bone, blood, and shrapnel into the windshield. There was no time for the smoke to clear before she heard Banks howling.

"Open wide, motherfuckers!" The trigger clicked, and the heavy machine gun boomed methodically over her head,

312

working like a massive saw. Lola watched intently as it cut through them, detaching torsos from legs, some rounds blowing them completely apart. The bullets were lightning bolts, spanning about a foot long as they sped from the barrel of the weapon. They struck much the same. The sounds upon impact were fleshy thumps producing webs of gore to spray over the oncoming dead behind. The entryway was a sloppy red ruin. The assault drove the corpses back almost too quickly to be believed. When the .50 caliber jammed, she could hear the lever being ripped back to clear it. In those brief moments, Burris would pump more grenades into the doorway. The windows remained silent and empty. The howling of the dead became more furious, raging against the trio's defense. Zombies tore and dug their way through the piling array of body parts, slipping and falling, toppling over each other, and ripping each other apart. She could see the faces appear through the red mass, only to explode like watermelons would.

"Bring me one, kid! Burris, light 'em up!" An empty box dropped down with a thud, and Lola hoisted a fresh one up. It didn't seem as heavy that time, mostly because her blood was boiling. Banks pulled it into place impossibly fast.

"I'm 'bout out of wrecking balls, man!" Lola heard Burris scream down to them. He shot slow, calculated bursts from the assault rifle, splitting heads and taking out knees and elbows. Though he was perfectly on target, the dead still surged, climbing through the rising mound of their fallen. Banks slapped the cover down, pulled the lever, and squeezed again. The shells blazed like hell unleashed, but as they thickened at the door, the walls collapsed on either side, and the spread of them became monstrously wide. Lola felt him turning the weapon to the left, then back to the right, but the ground the corpses gained in the meantime was alarming. *Come on,* she prayed. *Let it end. Let it stop.*

Another grenade erupted to her right, and she glanced over to see zombies pouring in through the windows. Banks screamed as the weapon jammed, but it was firing again as swiftly as it'd stopped. It sliced through the dead, repelling them at the center. Arms and legs flew in every direction, a spew of splintered bone and flesh. Blood rained onto the hood as if coming from the sky itself. *Twenty feet.*

"Another box, Lola!" She scrambled to get it up, the empty one narrowly missing her head as it came crashing down. She knew the reload would allow the dead more ground. Banks slung it into place, lifting the cover and slamming it closed. Another grenade rocked the crowd in front in merciless annihilation, but the dead fought on. *Ten feet.* They pushed against the barrier to the left and right, clumsily forcing themselves up and over or falling through it. Her breath quickened more. Hearing one last relieving click, she watched through the bloodstained windows as Banks reopened fire. The dead were close to them; the cop was firing just in front of the Hummer. The close range made the result look like a red wave, grinding and swallowing itself in place. The dead fell back a foot, then another. *Keep going,* she silently begged, watching the raging war in front of her. Burris did his best from above by free-shooting into the thickening crowd.

The assault rifle was storming in the prisoner's hands. When one corpse fell, two more would take its place. Two heads would pop, then four more appeared behind them, jaws chomping opened and closed, hands gripping for anything living. Lola glanced to the front, but the windows were so soaked it was impossible to see anything but the powerful flashes rocking from above. A metal, springy sound filled the air, and her heart sank. Banks was empty, and she knew they didn't have enough distance for a reload.

"Lola, load another box, and get up here on this gun!" She bolted into action, eager for her turn—eager to do her part. The third empty can bounced down, and she hefted the fourth in her arms. Banks's hands came down, and he lifted it the rest of the way, but that was all as he pushed himself out of the turret to stand on the roof. Looking through the hole, Lola saw Burris toss an empty rifle into the swarming dead. He grabbed his two shotguns and leapt down, landing with the assistance of his friend. Handing one of the weapons to the policeman, they flanked the turret and unloaded powerful blasts into the pressing crowd. Lola lifted herself up, grabbed the ammo box, and shoved it into the empty slot. She threw back the top and pulled a gold row free, laying it into the hot chamber and shutting the lid closed. Her eyes widened when she looked at the weapon, her gaze following the length of it down to the barrel, which glowed a deep orange. The cooling element must've been overwhelmed. *How long will it last?* The thought came and left, and she pressed her back against the rounded wall as she had before and gripped the handles of the weapon. The dead began to climb onto the hood, slipping as they maneuvered through the pile of red gore. It bought her just enough time to stare down the sights.

"Any fucking time, kid!" Banks barely got the words out of his mouth before her thumbs pressed down on the trigger and everything was drowned in the blast. It raged in her hands, obliterating any corpse that stepped onto the hood into minced meat. As the bodies pressed against the Hummer, they made for easier targets with only their upper halves visible. Lola sawed through them in long lines, stretching back toward the door, then returning and tracing the line again. When it jammed, she yanked the lever with hardly a blink, praying the barrel survived to continue the angry attack. She screamed, her whole body vibrating, but she couldn't hear her own voice over the fire. With the dead bursting to pieces just below, layer upon layer of the blood spray coated her. It was hot as it slapped against her skin, driving her rage and bloodlust further. As her hands were slick with gore, the steel slid in her grip until she readjusted. Large casings shot backward over her head and to the side, some grazing her cheeks and neck with a sizzle. Lola never noticed. What she did notice were the fallen corpses heaped in a mountain-sized mass all the way back to the door, slowing the oncoming ones. On the sides, however, they continued to push. They clung to the doors, reaching to the roof, desperate to pull themselves up. The shotguns were again slow to reload, so the dead pressed on, using themselves to climb. The .50 caliber spring popped, and Lola never hesitated.

She reached over and pulled one of Banks's pistols free. Lola squeezed it between sticky hands, taking aim. The closest corpse lost its head, as did the one behind it. Another took a bullet in the throat, its head tilting to the side, skin stretching hotly as the skull peeled from its shoulders. Turning to the other side, she unloaded more rounds. Banks and Burris were firing deeper into the pile, causing a blockage against the flow. She spared a glance to the front and saw the dead struggling with the blockade. They screamed, irate and desperate, their eyes and sockets alike burning with hatred. When she turned back in Burris's direction, a hand gripped the top of the Hummer, trying to hoist the weight of its body with it. Another hand followed. Lola blasted the first one to pieces, fingers exploding in all directions. She took aim to do the same for the other, but instead of gunfire, a metal click greeted her. Her breath caught in panic, and she reached for a magazine at Banks's hip. She brought it down, shoved it into place, and took aim, but she was moments too late. The hand gripped Burris's leg. With a shout, he put the barrel of his weapon against the zombie's teeth. Another click. *No.* Panic elevated, and her throat closed. The corpse howled, reaching and grasping the prisoner's other leg. Lola took aim at its head, enough room to make the shot, but another body of the dead appeared to her right, sliding on its belly across the roof. It grabbed her by the hand, and the pistol slipped free. It bounced once before disappearing into the mass below.

"*No!*" she screamed, kicking at the corpse as it struggled to maintain its grasp. Burris savagely drove the stock of his weapon down into the faces of the dead, but they clung like imminent death. Both of his feet were planted, but in a blinding instant, one was snatched free. He landed on his back on the roof, the breath leaving him before he bounced off into the screeching crowd. Lola screamed again, feeling her throat shredding to pieces as she did. She lost focus on everything else as the horde swarmed the fallen comrade. Hands and feet smashed and stomped, raining countless, merciless blows onto him, but she could barely see beneath the chaos. Tears bled down her face, falling in an uninterrupted stream as death once more found one of her friends. She couldn't hear anything as she watched, nor could she peel her eyes away. The silence pounded in her ears along with her throbbing pulse. In that moment, she didn't know if she felt anything anymore.

"I almost got them over here, Lola—" Banks's voice brought her vaguely back. He cut off suddenly as he looked in her direction, not comprehending the absence of his partner. She looked up at him, and when their eyes met, he knew. The grief twisted his features for less than a second before his eyes hardened again. He slid his last round into the shot gun and cocked it once before stepping around her, aiming down into the violent onslaught. The first blast seemed to shatter her eardrums, but it was nothing compared to the numbness permeating her mind. She slowly reached up to Banks's gun belt, pulling the other pistol free. She took aim down into the pile, currently being annihilated by the cop's firepower. Movement from the front caught her eye, and she swung in that direction, adrenaline flowing through her once more. The dead had eclipsed the mound, pouring over the top and onto the Hummer.

"Banks!" she screamed without hearing. Her first shot missed somehow, and the closest corpse tore forward, swinging a savage blow as the policeman turned in that direction. The fist caught him in the jaw, sending his head cracking back, but he maintained his footing. He yanked the shotgun around, and with the momentum of his arms and the weapon, slung the skeletal body from the vehicle. More dropped onto the hood, and Banks rained down on them. They looked up to see the inside of his barrel, darker than the blackness outside. It erupted in their faces, dismantling them faster than the flame could lick their cheeks. One blast after another sent them back, sprawling to land on the growing mountain. Lola turned back to the remaining dead near Burris and picked them off one at a time. That time, she didn't miss. Brains exploded outward, lips and teeth and eyes all becoming airborne with each shot.

Banks's gun clicked as he ran out of ammo for the final time. He only had a moment to glance in her direction before he was surrounded. He swung his fists desperately as they pulled him down, landing several vicious blows, but it wasn't enough. More of the dead slid down the heap, joining the circle around Banks as they finally wrestled him from the hood. Lola didn't scream that time. Her feelings were lost somewhere as she watched and numbly climbed back into the turret. She pulled the empty box free, squatting down to grab the last. It felt weightless in her hands. She slid it home, pulling the gold destruction from the inside and laying the sheet flat underneath the weapon's cover. It fell into place with a hollow click. Banks looked up from the thickening pile around him. When their eyes met, he let out a howling laugh that even caught the dead off guard.

"Don't give them the pleasure!" he screamed at her, their hands gripping and beating at his face, tearing into his shoulders. "Come on, baby, do it!" Lola knew the tears were hot on her cheeks, she just didn't feel them. *How many times did I say it?* She gripped the cold handles, fingers sticking to the steel as if frozen from the drying blood. *I said we'd walk out of here.* More blows struck the cop as the dead worked him to his knees. He spit a large red glob onto the hood. His eyes were still locked on hers.

"Do it, baby." In her ears, it was only a whisper. She squeezed her eyes closed, thinking of all that'd been taken from her. When she opened them, everything was a watery blur.

"I'm so sorry," she whispered before squeezing. The weapon erupted, and Banks and corpses alike disappeared in an

319

explosion of flesh and blood. More of them slid down the wet pile, and Lola kept firing. The rounds continued without fail, not jamming once as she poured hell into the corpses. Even as they stopped progressing, she continued, unable to release the trigger. The cracks pounded in her ears while the fireballs ripped through the motionless piles. Against the blast, the top began to lean and, in one massive heap, collapsed toward the door. The dead spilled in a million spreading pieces. Nearly simultaneously, the weapon clicked, and the spring popped, its last shell clamp snapping free.

Lola felt nothing. Even when the toppled mound revealed sunlight beaming through the door, no emotion found her. She stared outside, wet cheeks glistening in the warm, yellow light. Nothing moved. There were no sounds. Her thumbs were still firmly planted on the trigger, and all she could do was watch.

She didn't know how long she stood there in the turret. An hour, maybe two. Lola was in the center of a graveyard, all but two of the dead dying for a second time. Somehow, she was still alive, still sucking in breath, but her will was gone. *I was dead the moment Kalos took me.* The desire to go on, to survive, had dissipated somewhere. She felt no grief, no fear, no anger. She could only hear the echoes of her dead friends. Laughing, screaming, joking, fighting. The voices rang in her mind. *I've survived, but I saved no one.* Breaking free, she numbly ducked inside the vehicle, just far enough to grab her pack scrunched up in the corner. Even her journal brought her nothing. Lola stood and lifted a foot out of the turret, followed by the second. In her daze, she carefully pulled herself free and to her feet, stepping across the thick hood and onto the bodies of the dead. The blood came up to her calves as she waded through it all, making her way to the end, hesitating at the doorway and looking out.

Grassy hills rolled beyond with a setting sun. A small dirt drive lay to her left, stretching down and over the dips and rises, disappearing into some woods near the bottom. Beyond, in the distance, she could see a small town, but no movement or sound greeted her. Everyone was dead. She knew it in her soul. Lola stepped out into the light.

If anyone were to see her, they would no doubt think her one of the dead. The parts of her not covered in blood were pale. Head to toe, however, she was a red slaughter.

I can't, she thought. And she knew she was right, even if she didn't want to be. She couldn't watch any more people die. She had to be dead. It had to be hell. What made it worse was not knowing why. Why her? Lola felt like she'd never obtain answers to her questions.

"You'll never find out if you let go." It was Brandon's voice, but she dismissed it.

"I'm dead," she muttered to the wind. The pain of her shredded throat was the only feeling she'd be granted.

"No, Lola. Not yet."

"Leave me alone," she responded. The light around her got brighter, even if her world wasn't. The sun hurt, turning a pale white instead of the comforting yellow of before. She shut her eyes to feel it burning against her lids.

"Why…?" was all she could muster from her cracked lips, and she fell forward. Lola welcomed the feeling of the soft grass beneath her, but it seemed she didn't land. When she opened her eyes, she was falling infinitely down.

"Take me," she whispered as she fell. "Take me to another hell."

The Gaps: Mirrors

L ola couldn't recall details of the fall. The cold stone floor of the maze waited for her, and her face was pressed against it. But there was no impact—no tumbling or air knocked out of her. She was simply there. When her eyes opened, the light of the wall shone majestic and bright, imposing and absolute in its stature. It was a struggle to not close them again, lay her head on the ground, and rest peacefully. It was strange to ever think of stone as comfortable, but there she was, feeling like she was floating on a cloud.

She knew her journey was not complete. She felt utterly hopeless, but the image of her mother's face flashed through her mind. Her parents waited for her, no doubt dreaming of the day she'd return. Lola knew she had to get up, to continue. But she only had time to suck in one sweet breath and exhale before a shadow fell over her, dampening the sweet light. Alarms blazed in her head, if not in her bones. She'd encountered nothing in that place yet. Was someone behind her? Standing over her? *Something*, her mind offered, then the obscure memory once more found its home with her. Accompanying it, the sound.

Sssccccraaaaappppeeee.

Lola lay on her stomach and shot up to all fours before bolting unsteadily to her feet, her pack flipping up and landing with a pop on her back. She recalled fleeing the noise, but that was a lifetime ago. Her first inclination was to bolt forward, but an impenetrable white wall stood in her path, and the terrifying truth became clear. *I must turn around.* After everything she'd suffered there, the terror should have been purged from her. The things she'd seen, the blood, screams,

324

and death…but no. The fright was awake in her soul. The fear of the unknown was a storm inside her, its icy chill creeping up her spine like someone climbing a rope with a firm grip. Her throat was locked and mouth open wide as she turned. Lola couldn't force herself to do it faster. She never wanted to do it. But her feet shuffled around, body in tow. When she completed the one-eighty, her eyes remained on the ground. She could hear it. *It's breathing*. Heavy inhalations filled the air, followed by a hot gust that washed over her. It smelled of rot, something she'd recently become accustomed to. Lola had to peel her eyes from the stone floor, and when she did, the nightmarish sight loomed above.

It towered above her, a ten-foot hulk that was equally as wide. Its skin was the color of rich mud and just as slick. When Lola's eyes drifted upward, she saw its face was flat like a human's, but the upper half of its skull was dominated by pitch-black eyes the size of her head. A hundred teeth appeared as it opened its mouth, some sharp, though others broken and dulled. They lined the jaw of its misshapen, elongated head. When it leaned forward, dipping close to her face, it howled, a tornado of pure agony. The creature's mouth opened wide in an alarming stretch, its bottom jaw falling all the way to the ground, attached by a few deteriorating strands of rotten skin. Laced saliva dripped with it in front of a thick and spotted gray tongue that drifted to the floor. It slid against the jaw, scooping it up with the scraping noise she witnessed and sliding it back into its mouth with a wet pop. The creature stood as a gorilla would, on its fists, but starfish-like fingers stretched back to its knees. A long, thick tail, similar in color to the tongue, whipped beyond. It shifted toward her, the hand landing with a liquid splat not a yard from where she stood.

Shockingly, it lost balance and fell against the maze wall, letting out a deep, frustrated moan. Every instinct told her to run, but where? There was little space. Again, it roared, shaking the walls and vibrating the ground beneath Lola's feet, then raised a floppy hand to smash her flat. Lola watched, frozen in place. Did she want to move? Death was so easy, but her parents flashed through her mind again. Slime dribbled onto her face, but she hardly felt it. The beast swung its hand downward, but, in that moment, something closed around her elbow and yanked. Surprised, Lola was slung against the wall, and the blow crushed the empty spot she'd been standing in. A figure was suddenly beside her in black robes. After the shake of the impact, the mysterious person grabbed her again and began to run. Lola said nothing and followed helplessly until they darted into a small gap on the left she hadn't seen. *Was this here the whole time?*

The creature howled again, powerfully and emotionally, rocking the world around them. Hot wind blasted through the small gap, and Lola could feel it on her back. Not far behind the gust, a desperate limb forced its way through, clawing after them. Lola and the figure ducked under the first mad swing. The next, however, came low, and while the hooded person sidestepped it easily, Lola wasn't so fortunate. It caught her heels and swept her up. She hung in the air for what felt like forever until she fell back onto the ground, the breath knocked out of her.

"How'd you fail to see that coming?" asked the hooded one. A girl's voice. A hand reached out to clasp her by the elbow for a third time and dragged her out of the range of the beast. She painfully sucked in air and dared a look under the stranger's hood. It was dark underneath, too shadowed for her to make anything out.

"Who are you?" she managed, clutching her stomach.

"How about 'thank you' first? Come!"

They ran through the next area, rounding a bend, moving much too fast for Lola to protest. The howling beast faded from behind, furious it couldn't pursue them, and her body flooded with relief. And she *was* thankful, though she felt she could've gotten away from the clumsy creature by herself. The hand holding her arm maintained a tight grip, causing her to wriggle instinctively against it. A pathway came, low enough to have to duck, and they turned to the right and moved through another. It looked the same to her, as it always did, evoking the same feeling of helplessness. They were moving fast, and it struck her curiosity. The hooded figure was someone who knew the maze well—maybe another stolen soul? Nothing said Kalos couldn't have more than one plaything at a time. It was the best-case scenario. She needed someone to help her, someone with pure intentions. *Maybe there's hope.*

One of the wider paths emerged around a sharp corner. The figure pointed at a wall to the left as they walked, but Lola saw nothing. She looked at the stranger, puzzled, but as they walked further, Lola was shocked to see a small path reveal itself.

"Points and corners and bends," came the voice under the hood. "Angles are everything here." The sound unsettled her; it was oddly familiar. It wasn't Brandon, so who could it be?

"How do you know this place?" Lola asked, dipping her head to look again.

"Come," was the only response, and she was pulled through the hidden gap. Beyond sat a narrower route, and Lola consciously avoided looking at the words on the walls. It wouldn't be wise to be sucked into another place after everything. She needed answers, and if they were progressing toward the center, that was her best chance. Caution lingered, however, and Lola wouldn't let herself rule out a trap. At the end of the way, a pathway split two directions, and the hooded stranger took the left then slowed to a steady walk. Lola was glad, as she never had time to catch her breath. Ahead, a rounded room spread open. It was odd because she hadn't seen a place like that yet in the maze. She eyed an arched entryway on the left wall curiously. A rippling reflection danced on the walls beyond her, and when the stranger took her through, she gasped. A small, circular pool sat in the middle of the room, stacked stones surrounding it like a well. The light was faded here, but a white globe floated above the shimmering surface. The water was thick and black, almost the consistency of oil.

"You let that thing hang open long enough, you're going to end up like Slackjaw back there," said her hooded companion. Lola glared at her, but the figure's focus was elsewhere.

"What is it?" she asked, stepping nearer. A hand shot out to grab her, pulling her backward.

"Not wise," the stranger replied with a shaking head. Lola's interest was pricked, and she felt her impatience prodding her.

"Tell me who you are," Lola said again, staring hard into the shaded face. When she stepped closer, the figure eased back. "Why are you doing this?"

"The possibilities are endless here," came the familiar voice's serious tone. "It's your willingness to accept those that'll allow you to go on."

"I've seen too much that's been difficult to accept," she replied confidently to the riddling words. "And I'm still alive." The stranger had no way of knowing how close she'd been to giving up. Lola took another step forward, the hooded girl backing against the wall. "Quit dodging my questions!" She reached for her, wanting to shake some sense into her, but when she leaned in, a black-robed arm struck out like a lightning bolt, hitting her in the middle of the chest. The breath was knocked out of her, and the blow sent her to the cold floor. Lola yelped, and that time her glare could've lit the room on fire.

"What did you do that for?" she snapped, angry and hurt. The stranger knelt so close to her face that Lola could feel her breath on her cheek.

"I know what you've seen," came the voice, leaning closer. "I've seen it, too." A short hesitation. "In the same order."

"I don't understand," Lola replied weakly, working air back into her lungs.

"Nor will you. Not at first." The robed figure leaned back and put her hands to the cowl shrouding her face, shifting the hood back. The light from the globe at the center of the room illuminated her features, and Lola gasped. It was like she was looking in a mirror, the face matching her own. The eyes were weary, but knowledgeable. Dark circles clung to them, dug in deep. Lola tried to squash the rising panic as the world tipped on its side.

"How—" was the only word she could manage through gaping lips. Emotions sped through her, sadness and confusion and urgency. Her other self looked sad, too, but possessed her same smile. Something seemed more experienced about the face; maybe she was older? She looked so tired, and Lola suddenly felt ashamed for wanting to give up.

"There's much more that needs to be explained," Other Lola said, and Lola picked up on the urgency in her voice as well. "But first, you'll have to speak to Kalos." Alarms blared in her mind. *What game is this?*

"Kalos?" Lola said, heat coming to her cheeks. "I'd rather kill him than speak with him." She pushed herself to her feet, wary of her other self.

"This is known, but you must." Lola stared at her and couldn't wrap her head around it. *I meet myself, and she wants me to see Kalos?* Perhaps she meant at the center, which was her goal. It was a preferable thought, but still, the lure of a possible trap had her on her toes.

"What are you playing at? Who are you, really?" The girl across from her shook her head vigorously.

"I'm just surviving as you have, Lola. This is no game, no trap." The girl pointed at the dark pool. "The pool will allow you to communicate with the demon. He monitors your progression in this way." *How does this serve me?* She noted that Other Lola kept a safe distance from the waters, back against the wall.

"He's a ruthless, powerful demon. You want me to check in with my captor?"

"You must," came the desperate response. "Lola, he'll reward you for what you've survived."

"I want nothing from him," she declared stubbornly, but it was the truth. It was a trick of some sort. There couldn't possibly be two of her. If there was, it wouldn't be something she'd ever consider.

"If you don't, you'll die. The maze is vast. You have no idea what you've yet to be faced with. You need to be fresh." *Lies*, she resisted. She wasn't about to allow some illusion of herself to deceive her.

"That's what he wants," Lola said. "He wants me to die, so why would he gift me?"

"It's part of his game," Other Lola answered. Her tone carried the sound of true sincerity, but was it too much to think Kalos was clever enough to mess with her head like this? "I've been through it already; you have to use it against him!" She recalled the demon talking about the luxuries he was allowed because of his track record. Could that girl be telling the truth? Lola had a million questions lining up without expecting the first real answer. She eyed the pool and contemplated it. Indecisive, she played along.

"What is it that I have to do?" she asked, and a sigh of relief left her other self.

"You just look into the water," Other Lola replied, pointing again. "He'll find you, but you must not reveal my presence. It'll ruin all we've worked for." *We*? Lola frowned.

"Can't he see everything here?" she asked. The demon hadn't revealed all the details to his game, but she seemed to always feel his presence.

"Only near the pools and in the stories," Other Lola responded hurriedly, eyeing the water as if it'd jump out at her. *So there are more.* "He can't physically see inside the maze—his power doesn't work in that way—but the realities tell him where you are." When Lola thought of reality, it was constructed by God. How could evil possess the ability to create as such? Perhaps Kalos hadn't formed them, only opened their doors. Her head was pounding.

"How would I be rewarded?" she asked.

"The world will rise from your shoulders. Please, Lola. We can't waste any more time."

"If I do this…you tell me everything." Other Lola nodded impatiently.

"I promise."

The situation was surreal, but Lola turned to face the pool's murky waters, easing her pack to the floor. Other Lola backed up in the opposite direction, all the way to the entrance of the room. There was no breeze, no movement, yet the liquid rippled, alive and aware. She watched the surface but couldn't see anything underneath. When Lola was close enough to touch the stone encircling it, her reflection came to life. The white globe above made it little more than a shadow, mimicking her movements. No sound came with the tumbling fluid, which made the silence around more eerie than it was already. She knew a deep evil lurked beneath. If Kalos truly awaited her here, then the truth wasn't far. She placed both hands on the cool stone and leaned forward, not quite sure what to expect. Was she supposed to say something or touch the water? The urge to look back to herself for guidance pricked her. She eyed the shrouded mirror of her face and shoulders, not needing any detail to know what she looked like. *I look like shit.* Her newfound vulgarity, thanks to Banks, was a metaphor for her dilapidated physical state. She didn't need to see anything but the darkness. It told her all she needed to know.

The pool shifted in an unexpected direction—a subtle movement, but she caught it. The ripples acted as though they bounced off the wall, heading the other way in graceful humps. Her eyebrows rose, and in tune, the waters mimed the expression. She gaped in surprise, the pool joining the motion of her face before transitioning to a lighter grayish color. Her reflection faded, which caused an absurd panic to rise in her chest as if she were also disappearing. Lola clutched at herself, finding she was still very much there, but that didn't quell the anxiety building inside of her. Another reflection formed before her. A girl—no, a woman. Long, golden hair floated as if it were submerged, drifting away from the familiar face on either side. Eyes of green, shaped like marbles, regarded her, and for a moment, she couldn't breathe. *Mother.* She nearly choked in shock. A hand reached toward her, beckoning. Lola felt the natural need to answer the call, to reach into the pool. Anything to have that connection back. Tara Ray called to her without sound.

333

"Mom!" Lola cried desperately. She climbed onto the ledge, pushing herself to her knees and leaning down. Her face wasn't far from the pool. Her hair dropped toward it, touching the surface. A strange heat resonated from it, much like the warmth of her mother's embrace. Lola stretched her arm out, fingers shaking as they dipped in. When her tips brushed the top, the physical effect distorted the water more, and the face lost its clarity. *Don't go.* It was a silent plea, one she thought was answered when the image started to piece itself back together. The golden mane shrunk, pulling tight around the shoulders. The reflection's features turned gaunt, then thickened a shade, cheekbones rising slightly, then the eyes, her mother's beautiful eyes, twisted into a steel blue. Her chest tightened, an invisible force squeezing her from both sides. The ability to breathe left her. *Kalos…*

"Child," his voice boomed from the pool, vibrating the water to lap against the edges on all sides. Lola leaned back, tempted to leap from the wall and run. She fought to find words. The demon who'd wrecked her world was in front of her, and under the hate she felt was the urge to vomit.

"Not pleased to see me?" the demon continued amiably. His teeth gleamed too brightly under his smiling lips. Heat rose to her cheeks, but the words stayed in her throat. "I bear only compliments for you. Very impressive, I must say. There might be something a little devious in you." Her body remained as if trapped in stone, while she watched Kalos's intensifying smile. Something devious in her? More to stack on the pile of shit she didn't understand.

"You chose a rough path and have seen some unsettling things." His voice was smug. *Relax, think, breathe.* Lola almost wished he'd settle her emotions as he had when they met, but she squashed the thought against her pride. "You are so very tired." A low, bouncing rumble filled the air, originating in the beast's chest and spilling forth. His tone was mocking, and the anger she felt rising inside helped her work some moisture back into her mouth.

"I'm only tired of watching others die," she said, carefully pronouncing each word. Kalos's laughter died, but his smile endured, amusement dancing in his eyes.

"Perhaps. But that is why I am here. Your mind is a crumbling disaster, your body a broken shell." Lola didn't take her eyes from him as he spoke. The temptation to reach into the water and wrap her hands around his slender neck burned inside of her.

"A bath, maybe, to ease your pain." His casual tone caused her anger to spike. *He feels nothing.* "Some clarity, a fresh set of clothes."

"No," she breathed, tears welling up in her eyes. She didn't want it. She didn't want anything he offered. Lola didn't have to turn to look at her other self to know she was pleading with her, but she didn't care. "I'll do what must be do—"

The words stopped as she spoke them when a hand shot from the pool, impossibly large and the color of blue steel, almost black. The fingertips weren't rounded, nor were there fingers nails. They ended in sharp points. The dark palm met her face, and the hand closed around her skull, her anger and confusion all at once shifting to terror. The fight to hold her stomach ended there, and she sprayed chunks through the gaps of the oversized appendages. Her scream was a muffled grunt that fizzled to no effect. She beat against knuckles the size of her fist, desperate to break free. All it would take was one good twist, and her story would end; her soul would be his.

Abruptly, her scream became deep and powerful, filling the round room and racing around the walls. The water lapped angrily against the edges, and Kalos was gone. Lola, on her knees, gripped the stone ledge and lost the battle against her sobs. They poured from her and disappeared into the shifting liquid below, and for seconds, minutes, or hours, the burden of being alone controlled every ounce of her. Every emotion since the demon kidnapped her struck her with force. Lola leaned back and howled, a sound of pure, miserable agony that any would do well to avoid. Her head sunk to her chest.

The pool had calmed considerably. The water was very clear, as was her reflection. The numbness she felt masked the surprise when she took herself in. It was her own face, but her hair matched the grace of her mother's, layering around her shoulders as if freshly washed and dried.

No scum lined her face, and her little cross dangled in the smooth hollow of her throat. Her clothes were stripped of dirt and filth. As she sucked in a breath, she realized her exhaustion had fled. The fatigue was gone, and her uncertainty was the only thing remaining.

Reward or curse? Lola felt alive again, but the truth was clear. Kalos could see her suffering once more as if for the first time, and he watched her slow breakdown from beginning to end. The anger returned, chasing the fading fear.

"Come on," a voice whispered behind her. Two skinny, dirty arms encircled her waist and gently pulled her from the edge of the pool. *Other me.* She allowed the assist until her

feet drifted to find solid ground. "See? You're better now."
Am I? Lola heard the words, but her chest was hollow. Funny
how the demon couldn't fix that.

"I need answers," she replied, without much feeling. "I
need them fast."

"You'll have them."

Other Lola gave her a reassuring smile. She never realized
she was so pretty with whatever the girl was covered in. "We
have to go, however. Far from here." She pushed Lola's pack
into her arms.

"Where?" Lola asked.

"Between the lines." And then they ran.

Author Page

Bryan S. Godwin was born in Pensacola, Florida, growing up on the white sandy beaches of the Gulf Coast. His writing is propelled by his love for music and reading, all heavy influential characters in his never resting imagination. He currently lives in Tennessee with his girlfriend, enjoys time with friends and family, hiking and disc golfing, but also treasures the times alone, when he can do the thing he loves the most and attempt to tell an interesting story.

Made in the USA
Coppell, TX
24 September 2021